SHANN
Affaire
Five-Star Bestselling Author

*Praise for her previous novels
of love and intrigue . . .*

PRINCESS OF FIRE

"A master storyteller!"
—*Romantic Times*

LIE DOWN IN ROSES

"Drake [writes] high-quality, addicting romances."
—*Publishers Weekly*

ONDINE

"Each page keeps one eager to get to the next. A must read!"
—*Affaire de Coeur*

"A mesmerizing tale of Gothic suspense and intrigue."
—*Rave Reviews*

BLUE HEAVEN, BLACK NIGHT

"Sensual . . . Sweeps the reader into the vibrant Middle Ages."
—*Rave Reviews*

"A sweeping tale of medieval life . . . Sensual, adventurous and stormy romance."
—*Romantic Times*

"A web of hatred, passion, and intrigue."
—*Baker & Taylor*

EMERALD EMBRACE

SHANNON DRAKE

JOVE BOOKS, NEW YORK

EMERALD EMBRACE

A Jove Book / published by arrangement with
the author

PRINTING HISTORY
Jove edition / April 1991

ISBN: 0-515-10530-9

PRINTED IN THE UNITED STATES OF AMERICA

10 9 8 7 6 5 4 3 2 1

This book is dedicated to a very special lady and friend, Miss Anne Lucille Spence, with lots of love and many thanks for so many things!

Prologue

꧁❦꧂

She waited until she heard the clock striking midnight, then she slipped from her room and ran stealthily down the hallway. Her sheer white silk gown flew and fluttered about her, making her look for all like one of the ghosts that supposedly haunted the Castle Creeghan. Her loosened hair waved in her wake like a radiant burst of fire.

She paused outside the doorway to the lord of Creeghan's chambers, her heart thundering. Spinning around with her back against the door, she waited. The night was silent except for the wind that blew beyond the ancient stone walls of the castle.

She turned again and burst into his room.

It was an imposing place, imposing and dark, like the lord himself. A single candle fluttered upon the desk central to the room. A single candle, to light the master to his bed. The massive four-poster with its intricate carvings of demons and dragons was crafted from deepest mahogany. She shivered as she caught sight of the black bedspread with a red dragon emblazoned upon it. A Welsh princess bride had brought the dragon insignia into the family three centuries ago, and now it was everywhere.

1

A fine, hand-painted dragon stood atop the chest of drawers at the tower window, and the feet of the armoire were composed of dragon feet. The red velvet drapes were hung by rods with dragon heads. In the darkness of the night, it was eerie.

Banishing her fears, she raced to a large desk and hastily wrenched open the drawers. The bottom held Scotch whisky and tumblers, the second held nothing but farm accounts and mention of the tenants. The top drawer contained ink and pens and blotters . . .

And the massive dragon insignia of the lord of Creeghan.

With a cry she sank dispiritedly to the floor.

She needed to flee Creeghan soon, before the Dragon's Teeth could sink around her, and sweep sweet life away from her, as they had done to Mary, but she could not give up the search.

Desperate but determined, she rose. She almost headed for the armoire, then paused, and walked to the bed instead.

What better place for the lord to hide a treasure than beneath his own pillow? The bed sat raised up on a platform, and the frame, too, was high.

She climbed on top and drew back the covers, then wrenched aside the pillow. There was nothing there. No staggering, brilliant display of green fire.

"Lady St. James!" came a soft and wicked drawl in the night. "Are you so eager, then, to share my bed, that you ready it for me?"

She gasped, spinning around in startled surprise. She had not heard him come, but he was there. The heavy doors were open and he leaned within the door frame, nonchalant. His fiery eyes stroked over her like lapping tongues of flame.

"No!" She dropped his pillow, as if it were that that burned her flesh rather than his relentless stare. He moved into the room and slipped off his frock coat, hanging it over the back of the desk chair. He stood before her in a white ruffled shirt and ebony riding breeches and boots.

He smiled and placed his hands on his hips, watching her. "Then, pray tell, dear lady, just what are you doing between my covers?"

Her lashes fell over her eyes and her gaze dropped to his hands. They were bronzed, with long, strong fingers and clipped, neat nails. They could close around her throat. They could throttle the life from her in a matter of seconds.

"I . . . I . . . uh . . ." She inhaled quickly, desperately. He sat down, a Satanish smile curling his lips. His brow arched and his teeth flashed white against the bronze of his features.

"Yes?"

"My . . . earring!" she claimed defiantly.

"You lost it in my bed? Nay, my lady! I promise you, I would have remembered the occasion."

Martise inhaled and composed the most disdainful gaze she could muster. "Lord Creeghan, I meant no such thing. I thought perhaps it had caught upon some piece of your clothing—"

"You are not wearing any earrings," he interrupted her. He appeared so casual at his desk, one booted leg idly crossed atop the other, his hands set together, his fingers tapping against each other. Then the hands stayed curled, hard and cynical against the sensual fullness of his lip.

"How very rude of you to notice," Martise said coolly. "But alas, Lord Creeghan, when I lost the one, I removed the other."

"So . . . you think you might have lost the one upon my person earlier?" he asked politely.

She flushed angrily. "Perhaps—"

"But why would you assume that I had been in my bed already?"

"Sir, I say that you are no gentleman."

"And madam, I say that you are no lady."

He rose from the desk with purposeful, lazy menace. Her heart seemed to catch in her throat. She needed to escape. Now.

She cried out softly and sought to run by him. He reached out for her, missing her arm but catching the silk of her gown. In horror Martise turned back, stumbling, as the gown was wrenched from her shoulders, leaving her breast bared.

She stared into his eyes and saw the fire had kindled deeply there, and was vividly aflame.

"No!" she murmured. But his hands landed upon her bare flesh, and he swept her back hard against him. He caught her chin, tilted back her head, and kissed her lips, and then availed himself of the long white column of her throat. Fascination breathed into her. It feathered against her nakedness, and it teased her at the juncture of her thighs. From the second that they had first met, she had tried to deny him. But the fire had lived between them. Lived and breathed.

She pressed against him, barely aware that she did so. She felt his body pulse, and it beckoned to her. Her fingers touched upon his shoulders, then threaded into his hair. His lips moved further upon her, stroking her collarbone. His tongue created a trickle of fire upon her naked shoulder. He shuddered and groaned deep within, and she trembled at his touch.

"No!" She pulled away from him. A lock of his raven hair fell over his forehead. His ruggedly handsome features had grown tense and taut, constricted with emotion. She did not notice anything beyond his eyes. They were green and gold and blazing. They captured her senses . . . they burned upon her, naked, hot, and bold with desire.

She shook her head, backing away.

"Martise!"

"No! Leave me be!"

He smiled with cynical bitterness and shook his head. "You have lied and cajoled and taunted me for the last time, madam! If nothing else, by God, I will have the truth!"

She saw the intent in his eyes, and she screamed, but her cry went unheeded.

She beat against him, but he ignored her as he might the mere motion of a breeze. His hands gripped about her waist, and he carried her across the room, throwing her upon his bed. She tried to sit up, but he fell atop her, his anger now unleashed and free.

"What are you doing in here?"

"I told you."

"Liar!"

She tried to strike him, but he caught her hands and pinned them to her sides. He straddled her and stared down at her in a raw rage. "Tell me the truth!"

"I have told you—"

"Lies!" he finished.

She twisted beneath him frantically, then realized that not only had she bared her breasts, but the gown had crept high along her thighs, and now her limbs lay bare as well. She went still, seeing the anger seep from his eyes, but not the fire.

Effortlessly, almost thoughtlessly, he secured both her wrists with one hand, high above her head. She stared at him, spellbound, as he slowly cupped her breast and teased the nipple with his thumb. He rubbed it and watched it rise to a coral hardness.

Then he lowered his head against her and took it into his mouth.

She cried out with the searing brand of his lips and tongue so freely upon her. She trembled and burned, her blood simmering, her bones turning to soft clay.

His ebony hair grazed her flesh as his head moved against her, as he attentively tendered to the valley between her breasts, to the bare satin sleekness of her midriff. She grew dizzy, and burned, and fought it, but then realized that she fought nothing.

Her hands were free. Her fingers dangled upon his hair with a will of their own, and she yearned to kiss him.

He swept her back to her feet, and she felt something soft and glorious sweep around her. It was her gown, falling to the floor in a white wave of mist at her feet. He stepped away from her. She should have run. She should have left him then. She should have done something.

But she remained there, naked and proud. The moonlight swept in to spill over her shoulders and touch them with ivory, while her hair took on the glorious colors of a sunset, spilling over her high, firm breasts.

He emitted a guttural cry. The sound was harsh and hoarse, and brought her to life. She inhaled the virile scent of him and started to turn at last, but too late. He swept her into his arms. His hungry mouth found hers, and he savored the kiss with a savage need that brought her ever more vividly alive. He released her from the liquid magic of his mouth and tongue, only to bear them upon her again with the swiftness of mercury.

He cupped her breasts into his hands and sank before her on his knees. His kiss ravished the bareness of her belly, and her fingers fell upon his head. He caught her hands with his own, and held her. Casting back her head, she gasped as he invaded her with a sweet, savage intimacy that stunned and shocked . . .

And shattered all innocence.

The wind outside swept to new peaks, screaming and screeching against the rocks. In shock and splendor she cried out again, and the wind carried away the sound of her voice.

She fell against him, awed and amazed and at the shattering sensation he had taught her, at the burst of ecstatic fulfillment. He swept her into his arms and laid her upon the bed and whispered sweet endearments. She tossed her head, barely aware that he rose up again, then lay back beside her, naked and throbbing.

"What I have done . . ." she whispered.

He caught her chin and held her eyes to his. " 'What I have done,' my lady," he said, and laughed softly. Then his laughter faded, and the ruggedly masculine tension was all about him again. "You are a liar, and perhaps a thief, but a beautiful one."

"No!"

Flaming crimson, she tried to rise. He caught her against him. "Martise, what are you, witch or angel? I am enchanted against all wisdom, desperate to have you against all sanity." His lips found hers again, and he kissed her and kissed her until she knew no more whether it was night or day, or if the storm raged outside or within.

She felt her throat constrict and her heart quicken as his maleness probed against her. She felt the tempest and the storm and fire as he touched her, as his arms came around. Their bodies fused together, and then it seemed that he touched her everywhere. He stroked her arms and her breasts, the curve of her hip, and the length of her thigh. She felt the great wedge of his body between her knees and then she felt the burning thrust of him at the juncture of her thighs.

When the pain came, she fought the scream that welled in her throat and the tears that hovered in her eyes. He paused and went rigid, and she buried her face against his shoulder. She thought that he would speak, but instead he touched her. He stroked her cheek and kissed her, and found the tears that hovered on the edges of her lashes and kissed them away. And he found the fullness of her breasts with the gentle caress of his fingers, and he assaulted their crests with the graze of his thumb and his teeth and tongue. Slowly, sensually, he probed at the portals of her womanhood and moved gently inside her, catching her protests with the whisper of his lips against hers, until they faded into the sweet carnal knowledge that now was hers.

He began to thrust deep, deep within her again, so very deep she thought she would break and shatter and die . . .

She did not die. Or perhaps she did. Just a little bit.

The tempo of the storm increased again. The wind raged with wild abandon, and it sounded as if banshees had traversed the Irish Sea to come and sing on high. She did not know what had seized hold of her, what wild abandon had led her to this night.

She knew ecstasy then, as he stroked and thrust, felt pain become pleasure, a pleasure so unendurable that it might have been pain. She felt the wind, for she was a creature of it, felt the same savage desire of the surge that pounded against the rock. And when he drove with sudden, fierce force and locked above her, his head thrown back with a guttural cry, his features tense, his eyes a savage green blaze, she felt a swirl of silk and honey, of stars and splendor, burst forward within her. A rush of liquid fire took hold of her, and she shuddered with the violent climax, and then trembled and shivered as she drifted back to the truth that now lay between them.

As sweet as the ecstasy, so bitter the realization.

All that she had to give, all that was rightfully hers, she had cast away. And now he lay at her side, naked and savagely beautiful and graceful still, but already she felt his anger. He lay upon the bed, staring up at the ceiling, and then he turned to her, dark brows knitted over the probing sear of his gaze.

"What are you after? And who are you? Damn it, who are you?"

A sob burst forth from her, and she leapt from the bed where the proof of her innocence betrayed her.

He reached for her, and she jumped away from him, the fall of her blazing hair the only cover against her naked beauty.

"Damn you—"

"No! Damn *you,* Martise. We'll start at the beginning. Who are you really?"

"Lady St. James—"

He swore savagely, interrupting her, and she grabbed up her gown and ran out on the balcony. She gasped out a furious sound as she discovered the gown torn beyond repair. He leapt up, too, coming after her but ripped the top sheet from the bed first, and threw it at her. He came toward her then, sweeping his robe from where it lay upon the trunk at the foot of the bed. Martise wrapped the sheet around herself and backed away from him, along the length of the balcony.

"Martise—"

"No! *You!* Don't you dare question me! Who are *you*? Lord of Creeghan? Man or beast? You tell me, milord, what in God's name is going on here!"

"Martise—"

He reached out a hand, coming toward her.

"No!" she shrieked again. She was nearly hysterical and turned to flee. "I will find out for myself!"

"Martise, no!"

She did not listen; she did not want to hear. Not this night. She went to the dressing room and burst through the door, then hurried through the bath, and out to the corridor.

He was following her; she knew it.

She came to the winding stairway, and barefoot and heedless of danger, she started to run down the ancient and smoothly worn stone. Charles II was said to have trod the same steps. Creeghan had sheltered many Cavaliers, just as it had sheltered secrets, and wickedness . . . and evil.

Her breath was coming in pants and cries, her feet were worn and bruised, and still she ran. Some kind god overlooked her careless flight, for she came down, downward in safety, deep into the cellar.

Deep . . . as if into some dank and moldy pit of eternal hell and damnation.

She reached the bottom of the narrow curving stairway and paused, clutching the stone, catching her breath, trying to adjust to the dim light.

"Martise!"

He thundered out her name but she ignored him. She pushed away from the stone and headed to the right.

She had to know.

She pushed open the wrought-iron and heavy wood gate to the fourteenth-century crypt.

Stairs led downward. The smell of must and decay and death rose upward.

She snatched a lantern from the wall and braved the steps, wincing at the bitter cold of the stone as it bit through the tender flesh of her feet. She went down, twelve steps.

She looked straight ahead. She did not want to see the decaying bones and finery of the Creeghans laid upon their slabs centuries ago. She wanted only to reach the new coffin that had been hidden in the rear, beneath the beautiful marble crucifix.

Death visions danced before her eyes. The child in Tudor breeches and silken shirt and leather doublet might well come to life, and reach out with his bony fingers, claiming her . . .

Creeghan was such a place. Creeghan welcomed the living into its crypts.

"Martise!"

She gasped out loud, shivering so vividly that she could barely force herself to move. He was behind her; she was a fool. She did not know what she would find, but now he would know that she had found it.

She had to know . . .

"Martise!"

Any second now his fingers would close over her shoulders, and he would swirl her around, and in a blazing fury would tell her that she was losing her mind, that she was morbid, that she must not be here, and for God's sake, she must leave the coffin alone.

The coffin!

She found new courage then and raced forward, praying that the lid had not been nailed down.

She hesitated only a second, then lifted the lid.

She inhaled sharply, and her breath caught in her throat.

Her scream came then, shrill and long and hysterical, full of greater terror than had ever shattered the silence of the

ancient stone of Creeghan. She screamed again, denying
what she saw.

For it was his face.

The handsome features of the lord of Creeghan, the deep,
blue-black hair falling over the forehead, the bold sensual
lips, drawn white in death.

It was the face of her lover.

His hands were folded over his chest, folded in death. He
was cold and stiff and gone forever.

"Martise!"

She turned and screamed again, the sound rising higher
and higher . . . then fading abruptly.

Her lashes fell, her eyes closed, and she swirled, melting
into the earth as a cloak of sweet oblivion and darkness fell
upon her. She would have fallen, as cold and numb as death
itself, had he not come forward.

She spun against him and he caught her, and with a weary
sigh and painful regret, he lifted her high into his arms.

So much had happened since that first night, when she
had arrived with the storm, her hair a glowing flame against
the wind and the rain. She, in all her splendor, to haunt his
already complex life, to fall into this web of mystery and
horror.

To steal into his heart and rob him of his soul.

Aye, so very much had happened since that first night.

PART I

My Lady St. James

One

❦

It was a cold, windswept, storming night when Martise first saw Castle Creeghan. As the horses' hooves and the carriage's wheels clattered over the cobblestones of the drive, it seemed fitting to her that the night should be as volatile as the passions that had driven her here.

The castle stood atop a high tor, like a monster rising from the rugged and craggy earth. Lightning cracked and sizzled around the high turrets. The sky lit up again after each thunder crack, and the castle became a glowing silhouette against the sky, forbidding and evil, an ancient fortress in unyielding stone. The lights in the high slit windows were like Satanic, glowing eyes that watched for the unwary, and waited. The drawbridge over the chasm looked like a gaping mouth, waiting to consume the innocent, and when the sound of thunder ceased, the rage of the surf, far below the rocks, could be heard slashing against the stone, railing in tempest and fury.

15

Castle Creeghan . . .

Tremors seized Martise as she watched the castle from the carriage window. The sound of the horses' hooves was always with her, like the nervous beating of her heart.

She should not have come. There was time left, still, to halt the driver. To demand that he turn the horses and carriage, and carry her swiftly southward once again. There was time, still, to cease her charade . . . and run.

The carriage ground and jumped and twisted, causing her teeth to jolt hard and her head to bounce high and nearly hit the roof. Martise touched her head and rubbed it, clenching her teeth. Then she screamed out loud as the carriage veered wickedly, seemed to teeter, and came precariously to a halt.

White and frightened, she gripped the seat. The rain plummeted and the wind screeched as the driver nearly ripped off the door in his attempt to open it. "The wheel, milady, we've broke a wheel!"

As he spoke, the rain suddenly lessened. The wind, though, picked up to a more violent fury. Martise nodded, still clenching her teeth. The castle seemed far away now, while the darkness of the night and the ferocity of the storm seemed great, and very near. Struggling with the door, the driver sought his leave to repair the wheel. She did not want to be alone.

"Wait!" she cried, and he hesitated. "I'll come out."

"But milady, it is wet, and wretched—"

"The rain does not beat so hard," she replied quickly.

He was probably irritated, for his task would be compounded by her presence, but he did not refuse her. He paused just briefly, then brought down the stepladder and helped her down. She pulled the hood of her cloak high over her head against the soft spill of the subdued rain and the fervor of the wind.

She stared up at the castle again. High within a turret window she saw a shadow. It seemed that the shadow stared downward, watching the distressed carriage. She didn't know why, but the shadow seemed as evil and malignant as the glow of the house.

Something warned her of a presence. She didn't know what, for she heard nothing in the rain, nor did she see movement. She spun around quickly and cried out, startled, for a man stood not ten feet away from her. He had come in absolute silence, as if set before her by the eerie power of the night.

"Do not be afraid," he said, in what seemed like a whisper, carried upon the tempestuous air of the stormy night.

"I am not afraid," she lied firmly, and yet she was, for her reply was as much a whisper, and her heart beat with a startling furor. For in that very instant she was haunted by the sight of him.

He was tall, very tall, towering over her in a black cape that whipped with the wind, draping over tight black riding breeches, brocade shirt, and black vest.

His hair, too, was as dark as his garments, darker than the night, spilling over his forehead when the wind did not lift it. His features might have been cast of stone in those first minutes, for he did not smile. He assessed her grimly, eyes of green and gold fire blazing from a face with a hard, squared jaw, long, aristocratic nose, high broad cheekbones, and dark arched brows. His age was indeterminate except that he was in his prime, for he was straight as an arrow, powerful in his stance, and striking in his appearance. His mouth was tight in a stern line, but it hinted at fullness, at a sensuality that struck at her heart. It seemed that they were alone on earth as they stared at one another then. There was no moon, for the dark clouds obscured it. There were no stars, just the eerie glow that emitted from Castle Creeghan, and the meager light of the lantern at the front of the carriage.

Martise did not know what to do as she stood there watching the stranger. He stood, feet well apart, a riding crop held between his hands. The wind shifted his cloak again, and her eyes fell upon the tight fit of his riding breeches and boots, and she noted the hard muscles of his calves and thighs, the leanness of his hips, and then the breadth of his shoulders and chest. If such a man wished to offer her harm, then she was dead, for she could not seek to fight him.

He had not come to harm her! she thought quickly, determinedly. No man would be such a fool to come out in the night to do murder before a hired coachman!

But still, the fear of murder was why she had come . . .

"I am glad, for this can be a fearsome place. A man or woman must be of good courage to come here. Well, then, if you are not afraid, I say good evening, milady," the man said at last, bowing gravely to her. His voice was deep and resonant. It rose with no strain above the roar of the wind and surf. He continued to survey her, and she wondered what he saw. A slim young woman, encompassed in a cape and a blue gown with lace about the throat and sleeves. The wind had blown away her hood, and her hair, her crowning glory, a thick rich burnished copper, spilled from beneath it and was taken by the wind in a wild and lusty abandon. She sought to subdue it, reaching for her hood against the whimsy of the wind. She saw his smile of amusement, and her eyes, the blue of a summer's day, flashed with sudden anger.

"Good evening, sir! And the situation is not amusing," she assured him.

He nodded. His eyes moved upward along the craggy rocks leading to the high tor and Castle Creeghan. Then they fell upon her. He moved forward and spoke curtly. "You are on your way to the castle?"

"I am."

"And you are . . . ?"

"Lady St. James."

His dark brows shot up with surprise, and Martise thought nervously that he studied her with an ever more penetrating stare. Indeed, his eyes traveled the length of her, and with such a burning intent that she felt stripped of her layers of clothing. She braced herself against the onslaught, and assured herself that it was her own fear that caused her to believe he doubted her words. "You are Lady St. James?"

"I am, sir, and who are you?"

He ignored the question. Behind them, Martise heard the sound of the hammer as the coachman worked upon the wheel.

"You shouldn't have come here," he told her suddenly, fiercely, and with such confidence and supreme authority that she nearly jumped away, frightened and dismayed. She was Lady St. James, she reminded herself, and not to be intimidated.

"Well, I am sorry that you feel that way. But I am here, and as Lord Creeghan is expecting me . . ."

He cocked his head, studying her again as her voice trailed away with the touch of an imperious note.

"Look up at the castle, milady." He came even closer to her. Though a stranger, he touched her shoulders and turned her around to stare up at the rock and the towers and turrets. "Tell me, milady, do you see anything welcoming here? Do you feel welcome?" His voice came velvet and soft. It brushed down her spine and reached into her soul. She felt his heat and a tension beneath the civilized demeanor, strong, masculine. She trembled silently. Yet she was aware, too, of the pleasant smell of pipe tobacco about him, of leather and fine brandy, and of an attractively masculine soap or cologne. He compelled and repelled her in one, and though she was afraid, she was fascinated.

She pulled away from him, spinning around, and she stared into his eyes. They were green, deep, vividly green, with specks of gold, and flashing now with humor, and perhaps some darker emotion, too. "Have you heard nothing about Castle Creeghan, milady? Have you not heard that ghosts scream through the halls, that maidens were once sacrificed to Druid gods upon the rocks, that the Creeghan wives have been known to leap from the highest towers? Milady . . ." He shook his head as if in wonderment. "My dear, dear Lady St. James, I think that you must reconsider before traveling up these rocks to this place!"

His eyes flashed, and his lips curled into a devilishly wicked smile. He was like a handsome satyr who had caught an unwary innocent within a glen. Except that he was no satyr, but a man, strikingly handsome, powerful, and she was trembling despite herself.

"I am not one to fear ghosts," she stated. Nor, she vowed, would she fear *him*.

"Then come, and I will hasten you on your journey."

"What?" She frowned. "Sir, my carriage has broken a wheel, and I am afraid that—"

"I am afraid that the rain will come again, milady, and that you may well drown upon the road ere Castle Creeghan has a chance to offer its own brand of danger. I will take you onward, and then your coachman may bring your valises and portmanteau."

"But sir, I do not see—"

He whistled suddenly, a clear sound that cut through the wail of the wind. From the trees there appeared a great sleek bay horse, seventeen hands tall at least, shiny and magnificent with a huge lean head and fine dark eyes. The man did not turn around as the animal came to stand behind him. Together, Martise thought, they were splendid, large and muscled and beautifully lean and toned. They exuded the same hypnotic energy.

Who was he? she wondered anew.

"Sir—"

"Come, milady, for the rain will begin."

"Sir, you must realize that I cannot—"

"Pardon, milady?" he interrupted in a shout, for it was as if the very elements conspired with the man. The wind rose again, howling with the vengeance of a horde of banshees. The rain was beginning again, bringing with it a startling cold.

"Sir—!"

"I shall tell the coachman of my intent!" he shouted.

Long-legged, he strode from her on his high black boots. Had the bay not remained, she would have thought she had imagined him.

She shivered violently and drew her cloak about her as rain spattered cold and frosty upon her face. She could not allow this man to come too near her. There were strange things happening at Creeghan Castle, and he could very well be the cause of it. A man so striking, so powerful, so handsome, so alluring. She must avoid him at all cost.

He came back around the carriage, his crop tapping against his leg. "Milady . . ." he invited, lifting his free hand to her as he stood by the bay.

"Sir, I cannot—"

Once again, the weather conspired against her. Lightning zigzagged across the sky in an evil slash, and behind it, thunder hammered like the beat of a thousand drums. Inadvertently, Martise screamed, bringing her hand to her mouth, for the lightning raged again and struck upon a nearby tree. It burst into flames, so near her that she could feel the heat of the fire against the wet chill of the night.

His arms came around her, whisking her tight against the protection of his chest. "Milady, we will ride!"

He set his hands upon her waist and lifted her effortlessly upon the back of the massive horse. "Lucian will take us like the wind!" he promised her, and he leapt up behind her. His arms encircled her as he reached for the reins. He nudged his heels against the animal, and they were instantly off, racing the very forces of nature.

Behind them, the trees burned even in the rain. With the wind whipping her hair in disarray about her, Martise turned, and she saw the distressed coach in the glow of fire. Then she closed her eyes, for the rain was suddenly fierce. She lowered her head, and felt the power of the beast beneath her, and that of the man behind her.

She was not cold, despite the rain. She was not cold, for his arms were warm and encompassing. The horse moved with fluid, pounding grace, and the man moved with the horse, the heat of his thighs strong against her.

The castle loomed ever closer as the great bay snorted and churned away at the cobblestoned path. Martise gripped its mane as they rode, though she had no fear of falling. The man behind her was an excellent horseman; she sensed that he moved as one with the animal, and that she was safe.

Safe upon the animal . . .

But with the man . . . ?

She started to shiver, but then there was so little that she knew. She had come for answers, and perhaps there was no way to discover answers without seeking out danger. Perhaps the master of Creeghan could give her the answers that she craved, and she might sleep in peace again.

And if not . . . then she had cast herself to hell.

She gritted her teeth as the rain continued, and the horse's hooves thundered over the wood of the drawbridge. The lights from dozens of lanterns spilled down upon them, and as he slowed the magnificent bay, Martise thought that at least the man had delivered her unto the castle as he had promised, and he offered her no threat this hour. Yet as they rode beneath the archway of the drawbridge and the rain ceased, he spoke again, and she was not so sure.

"Castle Creeghan, milady, begun by Robert the Bold when the Vikings threatened this shore. He stole his bride from his very enemy, and she bore him ten children before leaping to her death from yonder parapet. Rebuilt by the sinner Caleb Creeghan upon the marriage of Her Royal Highness Mary of Scotland to the earl of Bothwell, and held firm until the ascension of the young James upon the throne of England, when peace was made. Dozens of men shed their blood here, for the castle was held again when the English chased the Jacobites, until even they tired of assailing the castle. Indeed, the stones are rich in their legacy of blood."

"I told you, I do not fear ghosts."

"Ah, a wise young woman. What do you fear, milady?"

"The living, sir."

She would have slid from the bay herself, but he dismounted with an agile flourish and reached for her. His hands encompassed her waist as he set her down upon the ground.

"Yonder lies the door, milady. Enter this world at your own risk!"

"You speak in riddles! You speak as if you're trying to scare me!"

"Alas, no, milady!" he said in mock horror. In the glow of the lanterns she studied him seriously. He was a very handsome man, she determined, with his noble features and fierce green-gold eyes. He smiled now, yet she felt that he was not so amused as he scrutinized her in return. She felt herself begin to tremble again, for he looked as if he could see through her. As if he knew all of her secrets, and was, for that, all the more dangerous.

He touched her cheek with his knuckle. She wanted to back away from him, to protest indignantly, but she was rendered speechless. "You are very beautiful, milady. The castle, so the rumor goes, is brutal to beautiful women. You must take heed. You must take great heed."

"Are you threatening me?"

"I gave you a history lesson, milady, and nothing more."

"Does evil really happen here, then?"

"Death happens oft enough," he said. "You should know that well. Your sister came here, an innocent bride, and soon enough joined the ranks of the dead in the crypt. That's why you've come, isn't it?" He was so very close to her. She breathed in the fascinating aroma of him, the masculine scent of leather and good brandy and tobacco.

"I have come because—"

"You have come to delve your nose into places where it does not belong. Perhaps you have come for even more. Beware."

"You *are* deliberately trying to frighten me!"

"I am trying to keep you alive."

"Why? Do *you* threaten my life?"

He did not answer her. His eyes penetrated hers with a brooding, simmering anger, and then he turned from her abruptly.

"Sir—"

He remounted the bay with the same flash and verve with which he had dismounted. She wondered where he had learned such horsemanship.

"Milady!" He brought his hand to his forehead, saluting her quickly. "Good eve to you, Lady—er—St. James!"

"Wait! Who—"

The bay rose upon its hind legs, swirled and plummeted back down to the earth. Yet hardly had the forelegs touched the ground before the animal was in motion again, clattering back over the bridge and disappearing into the night. Martise stared after the horse and the man for a long time as they faded into darkness. Lightning flashed, and the night came aglow, but the horse and rider were gone. They might well have been illusion, except that she now stood in the courtyard of Castle Creeghan.

She shivered, for she felt so very alone. Every dark nook and crevice of the empty archway and yard seemed to whisper of something hidden, and something evil.

Yet she had come here, and she would stay.

Bracing herself, she ran through the rain to the domed arch over the foremost tower door. Even as she stood there, she heard the sounds as the coach clambered and lumbered over the drawbridge, its wheel repaired.

The driver, clutching his cape, leapt down from his seat. He called to her, something that she did not hear in the driving rain. Then he was dragging her valises and her portmanteau to the doorway.

"Who was that man?" Martise shouted to him.

"What man, milady?" he demanded.

"The man who brought me here?"

"I saw no man. I thought that you had run in the night. You gave me quite a scare, milady."

"But there was a man! A man on a giant bay!"

The old coachman shook his head and looked from the castle walls to Martise, shaking his head. "I saw no man, milady."

"Well, he was to have told you—oh, never mind!" she said impatiently. The man had been no illusion of the night, and she was not about to let fear cloud her wisdom. She would discover the goings-on at Castle Creeghan, and she would not falter. She had to know the truth, or she could not go on.

Martise was about to bang the huge brass knocker, dangling from the mouth of a massive brass dragon, when the door creaked open, apparently of its own accord, for she saw no living person at first.

There was warmth, at least, she thought, peering in past the thick, gaping door. This first tower seemed the most ancient, for the walls were bare brick, hung with tapestries, like some old great hall. A long table that would surely seat at least twenty lay to the right; the great hearth with the blazing fire that warmed her against the wicked and sodden night lay to the left. Before it sat two large Queen Anne chairs, with a delicate cherrywood table between them. And far to the center were the stairs, broad and carpeted in rich red velvet, going straight to the curve of the tower, then taking a right angle to follow it to the floor above. A huge brass chandelier hung from the high ceiling, casting the glow of dozens of candles about the room already lit by the fire, as if someone, somewhere within the dwelling, feared the thought of shadows.

"Hello?" Martise said softly.

There were, after all, shadows within the room. An old man in black and white livery and stockings and breeches that belonged to the previous century stepped around from the pool of darkness created by the open door. He did not smile at Martise, but surveyed her gravely from a cadaverous face. He was tall and painfully thin, with a full white beard and mustache, hollow cheeks, and curious dark eyes that seemed to burn with a bright fire.

"Lady St. James?" There was the slightest note of surprise in his voice. Martise steeled herself against it and smiled brightly. Water dripped from her clothing and her person, and she was quite certain that she had never appeared less the lady.

"Yes, and you are—"

"Hogarth, milady, his lordship's butler and valet, glad to welcome you to Castle Creeghan. Your things?" He saw her portmanteau and valises on the step and dragged them inside. He was impeccable in his white shirt and black livery and white gloves. "You must be quite chilled, milady. I'll call Sam to bring your things to your room so that you might freshen up from your long journey."

"That would be wonderful. Thank you."

Hogarth pulled upon a bell cord, and a moment later Sam appeared.

Sam was tremendous, with the shoulders of a giant, slightly hunched, giving him an odd appearance. His hair was steel gray, and his eyes were a curious light blue. He smiled and bobbed to Martise, and she nodded and smiled uneasily in turn. He was a curious fellow, very ugly, and yet the smile seemed sincere and eager.

"This is the west tower, milady," Hogarth informed her, leading her toward the majestic curving staircase. "The lower floors of the north tower house the servants, the east tower holds the family rooms, and the south tower is the sole domain of the lord of Creeghan. I think you'll find your room hospitable. It is where your sister, Lady Creeghan, stayed."

A slight flicker of discomfort passed through Martise as she thought about Mary's letters, tucked away in her portmanteau. Had Mary's imagination run wild? Or was it true that evil had stalked the halls by night, that echoes of screams had carried throughout the stone walls . . . ?

"When shall I see Lord Creeghan?" Martise asked Hogarth.

"When you are rested and ready, milady."

At the top of the stairs stood a long gallery with mullioned windows looking out to the night. Martise paused to stare out into the darkness. Castle Creeghan was indeed a rugged structure. Even in the darkness she could see the endless rock that seemed to ripple down to the stream of the verdant valley below. The power of nature lay within the rock walls. The sea roared to the east of the castle, and the harsh rock protected it from any advance by land. No wonder the lords of Creeghan had reigned supreme for so many centuries, against their enemies, against the odds.

"Come, milady."

Hogarth hurried her along the gallery until they came to a set of heavy wooden double doors with brass handles and knockers. Hogarth tossed them open for her, displaying the room.

It was mammoth and elegant. A four-poster bed lay at an angle to the far right corner, and beautiful, huge Tudor chairs stood before the low burning fire, upon a muted Persian carpet. To the left of the fireplace was a round cherrywood table with two delicate matching chairs, and all stood just before the full length of the glass-paned doors leading out to the balcony.

"How lovely," Martise murmured, moving toward the sheer-draped doors.

"Allow me."

Hogarth hurried before her, opening the doors outward to the night. Martise stepped into the shadows of the balcony. She could hear the surf, far below her to the east. Even here, in this sheltered cove of the castle, the rock rose to create the walls of the balcony. But she need not look at the rock, for the flooring was Venetian tile and there were beautiful wrought-iron benches laid along the length of the balcony.

A touch of shadow caught her eye, downward, where the

balcony disappeared into the darkness of the night. Her heart beat suddenly, and she had the curious feeling that she was being watched. Again she wondered at her wisdom in coming. Castle Creeghan was dangerous.

As was the lord of Creeghan?

She lifted her chin, determined not to be easily frightened. "Hogarth, is someone down there?"

She started walking quickly along the length of the balcony. Hogarth hurried behind her. "Milady, no one goes this way now!"

She stopped abruptly and stared at Hogarth. "Why ever not?"

"No one goes there," he insisted.

"But someone—"

"Lady St. James, may I return for you in one half hour?" Hogarth asked.

She sighed. "Fine."

Hogarth nodded and left her on the balcony. Martise stared into the darkness that came when the light from her room was swallowed away by the night. Someone had been there. Someone, watching her arrival.

Well, it did no good to question Hogarth. She would wash and change, and await her introduction to the lord of Creeghan.

Martise came in from the balcony and surveyed the beautiful and spacious room in a pensive silence, her hands folded before her. She started to shiver but told herself that she was cold from the rain, and not frightened.

Her bags had been set at the foot of the bed and she set her portmanteau atop the mirrored dresser next to the armoire opposite the bed. She stared at her own reflection, finding her brush and trying to whisk through her abundance of hair. Her eyes were too wide, she thought. She had not been here long at all, and already her eyes were wide, and her cheeks were taking on a hollow appearance.

Nonsense. She tugged upon the hooks holding her gown in place and slipped out of it. In her corset and petticoats and pantalettes she hurried to the fire and let its warmth sweep over her. She closed her eyes and thought again of Mary's letters.

"He is fascinating, Martise, the most striking and arresting man I have ever met. He is tall and chivalrous and powerful and his voice could shake the very mountains. He is sometimes aloof and arrogant, and always the aristocrat, the great lord . . . but he loves me, Martise, can you imagine? He loves me."

And later . . .

"He is courteous, and he is pagan, and so vital! His eyes are fire and hypnotism and I cannot fight the power of his arms. He seduced me by moonlight, and I have never known such ecstasy . . ."

And later still . . .

"I cannot tell what troubles him, for he is not the man I knew. He is tense and quiet, and always brooding, and always listening, and always watching me. He holds me, and tells me to take care, to trust no one . . .

"Then he tells me that I must trust him.

"I heard the screaming again last night. I heard the screaming, and it was horrible and wretched, and it was as if the very walls of the castle themselves screamed with the horror and the pain. Martise, I am afraid . . ."

The fire snapped and crackled, and Martise spun away from it. Her hair had caught the highlights of the blaze, and might have been an extension of the flame that had warmed and dried her.

She would not falter; she would not fail. She would understand fully what came to pass at Castle Creeghan, and she would gladly live a lie to do so.

And . . .

She swallowed tightly, and with a certain amount of shame. She had come because of Mary.

But she had come because of the emerald, too.

She had loved Mary dearly; she *needed* the emerald.

For the moment, she wasn't going to think about it. She had to make it through this first, curious night.

She had to meet the lord of the castle.

"Someone should have come to unpack for me," she muttered aloud to give herself courage. She dragged her heavier bags around and onto the bed. Opening the first, she found a green muslin with delicate embroidery. She shook it out and laid it on the bed. Finding a pitcher and bowl, she scrubbed her face and hands and splashed the water against her, then dried and donned the gown, wishing that she could take a long bath with an endless supply of scalding water. Perhaps it could be arranged, once she had met the master of Creeghan.

She had just finished with the last of her hooks when she heard a soft tapping at her door. She opened it to find a wide-eyed young woman there, smiling and eager, and dressed in a white cap and white apron. "I be Holly, mum, and here to serve you."

"Thank you, Holly. I'd like my things hung in the wardrobe, if you would, please."

"Yes, mum, but first I'm to take you to his lordship."

"Fine."

"This way, Lady St. James."

Martise closed the door to her room behind her. Holly led her back along the gallery and toward the steps which had brought her to the second floor. Following Holly, Martise descended the graceful and curving stairway to the entry hall.

There was a man there. His back was to her as he faced the blaze, his hands folded behind him, his feet wide apart, his shoulders very broad beneath the fine-cut lines of his frock coat. He was very dark, a towering, striking figure, and it seemed that even the sight of his back might send fear scurrying into the unwary. He held himself with the power, with the authority, of the lord of the castle.

Holly hesitated, and Martise remained silent. The fire hissed, crackled, and sizzled, and he spoke.

"Thank you, Holly. You may leave us."

He turned around at last. Martise gasped out loud, startled to see the blazing eyes of the stranger who had swept her onto the bay and carried her to the castle through the rain.

He did not smile, he did not speak. He studied her again with what might have been an irritable care, seeking something.

"Welcome . . . Lady St. James."

"Really, *Lord Creeghan*? You told me that I should find no welcome here."

"You wrote and told me that you were coming. You are welcome, of course."

"You tried to scare me away."

"I am afraid that I did not succeed."

"Why?"

"I do not know. Why are you still here?"

Martise sighed with exaggerated patience. "My lord, why would you try to scare me away?"

"Because," he said quite simply, "you should not be here." He stepped around the Queen Anne chairs to the small table between them where a silver tray held a crystal carafe and several glasses. "Brandy, Lady St. James? It will ward off the chill of the evening, the dampness of the night."

"Yes, thank you."

She felt that he studied her still as he poured out two glasses of the dark liquid. His movements were graceful and effortless; he was indeed a man born and bred to be the lord of the castle.

He came to her, pressing one of the glasses into her hands. He was close again, towering over her with his leashed energy and tension and his masculine scent and his startling green-gold eyes. She longed to jump away, for she was suddenly very aware of Mary's words.

". . . the most striking and arresting man I have ever

met. His eyes are fire and hypnotism. He seduced me by moonlight . . . He is courteous, and he is pagan . . ."

He was all that, Martise thought, and so much more. For even as he stood so near her, not touching her but watching her with his bold and blatant stare, she felt a trembling seize hold of her. He seemed as rugged as the craggy tor, drawn to a pretense of refinement by the fine corded fabric of his frock coat and the silk of his shirt beneath it.

He tapped his glass to hers. "Do sip your brandy, milady. It has been a rough night for you, I dare say."

"I dare say," Martise heard herself repeat. She needed to back away from him, but she must do so carefully, for she would not have him think that she was afraid of him. She was not afraid.

She was . . .

Aye, afraid, for his threat did not seem to be one of violence, or maybe yes, violence was a part of it. What beat in the heart of the man? Martise wondered. She was certain that beyond Mary, many a poor innocent girl had fallen prey to the rugged excitement of the lord of Creeghan.

She was no lost innocent, but a wary woman of the world, determined to find truth and justice. She would not be touched, she vowed, and she would not be fooled.

But despite her silent avowals, he did touch her. He reached for her chin, raising it so that he might study her eyes, and her features, with blunt appraisal. She felt his fingers, warm and strong and hinting of their power, upon her flesh, and she could not draw away. She sizzled beneath his scrutiny, clenching her teeth. She saw his grim smile as he felt the movement, but when she would have broken from him in a fury, he abruptly released her.

"You do not much resemble your sister, Lady St. James."

"No," she said flatly, "we are not much alike."

"I assume, milady, that you would like to see the place of burial?"

Was there no emotion to him? Did he not grieve his wife?

Or had he cast her into her premature grave himself?

She hesitated, for the wind still moaned beyond the walls, and the night was a dark tempest. She did not know where he would take her, and though she had sworn she would not fear the darkness of night, she was eager for sunlight.

"I think, perhaps, in the morning . . ."

"Of course, how foolish of me," he apologized abruptly, but he moved away from her with his curious, mocking smile in place, and she knew that he was aware of her unease. She hated to allow him to see such a weakness on her part. "I shall take you to the crypt tomorrow, Lady St. James. Now, I suppose, you would like to retire to your room."

"Yes, perhaps . . ."

"I shall have dinner sent on a tray. Shall I send for Holly to take you back?"

"No, thank you. I can find the way."

He nodded. "Well, good night, then, Lady St. James."

"Good night, Lord Creeghan."

She started to walk away, but he called her back with a curious tone to his words. "It has surely been a difficult year for you, milady. Your husband dying in that wretched American war, and now, finding that your sister has perished, too . . . how strange, milady. You acquired quite an American accent in your few years in the raw wilderness."

Martise had just reached the stairway. Her fingers closed and tightened around the banister.

"It is easy to acquire an accent, Lord Creeghan." She spun around, lifting her chin, allowing the liquid flame of her hair to cascade down behind her. "May I say, milord, that you have lost a great deal of the Scotsman's burr?"

"Ah, milady, but I was educated at Oxford and Yale. And

when I've a mind, madam, my burr can be quite a wicked one, I do assure you."

"Oh, I've no doubt," Martise replied.

He smiled. "Forgive me, milady, but what is your Christian name? Margaret, is it not?"

She gritted her teeth tightly together and answered smoothly. "Martise, Lord Creeghan. Mary called me 'Maggie' for Martise, not Margaret. Good night, sir."

"Good night."

Martise fled up the stairs. She did not stop until she had reached her own room. When she was there, she securely latched the doors to the balcony, and then she carefully bolted the door to the gallery, and only then did she dare to fall across the bed, her heart thundering.

He suspected her . . .

He could not!

She steeled herself to courage as she lay there, listening to the sound of the violent surf far below, listening to the roar and churn and fury of the wind. The fire within her room brought warmth above the tempest. There was that warmth . . .

Soon there was a tap on her door. Holly had brought her a tray. Martise thanked her and bolted the door again. She was startled to discover that she was ravenous. Her dinner was roasted lamb with mint jelly, and the food was delicious. She ate it with great relish and sipped the wine that accompanied it.

Then she set the tray beyond her door and very carefully bolted it once again.

She dressed in a white nightgown and crawled into the four-poster bed with its crisp clean sheets and warm wool blanket, and she told herself that she must sleep. But as she listened to the howl of the wind, she wondered at the tales that the very stone walls of the castle screamed in horror . . .

At last, exhaustion came to her, and she closed her eyes and slept.

• • •

He came to her.

He came to her in the night, in the flickering red glow of the firelight, and she was bathed in it.

He stood close, looking down at her, and his eyes narrowed with suspicion, then he shrugged. He would discover her secret.

He had not meant to; he reached out and touched her. He touched her glorious display of blazing hair when it fell in silken beauty against the white of the sheets. He stared at her lashes, rich and dark as they fell in crescents over the softness of her cheeks, and he thought of the color of her eyes, bright, startling, cobalt and teal, eyes to defy the very color of day, sparkling with courage and determination.

And only hinting in the shadows of the slightest cast of fear.

"Damn!" he murmured aloud. She should not have come. He had enough on his hands, and the situation was grim indeed. Now he had this girl to cope with, too. This brazen beauty with her wild flame hair and clear blue eyes and silken voice.

He stiffened, for as he watched her, she shifted and moved, her breasts pressed fully against the white lace of her gown. Her covers were tossed and he was treated to a glimpse of long and shapely limbs.

With an oath he tossed the covers over her, and then he realized that tension had gripped his throat and his muscles, and that he shook with the force of it.

She was made for desire . . .

The heat and tempest and passion of life lay within her eyes, and within the bewitching curves and angles of her form, and in the blaze of her hair.

He wanted her . . . as he had forgotten how to want. He wanted to hold her and take her, until he slaked his restless yearning and doused the fire and tumult within.

He swore aloud again and pulled the covers high around her, and paused just a moment more.

Who was she?

He swore he would find out. She had come to seduce and trap him, he was certain.

But it would not be. She would be the one trapped and seduced.

It might very well be his only way to save her.

Two

❧

She dreamed in the half-light that filtered into her room with the coming of morning.

She did not dream of the stark walls of Creeghan rising out of the mist, but of a gentler, more tender scene. Of a white-columned porch shimmering in the sunlight, of rolling hill upon rolling hill of rich and verdant green, and beyond the manicured lawns, the fields of rich Virginia tobacco. The sun shone down so brightly and the sky was blue, dispelling any trace of gloom or fog or mist . . .

There was a man upon the porch, his hair golden and his eyes startling deep blue, and he was reaching out to her and she was running, running to cast herself into his arms. He smiled, welcoming her, but suddenly she was running through mist. The mist cleared, and she stopped dead in her tracks. The tall blond man was gone, and there was a dark-haired stranger in his place, oh, a man she had met, but a stranger, still. Tall, striking, his lips curling into a smile that might have been the devil's own, his eyes piercing her, seeing through her, knowing all.

And he was waiting for her, waiting.

She heard the burst of a shell, and the green lawn erupted between them. She was alone.

Alone with a horrible acrid stench, the smell of black powder from a thousand guns and countless cannons scorching the earth.

Martise awoke with a start, bolting up in bed.

She was no longer home, the war was over, and the endless green lawn of her dream existed no more. Her father was gone . . .

And Lord Creeghan belonged to this new life. He hadn't belonged in the dream. That was the past. It was about things lost to her forever.

No. Not Eagle's Walk.

Eagle's Walk still stood. She had sold off some of the land, but she was desperately hanging on to the house itself. It wasn't as old as Creeghan, but it meant every bit as much to her as Creeghan might mean to its lord. Her father had been an Englishman, but he had loved the property her mother brought to him through marriage as if he had been born and bred there himself. And as long as Martise lived, she would never forget the day not long before the awful war began when he stood with her on the bottom step of that beautiful porch. "Life is always fleeting, Martise, and we pass through it quickly. This war will sweep it away even more quickly for thousands of young men, for the idealists, for the zealots. They will all fall before the fire. Hold on to this home of ours, Martise. Hold on tight, because the present will be whisked away by the winds of time, and such places are all that we will have to remember. It will be your heritage. Your children's heritage."

She had made a vow to him then, not even understanding his words. She understood soon enough. Within a year and a half, he was killed, falling at Manassas in the opening stages of the war.

Martise St. James . . . That much was true, she reflected. It *was* her name. But she wasn't *Lady* St. James— that was Margaret. Margaret had married Martise's cousin Aaron, the son of Martise's uncle, her father's older brother,

Lord St. James. Then Aaron was Lord St. James and now . . .

Now they were all gone. Aaron had fallen at Sharpsburg, and Margaret had died outside of Richmond of the typhus not a year later.

She'd had to come here as Mary's sister, for it was unlikely that Lord Creeghan would have allowed her if he knew that she was merely his deceased wife's sister's cousin-in-law.

Margaret had been her friend, as close as Aaron, even though her cousin had led a very military life, being in the British service, fighting in Africa—and then choosing to take on the fight of the Confederacy, joining up with the Rebs to fight with Lee. And in the midst of the decay and destruction of her country all around her, Martise had learned that Mary had died, too. After all of her startling letters, after the things that she had said and written. Mary, Margaret's beautiful younger sister, carefree, a heartbreaker herself, being swept away by a man reported to be the catch of the season, the lord of Castle Creeghan. Mary, who was exactly the same age as Martise, who was her dear friend.

Tears were stinging her eyes, Martise realized. She had woken up very maudlin, and she was grieving again, missing people she should have learned not to miss so dearly.

Well, she was here. She was here now, and if she couldn't change any of the horror that had ravaged her past, perhaps she could discover the truth about Mary. She owed it to her, and to Margaret, and even to Aaron. She had loved them.

And she also needed the emerald. Desperately.

Martise rubbed her eyes and rose and walked to the balcony doors, throwing them open. The wind swept in upon her. Beyond the parapets the sheer rocks and cliffs rose high, yet looking out, toward the east, she could see the sea, wild, gray, beautiful, thundering against the rocks with a power of its own. It was a stunning sight, she thought, as beautiful as the green fields of home, in its way. The sky was clear and endlessly blue, yet offered up the harsh whisper of the wind, beautiful, deceitful.

She came back into the room and scrubbed her face, smiling. It was daylight. She was going to have no more fancies about Castle Creeghan. She was going to discover—things.

But when she finished washing, she realized that her hands were trembling. She sat down at the foot of the bed, hugging her shoulders for warmth.

She wanted very much to understand what had happened to Mary, and she also needed Mary's property, because the emerald had to be among Mary's things. It wasn't as if she was stealing a Creeghan family jewel—the emerald belonged to the St. James family. Mary had seen Martise briefly before her marriage, and they had decided that Mary should take the jewel, which might be important in time, to Scotland, where it could not be seized by an angry enemy.

Martise didn't know the emerald's exact value, but she knew that it was worth thousands of dollars. Enough to pay off the back taxes on Eagle's Walk, and that was all that Martise cared about. Her father was gone, her mother had died years before the threat of war ever loomed over the South, and now Aaron was gone, and Margaret and Mary, too.

The house, the home, the remaining land, they were all that she had.

She had hoped that Mary had entrusted her husband with the jewel, but that hadn't seemed to be the case when Martise first corresponded with him. Writing to Bruce Creeghan had brought her a reply, a solicitous, polite note, telling her that she was welcome to Mary's personal effects. An almost casual note.

Mary's effects. Simple things, combs and brushes, clothing, small gold chains, her letter box, her portmanteaus . . .

Not a single mention of the emerald. Either he didn't know about it or he intended to keep it from her.

There came a tap on her door, and she leapt up to undo the bolt and admit Holly.

"I let you sleep as late as possible, milady," the maid told her cheerfully. "Traveling being so rough upon the bones and all. But the master intends to show you to your dear sister's grave, and he's been up and about for hours, so I'm assuming he'll be ready for you the moment the midday meal is over. I've brought you tea and biscuits, but just a bite, for cook will have something fine in store in the main hall in an hour or so."

"Tea is lovely, thank you," Martise assured her, accepting the tray. Holly was so fresh-faced and pretty, so honest and down-to-earth that Martise felt some of the mystery and gloom of the night dissipating in her presence. She needn't have been so unnerved. It was only the storm over the castle that caused her unease last night. "Holly, I would dearly love a delicious hot bath. Would that be possible?"

It was possible. Holly left her with her tea and biscuits and went off for the wooden hip bath and kettles to heat above her own fire. She returned with a huge man carrying the tub and several kitchen lads toting water. The giant bearing the tub was introduced to her as Robert McCloud, the groom drawn in from the stables for assistance. He was well over six feet tall, burly and so muscle-hewn he seemed to have no neck. He nodded curtly to her as he set the tub down, but then seemed to study her with a boldness she found insulting—or frightening. A scar ran the length of his left cheek, his eyes were a startling light blue, and his smile indicated he appreciated all that he saw in her.

Martise ignored him, turning her attention to the lads Holly introduced. "This here, milady, our blond boy, is Trey McNamara, and the darker lad here is our Jemie, Jemie MacPeters." Holly's glance to her, over Jemie's head, indicated that something wasn't quite right with Jemie MacPeters. But the blond boy smiled very shyly and endearingly, and Martise found herself smiling gently in return, liking him the best of the three males she had just met.

Holly shooed them out of the bedroom, and Martise assured her that she was just fine on her own. "Well, if I can be of assistance, milady—I served your dear sister, I did. And I know of course that you were living in the South of the States, and that you were quite accustomed to the service of slaves—"

"Holly, I am quite accustomed to bathing and dressing myself," Martise said softly, gritting her teeth. She hadn't been accustomed to much help with anything over the last four years. Indeed, there had been slaves at Eagle's Walk. Dana had been with her for years and years, but her great kind heart failed as the war had gone on and on. Old Buff stayed there now, keeping up with all that he could. And there was Henry from the fields, and his wife . . .

And the hundreds and hundreds who had fled to the North, and out of them, the many who had come back, disillusioned, needing just to feed their hungry families when the North offered them no jobs, when the very people who had "freed" them refused to touch them, thinking that their color could come off on them like a disease.

Not that she defended slavery. She had known fine Southern gentlemen who were not averse to beating their people cruelly. She was just weary of the war, and weary of the concepts of others about the rebellious Southerners.

"If you're sure, then—" Holly began.

"Indeed, I'm sure!" Martise snapped, far more curtly than she had intended. She saw the surprise touch Holly's face, and the hurt, and she was sorry, but she would make it up at some later time. As Holly left her and she crawled into the steaming water, Martise thought ruefully that she must indeed seem a change from her "sister" Mary, for Mary was never brusque. She had always been gentle, always kind, and never raised her voice.

Her pulse quickened suddenly. Holly had served Mary.

She must know something of Mary's life here, perhaps even something about her secrets.

Just as the morning's light dispelled the gloom of the night, the hot bath and rich-scented soap seemed to wash away the last of the long trip to reach Creeghan. Martise dressed feeling a new strength about her. She studied her features as she combed out her hair, determining to leave it loose to fall about her shoulders and down the length of her back. She had chosen a royal-blue gown with a rich flurry of petticoats and she wondered even as she studied her own eyes if she had really chosen the day gown because it had traveled so well, or if somewhere, in the back of her mind, she might have chosen it to seduce the master of Creeghan.

There was a knock on her door. She swung it open. Holly was back, quiet, subdued. "Milady, shall I take you to the hall?"

Martise offered her a warm smile. "Please, Holly. I do believe I know my way, but I shall be happy for your guidance."

Holly brightened visibly before her. She smiled and turned, starting off down the hallway.

The sun streamed in through the mullioned windows. There were gorgeous draperies and tapestries along the walls, and the cold stone floor was covered with a red velvet runner held in place by brass rings. Every effort had been made to bring the castle into the nineteenth century, Martise thought. The master, it seemed, liked his comforts.

"So you were with Mary," Martise said softly, behind Holly.

Holly paused and looked over her shoulder. "Aye, that I was. No gentler lady have I known than your sister, milady. It broke my heart when we lost her, I do promise you."

"I'm sure."

Holly started walking again. "Tell me, Holly," Martise said. "Did it break the master's heart?"

Once again, Holly stopped dead, swirling around to stare at Martise with wide eyes. "Oh, indeed, milady, that it did!

Why, he just weren't the same, he weren't the same at all for months. He sat up night after night in the darkness, he did, missing her."

"I'm glad to hear that," Martise said, and smiled. "Thank you for telling me."

Holly nodded, turned about again, and led the way down the stairway. When they reached the hall, Holly did not remain, or even speak to Bruce Creeghan, who stood once more with his back to her.

When he spun around, Martise was newly startled by the fire in his eyes. It seemed that they had a devil's touch of fire, that they invaded her heart and her mind, and saw the very things she tried to hide. His raven-dark hair and striking features combined to give him the aura of the true master of the world, and yet when he smiled, slowly, as he did now, the arrogance did not seem to matter. He seemed to beckon her as a flame beckons a moth, and she felt the heat of his gaze deep within her. He was a sensual man. She stared at the fullness of his lips and was dismayed to realize that she wondered how the touch of his kiss would feel against her flesh.

"Good day, Lady St. James. Tell me, did you sleep well your first night in the castle?" he asked.

"Yes, I did. Thank you very much."

He walked across the room to the table that had been set for two. A crystal decanter of bloodred wine sat upon a silver tray between two glasses. He poured out two portions and offered her a glass, lifting it so that she was forced to walk across the room and stand before him to accept it.

"I'm glad that you were comfortable," he told her. "Castles are old, and they creak, and the wind streams through them and creates whispers in the darkness. For strangers, it is often difficult to sleep once the fear of the unknown sets in."

"The unknown?"

"Well, the whispers, of course. And the cries of the wind."

She fought the hypnotism of his eyes and brought a smile to her lips. "The castle is beautiful, Lord Creeghan. Truly beautiful by daylight. I missed so very much in the darkness last night. I do not fear the whispers—or the cries—of the wind."

"Aye, that's right, I had forgotten. You do not fear ghosts, only the living."

"And none of the living would threaten me here," she said sweetly.

"None," he assured her. He pulled back her chair. She felt the whisper of his breath against her neck as he seated her at the huge dragon-clawed table, bending low against her as he adjusted her chair. "None would dare to threaten such a righteous and determined beauty, I am certain!"

Warmth flooded her. He sat to her side, at the head of the table.

Hogarth appeared then to serve the soup from a large silver tureen. Martise thanked him, thinking that even Hogarth looked better by the daylight. He still appeared very old, but perhaps his cheeks weren't quite so cadaverous. To her amazement, he smiled at her and even seemed to wink.

"When we've finished with the meal, I shall see that you meet some of the household," Creeghan said.

"Well, I do know Holly and Hogarth, and I met your groom this morning, Robert McCloud, and the stable boys, Trey and Jemie."

He nodded and smiled. "But you've still to meet the other members of my family."

She set her soup spoon down. The beef broth was delicious, but he was watching her again. Watching her with that piercing gaze that seemed to seek answers even as it seemed to know . . .

"Your family?" she said. Mary had never mentioned his family. At first, her letters had been so filled with her obsession for this man that she mentioned nothing else. Then they had been filled with fear.

"My sister, Elaina, lives with me here, as does my uncle, Peter, and then there are my cousins, Conar and Ian."

"Where are they now?"

"About, I imagine. You'll meet them in time." She started as his fingers curled over hers, hot as fire. Her eyes leapt from their hands and looked into his. "I wanted this meal alone with you," he said. "I was curious about Mary's . . . *sister,* you see. I do hope that you will forgive me."

She quickly pulled her hand away and entwined her fingers in her lap. "You will take me to Mary?" she said softly.

"As soon as we have finished."

"Thank you."

"How long will you be staying here?" he asked her abruptly.

"I—I don't know," she faltered. "I'd like to go through my sister's things—"

"Of course. You mentioned that in your letter."

"If you are anxious for me to leave, then I shall try to move as swiftly with my endeavors as I can."

"Ah, my dear Lady St. James, I would not dream of rushing you. Your presence dearly graces this hall."

"You hardly gave me welcome last night, milord Creeghan."

"But then there was thunder and lightning, and danger in the darkness. I feared for you."

"Did you?"

"Just as I wonder what those endeavors might be that you will work at so swiftly."

She felt color flood her face, and she wondered again how this man could seem to know so much.

"Sentimental endeavors, sir," she replied quickly, her eyes downcast to hide her thoughts.

She was grateful when Hogarth came back into the hall with a heavyset and florid woman by his side. The soup dishes were removed, and they were served an aromatic meal of fish and new potatoes and small sweet peas. "This is Freya, Lady St. James." He smiled at the large woman. "I believe some of her ancestors to be as Nordic as my own. She is one of the rare wonders of our lives here, a cook far beyond the realm of any other in these parts."

Freya flashed him a broad, toothsome smile, and bobbed a curtsy to Martise. Martise murmured something, and then Hogarth and the woman seemed to melt away.

"Freya is a wonderful cook. You mustn't let your food grow cold," Creeghan told her.

Mechanically, Martise reached for her fork and tasted the fish. It was delicious, seasoned delicately, cooked lightly.

"Is it much like your cuisine in the States?" he asked politely.

She set her fork down. "Lord Creeghan, you must be aware that the States have recently been ravaged by a civil war—"

"A 'war of rebellion'—so it has been stated in your Northern journals."

She gritted her teeth and smiled. He was purposely trying her temper. "It matters not what one chooses to call it, Lord Creeghan. I was residing on the wrong side of it, since it has proven to be the side that has *lost,* and—"

"Aye, and indeed, but your poor husband was swept away in the midst of the turmoil—also on the wrong side of it, as it seems. My deepest apologies, Lady St. James. I had forgotten that you are a bereaved widow, just as I am a bereaved widower. Do forgive me. And pray," he said softly, and again his fingers curled over hers. She wanted to wrench them away, but she did not. She felt the heat. Felt it enter deep within her. Felt it become a trembling inside, even as she raised her eyes to his once again. "Pray, do know that I am very much aware of the war so recently fought, and of your losses within it. I shall try never to dwell upon it." He smiled. "I will, instead, haunt you with questions about the time your husband served with the

British military in Africa. Those must have been fascinating days."

Indeed, Africa *must* have been fascinating, Martise thought as she stared blankly at him. And the pity was that she didn't know a darned thing about Africa. Her cousin and Margaret had lived there for at least a year, but by the time they came to the States, the Civil War had become a way of life and Martise couldn't remember a thing Margaret had said about her life in Africa.

She forced a smile to her lips. It was cold and brittle, but surely, it passed as a smile.

"Africa . . . it was, of course, fascinating. The last years were so tumultuous, I fear that I've forgotten a great deal of everything that went on before."

"Of course." Lord Creeghan smiled gently, and his face seemed very near, and the heat radiating from him now seemed to engulf her and cause a simmering that filled her very blood. "I shall jar your memory with better times, milady." He paused and added softly, "I swear it."

They ate in silence, then he pushed back his chair and rose. Too quickly, he was behind her again. And again she felt the warmth of his breath against her flesh as he pulled back her chair that she might rise, too. "Come, milady. I will take you to Mary."

He offered her his arm. She had little choice but to take it, quickly lowering her gaze from his golden one. He walked her past the stairway to a heavy oak door. When he pulled it open, she saw the raw stone steps that led below and felt the cold of the stone reach up and wrap around her like a human arm. He gazed at her with apology. "I fear that the chapel and the crypts are cold, indeed. They had always been so. Excuse me, and I will precede you, for the stairs are also tricky when one is not accustomed to them."

It seemed that they walked downward forever. The cold remained. Yet even as he carefully led her down, Martise realized that someone had come before them, someone had prepared the way. Gas lanterns lit their descent into what otherwise must have been sheer darkness.

Finally, an endless distance from the main floor above, they came to the cold stone passage of the cellar and the crypts.

At the foot of the stairs Lord Creeghan paused, and Martise went still behind him, adjusting to the light and the cold. Down a long barren hallway she could see nothing but iron doors, some seeming to lead to darkness, and some seeming to offer a little light.

"These are all crypts?" Martise asked softly.

He smiled. "I warned you that the walls whispered here, Lady St. James. The ghosts of centuries are rumored to haunt the halls of Castle Creeghan. The edifice has changed over the years, but you must remember that there was a manor here even before the Viking invasions of the 800s. Remember, Lady St. James, you are not afraid of ghosts."

So she had claimed. Martise decided that she must fear the unknown and the dead just a bit if she was thinking that she wanted to get closer to the master of Castle Creeghan for protection. She almost smiled herself. "Milord, if you would be so kind, my name is Martise, and I am not afraid of ghosts. I had simply not expected the crypts of the castle to be so very vast."

He slipped his arm through hers, chuckling as he led her forward. "To the left, Martise, there is nothing so haunting except for our wine cellar. And both doors yonder lead only to the chapel, which is very beautiful. Come, I'll show you."

The chapel was indeed beautiful. The earth directly beyond it must have been dug out, and the castle walls built beyond a path, for magnificent windows of elegant stained glass had been added to old arched openings. They faced the sea, Martise thought, and the afternoon light flickered in, creating a rainbow of colors. St. Luke, St. Mark, and a number of others adorned the stunning windows. The pews were new and smelled of pine oil and wax, and the center aisle was lined with handsome brass candle holders. The altar was of white marble, and fresh flowers sat upon it.

"The Creeghans remained obstinately Catholic, just as many Stuart royalty were known to do," Lord Creeghan informed her with a touch of humor. "They weren't the type to lose their heads over their religious preferences, though. While the country turned largely Protestant, the Creeghans came down here in quiet. We seldom use the chapel anymore, except for private services. Father Martin, in the village, does well enough for all of us." He was quiet for a second. "Yet Elaina keeps up the flowers. Bless her, else this place should surely fall to decay."

"That would be a pity, for it is truly beautiful," Martise remarked.

She felt his eyes, and their touch of fire. "Aye, an oasis of peace perhaps," he said, and she sensed the laughter behind his words. "Come, you must see the rest of the cellar." He led her out and they were in the cold and drafty hallway once again. Where the chapel had seemed to offer warmth, the hall was decidedly cold and led into endless darkness.

Following close behind Bruce Creeghan, Martise noted the wrought-iron doors along the way. Through most there was nothing but darkness, but as she came closer upon them, she realized that each door led to an inner crypt. Row upon row of coffins lay on stone slabs. Coats of arms often entwined in the gates, dates were set above them in brass, and a cross hung heavily above the wrought iron. Farther down the hallway, in intense darkness, there was another gate that blocked the way.

Her heart beat too quickly even as they walked along the hall. Their footsteps seemed extraordinarily loud to her ears. She wanted to touch him, or she wanted him to take her arm again, but he did not. She gritted her teeth. She was not afraid of ghosts. Yet, if she were to be down here, alone, in the total darkness of the night, she might well be tempted to think that the corpses of these endless Creeghans did rise to dance within the ebony shadows of the night.

He stopped directly before the iron doors that blocked the hallway. Martise thought that he meant to open the ancient and rusting lock there, but he did not. He turned to a set of doors to the left of those blocking the hall.

"Wait!" Martise said. "What—what lies beyond those gates?"

He arched his brow. His face was doubly handsome, and doubly Satanish, in the muted candlelight of the crypt. "Those, Martise, are the truly ancient crypts. They did not lay the dead within coffins then, milady; rather, their custom was to set the deceased upon their stone, cover them with a shroud, and leave them to the damages of time. I had the gates erected years ago after Elaina was lost in here as a child and nearly frightened herself to death. None of us go there now. I intend to have the crypts walled in."

Martise shivered anew, imagining the dead of hundreds of years gone past, decayed to bone now, and still gowned in their silks and velvets and furs.

"This," he said very softly, "is where Mary lies."

This crypt, so close to those that were so very old, was new. When the gates were opened, Martise stepped through them. Fine wooden coffins lined brick shelving. There wasn't a trace of a spiderweb in here, and lanterns had been lit to illuminate most of the shadows.

Mary's was the most recent interment. Her coffin lay in the middle aisle, with a beautiful marble effigy of an angel set upon the slab to guard it. Her name was set upon the coffin in shining brass, MARY ELIZABETH CREEGHAN, along with the gentle, consoling words: "Her beauty of spirit was too great for this our earth and she now resides with the angels."

Fresh flowers were laid next to the coffin.

Heedless of Bruce Creeghan, Martise remembered Mary, and tears flooded unbidden to her eyes. She stepped past him and knelt down before the coffin, lowering her head.

And then she heard the sniffling sound. A low but anguished sound of loss and misery, and it seemed to come from the very coffin itself. Perhaps the unfettered dead had risen from the crypts beyond, and ghostly creatures had come forth to mourn new losses . . .

Martise leapt up, amazed, a scream racing to her throat and hysteria rising within her.

Strong arms swept around her shoulders and she was only too glad of them as an apparition rose from beyond the coffin. In the shadows, she thought that Mary herself had come back to life, for the apparition was of a small dark-haired woman in an elegant sea-green contemporary gown.

The scream continued to grow within Martise. She felt the heat and power of the man behind her and fought for sanity even as she seemed to lose her grip upon it. But then he spoke, quickly, harshly, shattering the illusion before her.

"Elaina! By God, what are you doing there! You've quite scared Lady St. James near to death!"

"Oh, I am so very sorry!" the woman said, and coming around the coffin, she reached for Martise's hand. "I didn't mean to frighten you. I brought the flowers and found myself staying."

Her speech was beautiful, softly, wonderfully burred. Her eyes were wide and luminous, shimmering green, and framed, as were her brother's, by the darkest lashes. She was a woman in her early to mid-twenties, delicate, fine, and seemingly earnest and sweet.

"Martise, my sister Elaina. Elaina, the Lady St. James."

"Please call me Martise," Martise said quickly, taking Elaina's hand. "I've very glad to meet you."

"And we are so very glad to have you, except that we are sorry that you have come here to find Mary . . . to find her so," Elaina said, indicating the coffin. She seemed to straighten, rising in height. "We do care for her tenderly, even now. My parents lie there yonder, and Mary is here, and I bring them flowers and pray for them quite often, I promise you."

"Indeed," Lord Creeghan said, and he sounded somewhat irritated, "Elaina is quite frequently upon her knees."

She gazed at her brother and seemed uneasy but made no reply to his words. She smiled at Martise instead. "This is not a warm or welcoming place. Perhaps my brother and I should step outside and allow you a moment with your sister. Then we can leave the coldness and the dampness behind. There is so much about the castle that is warm and beautiful." She shivered suddenly. "I hate the crypts."

Martise smiled in sympathy. "Your brother told me you were once lost beyond the gates. It must have been horrible."

"It was, indeed. You cannot imagine the bones within their shrouds, the bits of decayed flesh, the eeriness of the silence . . . I'm sorry. Excuse us. We'll await you."

Bruce Creeghan's hands were still upon her shoulders, Martise realized. And she had wanted them there. She had wanted to feel the searing heat and the strength, the very life of him, behind her.

Now he moved away, slipping his arm around his sister's shoulders. His eyes touched upon Martise in the shadows. "Say your prayers, milady," he told her. She watched after him as he led Elaina from the crypt.

Martise sank back to her knees again. She wanted to pray for Mary. She wanted to pray for her immortal soul. Instead, she found herself bowing her head and envisioning the lord of Creeghan, remembering the feel of his touch. She saw him again, coming from the darkness and thunder of the night, sweeping her up upon the gigantic bay horse. She felt his arms . . .

She rose from her knees quickly. As she moved toward the gates she could hear Lord Creeghan talking to his sister. He spoke low, but his voice was impassioned, and his burr seemed more prominent, though still not nearly so strong as his sister's.

"Elaina! 'Tis not healthy that you come here so continuously. You must promise me to stay away from this realm of the dead."

"Oh, Bruce! I cannot help it! I think that if I come here, God will look down more gently upon those who are far away from me!"

"God had little part in that war, Elaina," Creeghan said gruffly. "And drowning yourself here in the dampness and the darkness will not change the future. You will cease to spend so much time here."

"Bruce, you mustn't—"

"Elaina, I command you to obey me."

There was the sniffling sound again. Elaina was crying. Martise paused awkwardly, realizing that Elaina Creeghan was being held in her brother's arms.

"Bruce, what of the coffin beyond the gate?"

"Elaina, you will not talk of it."

"But Bruce—"

"That, too, is my command."

The coffin beyond the gate? Martise wondered. Beyond what gate? The one that blocked the ancient Creeghan dead from the modern crypts?

But there were no coffins beyond the gate. He had told her that in those crypts the dead were laid out upon their stones, and covered only in their shrouds . . .

Martise suddenly realized that she was not standing in the shadows. Lord Creeghan was holding his sister, but his eyes, blazing even here in the candlelight, were fully upon her.

Challengingly upon her.

He knew that she had been standing there. He knew that she had heard his words.

He moved away from his sister. "Elaina, it seems that our dear Lady St. James prays with *admirable* speed. Shall we go up?"

"Oh, indeed!" Elaina said, spinning around and smiling

at Martise. "Please, let's do go on up. I should love a sherry. Wouldn't you, Martise?"

Actually, she'd love a damned good shot of whisky—she'd learned to enjoy such decadent pleasures during the war. But she smiled, or she tried to smile.

"Yes, I'd love a sherry."

"I'm quite sure she would," Lord Creeghan said, and his lip was curling.

He stepped past his sister and offered Martise his arm. She hesitated, feeling the compelling fire of his eyes. He touched her hand, and the heat was searing as he tucked her fingers against his arm. "But bear in mind, Elaina, this visitor of ours, this Lady St. James, does not fear ghosts. The crypt holds no haunting images for her. It is only the living that she fears. Is that still true, Martise?" he asked.

She felt his touch, felt the power. She felt the slight rippling of his muscles beneath the civilized elegance of his apparel, and she felt the lightning probe of his eyes.

"It is only the living I fear," she agreed, meeting his gaze. "*When* I am threatened."

He smiled slowly, wickedly, a raven-black brow arched, and Martise knew then that he was very much aware that she *was* afraid of the living. She was afraid of him.

Or afraid of herself.

She really knew not which.

Three

❦

The hall seemed very different for supper that evening.

Martise dressed carefully for the occasion. Holly had seen to the pressing of many of her garments that afternoon. Styles had made numerous subtle changes between the beginning of the war and the end of it, what with the bustle coming in and the petticoats toning down ever so slightly. She hadn't been able to afford any of the new fashions being shown in Lady Godoy's, but she had managed to taper down her old skirts and create bustle effects from the extra material. That evening she was able to dress in an elegant royal-blue velvet bodice and overgown with an underskirt of flower-strewn linen. She weaved blue ribbons through her hair and stood back, pleased with the effect. Her eyes seemed larger, wider, and more luminescent. Her cheeks were naturally flushed and she realized that it was with excitement. She was about to meet with Bruce Creeghan again, be it in challenge or battle, and although she was still made uneasy by his probing eyes and questions, she could not deny the fascination.

"Forgive me, Mary!" she thought, giving her reflection one last glance before leaving her room.

Coming down the stairs, she was certain that Bruce was already in the room when she saw a tall man standing before the fire. He was immaculately dressed in fawn trousers, a rich frilled shirt, and a handsome maroon frock coat. When he turned about, though, she saw that he was not Bruce at all, but a younger version of the lord of Creeghan. His light, dancing green eyes had a definite mischief to them.

"Lady St. James," he said gallantly, and came up several of the steps to take her hand and assist her down, making no pretense of hiding his intense interest in her. "I do admit to being highly intrigued. Bruce was so quiet about you, keeping his own counsel, that I was quite fascinated to meet you. And then Elaina told me that we had a true creation of an elegant, beautiful and glorious Southern belle in our very presence—of course, dear lady, you really are an English-woman, aren't you?—well, never mind, the fascination was there. And you are astonishingly lovely, but then you must know that, don't you? No matter, how rude. We're de-lighted to have you, and ever so sorry that you have come under such circumstances."

"Thank you," Martise said, smiling, and trying not to laugh. She still didn't know who the man was, but he was definitely handsome and far more welcoming than ye olde lord of the castle.

"I'm Ian," he informed her quickly. "Bruce's cousin. The poor relation. Well, not so terribly poor, really, I'm just not so rich as Bruce the Laird, you see. I own an estate about fifty miles from here, but we keep our livestock pooled and use Bruce's land. Since I am a single gent with no wife or wee bairns as yet to care for, I'm glad enough to keep my rooms here in the castle."

"Ian," she said, spinning around as they reached the landing to study him. She held his hand still and told him, "It's a pleasure, Ian. I am delighted that you are at the castle."

"Aye, as well Lady St. James should be!" Bruce Cree-ghan's rich, softly burred voice came to her across the room. He strode toward her, inches taller than his charming cousin, and seeming to ignite the air with his dark presence. He smiled at Ian. "Lady St. James must not feel that her welcome on her first night here was the warmest. I felt compelled to warn her that Creeghan is rumored to be full of haunts and evil beasties."

Ian grinned. "Take no heed. Bruce is the evil beastie here, as any man can tell you."

"Ah, cousin, you mustn't joke with her so," Bruce said, watching Martise's eyes. "I'm quite certain that she came here believing I was a beast or dragon as it is, and that I did, perhaps, devour my poor wife, her sister."

Elaina, entering the room, gasped, and stood deathly still. Bruce looked to her quickly and strode the few steps to the stair to take her hand. "Elaina—"

"It isn't true, you know!" Elaina said, looking desperately to Martise. "None of what has been said is true, and you mustn't believe it!"

Ian cleared his throat. "Elaina, I don't believe that Martise *had* heard anything."

"Whatever she has heard," Bruce said, leading his sister to her seat at the table, "she must judge for herself. Don't you think that is only fair?"

"Ah, fair!" came another voice, and Martise turned to see that an older man had entered the room. Unlike the others, he was light, his blond hair turning white, rich and thick, though, and a handsome complement to his gray eyes. And unlike the others, he was dressed in Highland style, wearing a kilt with his plaid draped well over his shoulder, a traditional sporan swinging from his waist.

The older man came quickly to her, taking her hand, his eyes dancing as he kissed it and introduced himself. "I am Peter, father to that rascal yonder"—he indicated Ian—"and uncle to the laird, Bruce there. And I'm might glad to have ye, lass, but I'll give ye a warning meself. We're here in the Highlands"—he pronounced the word as "*he*lands"—"and superstition runs fast and furious, and the tales that ye'll hear can curdle milk, I swear it. So keep that in mind when ye hear tales of Castle Creeghan, and maybe ye'll not find us all so sorry a lot as ye imagine at first."

"Well, I thank you for that, Peter," Bruce Creeghan said, not addressing the older man as "uncle," but nodding to him politely. Elaina was already sitting, and Bruce stood at the head of the table, opening the bottle of Burgundy that had been set at the table for them. The room seemed truly gracious this evening, the table set with a snowy-white linen cloth, and the silver so well polished that it shimmered in the candlelight.

"Shall we sit?" Lord Creeghan suggested. He poured out a glass of wine, tasted it, and began to pour the others as his family took their seats, Peter guiding Martise to a place at Bruce's left side. Hogarth made his silent appearance and took over the task of pouring the wine as Bruce took his seat. Freya joined him, and the meal, an aromatic stew, was swiftly served.

Frowning, Bruce asked, "Where's Conar?"

"Running late, I imagine," Ian offered. As Bruce's frown deepened, Ian added, "Bruce, you asked him to see Father Martin about the memorial service."

Bruce nodded. "Aye, that I did. And I imagine he stopped off then for a wee spot of whisky."

Ian said nothing more to defend his brother, nor did Peter rise to speak for the missing Conar, either. Her first start of the evening over, Elaina seemed determined to ignore her brother's ill temper and poor manners and recapture the warmth. "I do hope you'll still be here for the Highland games, Martise. They're coming up very soon and I'm sure you will find them quaint and so much fun."

"I'm quite sure that Lady St. James will be gone by then," Bruce said coolly.

"Perhaps not," Peter said. "And ye would enjoy the day, lass. There is dancing and singing and the endless cry of the pipes and there'll be dishes I'll wager ye'll not see again, anywhere. And all the lads and lasses wear their colors—"

"And that's important!" Elaina said, her cheeks flushed with excitement, heedless that she had interrupted her uncle. "You see, Martise, after the Jacobite uprising, the men were not allowed to wear their plaids, their colors. Many rushed off to America to fight in the Revolution, because there, in British regiments, they were allowed to wear their plaids."

"Aye, and for all of that," Bruce continued, a touch of bitterness in his voice, "many of the Scotsmen were deserted there when the war was lost."

"Or won," Martise reminded him pleasantly, "depending upon one's point of view."

"Aye, of course," Bruce agreed. "Except that you are a born Englishwoman, Lady St. James. Did your years with the Yanks convince you otherwise?"

Martise very carefully cut a piece of carrot that lay within her stew. "Yanks?" She smiled very sweetly. "I lived in the Confederacy, Lord Creeghan. Yanks referred to the Americans in general of nearly a hundred years ago. Southern gentlemen highly resent the term 'Yank' being tossed upon them, I do assure you."

"That's right, we've welcomed a little Rebel into our midst, I had quite forgotten," Bruce said. Martise sensed the tension in his voice, the same tension that had tightened her own.

"Bruce!" Elaina exclaimed, distressed. "How can you—" She broke off and turned to Martise. "Don't let him taunt you so. He is very much aware of the American situation, and I assure you, all of us here had our hearts with you in the South." Tears shimmered in her eyes as she challenged her brother. "Isn't that true, Bruce? Isn't it, please?"

If Bruce Creeghan had anything whatsoever that might be considered a soft spot, that soft spot was Elaina. The tension left his features. Across the candlelit table he stared at his sister. Martise felt a warmth at her spine as she wondered what it would be like to feel the tenderness he cast upon Elaina turned her way just slightly. The years left his features, and the fire of his eyes seemed amber with warmth. His appearance was ever more striking.

"Aye, Elaina," he said very softly. "We have sympathized with the South. And we have prayed. And all will come well."

All would not come well! Martise wanted to scream. The war was lost, the land was ravaged and bathed in blood.

"Martise lost her husband," Elaina reminded him. "Fighting for the Confederacy."

"Indeed," Bruce agreed. But he said no more, and gave no apology, and Martise felt the fire of his eyes upon her once again. He did not seem to sympathize with her at all. He did not even seem to believe that she had lost a husband in the war.

There was an awkward silence.

"Well, the war is over," Martise said. She sipped her wine, ignoring the laird's eyes as she felt then sizzling upon her. She smiled down at Elaina. "The games do sound wonderful. Once, when I was very young, I went to something similar in North Carolina. Some of the Highlanders left over from the Revolution must have planned them."

"You were in the States when you were young?" Bruce asked politely.

She froze, then felt heat flush her cheeks. She fought against the color and made herself smile very sweetly. "Yes, you see my father had a brother who moved to the States, and we visited there that one year."

Elaina saved her then, plunging in once again with enthusiasm. "The bad is all in the past, isn't it? The Jacobite uprising and both of the American wars are over, and now, in the Highlands, we wear our colors and play our games. Mary loved the plaid, you know, the Creeghan plaid. And Bruce plays the pipes wonderful—well, so does Uncle Peter, and Conar and Ian, for that matter! But it's the caber throw where we are known to excel. The laird of Creeghan always wins the caber throw."

"The caber?" Martise asked.

"It was very important once," Bruce said. "The caber is a great log, and the laird who could throw it the farthest would be deemed the strongest. In the days when we were known for our endless feuds—and when we battled the English with swords instead of words—it was important to prove our strength."

"But now it is fun," Elaina said. "We shall have to find some colors for Martise to wear. We'll have a kilt made for her."

"Ah!" Uncle Peter said. "Shall we get her a kilt, or have her kilted?"

"What's the difference?" Martise asked.

"A kilt is a skirt, lass, a garment, made and ready. To be kilted, a man rolls in his fabric, and in the rolling, creates his skirt and his scarf from the one piece, as I be awearin' it now. But the lasses, they choose their colors as they would, some making fine long woolen skirts, and some choosing only to have scarves about their necks. But indeed, lass, ye'll have to come in colors of some sort! What shall they be?" he asked Bruce.

The master of Creeghan lifted his wineglass to his lips, watching Martise with his burning gaze. "Why, she must wear the plaid of Creeghan, of course. She is a guest in this castle, and Mary's sister. She must take Mary's things."

"Then it is settled!" Elaina said delightedly. "And she will stay until the games, at the very least."

"Aye," Bruce agreed. "She will stay until the games, at the very least."

He did not ask her, Martise noted. It seemed that he did not ask much, but assumed that when his will was determined, it would be as he said.

Not with her.

"We shall have to see," she told Elaina. "I'm not sure how long I can stay."

"Oh? Do you have a pressing engagement awaiting you elsewhere?" Bruce asked, courteously enough. Why did his every question seem double-edged? she wondered.

"We shall see," she repeated firmly, and once again, it seemed that another member of the household saved her, or saved her pride, for at that moment the great outer doors opened, and then were closed, and they heard footsteps upon the stone. Seconds later a man appeared in the hallway, unbuttoning his heavy overcoat and apologizing as he did so. "Sorry, that I am late, but Father Martin was not so easy to find this night," he told Bruce. With his coat gone, the man very much resembled Ian. His eyes were lighter, his hair had a reddish tint to it, and he was, perhaps, a few years older. He, too, was a handsome man, and his smile, when it touched upon Martise, was warm.

"Conar," Bruce told her, rising to his feet. "Lady St. James, I give you my cousin Conar, and the last resident here within the castle."

Conar came around the table. His smile was open and very pleasant when he welcomed her. His hand was cold upon hers, but he had come from outside. "How delightful, and yet how sorry we are, Lady St. James."

"Martise," she said softly. "And thank you."

Conar took the empty chair at the other end of the table. Hogarth seemed instinctively to know that Conar had arrived, and within seconds the old man was back in the room, serving him. Martise was glad to see his comfort and ease with the servant as Conar thanked the man and apologized again for being late.

Martise was glad, too, that she had smelled no whisky on the man's breath, for he probably would have gained the wrath of Lord Creeghan.

She didn't need to defend these people, she thought to herself. They had lived with one another for years and seemed to do well enough.

"Did he say when he would come?" Bruce asked Conar.

"Aye, he agreed that tomorrow would be fine."

"Good," Bruce said. He turned his attention to Martise, smiling. "I had assumed you were anxious to leave us. And I was quite certain you would want a service for your sister while you were here. That is why Conar went for the father. Tomorrow afternoon at five, we will have a memorial in our own chapel below. For Mary."

"Oh! That—that was very thoughtful of you," Martise said.

"Not so thoughtful, merely proper," Creeghan said abruptly. "Tell me, Conar, what is our status with the Flemish wool merchants?"

The tone of the evening meal changed to one of business. Martise soon realized that castles were difficult to maintain these days and that Lord Creeghan was involved in many and diverse enterprises. Wool was their largest export, but they were also involved with certain fishing industries and owned a harness-making shop, which Ian spoke to Bruce about.

" 'Tis doing poorly the shop," Ian informed Bruce. "We should pull out."

"We can't pull out. At least twenty families in the village are dependent on that shop. We'll have to find a way to make it work, and that's that." He rose suddenly, staring down at Conar. "If you've had time to finish, we'll take our brandy in the office and continue there."

Creeghan rose and bade Martise a good evening. Conar, Ian, and Peter did the same, leaving her and Elaina alone.

"Truly, I am so glad that you have come, Martise!" Elaina told her.

The welcome was real. "Then I am glad, too," Martise responded. She smiled. "Tell me, what are we to do now?"

"Well, I know that I, for one, am going to indulge in more sherry," Elaina said, and rising, she went to the sideboard for the sherry bottle. She smiled, and poured the sherry into her wineglass. "Hogarth will bring us tea. Shall we have it by the fire?"

"Lovely," Martise agreed. "Except that I've a better

idea. Let's have it in my room and we'll steal the sherry bottle and have that, too."

Elaina was delighted. When Hogarth came, Martise informed him that they would like the tea in her room. Hogarth seemed surprised at first, and then very glad that Elaina seemed so happy.

Up in her room, Martise did her very best to draw Elaina out, but Elaina proved herself to be quite a Creeghan, subtly evading questions while asking Martise many of her own: what had the war been like, what had the South been like, there had been so much said, and so much romanticized. Martise did her best to answer many things honestly, but when Elaina turned her questions to Africa, Martise found herself in trouble once again. She shifted the conversation back to Elaina. "Why were you so distressed at dinner this evening? With your brother. When he seemed not to know that my husband was a Confederate—and definitely not a Yank."

"Oh!" Elaina said. "Oh . . ." She rose, agitated. "It's quite a long story, truly it is. And it's late, really late. I hadn't begun to realize just how late it had gotten. I'm quite exhausted. You must forgive me. I've had a wonderful night. I haven't had a friend such as yourself in so long now . . . since Mary. Oh, I am sorry, I—"

"Elaina, you must not apologize each time her name is mentioned. I loved her dearly, but then I believe you did, too, and truly, you were the one most frequently with her at the end, so, you see, your loss is all the greater."

"How very kind," Elaina murmured. Impulsively, she hugged Martise, but before Martise could say another word, Elaina fled. "We'll talk soon, sometime soon, I promise. Good night, now."

And then she was gone.

Martise looked around the room, and it seemed as good a time as any to begin a thorough search of the place.

The emerald had to be somewhere.

Deep in the armoire she found many of Mary's belongings. She searched through the beautiful silks and velvets and brocades, and marveled at the lovely corsets and elegant bloomers that Mary had acquired after her marriage. She suddenly found herself wondering about the relationship between the tall dark lord of Creeghan and her petite friend, and then she felt her cheeks burning and she touched them with her hands. She knew why Mary had fallen in love. She knew all too well.

And yet . . .

And yet, she told herself harshly, the emerald was not among Mary's things.

She thought about calling Holly to help her disrobe for the night, but she determined to struggle with her numerous hooks and tiny buttons herself. She laid her gown out carefully over the back of a chair, then wearily left her petticoats to lie where they fell. She breathed far more easily once she had untied her corset and stepped from her pantalettes, but then she shivered in the evening coolness and quickly slipped into her sheer white bed gown.

Beneath the covers, she discovered that she still shivered.

And when she closed her eyes, she discovered that Bruce Creeghan was with her still.

She drifted, and in her dreams, he came toward her. He was dressed in black, and the very darkness combined with that of his hair and the fire of his eyes gave him a Satanish appeal. He smiled, and in his eyes she felt the curious power that so beckoned to her. And in the darkness all around him he was before her, and his hands were upon her shoulders, beneath her gown, and the gown was falling to the ground in a rustle of lost purity, of lost innocence. And then she felt his kiss against her naked shoulder, slow, lingering, and then the fire was stoked in a line to center and swirl within her breast, for the liquid flame of his tongue touched her there . . .

She jerked up, wide awake, very aware of the dream, shaking and horrified . . .

And yet, wondering what it was that had awakened her.

There was no light in her room. The single candle she had left burning had died out.

The doors were opened, she realized. The doors to the balcony beyond.

And she had heard something. Not something near. Something far away. Something tremendous, like thunder.

She leapt from her bed and slipped out onto the balcony, hugging her sheer gown to her as the night wind ripped upon it.

She heard the wind, and again she heard a sound like thunder. She walked to the wall and listened, holding tight to the ancient stone. Far below her, she could hear the sounds of the sea, slashing hard against the cliffs.

She blinked, thinking that she saw a flicker of light on the cliffs below. But then there was nothing. The light was gone.

She waited, but there was nothing more. Just the wailing sound of the wind, and the crash and thunder of the waves upon the stone. No more lights appeared. The wind was cold, and it was seeping through her fragile clothing. She started to back away from the wall.

As she did so, she came against something as hard as the rock, but not cold, not cold at all. She felt the touch of something living, vibrant, pulsing. She nearly screamed, but she did not. She could not. A hand clamped down firmly upon her mouth, and a searing whisper touched her ear. "Don't scream, milady. 'Tis me, Bruce. Laird Creeghan."

Terrified, she raked at his hand with her nails. He swore furiously and his arm locked around her waist. Lifting her feet from the ground, he carried her squirming into her room and there set her down. "By all that's holy, woman! Would you be a wailing harpy this night and waken the very dead? Hush, I'm tellin' you, hush!"

Within the circle of his arm he spun her around. When her eyes met his, large and luminous, he smiled slowly, and held still, but then began to ease his hands from her lips. "Don't scream!" he warned her.

She still wanted to scream. He had startled her at first. Now he was in her room. And she was scarcely clad, and his legs were bare and he was dressed only in a velvet smoking jacket.

"What in the hell were you doing out there?" she demanded heatedly.

"On me own balcony, you mean?" he cross-queried.

"Behind me!" she exclaimed.

"What were *you* doing out there?" he demanded.

"I—I thought I heard something," she said. "But you! Your chambers are in the other tower. Hogarth told me—"

"Milady, my chambers may be elsewhere, but the door next to this one leads to my library, and if I may remind you, Martise, I am the master of this castle. I roam it at my liberty. But tell me, milady. It is late. Atrociously late. It is near dawn. What brought you awake, and to this balcony?"

"Nothing," she murmured.

"What?" he persisted.

"A noise, something, a sound."

"That is all?" he demanded quickly. He was very intense.

She shook her head, at a loss. "I don't know. Something woke me. I came out. And then . . . I backed into you. And there was nothing wrong until then."

"Nothing wrong? Noises in the night did not frighten you?"

"Should I be frightened?"

"Aye, lass, you should be frightened. Very frightened. If you hear noises in the night, you should run. You should lock your door tightly and ignore everything that you hear. Aye, indeed, lass. As it is, you should run. As far from Castle Creeghan as you might!"

She should have had some quick retort, but suddenly, she had none. The moonlight was pouring in upon them and she realized that she was in his arms, or at least, his arms were still about her, his hands upon the small of her back.

And she was certain that he wore nothing beneath the jacket, and she was achingly aware of the breadth of his shoulders and the ripple of muscle in the bronzed and richly furred chest that was bared to her by the deep V of the jacket. His body seemed to emit heat and energy in waves as wild as the slash of the sea against the rock, and the fire in his eyes was unmistakable. Her mouth grew dry as her eyes met his, suddenly naked, suddenly bared. He wanted her. The master of Castle Creeghan wanted her, and she knew that she responded to that wanting in a way that she had never imagined possible before. She wanted her dream to be truth, wanted to feel the brush of his fingers upon her naked shoulders, wanted to feel the burning heat of his kiss upon her bared flesh. She wanted to brush against him, to press close, to feel his arms wrap around her and hold her still to the leisure of his forage upon her lips and form . . .

"Aye, lass, you should run," he murmured. "Hear the wind, hear the cries, hear the savage tumult of the sea. Perhaps the dead do rise, and haunt us all."

"Lord Creeghan, I do not run," she whispered, trembling. She was fiercely aware of his nearness, and the raw power of his maleness. "Even when I am threatened."

He touched her cheek very gently, stroking down the length of it with his knuckles and following through so that his touch just seemed to breathe against the length of her throat and collarbone, and rest against her shoulder.

He smiled then, the moonlight touching his eyes and causing his teeth to flash very whitely against the shadows. "Do I threaten you? Aye, lass, that I do. For if you stay, I will have you. Do you understand me? 'Tis not by choice, but by the yearning alone. I will have you, *bed* you, lass, if you do na comprehend my words. Bear that in mind when you make your decisions."

She gasped at last, and stepped away, staring into his eyes, unable to believe that he would be so bold as to say such things—even if he was thinking them. What did he think of her?

She was illuminated by the moonlight, the gauze covering her from breasts to ankles, and yet she knew that he saw her clearly, saw her form defined and delineated, beneath the mist of sheerest white. "My dear Lord Creeghan, you do flatter yourself," she claimed.

But his smile remained and he came toward her. His hands fell upon her arms and moved the soft material against them, and then he was lifting her, and she was suddenly stretched out on her bed, in the tangle of her covers, her hair a wild splay upon them. "Perhaps I do not threaten, perhaps I warn," he whispered, his breath feathering her cheeks and lips as he leaned over her. "Indeed, lass, know this: you'll have met the dragon or the beastie in truth if you stay, for I will have you this compliant, this willing, this sweetly, within my bed. Yet, you are a widow, milady. Maybe I am misled, maybe you are the one stalking the dragon . . . ?"

Her heart beat rampantly as his words sank into her mind. Her temper rose at long last to save her from the seductive quality of his words and of the night and the moonlight.

"Beast, indeed!" she spat out suddenly, striking out. But he was quick, and caught her hand, laughing. He stepped back, releasing her. His smile broadened, and he bowed deeply to her. "So run, lass, run if you would have the chance. And if not . . ."

A dark brow arched high, and he turned silently and disappeared through the balcony doors. With a startled gasp she followed him out, longing to do real battle, ready to tear into him and his arrogance with a vengeance.

But he was gone. The great laird of Creeghan had disappeared into the darkness, and she might well have dreamed the entire episode.

She came back inside, and she closed the balcony doors tightly behind her, bolting them securely. She shivered fiercely and dived back beneath her covers, drawing them to her chin for warmth.

She had dreamed of him . . .

But he had come, too, in truth, to her room. The rich, subtle scent of his cologne lingered upon the air.

And upon her flesh.

He was dangerous. So dangerous. But when he touched her, she did not care. She wanted to explore the fever that came to haunt and singe her blood. She wanted to feel his eyes touch her again, just as they had this night.

She closed her eyes. She could not face another day. Not in this castle. Not with Creeghan.

Her eyes opened, and she saw that the light of dawn was beginning to filter into the room.

It was too late. She had already stayed for another day. And now there would be another night.

Four

֎

Martise did not sleep in the dusky hours of the early morning.

When Holly mentioned that she had dark shadows beneath her eyes—in a beautiful shade of mauve, mind you, but dark nonetheless—Martise agreed to have a tray of tea and biscuits brought to her room. She was tired, exasperated, and restless, and it seemed like a wonderful time to begin a more thorough search of the room.

She convinced Holly that she meant to sleep, but when she finished with her tea, she began a probe through Mary's clothing. Touching Mary's garments was disturbing at first. The soft scent of roses lingered upon them, and guilt weighed down heavily upon her; but in truth, Martise needed the emerald, and Mary would have understood.

After a while, she had gone through every garment, every skirt and scarf, every fine petticoat, in Mary's trunks and drawers and armoires. She spent hours running her fingers over every swatch of cloth, thinking that Mary might have sewn the emerald into a hem, but she found nothing.

By the time the midday meal came round, Martise was forced to admit that the emerald was not among Mary's things in the room. She had searched the drawers for false bottoms, she had gone through the bedding, she had looked through the drapes and tried to imagine every nook and cranny in the large room.

She was running out of time. She could refrain from going down to the hall for a meal, but she had to dress for the memorial. After all, the proceedings were being carried out for her benefit.

She pinned her hair in a secure and staid knot at her nape and dressed in a dark and somber blue, a gown with tiny buttons that crawled nearly up her throat. She had tried not to spend the morning thinking of the master of the castle, but now, aware that she would have to see him sooner or later, the floodgates upon her emotions were slowly cracking open and she realized that she had not really ceased to think of him at all, not even for a moment. As she had carefully searched through Mary's things, she first told herself that she was grateful that Mary had kept this large room while the laird maintained his own quarters in a separate tower of the castle. Then she found herself wondering at that arrangement. If Bruce Creeghan had truly loved his lady, why had she been so very far from him? Not that it was so unusual for a wife to maintain separate quarters, but in such a case . . .

Mary had been in love. She could not imagine anyone loving so rugged and vibrant a man as Creeghan and keeping such a distance from him. Stretched out upon her bed, she pondered the problem and realized that it seriously complicated her own. The laird kept a library next to this room, a library that adjoined the room by the balcony. Perhaps they had spent time there together. Perhaps they had supped in intimacy, and the dark towering laird had carried her across the moonlit balcony and to her bed.

Her fingers were shaking. He hadn't behaved at all a gentleman. But then, maybe such a man as Creeghan would never have to pretend that he was what he wasn't. He had been blunt, crude. He had told her that he wanted her . . .

She stood up and smoothed down her dress. It was time to arrive deep down below for the memorial service.

She did not wait for Holly or anyone to escort her. She left her room, closing the door softly behind her. As she hurried for the stairway that would lead her down to the crypts, she reflected that she would have to extend the realm of her search. And to do that, she would have to have Laird Creeghan's permission to peruse his collection of books. Surely, he could not be so crass as to deny such a request.

Unless he was afraid that she would find something.

Unless he *had* murdered Mary.

She swept away the thought as she passed through the great hall and realized that no one was about. She glanced at the timepiece that hung from the slender chain upon her neck and rested at her breast. She was late. The family had surely assembled already.

The rough stairway leading to the crypts was well lit, but she bit into her lip to remind herself that she must not think of things such as murder. And she must not think that Laird Creeghan had murdered Mary, for if the library yielded nothing to her, then it would be necessary to prowl through his private quarters.

Did he take Mary there? Were his rooms as dark and dangerously intriguing as the man? Had he carried his laughing bride there to be with him?

Her palms were wet, her throat was dry. She was descending deep into the valley of the dead, and for a moment, in the twist of the stairs, it seemed that she was alone in the world. Alone with the cold damp stone and the threat of eternal darkness. Alone with the corpses of hundreds of years arrayed in their finery to come up and meet her and greet her, and welcome her to Creeghan when it seemed that the present master would not . . .

She heard voices. The fit of fancy left her and she nearly laughed aloud. What a liar she was to say that she was not afraid of ghosts! How odd that she could have endured so much for so long, that hellish war, only to come here and find that she was frightened by the thought of a long-deceased chieftain or his bride.

She came to the last step. Nothing more frightening than the wine cellar to her left, she reminded herself. And before her, there was the chapel, the chapel so beautifully kept, and alive with the light from its exquisite windows.

She hurried for the chapel and stepped inside. The family was all there, and the servants of Creeghan, so it seemed, and half of the village, too, perhaps. She nearly laughed, despite the solemnity of the occasion. She had thought herself alone. There were at least fifty people within the small chapel.

And all of them staring at her as she entered. Some openly, some covertly, yet all with suspicion. She was a stranger here, she realized.

And these people belonged to Creeghan. Just as the castle, just as the land, just as the great bay horse. They made their livelihoods through the laird's largesse. She wondered if they weren't every bit as tethered to the lairds of the castle now as they had been hundreds of years ago.

She tried to smile, and yet her effort faltered, for it seemed that she was being boldly studied by young eyes and old.

A hand slipped through her arm and she turned to see Elaina. "Martise, I was about to come for you! Holly informed us you were tired this morning, the travel catching up with you, no doubt. But when you didn't arrive here, I grew quite worried."

"I did not mean to be so late; I apologize."

"Oh, it's quite all right!" Elaina assured her. And then Martise realized that Bruce Creeghan was standing behind her.

"Ah, so our dear Lady St. James has come to make her appearance at last!" he said. "Excuse me, Elaina," he said smoothly to his sister, his hand then upon Martise's elbow as he led her down the aisle toward the altar. It seemed that he was bringing her to the priest, but then he paused and lowered his head, his whisper for her ears alone. "Have you decided to run and hide at last, milady? The wise course of action, I promise. If you wish it, I can have a carriage head you for a port this very evening."

She spun around, lifting her chin, trying very hard to maintain the dignity and maturity she was determined to believe her apparel gave her.

"I am not running, Laird Creeghan." She spoke his name softly, in a long drawl that mocked the Highland accent. He smiled and inclined his head to her.

"Not from ghosts, milady?"

"Not from ghosts."

"And not even from the living—whom you do fear?"

"Again, you flatter yourself, milord, if you think that I am afraid. It's what you want, *isn't* it? You want me to be afraid."

His smile deepened and even as he replied, he was stepping aside casually. "*Forewarned,* milady. Forewarned, and nothing more. Ah, here's the good father—he's been waiting for your appearance. You must meet him, of course. Come."

He took her hand. As always, she felt the heat and the all-powerful energy that seemed to exude from him.

She was drawn up before the father, an elderly man with dark, sharp brown eyes that belied the age in his snow-white hair. It was a wrinkled face, one well weathered by age and time, and yet a fascinating one, interested and interesting. "Ah, Bruce, so here's our lass, eh?"

"Aye, Father," Bruce agreed. "I give you the Lady St. James. Martise, Father Fenen Martin."

"Lady St. James," Father Martin said. "Welcome, welcome to the Highlands, though it be a sad occasion on which we do so. I knew your Mary and loved her well. So did all assembled here. She was sweet and dear."

His accent was not so pronounced and Martise wondered

if his religion hadn't sent him about the world before returning him to his home.

"Thank you," Martise said, and added innocently, "Did you see—my sister, then, at the end, Father?"

"Alas, she was gone when I arrived that night!"

"Was she ill? Had she come to you?"

"Nervous, perhaps, pale, wan. Aye, she must have been ill, but wanted no one to realize. When the end came, she was gone so very quickly."

Martise was aware of Bruce Creeghan behind her—so supportively!—and yet she could not caution herself to silence. "Mary was afraid, Father, of something here."

"Was she now? But she needn't have been, she had her husband. And she did not let on. I'm sorry I canna say that I was there in her final moments, but I am convinced she has taken a proper place in heaven. Aye, indeed, if ye've a mind, I'll start with the service now."

"Of course," Martise said.

A hand landed upon her shoulder. Heat waves coursed through her as she found herself being led—or manipulated—into the front pew by Bruce Creeghan.

And then Father Martin began his service.

She should have been listening; she should have been paying grave attention, and yet Martise could not concentrate on the service going on before her. She was too keenly aware of Bruce Creeghan, knelt by her side, and of Conar, to her left. And when she lifted her eyes when she should have been at prayer, she noted a young, dark-haired girl on the other side of the church.

She was dressed in the simple clothing of a village girl, a full cotton skirt and well-scrubbed blouse, but that blouse sat low upon an abundant chest, and the charms of her physique were enhanced by the huge dusky gray orbs of her eyes and the rich length of chestnut hair that curled lushly about her shoulders.

Her eyes were upon Bruce Creeghan, and they seemed

naked of shame and hindrance. One emotion reigned within them, and that emotion was adoration.

Then the girl turned just slightly and she was staring at Martise. Their eyes met and locked, and the emotion turned swiftly to a surefire hatred so intense that it almost seemed a physical blow.

Martise almost turned away, but then held fast. This girl had no right to stare at Creeghan so. He had been Mary's.

Aye, Mary's. And yet Martise had felt the power and the danger and enchantment herself. She could not blame the girl.

And she could not help but wonder if Bruce Creeghan had ever told the girl that she should run, else he would bed her. And once he had given her the warning . . .

Had she run? Or had she stayed to warm the master's bed?

Martise waited determinedly until the girl lowered her eyes, then she cast her own lashes down in prayer again.

She was startled when they rose, Bruce's hand upon her elbow. The service was over. Mary's service. And she had scarcely heard a word of it.

There was a murmuring, but Martise quickly realized that the ceremony had not come to an end. A young girl beautifully and plainly clad in a white gown came toward her, a ringlet of flowers in her hand that nearly matched the circlet she wore atop her head. Martise realized that she was to take the flowers, and she did. Bruce's hand was still upon her elbow, guiding her.

"They are for the grave," he said very softly.

She nodded. They walked then from the chapel in the lead, almost as if they had just been proclaimed man and wife, and Bruce opened the wrought-iron gates to the contemporary crypt and Martise followed.

All of the assembly did not come with them, yet she knew that Father Martin was behind her as she laid down the flowers and went to her knees once again.

She also knew, without looking, that the buxom farm lass with the chestnut curls had followed her, too.

She rose, again with Bruce's assistance. The people were filing out of the chapel.

" 'Tis time to come now. There'll be refreshments for the mourners in the hall, yet nothing can begin until I appear."

"Then you must appear quickly," Martise said coolly. "I am not quite ready to leave as yet."

He looked as if he were about to argue, to command her differently, and she wondered if she could have withstood a direct order from him. But he did not argue. He smiled grimly and lifted his hands. "I leave you, then, to our honored dead, milady."

She was alone, she thought, as she watched his tall shoulders and broad back disappear beyond the gates. The moment that he was gone, the candles seemed to flicker. Absurd, she thought. She knelt again before the coffin and tried to make amends for the fact that she no longer seemed to be able to pray. Oh, Mary! Let me do right by you, oh, please, Father in Heaven . . .

Her thoughts trailed away. She had heard a scuffling, a noise. The sound of breathing . . .

The sound of a heartbeat.

She jumped up and spun around, trying to calm herself. She had been frightened once, and it had only been Elaina, praying on the other side of the coffin.

She had wanted to defy Creeghan, and so she was alone.

Not alone. Entombed with all these dead.

"Elaina?" she said sharply. But there was no answer. It seemed, though, that she still heard the breathing, still heard the heartbeat.

And then . . . the laughter.

And the wrought-iron gates to the crypt came slamming closed.

"Elaina! Is that you?" she cried out, determined that she would not panic again. Someone was taunting her, someone wanted her to be afraid. She could not give that someone the satisfaction.

"Elaina, Bruce . . . ?" She tried to keep her voice steady and her footsteps sharp as she walked across the cold stone floor. But when she reached the wrought-iron gates, she found that the bolt had indeed been slid shut and that she was, in truth, entombed with the dead.

It was not so bad, she assured herself. These dead were safely, neatly, within coffins. They were not lying as the dead that Elaina had described to her, decaying in mortal splendor, flat upon their slabs, hidden only by the gauze of their shrouds. There was no need to panic, no need at all . . .

"Someone!" she called out sharply. "Help me, please! Oh, this is ridiculous!"

Then her words faded away. *Someone was coming toward her.* Coming from the gates to the older section of the crypt.

The candles were dying out. Darkness was fast descending. And even as the figure came closer and closer, it paused to douse more and more of the light.

She must not panic . . . she must not! she told herself. And then she remembered Elaina's whispered words to her brother. There was a new coffin in the old section. Elaina had seen it. A new coffin.

Yet why be afraid of the new when it was the bony finger of an ancient decaying corpse that might be coming forth, the shroud flowing about the frame in the darkness of the crypt as it came ever closer and closer . . .

"Who—" Despite her resolve, she had to try a second time to speak. "Who are you? What are you doing? Open this gate at once."

Then she heard the laughter again, and just as panic nearly engulfed her, she saw that it was the girl.

"Lady St. James!" she whispered, and her voice was sweet. " 'Tis sorry I am, and yet perhaps I shouldna be so, fer ye craved the time with yer dear dead sister, did ye not?"

"Indeed, I did," Martise said carefully, wanting the girl to open the gates before taking any chances on upsetting her. "But now I believe that we shall be missed; we should go upstairs."

"Oh, aye, we must!" The girl's eyes were innocently wide, but vengeance lurked well within their depths. "We must indeed, fer ye're so very, very pale, milady! Did ye think that the ghosts of the Creeghan dead were welcoming ye to their bosoms? Alas, I didna mean to frighten ye so!"

It was a lie. A bold, taunting lie. The girl had very much wanted to scare her.

The girl shivered, staring at her through the bars. "The ghosts only come out at night. I've seen them, mind ye. I've heard their wailin', and I've seen their lights. So much death, and so much murder. Aye, murder, Lady St. James. And 'tis the victims of the murders, they do say, who walk the halls. Dear Mary is perhaps among them."

"Lord Creeghan will come looking for me very soon," Martise said sharply.

The girl's smile faded to a sullen frown. "I didna mean to shut ye in. I didna see ye there upon yer knees. Of course now, 'tis not like being locked in the other, ye know. When the eyes lay open and gaze at ye and the bones slowly lose their flesh and the smell of decay is all about . . ."

"No, it's not like that at all," Martise said evenly. "Now, if you would be so kind as to slide the bolt once again . . . ?"

The girl did so. And the second that Martise was free, the girl turned and fled.

Martise felt like doing the same, running as fast as she could. Now, she knew, she *was* truly alone in the crypt.

Her footsteps moved swiftly over the stone. Then she couldn't help it. She started to run. And when she reached the winding stairs, she continued to fly up them until she almost ran into a body. Her hand flew to her mouth as she tried to hold back a scream.

"Martise!" It was Ian, smiling, charming, elegantly

dressed. "We'd wondered what was keeping you. I ken your need to say a prayer, but . . . Bruce missed you."

"Did he?" Martise murmured sweetly. "I am so sorry. I was, er, waylaid."

"Waylaid?" Ian took her elbow and escorted her on the narrow stairs. She looked down. A tumble from this distance to the floor below would almost certainly mean death.

But Ian's hand on her arm was prodding her up the stairs, and she continued, Ian behind her. "Aye," she said. She was at the top of the stairs. She could hear voices from the hall. She turned around as Ian joined her on the landing. "A certain young lady 'accidentally' bolted me into the crypt."

A grim smile slashed across Ian's handsome features. "That would be Clarissa," he told her. "I believe she was quite jealous of your sister. I don't imagine she is happy to have another beautiful St. James woman in the castle."

"Was she engaged to or involved with Bruce?"

"Of course not. She's simply a village lass. It would not have been proper."

"Ah," Martise said softly.

Ian grinned. "Well, you may raise your Americanized nose if you like, milady, but here, well, there are traditions which much be maintained, and that is that. She would never have been a proper bride for Bruce."

"Not a bride, but perhaps something other?" she questioned, searching out his eyes.

He cast back his head and laughed and seemed very much like his arrogant cousin at that moment. "Village girls by the scores have adored Bruce with their eyes. 'Tis the Creeghan mystique, so they say. He has not bedded them all, I assure you."

"Ian—" she began, but she broke off, aware without looking that Bruce Creeghan was coming upon them. His footsteps were silent, so it was not that she heard his movement. She was simply becoming so attuned to him that she sensed him; she felt the electricity, the tension, in the air.

She spun about.

"Why, milady, we were beginning to fear that our ghosts, in vengeance for your disbelief, had swept you into their fold," he said lightly. His eyes burned into her despite the soft tone of his words.

"I met a friend of yours," Martise said sweetly. "Clarissa."

He arched a brow to Ian. Ian shrugged.

Bruce said nothing about Clarissa. He offered an arm to Martise. "Milady, there are many waiting to meet you. And there's one introduction that I've been anxious to make. Dr. MacTeague is here, and I know that you want to talk to him."

"Dr. MacTeague?" she said.

"Mary's attending physician. Well, you do want to ask him if she wasn't really strangled, don't you?"

She could read nothing in his eyes, but his touch made her tremble as he curled his fingers over her own and placed them on his arm. "Indeed, I do," she assured him sweetly. He smiled wickedly. They entered the hall with Ian behind them, and a moment later, she stood before an attractive dark-haired man with grave blue eyes and a crisp neat mustache.

"Dr. MacTeague, Lady St. James. I will leave the two of you to get acquainted."

Bruce left them, and she was facing the doctor, who seemed to watch her sorrowfully. And it still seemed that there were people all around them, people listening to her every word.

Dr. MacTeague had mercy. He caught her arm and said, "Shall we take a walk in the courtyard?"

"Yes, please," she agreed.

Seconds later, they left the hall by the same great doors by which she had first entered it. Darkness had fallen, night had come, but the courtyard was very well lit, and it was pleasant to walk along the arched stone gallery where someone had planted flower beds. Without the storm, the place did not seem so sinister, and Martise was glad to be out of doors.

"Bruce seems to think you feel the need to talk to me, milady," the doctor offered politely after a moment.

They had come to a wrought-iron bench. It was new, a style favored by Queen Victoria, ornate and elegant. Martise sank down upon it, watching the doctor. His dark eyes seemed so grave, and so honest.

"My sister was very frightened of something or someone here, Doctor. She wrote me frequently. I was very disturbed when she died."

MacTeague nodded slowly and then shrugged. "Mary did seem nervous, but I thought it all in her mind." He hesitated. "Lady St. James, I can only tell you that Castle Creeghan is very old. It has its share of legends and horror stories. But your sister died of heart failure. I arrived moments after her death, I signed the certificate, and I would defy any physician anywhere to dispute my findings. And I can tell you this, too: I have never seen a man more grieved than Bruce Creeghan when he held her there, so, in his arms."

Martise lowered her eyes. She could not imagine Bruce Creeghan so grieved. She lifted her gaze to the doctor once again.

"You said horror stories. Are they true?"

"Things have happened here, of course. This place is ancient, these people are very superstitious. They dance each year to their May pole, and, I swear, that night, dozens of children are conceived. They still seem to worship the gods of fertility for themselves and for their harvests, and—"

"They still seem to worship Lord Creeghan, do they not?" she inquired.

"Bruce has always been a good master here. He allows no man to remain idle, and no widow to starve."

She nodded absently. All the more reason for the people to adore him.

"Doctor, what type of thing has happened here?"

He smiled broadly. "Well, in 1205 one Lady Creeghan did throw herself to her death from the battlements. They say that her ghost haunts the north tower."

"And the west tower?"

"I'm afraid I haven't kept up with all my ghosts," he said with a grin. But then he shrugged again. "We are no better, and no worse, than others here, milady. Full moons sometimes seem to bring out violence in people. No one knows the truth of it all. But I do know this—Mary Creeghan died of heart failure, pure and simple. My lady, I swear that to you."

"Thank you," she told him. "I appreciate your speaking with me so frankly."

He paused, a grave, attractive man, staring up at the sky. Martise followed his gaze. Soon there would be a full moon.

"Perhaps you should not stay very long, though," he said.

"Why?"

He shrugged. "Like I said, full moons . . ." His voice trailed away but then he smiled. "Perhaps we should return. I fear it is growing late."

It *had* grown late, and only Bruce remained in the hall when they returned. He stood with his back to the fire, still handsomely adorned in a dark and somber frock coat, ribbon tie and vest, and high boots. His eyes reflected the flames as he watched the doctor and Martise come back into the hall. MacTeague said his good-nights, and Martise was left alone with Bruce.

There was a silence in the room. She felt Bruce's eyes upon her. She turned to him, and was startled by the depths of the anger within them.

"Just *exactly* what is it that I am suspected of having done, milady St. James?" he demanded sharply.

"I—I don't—"

"You don't know what I mean?" His brows shot up in scornful disbelief. "Ah, let's see. You've questioned the priest and the doctor, and surely my sister, perhaps my cousins and uncle, and I dare say you've tried to deluge the corpses with your insinuations."

"I haven't insinuated anything," Martise snapped back, very glad of the distance between them. He had not moved. He still stood there, his back to the fire, his legs firm and far apart on the stone, his hands locked behind his back.

"She died of heart failure, but you still accuse *me*. Obviously," he said, his voice suddenly soft and therefore sinister, "you think I am to blame. And so the questions." And then he was moving, seeming to circle around her like a hawk looking down upon its prey. She spun around, watching him, in no way willing to have her back to him. "Did I perhaps throttle Mary? Strangle her with my bare hands?" He offered his hands up to the light, studying them himself, flexing his fingers. "Indeed, they are powerful, milady. More than strong enough to snap the fragile throat of a gentle creature like Mary. Poison perhaps? Ah, I think the strangling more my style." And then he was a foot away from her, staring at her with a violent fury. "*Why* in God's name do you accuse me of having killed her?"

"I didn't—"

"But by God, woman, you did!" he thundered.

"Mary was frightened, terribly frightened. She wrote to me."

"She was frightened *of me*? I don't believe it!"

"No . . ." Martise admitted softly. She lifted her chin. "She did not say that she was afraid of you. She was just . . . afraid."

He came closer. So close that she could feel the warmth of him, the heat, the burning tension. "If *she* was so afraid, then why in heaven and hell are *you* still here?"

"Because I intend to know!" Martise cried.

"There is nothing to know!"

She backed away from him. "There is—*some*thing!" she managed to gasp out. And then she realized that she had backed herself against a wall, and that his hands were flat against it on either side of her head, his face disturbingly close to hers. "If you stay, milady," he began, and he said the last with such mockery that she cringed inwardly, "if you stay, be prepared to feel me as your shadow, Martise, day and night. And don't ever disappear, as you did this evening in the crypts!"

"Disappear!" she gasped, her eyes narrowing with anger. "I was locked in, you arrogant—" She stopped, biting off the word "bastard" just in time.

She was still a guest here. And still supposedly a lady.

She smiled. "A *girl* detained me, Laird Creeghan. She bolted the crypt. I think that it has something to do with you. I wondered, indeed, if you hadn't forewarned her, too, at some time or another, that you wanted her and would have her."

For a moment, she thought that his wrath had risen so greatly that he would strike her, but he did not. He smiled instead. "Nay, lady," he whispered, "you are the only woman I have ever wanted in so desperate and determined a way."

And his lips, so close to hers, touched upon them. Lightly, as if the kiss were a part of the whisper.

And as the touch was so subtle, she did not think or reason to protest it. She only felt it. Felt the shattering, masculine persuasion, felt the heat and the fever, and the parting of her mouth beneath his. And then she felt the full force, the passion, the violence, within him. Felt his tongue, and his touch, and a power of seduction and force so great that she thought she was falling. Her hands clung to his shoulders and she clung for life, it seemed. She tasted blood within her lips, and still, she could not protest the rape, the invasion of his kiss. The fire of his eyes had touched her body and her soul, and she knew that she felt within herself that he was right, that there was something there, within them both. He had to have her . . .

And she had to know, somewhere in time, the sweet ecstasy that he offered, the excitement, the sweeping, volatile passion . . .

"No!" she gasped, tearing away from his lips at last.

His eyes were still alive with the flames of both fury and desire.

"If by chance you do fear me, lady, there are things you should know are true. My temper is fierce, my passions are great, and indeed, perhaps, there is a simmering violence within me. But I did not kill Mary. I did not hurt her, and she was beloved as lady of this castle until the day she died. Stay, then, haunt the place with your suspicions and aspersions. But know that I will be here, stalking your every step. And remember that it is all true. I am a passionate, volatile, temperamental—arrogant!—man, and I will have my way!"

She wrenched free, afraid that she could not fight him if he tried to stop her.

But he did not.

She ran for the stairs, feeling the fire of his gaze within her soul all of the way.

Five

⚜

That night she dreamed about Castle Creeghan.

She was seeking out that elusive room, the master's room within the castle.

She moved along the stone passageways, and the moonlight filtered through ancient arrow slits and played upon the tapestries depicting ancient battles and victories. She walked along the bloodred carpeting, seeing the darkness before her as she approached the laird's tower.

The hallway stretched into the darkness. It seemed endless. And then, from behind her, she heard the whispers.

The sound was like the wind, like a moaning, like a cry. It seemed to grow and swell, even as candles lit along the way began to flicker and fade. It seemed that there was no sound, none at all, except for the beating of her heart, but she turned, and she saw the white shadows, and the moaning whispers began again.

They were behind her.

Creatures, beings . . . no, the dead of Creeghan Castle. Bony fingers, covered with their gauze shrouds, rose and pointed toward her. Sightless, empty eye sockets stared upon her as if they could see. They did not need to walk upon the floor, but they floated slowly and surely toward her.

She turned to run again. But the corridor seemed to lengthen with her every step. And she was running and running, so very desperate.

She was almost there. Almost to the master's tower. Almost to safety.

But then she realized that there was a large towering figure standing there. Tall and dark, a black cape rippling from his shoulders. He stood with his feet well planted upon the floor, his arms crossed over his chest. And there was laughter, deep, rich, taunting, and filling her being.

And then she saw the white flash of his smile, and she stood still, for the searing fire of his eyes touched down upon her and she cried out, startled by the sense of evil . . .

Behind her, the white-clad death-ghosts began to whisper her name, and before her, Bruce Creeghan reached out his arms. She thought that to turn back would be certain death . . .

And yet to run forward would surely damn her soul forever.

She awoke, jerking up. There were arms around her, someone was shaking her, and indeed, something was whispering her name harshly.

She opened her eyes and a scream caught in her throat. He was with her. He was seated beside her on the bed, holding her up, shaking her. His hands upon her were strong, arresting, and she stared from his eyes to that touch, and then met his gaze and shivered again.

"Creeghan!" she cried. "What . . . what . . ."

"You were screaming," he told her. "I came as quickly as I could, since it sounded as if you were being attacked by a thousand vicious demons." She didn't say anything, but stared at him blankly. "You were dreaming, Martise, I assume. A nightmare. Unless you outran the demons and returned to your bed."

Her bed. He was sitting at the foot of her bed. He was in his smoking jacket again, naked beneath it, she was sure, and she was once again clad in white that concealed no more than had the white shrouds that covered the moving ghosts of her dream.

He had lit the lamp, so the room was not dark, but cast in mysterious shadow. And, it seemed, they were as alone in those shadows as they might have been had they ventured to the ends of the earth.

"Oh!" she whispered, and it all rushed home to her. She had been having a nightmare, and she had screamed and screamed in truth just as she had in her dream. She met his eyes again and pulled her bedcovers close to her chest, trying to smile and failing, and then managing to apologize. "I'm sorry that I've disturbed you. I suppose that I *was* dreaming."

"It's all right," he told her. He hadn't moved. She needed him off the foot of the bed. There was a magic about him. He brought decadent, forbidden thoughts too quickly to her mind. If he reached out to touch her . . . she might want him to stay.

"Then there is nothing wrong, you are all right?" he asked.

She nodded her head vigorously up and down. "I'm fine. Again, I apologize. I—" She paused, staring at him, exhaling through clenched teeth.

He shouldn't have been in there. She was certain that she had bolted both the doors to the balcony and the door to the hallway. "How—how did you get in?" she demanded.

He rose then. His eyes were cast in shadow. "By the door," he told her.

"I bolted it."

He shrugged. "You must have forgotten."

"But I—"

"But bolting the door is a good idea, a very good idea, while you are here. Make it a practice."

He walked to the door, his strides long. But when he

would have opened it, he turned back suddenly. "Tell me, milady, has the dream faded now? What caused it? When your eyes opened and you saw me, I might have sworn that *I* was the demon of your nightmare."

She laughed uneasily. "No, milord Creeghan. 'Twas merely the thought of your ancient ancestors, prowling about the halls."

"Ah, yes, the haunts of the castle. Are you sure that you wish to brave them longer?"

She thought that there was a challenge to the soft taunt in his words, and she did not know if he wanted her to stay or to leave. And she wondered if he knew himself just what he wanted.

"I told you—"

"But you see, Martise, you *do* fear the ghosts."

"I dreamed, and nothing more."

She felt his gaze, though she could not see his eyes in the darkness. "Bolt the door, then. Rest well," he said, and then he was gone.

For a moment she was still, but then she leapt to her feet and raced across the room to slide the bolt. She hesitated there. She could have sworn that she had done this before, but then . . .

She walked across the room to the doors to the balcony. She tried them and discovered that they were firmly bolted. Exhaling slowly, she returned to her bed and lay down upon it.

His scent seemed to linger on the air. She ran her hand over the bed where his heat still remained.

She closed her eyes and prayed for sleep. Images of the day kept running through her mind. She saw Clarissa, laughing through the wrought-iron bars of the gate. Beautiful, bold Clarissa, who so evidently wanted the master of Creeghan . . .

Faces swam before her, Father Martin's, Dr. Mac-Teague's. Elaina's . . . the doctor's again, earnest before her as he swore that Bruce Creeghan had been devastated.

But things happened. He had never told her what, he had just alluded to the full moon. Strange things happened by the light of the full moon. The people were superstitious. They still worshiped, in their ways, phallic symbols and fertility gods and goddesses.

As last, the images began to drift away. And in time, she slept.

And she dreamed again.

But this time, there was no horror, no terror-filled run along the stone halls of Creeghan. This time, she was here, within this room, and she was alone with Creeghan.

And in the dream she met his eyes. He cast the elegant smoking jacket from his shoulders and began to walk toward her. He was naked and sleek and magnificent, and she should have been shocked, and she should have looked away, but she could not.

She waited, barely breathing, waited, with her arms outstretched. And then he was with her, and he touched her, and it seemed that she was consumed with flame, and the sweet magic overwhelmed her . . . and she knew no more.

But it was with her, the dream was still with her, when she awoke to the bright light of morning. Mortified, she drenched her face in the wash water again and again, and even then, she sat at the foot of the bed and shivered, and wondered just what power it was that he wielded that could do this to her. Was it something in the wine, or in the water?

She knew that it was not. It was in the man, and in the man alone.

Elaina was the only one in the great hall when Martise came down for the day and was quickly up, pulling back one of the dragon-footed chairs for Martise to have a seat. "I'm so glad to see you. I thought that I was all alone for this meal. Ian and Conar are out in the fields and Bruce has gone to see the harness makers. And even Uncle Peter is occupied this afternoon, something about water seeping into the cellar. Castles, you know," she said with a wry grin. "They are the very devil to keep up."

Martise smiled, taking the chair that Elaina had drawn out for her. "I imagine that it must be so. I've never lived in a castle, but I have seen many rather great manor houses, and even those are often victims of time."

"Of course. Tea?" Elaina asked her. "Hogarth has left us to serve ourselves since we are alone. We've chafing dishes on the buffet. May I fix you a plate?"

Elaina seemed so eager that Martise smiled and agreed. "Please."

Elaina poured the tea first, then set about preparing a plate for each of them. Then she sat once again herself and picked up her fork, but she did not really seem to want anything to eat, and merely prodded her food about. "I heard that Clarissa locked you in the crypt yesterday." She shivered fiercely. "I'm so sorry. It's such a horrible experience. And Bruce was furious. He was like a beast this morning, swearing that we must all take care that such things should not happen again."

"It was not so horrible." Elaina looked doubtful. "Really, it was all right. I was in with Mary, Elaina. Not a lot of ancient bodies."

Elaina shivered again. "Bruce said that you had awful nightmares in the night. I imagine he'll find Clarissa and speak with her. It seemed that he was about to explode."

It seemed that he was about to explode . . .

How furious could he be with Clarissa? The girl was beautiful, really beautiful, and very young. And her adoration for Bruce Creeghan was obvious.

"It's not so serious as all that," Martise said. She tasted a bite of her food, stew again, but delightfully different, a mixture of fish and shellfish in a cream sauce. She looked across the table. Elaina was still playing with her food. "I really am all right. It's you I worry about," Martise said.

Elaina started, staring at her. She set down her fork and folded her hands in her lap. "Why?"

"This is none of my business, of course," Martise said, but she rushed on, not giving Elaina a chance to tell her that her words were very true. "It broke my heart to see you when I came in just now. You looked very, very sad. Is there anything at all that I could do for you?"

Elaina just stared at her. Martise thought that the girl was highly attractive, slim and lithe, with her beautiful green eyes and startling dark hair and fine features. And she came from such a distinguished—and affluent—family.

"Please!" Elaina murmured. "You mustn't say anything to Bruce. He gets so upset when I . . . when I brood."

Martise frowned. If Bruce Creeghan had betrayed any emotion whatsoever, it had been for his sister. "I certainly won't say anything to anyone," Martise assured her. "It's just that I hate to see you suffer so. If I could do something—"

Elaina shook her head. "There's nothing that anyone can do. I just wait. I've got no choice." The last sounded desperate. She met Martise's eyes with a trace of moisture flooding her own. "And you are here. My God, your war has ended, long ago now . . ."

Confused, Martise shook her head. "It hasn't been that long," she said. "General Lee surrendered in April, but Edmund Kirby-Smith fought on awhile and they say that some troops didn't know that the war had ended until it was over for weeks. Months even. I don't understand—"

"Then we must enlighten you."

It wasn't Elaina who spoke, but Bruce Creeghan. Martise hadn't heard him come. But he was there, walking toward them at the table, then walking around the head to his sister's seat and bending down to kiss her cheek. When his gaze flickered over Martise, she felt a glacial chill. He kept his temper so well in control, but she could always feel his anger, feel it simmering beneath the exterior that he so often offered them all.

Perhaps he did not pretend with his family. Elaina said that he had been furious that morning. Perhaps he had ranted and raved then, the true ancient chieftain, supreme in his world.

Or maybe he was newly angered now, watching her, condemning her, as if she asked questions which were surely none of her concern. As if she had set her nose into his life and had no right to be doing so.

Martise lifted her chin. Mary was dead. She had her rights.

"Enlighten me, then," she said.

He pulled back his chair and sat watching her.

"I'm so glad that you find the family so intriguing, Lady St. James," he said.

"Bruce," Elaina murmured uncomfortably.

"I've a brother still in America," Bruce said sharply.

"What?" Martise said, startled.

"My younger brother, Bryan. He went to school in America. He became friends with any number of Virginians, and like your husband, madam, he decided to make their war his own." He turned from her to study his sister, and his voice softened. "For Elaina, it has been worse. Her fiancé, Niall MacNeill, was with Bryan. Neither has returned."

"Oh!" Martise said.

It was so sad—and frightening. Had this Bryan Creeghan had any correspondence with Mary's sister, Margaret St. James, during the war? How easily this could jeopardize her own position!

"I'm so sorry!" she said to Elaina.

"As we are," Bruce said, "for you. After all, Lady St. James, you were there through the hardships, were you not?"

"Yes, but not to know!" Martise said. "And to miss both brother and beloved to a war that was not really your concern—"

"But that was *your* same circumstance," Bruce Creeghan reminded her politely.

"What?" Martise said.

He leaned across the table toward her. "Your husband was an Englishman, Lady St. James. And you lost him to a war that was not his own, or your own."

She lowered her eyes swiftly. "Yes, yes, of course."

"It so often sounds as if you embraced the Southern cause yourself. As if you had been born a true daughter of the Confederacy," Bruce said politely.

" 'Twas easy to become involved," she said. "I *was* there through so much, you see."

"Of course. The exploding shells, the land ravaged. No matter where you were, how could you have missed involvement? The Shenandoah Valley ravished, the Peninsula campaigns, two battles at Manassas, Cold Harbor, the Wilderness, Chancellorsville, the Siege of Petersburg, the evacuation of Richmond—the war must have come very close to you."

She stared at him, wondering how in hell he could be so informed on all the different battles.

His brother. His brother had probably written home. That had to be it.

"I was living outside of Richmond," she said smoothly, "so naturally I heard the roar of the cannons and saw the soldiers passing by often enough. And we tended the wounded from many battles, Lord Creeghan."

He nodded, and took a sip from the mug of ale that Hogarth brought him. "A hard life, I dare say, yet the time that Lord St. James spent in Africa must have prepared you for it well."

Africa, again! Damn him. Well, his little brother couldn't have served in Africa, too.

"Of course. But then the war among the tribesmen was quite different. The fighting seemed far away. We tended wounded, of course," she lied, "but this was very different. The enemy spoke the same language, worshiped the same God."

She thought that Creeghan was smiling, and it was

unnerving. He didn't seem to believe a single word she was saying.

And she was actually lying damned well.

"Well," Bruce murmured. He looked at Elaina, then squeezed her hand where it lay upon the table. "We will keep waiting. But I tell my sister that she must live for the present, and not wait for the past forever."

He stood, pushing back his chair. "I am riding into the village, Lady St. James. If you wish to accompany me, please be ready within the half hour. If you haven't the proper clothing, I'm sure that there must be something of Mary's that will suit you well enough."

He didn't wait for her reply, but turned around and left the hall.

Martise finished the meal with Elaina, then hurried for the steps herself.

She didn't need to take any of Mary's clothing—she had ridden all of her life and was a very good horsewoman and her wardrobe still consisted of several fine riding habits. But when she would have chosen one of her own, she paused, and delved into Mary's trunk.

It would be interesting to see Lord Creeghan's reaction to her in Mary's clothing.

She chose a beautiful, rich kelly-green habit with a tailored jacket and smart matching hat with a dyed pert plume. The hat pulled slightly over one eye, and she was startled by her own appearance in the garment. Her hair seemed as rich as fire against the color of the habit, her eyes seemed wider and bluer, and the angle of the hat gave her the air of a woman of the world, an attractive woman . . .

A sensual woman.

She turned quickly away, not wanting to dwell on such an idea when she was already living with such distressing dreams. Lord Creeghan might have his arrogance and confidence, but she had her pride. If they were engaged in battle, then she must win. It was that simple.

She left her room and hurried back down the stairs to the hall. He was not there, and so she immediately left the castle, exiting by the main archway.

He was with one of the young grooms, the lad Jemie, awaiting her. His great bay was saddled and ready, and beside it stood an elegant silver mare with a mane and tail so long that she resembled some mythical beast.

"You're late," Creeghan told her. "I waited this once, milady, but I do leave promptly." She didn't have a chance to reply. He was at her side, sweeping her up and lifting her atop the mare. He took the reins of the bay from the lad without a word.

"Good afternoon, Jemie," she said, ignoring Creeghan.

Jemie blushed. "Good afternoon, my lady."

Creeghan was staring at her. She met his eyes, but they gave nothing away. Whether he was displeased with her apparel or her words to Jemie she wasn't sure.

"Come, milady," he said, and turned the bay. He trotted the horse across the bridge and out of the castle to the roadway. Then he set a quick and wicked pace along the road that a less experienced horsewoman would have had difficulty in maintaining.

Was he wishing she would catapult from the mare and break her neck? Martise wondered as they raced along the roadway and the wind tore at her hair and the dirt and stones flew beneath the horse's hooves.

But then he slowed his pace, and she pulled in the mare. He waited for her, to ride beside her, and she felt the power of his gaze upon her.

"She's a fine animal," he told her of the mare. "An Arabian blend with some of our local stock. She is graceful and surefooted, a virtue necessary in our country of high cliffs and ragged tors."

"She's a very fine animal," Martise agreed, patting the mare's neck.

"Desdemona," he informed her. "You must feel free to take her out whenever you desire."

"How kind."

"Not at all. She belonged to Mary."

"Did you ride with Mary as you have been riding with me today?" Martise asked him. The sun was warm on her face, despite the coolness of the day. Birds whistled and sang from the forested fields around them.

"Why do you ask?"

"I—" She hesitated. "I had never known that Mary had become so accustomed to horses."

He smiled, and she sensed the devil's curve to his lip. "Ah, and if I took Mary out on such a ride, I would indeed be risking her life. Mary did not die upon a horse, milady. Nor had she been riding the day that she died."

"Still—" Martise began.

"Still. No, Martise. I never rode with Mary as I rode with you today. Mary was no horsewoman. She loved Desdemona, but we were very careful with Mary and the horse, and her riding was limited."

"And yet you took me out like this—" Martise said.

"Ah, but you see, I knew that you were an excellent horsewoman, Lady St. James."

"And how would you know such a thing?"

"How could you be any other, married to Lord St. James, traveling here and there in his reckless world?" He arched a brow to her, smiled, and added, "I am not after your throat, Lady St. James, no matter where it is that your thoughts may lie."

He nudged the bay, and the horse leapt to life again, racing away like the wind. She did not need to touch the mare Desdemona—the horse tore after the bay with her beautiful, smooth gallop.

Martise seethed even as she leaned against the mare. Her temper eased as she felt herself become one with the fluid motion of the horse, as she felt the power thundering beneath her, and the wonder of the wind and the air and the sky all about her.

They cut through the woods and rode southward, and

soon enough Lord Creeghan was slowing his pace again. She came up behind and could see the village stretching before them. It was enchanting in the waning sunlight. The village sat upon the water as did the castle, except that the bluffs and tors were worn here, and there were several docks with dozens of fishing craft lining them, and there were stretches of cream-colored sandy beaches, and behind all that, rising again into the tors, was a multitude of thatched-roof cottages and houses.

"Creeghan," he said softly, and his arm stretched out to encompass the land and sea as he showed it to her. "Across the sea lies Ireland. Our people, the 'Scotia,' came from Eire in ships long ago, and so many settled here that we became Scotland. The Vikings ravaged all these lands. But the Romans never came. The mountains and the tors stopped them. They couldn't fight the Highlanders, the people who ferociously clung to their clans and families, who fought by darkness, and melted into the earth by night."

He turned to her and smiled suddenly. "Do you like it, milady?"

"It's very beautiful," she told him.

"Good," he said simply. "Come, then, I've business below."

They rode down by the docks, past the many dwellings there that also housed businesses. There was a large blacksmith's shop as they first left the trail and reached the valley, and beyond that, there was a cabinetmaker and a shop filled with farm machinery. There were also numerous fisheries. It was a small village, but it seemed to be thriving.

The fishermen, just bringing in their catch, stopped as they rode by, the men lifting their hats and even bowing to Creeghan. He waved to them all in recognition.

They turned a corner, and Bruce dismounted from the bay before a small quaint house. He came around to lift Martise from the mare, and she was much aware of his arms as they came around her, sweeping her easily to the ground.

"Me Laird Creeghan!" came a woman's voice. Martise turned to see a slim graying woman with beautiful light eyes coming their way, wiping her hands upon her apron. She paused before him, bowing her head, then smiled up to him anxiously.

The woman had been at the memorial service, Martise recalled.

" 'Tis a privilege to see you, milord."

"Thank you, Peggy," Bruce said. "I've a bit of business with your man. Mind if Lady St. James has a sip of your chamomile tea and a taste of your fine shortbread?"

"Oh, me lady, 'tis an honor!" Peggy said, smiling broadly. Martise looked to Bruce but he was already mounting the bay. "Tell your boy to look to the mare, Peggy. And I'll return soon enough."

He was gone before Martise could protest any of his arrangements. Not that she really wanted to. She was curious about the villagers, and Peggy seemed friendly enough.

"Please, ye come in, now, I donna wan' ye catchin' yer death of cold in this weather!" Peggy told her, leading the way to her house. Martise entered the cottage behind her and found herself in a warm kitchen that was surely the center of the family's existence. A fire burned, with something bubbling in a pot above it. Herbs and leaves lined many walls and the rough wooden table in the center of the room was covered with jars filled with jellies and jams and pickled fruits and vegetables.

"Sit, sit, me lady, if it please ye," Peggy encouraged her. Martise smiled and sat at the table. "It's very warm and comfortable. And I'll have yer tea in a wee bit," Peggy said, coming forward with a crockery dish and placing it before Martise. " 'Tis the very best shortbread in the Highlands, I promise ye!" Then she paused, and studied

Martise openly. "Ye don't look much like her," she said flatly.

Martise smiled. "Like Mary? No, I suppose that I don't resemble her very much."

"Not at all. Ye're prettier. Not that milady of the castle warn't a sweet beauty, aye, that she war! And we loved her, we did. 'Twas a sad day when she left us. And sad fer his lairdship, too. Why, they say that they could hear his roar of pain like that of a cat, filling the hills." She crossed herself. "She rests with the Saviour now, she do. Alas, 'tis sad when they're young, is it not? Yet it seems that God do take the young ones when he do so desire."

"Yes, of course," Martise murmured.

Peggy turned around, going to the fire and the kettle against the bricks. She prepared the tea, strained it, and came back by Martise.

"Did my sister come to the village often, Peggy?"

"Oh, aye, she did!"

"With Lord Creeghan?"

"With him, without him."

"Oh?"

"She was always willin' to be of help, Lady Creeghan was. I remember once, when there'd been a shipwreck, she was here, and so distressed, and with her hands in the dirt and the sand like the rest of we, trying to save a child, she were. But the ship, it had broke up too bad, and none of them did make it, not the sons nor the daughters." She shrugged fatalistically. "It do happen."

Martise nodded.

Peggy looked to the door, then clicked her tongue against the roof of her mouth. "Where is that lass of mine? She should have been about the house long ago. Her da will be home with the master now, and he'll no be pleased."

"You've a daughter?" Martise asked her.

"Aye. Why, ye saw her yesterday, milady, so ye did. Clarissa. She's me lass. I've three sons, mind ye, and not a spot of trouble among them, but that one . . ." She shrugged. "Men do turn her head. The village is not enough fer her. She yearns fer the city life, and I fear fer her, I do. She is too quick to speak with the sailors." She sighed softly. "Her heart is set too high, ye see, milady."

She rose suddenly and looked out the window. "Ah, here they come. My man, Henry Cunningham, and Laird Creeghan."

The door opened. Peggy's husband, white-haired and kindly looking, and hardly the ogre who would lash into the wayward Clarissa, entered with Bruce. His cap was in his hand and he wrung it around and smiled a hesitant greeting to Martise. "Lady St. James, 'tis honored we are to have ye in our wee home."

She smiled and told him, "I've just enjoyed the best shortbread in the Highlands. It has been my honor, Mr. Cunningham."

"Henry, milady, Henry," he offered quickly and shyly.

"Henry, then," she said.

Bruce was watching her. And she thought that, for once, he seemed to approve of her.

"Is the lass home?" Henry asked his wife.

She shook her head broodingly. "I've not seen her, Henry, since she set to her bed last night."

"She's nowhere about?" Bruce asked.

"Nay, Laird Creeghan," Peggy said.

"I'd a mind to talk to her," he said.

"Is there something amiss?" Henry asked worriedly.

"Nay, no more than what we've been seeing already this day," Bruce told him.

"Why? What's happened?" Martise asked.

Bruce looked at her across the room. "There's been another shipwreck along the rocks. The children began to see the bits and pieces of salvage breaking up upon the beach today."

"Oh, dear God! How horrible!" Martise said.

Bruce nodded. "I cannot take you back to the castle,

Martise, I've got to stay and go out with the men and see if there is any help to be given."

"Of course, of course," she said quickly.

"I can have me lad lead the lady to Castle Creeghan—" Henry Cunningham began, but Martise cut him off.

"No, please, I'd like to stay. Perhaps there is something that I can do that will be of assistance."

"You should go back," Bruce said curtly.

"But I do not care to," Martise said, staring at him. Then she suddenly felt that to argue with Bruce Creeghan would be futile. He was the laird here—not just of the castle, but of the village, and of the people. She didn't mind fighting, but she preferred to do so with a chance at winning.

And if he wanted her gone, there would be no help.

"Please!" she said. "Really, I could help."

Bruce Creeghan turned around, slamming out of the house. Henry and Peggy were still, and Martise flashed Peggy a fleeting glance, then hurried out behind Bruce.

"Please!" she called to his back as he walked toward the bay. "Wait! Honestly, I have helped through battles, and if there are any wounded—"

He swung around with a sudden violence and fury so startling that she backed away from him. "There won't be!" he said savagely, striding toward her. She wanted to run as he gripped her shoulders with a startling, almost cruel force. "Don't you understand, there won't be! There are never any survivors!"

For once, she realized, he wasn't angry with her. There was pain and sickness in his eyes along with the fury. He didn't even seem to really be seeing her. His anger was directed elsewhere.

"By God, this time I am going to London! Something must be done, something to better chart the waters and warn these captains about the Dragon's Teeth!"

"The—the what?" Martise gasped. His fingers were biting painfully into her, and still, she wasn't at all sure that he was aware of her.

Then his eyes focused on her at last. "The rocks," he said more quietly. "These cliffs and tors you see here, the rock . . . it does not go out into the water and disappear. They extend, like teeth, and dear Lord, over the centuries they have trapped endless ships." His voice took on an edge of harshness again. "The ships should not flounder! There are lights set for them, here, in the village, to follow a course away from the rocks. Yet sometimes the ships come in, fools! As if they are beckoned to the very bloody rocks themselves." He paused, still tense, his features stark and strained. He looked at his hands, where they lay upon her shoulders. His grip upon her eased, and his gaze caught hers once more.

"There will be no survivors," he told her softly. "There never are. Go home. This is not your affair."

"Let me stay—"

"Martise—"

"Peggy is distressed. Perhaps Clarissa will come home."

He stared at her several long moments. Then he looked past her and she saw that Peggy and Henry had come from the cottage and were silently awaiting Laird Creeghan's next command.

He looked at Martise again long and hard, and then shrugged. "Stay with her, then. I'm surprised that you've a mind to, after Clarissa's behavior yesterday."

"I'd not punish Peggy for that. Clarissa is in love with you. She's jealous of anyone in your house."

His brows flew up and he looked at her with a great deal of surprise. Then he managed a crooked smile.

"Fine, then. Stay."

He was about to walk away. Martise stopped him, feeling a ripple of fear snake along her spine.

He stared down at her hand upon his arm, then looked into her eyes. "Aye, lass?"

"You haven't seen her today, have you?"

"Who?"

"Clarissa." She didn't know why, but she had to pause,

and wet her lips. His eyes were darkening at the question, their color growing deeper. "Your sister told me that you were very angry with her, that you . . . that you might speak with her."

He pulled away from her touch and responded coldly. "No, Lady St. James, I have not seen Clarissa. Not since yesterday. Now, if you'll excuse me . . ."

It wasn't a question. And it wasn't polite or courteous. He swept past her, whistled to the bay, and called to Henry. "Come, let's see of what good we can be."

He was up on the bay, staring down at Martise, and his eyes were all fire, scornful, condemning fire. "We may be late, milady. But 'tis your choice."

Then he was gone, riding back toward the sea.

Martise closed her eyes, miserable, and not at all sure why. It was the tragedy of the sea, the horror of the breakup of a ship, any ship, the lives that could be lost, dashed against the shore.

But there was more. She felt as if she had betrayed him. What did it matter? She owed him nothing, nothing at all!

But she had felt his passion, felt his distress at the death upon the Dragon's Teeth, felt his fury and his tempest.

Clarissa was missing . . .

And Martise had a very uneasy feeling deep inside of her, and not even the rise of the wind and the rush of the surf could seem to sweep it away.

She wanted to run after him. She wanted to stop him and beat against him and cry out, "Swear! Swear to me that you did not see Clarissa!"

But he was gone, and she could not reach him, and if she could, he would surely stare at her with fury.

He wanted her belief, she thought, her trust. He demanded it, in fact, and when he did not receive it, he was angry.

But she could not give him her trust! she told herself firmly.

And then, even as she turned toward the house, she

realized that he already had much, much more of her. With each new encounter, he was beguiling her ever more beneath the simple but shattering power of his will . . .

And his desire.

Six

֍

It was late when Bruce Creeghan returned for her.

And Clarissa Cunningham had still not come home.

The men came into the cottage tired and drenched. Peggy was quick to pour tea to warm them.

Martise, very aware that Peggy would tend to her "dear Laird Creeghan" before seeing to her elderly husband, took to tending Bruce herself. If she had begun the task of bringing him his stew and tea with a trace of resentment, that feeling quickly faded, and for the time they remained within the cottage, she was convinced that Creeghan was a man of honor, deeply concerned about the events of the day.

His eyes touched hers with a weary thanks as she set down the hot stew, and she almost felt his exhaustion. Henry was quick to tell them that Creeghan had dived into the frosty northern waters when necessary, frantic to save lives. But it was too late. The bodies they discovered were long past life.

"She went down in a full moon," Bruce commented broodingly. "I canna understand it, Peggy, I canna," he murmured, his accent growing stronger with his weariness.

Peggy sighed. "There's none can do anything, Laird

Creeghan. The ships, they will smash up on the Dragon's Teeth."

"Aye, but it seems they fall upon the rock too oft in recent years," he said. He finished his tea and set down his cup. "Did your girl make it home?" he demanded of Peggy.

Peggy cast a quick glance to her husband. "No, she dinna."

Henry looked up, anger and worry contorting his weathered features. "I'll have me a switch to her, I will," he muttered.

Peggy said nothing.

"We'll have a search for her tomorrow if she doesn't make it home soon, Peggy. You mustn't worry. The young will be young," he said reassuringly.

Peggy nodded. They came outside. The moon was still nearly full. Peggy's son Michael brought their horses and Bruce helped Martise up into the saddle.

He did not head home with his customary breakneck pace. His sluggish journey seemed to match his mood. He was very quiet, barely speaking.

When they reached the castle, he lifted her down and told her to go to bed, he would tend to the horses himself. She turned, wishing that she could say something, and yet she could not. As she headed for the door he called her back. "Bolt your doors."

"I always do."

"Be sure. Be doubly sure. Do you hear me, girl?"

She nodded, irritated, but his attention was no longer upon her, and he was already leading the horses away.

Martise hurried through the empty hall. A fire still burned in the hearth, she noted, and realized that Hogarth probably never turned in for the night until the master had done so himself.

She did not tarry in the hall, but hurriedly ran up the steps to her room. She was cold, very cold, and she shed her night-dampened clothing and donned a gown. She was ready to dive into her bed when she paused and went back to try the bolts once again.

The doors were definitely locked.

The events of the day played over and over in her mind when she went to bed.

But then she fell asleep, and if she dreamed, she knew nothing of it.

She awoke once, with a start. She sat up in bed, hugging her pillow and looking about.

She had thought that someone was with her. There was no one. She was alone.

And yet . . .

It seemed that the masculine, alluring scent of the lord of the castle lingered on the air, haunting her heart and her mind.

She turned back into her covers, and it was a long, long time before she slept again.

In the morning, Martise discovered that the men were preparing to ride out and search the forests and the cliffs.

Clarissa Cunningham had not come home with the dawn, and her parents were frantic.

Bruce was already outside when Martise heard the news from Ian. She ran out herself, catching him before he could mount the great bay.

"I'd like to come, perhaps I can help!" she told him.

"You'd be in the way, lass. Stay home," he told her.

"I'm an excellent rider, you know that. I *can* help."

He leaned forward, exasperated. "And what do you ken of this land, lass, eh? Do you know the cliffs, or the beaches, or the forests? Or the rocks, by God, the rocks are deadly. Above the water and below. You've been told what they do to the unwary."

"I don't want to take a ship out. I want to ride with you."

He threw up his hands and called out to one of the stable boys. It was Jemie; it seemed that Creeghan liked the lad and called him most frequently.

"Bring out Desdemona for Lady St. James, lad." His eyes fell upon Martise. "She'll be ready to ride within ten minutes."

Ten minutes. She gazed at him for a single second, then spun around and raced for the stairs.

She did not wear Mary's habit that day, but chose one of her own. It was a cobalt blue, and severely tailored, lightened only by the white ruffles of the blouse she wore beneath it.

When she came running back downstairs, she found that Conar and Ian and Peter were already mounting as well as Bruce, and that they all waited for her.

She hurried toward the mare, and Jemie helped her mount. She turned to Bruce.

"Nine minutes," he said with a trace of amusement. "Very good, Lady St. James."

They rode first for the village. Bruce was ahead with his uncle, Peter, and Martise found herself riding beyond them, between Ian and Conar.

"Do you think we'll find her?" Martise asked anxiously. She couldn't bear thinking of Peggy having to deal with the disappearance of her daughter. "She could be lying hurt somewhere—"

Ian interrupted her with a scornful snort. "Clarissa? No, I think not. The girl is as wild as the weeds that grow upon the cliffs. Mark my words. She's run off—she's found some man, and she's run off, and we'll not hear from her again until she comes running with a brat in her belly—"

"Ian," Conar said sharply.

"My apologies, Martise. That was crude."

"It was *incredibly* crude," Conar said flatly. He grinned at Martise. "Do forgive him. It's a small world we live in."

"What did Bruce say?" Ian asked his cousin. "I had thought that he intended to talk to her yesterday morning. He rode out to see her, I know that he did."

Martise felt a ripple of unease sweep along her spine as she waited for Conar to answer.

Conar lifted his shoulders and let them fall. "Bruce says he never spoke with her. She was not about."

Bruce had been angry, Martise thought. Angry about the crypts he had warned her about so constantly.

Clarissa had really disappeared on the night of the full moon. On the night that the ship had evidently wrecked upon the rocks.

On the night that she had awakened because of the noises far below her on the cliffs. When the wind had been high and cold, and she had seen the lights running along the cliffs.

On the night that she backed into the arms of Bruce Creeghan, and he had carried her into her room to promise that if she stayed, he would have her . . .

She shivered. "Let's pray that she did run away with some man, a sailor briefly into the village or some other."

Ian's hand rested upon hers on the saddle. "I'm sure of it, Martise. You needn't fear discovering her twisted and torn body upon the rocks."

"Well, now, that was a wonderful and thoughtful comment, too," Conar told his brother with exasperation.

"Sorry!" Ian said, and grinned at Martise. "I meant to make you feel better, honest, milady, I did."

She smiled. "It's all right, Ian. And thank you, Conar." She smiled at them both and then urged her horse forward. Peter was commenting to Bruce that they should take the cliffs, since they knew them best.

"Father Martin was making the arrangements for the search, so I was told," Bruce said. His gaze fell upon Martise as she rode beside him, but he made no comment to her.

"Aye, and ye know that they'll all be waitin' until ye make yer appearance, Bruce, and that ye'll be leading the party. 'Tis the way that it is, and that's a fact, and that's that."

"Then we'll take the cliffs," Bruce said, and Martise

realized that he was watching her again. "And ye'll stay by my side, my lady, do ye ken? The cliffs are dangerous."

She smiled sweetly. "As you wish."

Bruce nodded and nudged the bay, and the horse broke into a smooth canter. The mare leapt to life behind him, and she and Peter followed his pace.

Within moments they reached the village, Bruce leading the way through the winding paths to the church, where it seemed that all the men and older boys had gathered.

Father Martin and Dr. MacTeague seemed to be organizing some kind of effort, and, watching them, Martise understood the social structure of the village. Things had not changed so much from ancient times. There were the simple folk, the fishermen, the farmers. And there were merchants, and the shopkeepers, and some of the larger landholders. Above them in status were the doctor and Father Martin, and at the very top of the pinnacle was Laird Creeghan—supreme, she thought, beneath only God himself.

The villagers, it seemed, were becoming more accustomed to her. Grave but respectful and perhaps even friendly nods came her way as she quietly waited astride Desdemona. She returned them all, surprised at how fond she was already becoming of the villagers, and of their quaint and charming lives.

As Peter had said, the men had awaited Bruce to make definite decisions. And the master of Creeghan was quick to take charge, leaping atop the stone fence that surrounded the church to map out a plan of action. He sent some men forth to the forests, some along the trail, some to the beaches—and himself and his family to the cliffs.

Bruce mounted his bay once again and trotted around by her side, murmuring to her, "At my side, milady. At my side."

"Aye, Lord Creeghan," she said humbly, only her excellent adaptation of the Highland accent giving a hint of her sarcasm.

He cast her a fiery glare, but continued on, and she followed closely, Ian, Peter, and Conar behind her. They left the village and rode along the beach. The path gradually became littered with rocks, and then with boulders, and then they came to a high rise of sheer cliff that Martise could not imagine scaling.

But there was a trail. Bruce led the way, and they wound between the gray rises of jagged rock. The trail beneath Desdemona's feet was dirt and sand and scraggly grass, and yet, as they climbed, more foliage began to take tenacious root until they reached a plateau area with more rock rising ruggedly to the sky beyond them. From here, Martise could clearly see Castle Creeghan, still in the distance, so high above them that it seemed to sit in the clouds, and yet at the same time, it was all part of the landscape, harsh, challenging, and somehow as supremely confident as its master.

"We'll split here," Bruce was saying as they dismounted. "I'll take Martise along the lower levels."

"Aye, fine," Peter muttered. "And I'll—"

"Da, you'll take the left pass. You're a wee bit too old to be playing mountain goat. Ian and I'll take the rock trail to the right."

"A wee bit too old—" Peter began with a bluster.

"Da, behave now," Ian said with a grin. "All of the paths must be taken, right, Bruce?"

"Right. We'll meet back here. There's brandy in my saddlebag if you make it back first."

They split. Bruce started for a narrow, overgrown trail and then paused, looking back to Martise. He reached out a hand and she scampered over the pebble-strewn earth to take it.

His fingers closed around hers. Their eyes met, clashed, and Martise allowed hers to fall. He did not say anything. Martise thought that perhaps there was nothing left to be said. She could feel the vibrant heat and pulse of him through the touch of his fingers, and she meekly followed behind.

It was not an easy trail. It seemed that they had only gone a few feet before Bruce released her to leap about four feet to the slab of rock beneath him. He turned back to her, his arms up. She hesitated, then stepped forward and reached toward him. His hands slipped around her waist and he lifted her down.

Her body touched his. Slid against it. And then her feet were on the ground but his hands were still upon her and she felt the ripple of muscle beneath his clothing as her body pressed hard against his.

And then there were his eyes . . .

Emerald and fire as they tore into hers. The sun was high overhead and a bird called out and the sea breeze picked up, swirling around them. She wanted to close her eyes but she could not; she could not take them from his. And she thought that he must truly be some devil, demon, or satyr, for had he touched her then, had he chosen to kiss her, strip her . . . have her, there upon the rock beneath the hot sun, she could not have spoken, she could not have protested.

"Come on. We'll take the caves below first," he told her. His eyes hadn't left hers. But then they did. He had turned, and he was dragging her along, and it seemed that he was furious all over again.

They came to a second jump, and though he helped her down, he released her as soon as he could, caught her fingers once more, and hurried still downward. As they rushed along the path, Martise cried out in pain when her ankle twisted, caught in a crevice. She tugged her hand free and sat back upon a slab, fighting the scissors of pain that slashed from her ankle to her thigh.

"Martise, will you—" he began angrily, then spun around. He caught sight of the pain in her eyes, then knelt before her, lifting up her foot. He ran a hand along the length of her calf beneath her skirt, and even as a sound of protest escaped her lips, he was untying her boot and removing it. He swore softly, and offered no apology, and then looked up into her eyes.

" 'Tis sprained, at least, not broken," he said irritably. "I told you that you should not have come!"

"What?" she snapped, and her eyes narrowed. "If you were not so damned all hell-bent on leaving me behind—"

"I'm hell-bent on hurry. We've a great deal of land to cover while we've got the light."

"It was your fault, Laird Creeghan, and that's a fact!"

He rose, her boot in his hand, and he pointed it at her as he opposed her flatly. "You'd not be hurt if you'd stayed behind, and *that's* a fact. But you've always got your wee nose into things, haven't you?"

She gasped in fury and rose, and the pressure on her ankle caused her to cry out.

Then she was swept up into his arms, and his eyes softened somewhat as he stared down at her. "You haven't the good sense you were born with, lass," he told her.

"Set me down," she commanded him.

"I canna do that, lass. You'll come a little farther with me, to the caves, and there I can see you and reach you quickly if there's a need."

He was walking again. Involuntarily, she wound her arms around his neck. She closed her eyes against the sight of his clean-shaven jaw above her.

He was surprisingly agile, holding her so as he scampered ever downward until they came to the sea again. From here, arms of the cliffs stretched out into the water, and Martise could easily understand why they hadn't been able to ride here: the beach itself was totally blocked by the rise of the rock.

She saw, too, why the rocks were called the Dragon's Teeth, for they rose before her, and far out into the water, like huge, monstrous canines, jagged and sharp and dangerous.

Bruce set her down upon a water-worn slab where she could see the waves as they lashed in.

"At high tides, the beach floods here," he warned her. "But we've hours yet. I'll be in the caves, not too far. If you need me, call for me."

She said nothing, but stared out at the deep blue sea.

"Martise!"

Startled, she looked into his eyes.

"Do you ken? Call me if you need me."

"Aye!" she heard herself saying. Then something about his eyes touched her deeply and she promised, "Yes, Bruce, I hear you, and I will. But what . . . could happen?" she asked.

He shook his head, and she realized that he didn't know.

Still he was reluctant to leave her. Suddenly, he was walking back toward her, and then balanced down upon one knee, smoothing back that soft wayward strand of hair for her. His fingers brushed her cheek, and she wanted to catch his hand and stop him. But her eyes were locked with his once again, and the sizzling amber mystique was filling her with longing, with the golden edge of his fire . . .

Her hand fell upon his shoulder, and she feathered her fingers through the raven wings of his hair, and she closed her eyes, overwhelmed by the fascination. She felt the salt ocean breeze against her cheeks and then the touch of his lips, caressing, soft, against hers. And she felt the heat of the sun again, too, against the damp chill of the day, for he pressed her back against the rock, and its warmth seeped into her. "By all that's holy," he murmured, his lips paused above her eyes as he gently brushed them both with his kiss, "I should play the demon indeed this moment. The waves and sea become a part of it, coursing through the blood, demanding the rhythms of Eden." His whisper was seductive, lulling.

But then his hands were upon her, pulling her up, and a taunting gleam was in his eyes as she opened her own to them. "Indeed, milady, I've warned that I shall have you, and that I shall. If you do not have me first."

Her eyes widened at his insinuation, and then she realized

that, rational or not, her hand was flying and she was determined to see that her palm smacked hard against his cheek.

But he caught her wrist, and his laughter was subtle, and she was suddenly pulled hard against him, aware despite all her layers of clothing and his own that he was most certainly very male and very aroused, and more than ready to carry out any threat.

She struggled against his arms, but he held her close, and his kiss caught hold of her lips then, hard, rugged, as forceful as they were persuasive. She tried to fight him, tried with fury, and yet her strength waned and the taste and the scent and sheer power of his touch prevailed in the end, and he killed her then at his leisure, tasting her lips, knowing them with his tongue, with the gentle graze of his teeth. And then he was tenderly holding her against him, and his murmur touched her ear softly.

"Do I hold the rabbit or the hawk? The seductress is always there, bold, fighting, demanding. And you should know the ways of the world, and the ways of men, and yet then again I think that I am misled, that there is innocence there. Who are you, Martise?"

She pulled away from him, dismayed. Her hand flew to her throat, and she stumbled back upon the rock, wincing as she placed weight upon her ankle. "Mary's—Mary's sister!" she cried out. "You—you must remember that!"

He arched a brow to her, and it seemed that a golden gleam came down to hide all the emotion within his eyes. "I try," he said quietly, then turned toward the caves, pausing. He cast his head back and closed his eyes against the sun, and then he opened them again and turned back to her. "*You* must try to remember it, too," he said.

But before she could begin to ponder the true meaning of his words, he was gone, heading into the caves.

For the longest time, she just sat there on the rock, listening to the sound of the surf. She was falling in love with him, she thought.

She could not be . . .

And yet she was.

Her thoughts about Bruce faded as she realized that she was staring at a piece of fabric that seemed to trail from behind a rock, perhaps sixty feet away from her.

She hadn't seen it before, she was certain.

Then she noted that the tide was rising, and she thought that perhaps the rise of the water had loosened something behind the rock.

She stood slowly, and then she felt as if her heart congealed. Fabric . . . it could be Clarissa behind that stone.

Or her body.

Martise inhaled on a sharp gasp, but then quickly came to life. Hobbling on her sprained ankle, she made it as fast as she could across the sand. She rounded the huge rock and then her hand flew against her mouth to hold back a scream as she saw that the fabric indeed housed a body.

But it was not Clarissa's.

Beneath her, pinned by the weight of the rock, lay a man. He was clad in the simple garb of a sailor. His graying hair was flat against the sand, tangled within it. The fabric she had seen had torn free from his pants where his leg had been snapped like a match, and now lay at an awkward angle, the bone protruding.

His shirt, too, was stained with blood.

For a moment she thought she would be sick.

She closed her eyes and remembered the days in Richmond at the hospital when she had tended the battle-injured. When she had smelled the rot of gangrene. When she had heard the horrible screams of the men as such injured legs were amputated.

She fought the nausea, and then she opened her eyes, determined. She fell down on the sand beside him, trying to remember any little thing that she had learned from the doctors.

Then she wondered why she had worried. The man was so obviously dead.

She pressed her fingers against his throat and laid her head on his chest. She jerked up, certain that he had a heartbeat.

But there was little that she could do for him here. She ripped open his shirt and saw that the wound had torn his lower diaphragm. She sat back and ripped at her petticoat. He was heavy, and it was difficult to move his upper body to bind up the wound, but she tried to do just that.

Then she started to scream. "Bruce! Bruce! Please! I need you."

The man was alive; he was still bleeding. Fresh marks of blood welled into the bandage and she ripped more material to pack the wound more tightly.

"Bruce!"

The man's eyes opened. Unfocused, dazed, they stared into the sun. The man cried out.

And then he glanced at her, and his eyes were filled with fear and terror.

"It's all right," Martise tried to assure him. "I'm trying to help you. Please, lie back. We'll get more help. We'll splint your leg. It's going to be all right."

But he opened up his mouth and screamed again. Martise leaned forward, using her skirt to mop at his forehead. "Please, it will be all right. It will be all right."

He was trying to say something. She leaned low against him as his lips moved and no sound came. There was just a whisper. She couldn't understand him.

And then she thought that she did.

"Creeghan," he mumbled.

She couldn't have heard him correctly; it was her imagination. She tried to talk to him again, to keep talking, to say anything. "It's going to be all right . . ."

But it wasn't. The tide was coming in, and the man was still stuck beneath the rock.

Frantically, she began to tear at the material that was caught, and pinning him down.

And then Bruce appeared.

"Martise!"

She was not sitting upon her rock, and so she thought that she heard a note of anxiety in his cry. "Bruce, over here! Please, help me!"

He was there in seconds. His tall black riding boots slashed through the water and he quickly assessed the situation. He rolled back his sleeves and set his strength against the boulder.

She watched as the cords in his neck tightened, as his face strained, as the muscles within his arms rippled and tautened out like whipcords. The rock didn't move. But then he braced himself and pushed again, and the huge boulder floundered over several inches.

The man was free.

"His leg!" Martise warned, looking about frantically herself. They had left the area of any ground that resembled woods, but Bruce disappeared into the cave again and returned almost immediately.

She wondered how he had found a length of split lumber so easily, but it did not seem the time to ask. As he gritted his teeth against the pain he would cause the injured man, Bruce straightened the leg, snapping the bones into place.

The man screeched in agony.

Then he passed out, and Martise took more strips of petticoat to bind about him, and when she was done and the leg was secured, Bruce carefully caught him by the shoulders and pulled him from the path of the oncoming tide.

"You can go for Ian and Conar and Peter," Martise said. "I'll stay here with him—"

"Aye, lass, but I think that we need the doctor here. That's severe. And he's suffered more injury than the leg, I'll warrant. A man gnashed by the rocks seldom breathes again." He drew off his black frock coat as he spoke, placing it around the man. "Aye, stay with him, and I'll send Conar to bring Dr. MacTeague, then we'll move him with the doctor's supervision." He paused just a moment. "He'll probably lose that leg. I've seen such wounds before."

"Yes," Martise agreed, then she looked up at him, startled, wondering where he had come across such a woefully shattered limb before.

He was already leaping up the rock, graceful, agile for his size.

Martise bent close to the man's chest again. At first, she did not hear a heartbeat. Then she caught just the faintest murmur, and she sat back, relieved.

There was nothing else that she could do.

She was sodden and wet from her foray into the rising surf. Her feet were drenched, as were the hem of her skirt and what remained of her petticoats. She shivered fiercely. The daylight was leaving them. The surf was still rising, and a bitter chill seemed to have settled over the sky. She looked up. It would rain that night, and the air would become cooler.

She looked back to the sailor. "Live!" she whispered to him. "Please, live. You must tell us what happened, why . . . it happened. And why you whispered the word 'Creeghan' to me."

Creeghan. Because Castle Creeghan had brought about his downfall?

Because the great laird of Creeghan . . . had what?

She swirled around as she heard a sound on the sand. Bruce had come back, and Conar was with him.

"Ian has ridden for the doctor," Bruce said. "It should not be long."

"It had better not be," Conar muttered. "Watch the tide, Bruce. It will be up to the cave in another hour." He rubbed his hands together, shivering in the wind. "How he's made it this long is surely a miracle. Bejesu, Bruce, but 'tis freezin' here!"

"Aye, that it is," Bruce agreed, and his gaze landed upon

Martise, who still shivered and shook. Then she gasped out a protest as he reached down and swept her into his arms.

"Lord Creeghan, whatever—"

"I'm taking you into the cave, out of the wind," he told her with an angry crack to his voice. "We'll have you down with a bad ankle *and* pneumonia if you don't listen to some sense."

"But the sailor—"

"Conar is there. We've a blanket to set over him. Martise, there's nothing that you can do!"

He was right. As they entered into the darkness of the cave, she unwillingly tightened her hold upon him. He slowly, carefully set her down, and then rose to tower over her.

"Are you all right there?"

She nodded.

"I'll go back out, then."

She could see him and Conar by the sailor. They sat on either side of the man in the sand, their knees up, their elbows rested upon them. Their voices were very low. She could not hear their words, though, and she leaned her head back against the stone of the cave and listened to the wind.

It was growing shrill. Passionate, raging, and shrill. It swept through the cliffs, and it seemed to cry and moan and to have a haunted life all of its own.

She shivered. Even in the cave it was cold. Perhaps it was even worse, for the wind sounded more terrible here.

The rains would begin soon.

But it was not that long before Ian and Peter returned with the doctor. And Dr. MacTeague instantly sat down by the man, nodded his approval of the splint and bandage, and then leaned low against the man's chest.

"We can lift him painlessly enough, I think, the three of us," Bruce was telling his cousins. "One at the shoulders and two at his feet. It will be a blessed mercy if he stays unconscious—"

"We need no mercy, Bruce," MacTeague said quietly, looking up. "He's dead."

"What?" Martise cried in horror from the cave.

She stumble to her feet and then lumbered heavily across the sand. She fell by the man and cared not if she insulted MacTeague. She leaned against the sailor to seek a heart-beat herself, and then she frantically felt at his shoulders and at his breast.

There was nothing.

MacTeague was watching her over the body of the fallen man.

"I'm sorry, Lady St. James. The man is gone."

"But he was alive!"

"Aye, milady. And you did well, miraculously well. You made every effort . . . but he's gone now."

"I'll take him up," Conar said briefly, bending down to lift the body over his shoulder. He straightened. "It will not matter now to him if it be a rough and rocky road."

He started up the cliffs. Martise sat in the sand, shivering anew, unable to accept the man's death.

Then she felt Bruce's hands upon her again, lifting her to her feet, sweeping her up into his arms. His eyes touched hers, but he spoke to MacTeague.

"The Lady St. James needs her ankle bound. Can we tend to it at the plateau?"

"Aye, that's fine," MacTeague agreed.

Her eyes remained on Bruce's as he carried her surely up the cliff. The wind ripped and tore around them both, and screamed and cried.

"He was alive," she whispered.

"Aye, he was alive," Bruce agreed. And then he looked ahead, climbing. "He might have told us—something," he said.

"He did," she murmured.

Then he was staring at her again, staring hard.

In the gray murky air that swirled around them, he seemed to be cloaked in darkness. Fear and longing mingled within her, along with the terrible sense of danger she felt whenever he was near.

She knew not if the danger was within the naked, all-powerful charisma of the man, or if it lay in something more evil.

"What did he say?" he demanded harshly.

Conar and Ian and Peter and the doctor and the dead man were far ahead of them then.

They were alone on the cliffs, alone by the sea, and she was powerless within his arms.

"What did he say?" Bruce repeated, his voice like the thunder that would soon crack the sky.

"Nothing, nothing, really!"

"You're lying, girl."

"No!" she cried. "He *tried* to speak. He barely had a voice left. I leaned against him. I tried to hear—"

"Don't you understand! We might have learned something!" he snapped back at her.

Oh, yes, she understood.

The man might have told them all something . . .

Creeghan. The word that he had whispered was "Creeghan" . . .

The wind screeched and moaned again, and then suddenly, with a violence all its own, the rain came.

Bruce ducked his head low against her, and for the fraction of a second, Martise caught her breath, certain that he meant to throw her . . .

Down to the Dragon's Teeth far below.

But he did not. He held her more tightly to leap his way across the rocks, and hurry for the plateau and the waiting horses.

There was no question that her ankle could be bound then and there. Nor did Bruce even take a step toward the mare. He set her atop the bay and leapt up behind her, and called out that they would head straight for the castle.

He sheltered her from the wind, and from the rain, and though her heart beat too quickly at first, she was glad enough to lean against him and let him take the brunt of the wind and the rain. Lightning flashed, and thunder roared, and she closed her eyes, tucked close against him.

He was in his element, it seemed. Undaunted by the wind or the sheeting rain or the sizzle of the lightning or the heartless crack and peel of the thunder.

Indeed, he seemed immune to it, a lord of the wind, a lord of the thunder. She could not care at the moment, she could not think. She could only hold tight throughout the reckless ride and seek her harbor in the hard warmth of his chest.

They came to Creeghan. Bruce burst through the door with her in his arms. Elaina and Hogarth, both in the room, cried out at her appearance.

"What is it?" Elaina cried.

Bruce set her in the chair before the fire.

"It's nothing—" Martise tried to say.

" 'Tis her ankle. Brandy, Hogarth, we've a need of some warmed brandy." His eyes met hers as he loosened the button at her throat, then he stepped back and MacTeague took his place. Hogarth was there with the brandy, informing her that there would be a steaming bath in her room as soon as she was ready.

"Thank you, but I'm fine, truly I am," she said.

MacTeague was pulling off her stocking and carefully feeling her foot and ankle. Ian drew off his soaking frock coat and set it upon a hook in the wall and walked across the room to the table, pouring out whisky for the men and handing a glass to his father before bringing glasses to his brother and Bruce.

And then they all stared at Martise. She tried to smile wanly.

"Well, 'tis a sprain, and Lady St. James might want to soak it in her bath before I bind it. It will do well enough, but"—he pointed a stern finger at her—"ye must stay off your feet, milady, for a good week."

"A week!" she cried with dismay.

"A week," he said firmly.

Bruce set down his whisky and stepped forward again. "Come on, I'll carry you up for your bath."

"I'll come, too," Elaina said, "and tend to her."

Bruce paused, looking at his sister. "Well," Elaina reminded him softly, "I can help her where you must not, Bruce."

Bruce's look conveyed that he could help her very well, and that he really didn't give a damn whether he must or must not. But he smiled at his sister and agreed, and started for the stairs.

And his eyes upon Martise's as he walked indicated that he really could and would do whatever he chose.

Whenever he so chose.

He opened the door to her room with his shoulder and carried her in to set her on the bed. Holly was there, pouring a last kettle of steaming water into the bath.

"Oh, my Lady St. James!" Holly moaned.

"I'll stay with her, Holly," Elaina said.

Bruce was down upon a knee, removing her other boot, his eyes upon hers. His hand moved subtly against her stocking, and his gaze was wicked. But then he smiled, dropped her boot upon the floor, and rose.

"Call me, Elaina, when Lady St. James is ready to come down and see the doctor again."

He strode to the door. Martise watched him, then she struggled to sit up. "Wait, Bruce, please!"

"Aye?"

"Where—where is he? The sailor."

"Tenderly wrapped within the archway, I assure you. We'll bring him back to the village. MacTeague will want to examine him at greater length."

He was stepping out the door.

"Bruce!" she called once again.

He paused, watching her, waiting. Was it warily? she wondered. She could not tell. His fire eyes burned into her.

"What about the girl? Clarissa. Did any of the others find her?"

He hesitated. "No, I'm afraid not," he said. He stared at her a moment longer, then looked to his sister. "Call me, Elaina," he said, and then he was gone.

And even though Elaina chattered and sympathized, Martise felt as if she was very much alone.

She felt cold. So very cold.

Even when she had stripped away her sodden clothing and sunk into the steaming water, she still felt a chill deep within her, because he was gone.

Like any childish, wayward girl, she was falling in love without wit or reason.

No, she was no longer falling. It was too late.

She loved him . . .

She feared him . . .

But like a fool, she loved him more.

Seven

It was later that night, when Bruce Creeghan had carried Martise back down to the hall and Dr. MacTeague was busily binding up her ankle, that Bruce announced his intentions of leaving the following morning for Edinburgh.

Startled, Martise looked from MacTeague's gentle hands upon her foot to Bruce Creeghan's eyes.

He was watching her.

"I want something done," he said simply. "There has to be a better warning system for these ships."

"But can anything be done in Edinburgh?" Ian asked his cousin.

Bruce's gaze fell upon Ian. "I hope so. If not, I shall take the problem on down to London, and to the Queen herself. By God, this is the third wreck we've had within four months! And we don't even seem to be able to pick up enough pieces to learn where the ships are coming from, or going to." He paused, staring into the fire. "Except for this time. We know that she was the *Lady Anne* out of Glasgow. Part of the mast washed up on the shore." He was looking from one to the other of them, around the room. No one said anything. There was an acute and painful silence, and then a log snapped.

Watching him, Martise felt his anguish over the downed ships. But then she found herself wondering about the sailor again. The man had been alive.

And she had been sure that he whispered the word "Creeghan."

And if so . . .

She closed her eyes. She didn't want to think about it. Bruce couldn't have murdered the man, he hadn't been alone with him. But after he had carried her into the cave, he might have asked his cousin to fetch something by the rock, or walk toward the cave and check on her. And perhaps, in those fleeting moments, he had snuffed out the small breath of life that had remained within the sailor. To hide something.

To keep the man from whispering. "Creeghan" again . . .

She opened her eyes. He was staring at her. Seeing into her, seeing through her. His lip curled with a certain mockery. "Perhaps nothing can be achieved," he said. "But still, I must go."

"You might want to keep your eyes open for the young Cunningham lass, too, Bruce," MacTeague advised him. "I say the lass has gone and run off. And without a word to her poor mum."

"Aye, indeed, I'll ask after her," Bruce said.

After Martise's ankle was bound, the chairs were drawn all about the fire and they sipped warmed brandy against the wet chill of the evening. The men were still talking. Elaina broodingly studied the fire, and Martise wondered if she wasn't thinking of her own lost love.

It occurred to her then that if Bruce Creeghan was going to be absent, it would be a wonderful time to search his library.

He was watching her again, and she lowered her eyes quickly, staring at the flames in the hearth. She would have to ask him tonight for his permission to use his library while he was away.

MacTeague rose. "I imagine that the rain has stopped by

now. I'll be getting on home, then. Thanks for the warmth and hospitality, Bruce."

"Thank you for coming to the cliffs so quickly, and returning here for Lady St. James's ankle," Bruce responded.

MacTeague included them all in wishing a good evening, and then Bruce walked him to the door. While he was gone, Peter yawned, excused himself, and said good night.

Only Elaina, Ian, and Conar remained with Martise. They all looked expectantly at Bruce as he returned. "There's naught you need before I leave?" Bruce asked his cousins.

Ian shook his head. "We'll be fine, Bruce. And if anything comes up, why, we'll wire you in Edinburgh."

"Then I'll take Lady St. James up to bed," he said. He bade them good night, tenderly kissing his sister on the cheek. Then he swept Martise up into his arms. She wound hers around his neck, and thought how quickly, how easily, how trustingly she had come to do this.

Trustingly . . .

He carried her up the stairs, and she knew that he was going to speak, but he did not do so until he brought her into her room and laid her gently upon her bed.

He moved away from her, standing by her side, arms crossed over his chest, and she was suddenly aware that she was going to receive a lecture.

"You must take care, which may not be so easy now, but MacTeague means to send up a pair of crutches in the morning, so you'll be able to get about a little. Your door bolts must always be locked. Do you ken?" He took a step toward her again. "It's very important. Keep your bolts locked at night."

"Against the ghosts?" she asked.

She saw his jaw twist and set. "Against any intruder," he warned her.

He turned around and headed toward the door.

She sat up on the bed and called out to him. "Who is it in this house that I should be afraid of?" she demanded.

He stopped, and slowly turned to her, and she felt the fire of his eyes like something that could devour her very soul. "An intruder need not come from within a house, milady St. James. No castle was ever truly impregnable."

She moistened her lips. "But if you're so worried . . ."

"You'll be safe, I'm certain. There's no full moon in the few days ahead."

"Full moon," she whispered.

He swore softly. "Just keep your doors bolted, and you'll be fine. For now. Do you ken?"

"No, I don't ken!" she retorted angrily. "Tell me, explain to me—"

"What would I explain?" he asked. "I am the beast in your eyes, am I not, milady?"

He took a step toward her. A trembling shook her body, and yet she was not afraid. No matter how he stalked her, she was not afraid.

She thought that he would touch her, that he would kiss her. And she quivered within because her imagination would travel to dangerous paths, and because, if she closed her eyes, she would see him in her dreams, naked, agile, a panther of the night, moving toward her, magnificent and hungry, taking everything . . .

And giving everything.

But he didn't touch her. Not in any way evil or forbidding. He stopped by the bed and his thumb and forefinger moved gently over her cheek.

Seductively. Just a brush . . .

But his words were of warning, and almost tender. "Martise, take care. I beg of you, heed my words. Trust me in this. I will return as soon as possible."

His hand fell away. He turned and left her. The door closed behind him, and he warned her again to slide the bolt. She stumbled up and hopped to the door, wincing as she put her injured foot down on the floor.

"Martise?" It seemed he had even sensed her expression of pain from the other side of the wood.

"Yes, I'm here. I'm bolting the door," she said. But she didn't do so. She threw it open, remembering that she had not asked him about the library.

His dark brows rose in surprise. He was very tall there, dark in the shadows, fascinating.

Her voice failed her for a moment. "Lord Creeghan, may I use your library in your absence?" She lifted a hand prettily and let it flutter back to her side. "Since I shan't be able to move about much, I would dearly love to peruse your books."

He bowed to her very formally. His voice was cool and mocking as he said, "My dear lady, you must be my guest in all things. Roam where you will. Take what you choose. I'm rather surprised that you have bothered to ask me."

She smiled sweetly. "Ah, but, milord, *you* are one prone to taking without asking!"

"Only what I know is mine to receive," he returned swiftly. Color flooded her cheeks, but he bowed courteously and pulled the door shut.

"Bolt it!" he said flatly through the wood.

She did so.

"Good night, milady," he murmured.

"Good riddance!" she muttered to herself.

But he had heard her. Miraculously, he had heard her. And his soft, haunting laughter seemed to follow her all the way back to the bed, and even beneath the covers.

He was gone, and Creeghan itself seemed empty without him. Hogarth was quiet and not his usual cheerful-if-cadaverous self. Elaina seemed to have withdrawn further into herself. Even Holly seemed more subdued.

The cousins and Peter were out the majority of the day, and in the first two days that Bruce was gone, they did not even return for the evening meal. The weather was bad, and counting the sheep had become more difficult with it. A work horse had slipped and had to be put down, and there were all sorts of complications about the estate, so Hogarth informed her.

She was somewhat morose herself, for having been granted Bruce's blessing to tear apart his library, she discovered that she did not have the power to do so.

The first day her ankle caused her horrible pain if she even tried to take a step. And managing a search with crutches was difficult at the very best.

That day she went through many of the volumes on the first row of his shelving, looking for she knew not what. Then it occurred to her that she really needed to go *through* each book, all of them, for that might be the ideal place to hide an emerald. If pages were torn out, the stone might well be fit into a perfect groove.

But since the library housed hundreds of volumes, she faced a dismaying task. One that must be completed before Creeghan returned.

On the second day after his departure, she tore through the desk in the library. She was disappointed to discover that he did not seem to keep much in it. There was a calendar with simple remarks, tobacco, a few pipes, paper and writing utensils, an almanac, a few notes, and no more. Discouraged, she left the desk and stared again at all the volumes.

She sank down upon the velvet-draped day bed and wondered if Mary had come here often. It seemed a fitting place for a lady to curl up with a book and read while her lord worked upon his business. It was a large, full, four-poster bed with dragon-claw feet, covered in gold damask, masculine and inviting, and a multitude of decorative pillows was spread upon it. The bed was recessed so that the room kept its character as a library, and yet when one looked at it, it almost seemed to beckon one to stretch out . . .

She wondered if the master of Creeghan had slept here often. She forced the thought from her mind, but it would not stay gone, and she could not help but wonder, too, if

Bruce Creeghan had slept in the bed since she had come to the castle. If he appeared on the balcony that night behind her because he had been here all along, because he had sensed her very first movement . . .

This was getting her nowhere.

She threw herself down on the large gold-covered bed, nearing despair. She needed to leave, before she fell any further under the spell of fascination, of danger, of hypnotism, woven by the master of Creeghan.

She needed to find the emerald and run.

But what of Mary? And what of ships that floundered in the night beneath the glow of a full moon? What of Clarissa Cunningham?

It was not her concern.

And yet it was. Every day that she stayed, it became more so.

The library was yielding little to her, but then there were only so many hours a day she could use to sift slowly through the endless volumes. Elaina would seek out her company, determined to take care of her while her ankle healed. Then there were meals to be taken with the family. Every night as they sat around the table, she hoped she would learn something new about the castle.

Or Bruce.

But she did not.

By the sixth day after Bruce's departure, she took to prowling through the library at night. Her ankle had gotten to where it was only slightly sore, and by night, she moved the library ladder up and down the shelves to search out the upper levels. She was thus involved on the night when Bruce Creeghan had been gone for ten days.

She had gotten the search down to a frantic but methodical and even mechanical task, quickly taking out one book, returning it, slipping out the next, running her fingers over the fine paneling of the shelves. She had become very involved.

And very accustomed to the castle. She paid little

attention to the creakings she heard within it, stone shifting ever so slightly, ancient wood adjusting. And then there was the wind, the constant wind. Always whispering, sometimes moaning and wailing, and often screeching and screaming like a soul in torment.

It was just such a night. The wind outside the castle blew with a vengeance, and its cry seemed high and anguished. That night, she could even hear the sound of the surf crashing far below, against the rocks.

She had finished with the top row the night before and now had moved down to the second row of shelving. She moved her fingers over the paneling, then started with the books. They were volumes of the works of Shakespeare, Bacon, and Tennyson. She had paused to study the beautiful binding of a book when she suddenly felt a chill swirling around the base of her spine. She was being watched. Someone had come into the room.

She held very still, then turned around on the ladder to stare at the door.

Lord Creeghan had come home.

The gas glow within the room caught the color of his eyes, and they were gold and seemed to sizzle. His stance was comfortable as he leaned against the door, his arms idly crossed over his chest. His hair was tousled, as he had come from the wind, and ebony-dark locks lay heavily over his forehead. He had shed his overcoat, but wore an attractive dark corded frock coat, snow-white shirt, and his inevitable high black riding boots.

His lips curled into a slow, taunting smile, but his eyes were slightly narrowed, a dangerous sign. Perhaps, if she had not come to know him as she had, she wouldn't have even noticed the anger that simmered beneath that smile.

But she did know him, and his gaze was frightening.

"My dear Lady St. James," he said. "What on earth are you doing?"

"You're back," she said, almost in a whisper.

He arched a brow. "Aye. Obviously."

"Oh . . . well . . ."

She was in a rather precarious position, she decided. She was clad decently enough in a long peach nightgown of cotton which buttoned to her throat. Still, there was nothing beneath it, and posed there, upon the ladder, she was surely caught in light and shadow, delineated by the glow of the two lamps in the room.

And it was well past midnight, she was certain.

How long had he been standing there, just watching her? Watching her search through his things?

"I repeat, milady," he murmured, his words polite, just the slightest edge to his voice, "what *are* you doing?"

"You . . . you said that I might use the library," she reminded him hastily.

His brow arched higher. " 'Tis well past midnight," he informed her pleasantly.

She tried for a brilliant, innocent smile. "Ah, well, yes, I do still have some trouble sleeping when the wind blows so fiercely. I thought that I would read for a while." It was logical, it was believable, she determined.

Except that he didn't believe her. He dropped his pose at the door and walked into the room, pausing at the foot of the ladder, staring up at her. "Do you look through so many books so frantically and with such brutal disinterest frequently? It's a most intriguing way of choosing a volume."

She clasped the one that she had been holding to her chest. It was *King Lear*. "I suppose I *was* rather in a hurry," she mumbled.

"Oh," he said. He was still staring at her. She warmed where she had been cold before. She felt the sizzle of his gaze raking through her, heating her, setting her aflame.

She had to get by him quickly. It would be difficult, as he blocked the way down the ladder now.

"How was your trip? Was it successful?" she asked in a rush.

"Aye, I believe that it was," he said, and offered no more.

"It's good to have you back."

"Is it really?" he asked courteously. He didn't believe for a minute that she was glad to have him back in the castle.

It was time to make a quick retreat. Whether he stood there or not, she had to get by him.

She came carefully down the steps, hoping that he would move away.

He did not.

His hands settled about her waist and he lifted her from the final rungs. He turned her in his arms and she slid against him, her breasts brushing his chest, stinging slightly, swelling, coming alive to the contact.

She jerked away from his touch. He did not hold her. His gaze seemed dark, as if it could impale her and hold her with the power of the knife.

"What are you looking for?" he demanded.

"Nothing!" she said, and she turned to run from the library.

He caught her wrist, and she was forced to hold still, staring at his fingers where they curved around her wrist. "You're going to tell me," he said softly, and the sound of his voice seemed to touch her bare spine, sending tremors shooting to her abdomen, and below. "You're going to tell me, in time."

She jerked her wrist free and returned his stare, her chin high. "I thought that I was going to sleep with you in time, milord!" she retorted.

He smiled. "That, too, milady. That, too."

She uttered a sharp expletive and turned to run at last. His soft laughter fell around her as she did so, ridiculously like a warm caress.

He was back. Bruce Creeghan was back.

And that night, he was within her dreams again.

She was so very aware that he was back. The castle seemed alive once more, filled with warmth and vibrance.

She had heard his voice early in the morning, deep and rich, filling the corridors.

She had stayed away from the great hall at breakfast time, and soon after, she determined to slip down to the village, to get away for a while. It was well over a week since she had injured her ankle, and she was certain that she could ride. She was very anxious to do so.

She dressed in her own blue habit and boots and slipped quietly down to the hall. It was empty and she exited by the main tower door. The courtyard was empty, too, but she saw a form in the stables and hurried on over.

The smell of hay and horses was strong, but when she stepped from the sunlight into the shadows, she saw that the stalls were kept as immaculately as the castle. Only the horses were housed here, she knew from Ian's dinner conversation. Sheep, he had informed her, in a quantity, did not smell anything like roses, and so the farm animals were kept in barns just down the hill, along the valley and the craigs that the surefooted animals loved so well.

"Hello!" she called out softly.

Jemie appeared, shyly nodding but saying nothing. The boy might be somewhat daft or fey, Martise thought, but he was very sweet. She smiled. "I'd like to take out Desdemona, Jemie. Would you saddle her for me, please?"

He nodded eagerly and set to the task. She looked along the rows of stalls. The horses' names were all set upon the individual gates, carved into wooden placards. Black Satan, Beauty, Lord Timmons, Ebony, and Star were in residence. Cera, Siren, MacGregor, and Lucian, the great bay, were gone.

The master was home, she thought wryly, and riding over his domains.

And now Desdemona, too, for Jemie had brought her out. She was already well groomed, and Jemie was quick and agile and competent as he threw the blanket and then the sidesaddle over her haunches and quickly adjusted the girth. Her halter was exchanged for a bridle, and then Jemie

led the horse out to a block directly in front of the stables for
Martise to mount the mare.

When she had done so, she thanked him sweetly, and was
rewarded by another shy smile.

She started off.

It did not take her long to reach the village. She walked
Desdemona along the docks, watching the fishing boats
way out on the water. The sea seemed calm that morning,
calm and blue and deceptively serene. Nothing of the
Dragon's Teeth could be seen from here. The whole world
seemed peaceful.

She turned toward the village, hoping that she would be
able to find the Cunninghams' place. She did so, easily
enough.

Young Michael was in the front, chopping wood. He was
a big lad with heavily muscled shoulders. He nodded her
way with a courteous respect, but it seemed that he watched
her warily, as if she might be the enemy.

"Hello, Michael, is your mother about?" she asked him.

He shook his head. "Me mum is helpin' out at the inn," he
told her. "Can I give ye tea or aught, meself, milady?"

"No, thank you, Michael," she said, and knew that he
had been hoping she would refuse the invitation. "I didn't
know that there was an inn. Could you point me toward it?"

"Aye, and surely, that I can," he said, and dropped the ax
he had been swinging. He walked toward her, and one of his
heavy hands fell upon Desdemona's neck as he pointed
down the road. " 'Tis there, on ta other side of the church,
there. Ye canna quite see it from here, but 'tis there."

She was looking down at his hands. They were very large
and broad, and even his fingers were powerful and heavy.
She realized that he had ceased speaking, that he was
looking at her. She smiled quickly. "Thank you." Then she
paused. "Michael, has your sister come home as yet?"

He shook his head, some invisible mist falling over his
eyes like a shield. "No, lady, she's not," he told her.

She bit her lip. "I'm sorry."

He nodded. What he was really thinking, she did not know.

She thanked him for the directions then and nudged Desdemona and followed the trail down the hill along several more cottages very much like the Cunninghams'. And then she passed by a field of bracken and wildflowers and came to the church. Beyond it, she saw the inn.

There was a wooden sign swinging from a handsome iron pole in front. It simply announced that this was the Creeghan Inn and that all were welcome.

Martise dismounted from her horse and stared up at the building. It was freshly painted in a bright white. There was a wide porch with tall handsome columns, and the windows were trimmed in a forest green that seemed to blend with the natural beauty of the Highlands.

In front of the porch were rows of artistic rings set atop heavy brass horses that resembled the knights in chess. Martise tethered Desdemona and climbed the steps to the porch, then entered by the large double doors.

The hallway offered a hospitable warmth. Martise stood there and looked about. To her left was a large room with a crisply burning fire in a big bricked grate and numerous covered tables strewn about. To her right was a second room, but the door was more than halfway closed, and she could see little within it. She heard laughter, though, and men's voices, and assumed that that would be the private pub, the men-only room, where the workers and fishermen would come to wet their dry and weary throats. The room to her left was for ladies and children—and husbands, if they had a mind to join their wives.

It was an inn, and she was sure that, up the long stairway, there would be rooms for guests. She was equally sure that Creeghan was a small and out-of-the-way village, and that guests could not be very frequent.

The door to the room for men opened wider and a plump figure appeared, wiping her hands upon her apron. She looked up.

"Can I help ye—why, 'tis Lady St. James!"

It was Peggy Cunningham herself. Martise smiled. "Yes, Peggy. I rode in to see how you were doing."

Peggy shrugged. "Well and good, I reckon, milady. But come, come in. The wind is down today, she is, and still the air grows sharp and chill already. We've sweet mulled brandy with cinnamon, and if I say so meself, 'tis grand as any anywhere. Sit, Lady St. James, and I'll see to your comfort."

"Oh, I don't really need—"

"But ye must!" Peggy insisted.

Martise took a seat at one of the tables before the fire. There was a young woman with a child at one of the tables toward the far corner of the room. She nodded to Martise and smiled shyly. Martise returned the smile.

And Peggy was back, and there was another plump woman at her side, and a very tall, very slim old man with her. "These be the Douglases, Lady St. James, Katie and Micky, and they do run our inn here and were most anxious to make your acquaintance."

Katie Douglas bowed as if she were meeting royalty, and Martise rose and took her hand and smiled. "'Tis my pleasure, Katie, Micky," she said.

"We're ever so pleased to have ye," Katie said. Peggy set the mug of brandy down before her. Martise saw, beyond her, that several of the men had come quietly from their own section to stand behind Micky.

"We heard tell about your ankle, Lady St. James," said one of the men, twirling his red fishing cap in his hands. He said the last with a wickedly strong accent. He went on. "Doc MacTeague told us yer efforts to save the poor downed sailor, and we were all proud ta have ye, we were."

She arched a brow, startled and surprised, and smiled. "Well, I'm glad to be here." She was, she realized, quite a curiosity. Perhaps any stranger would be a curiosity in such a small place.

"It was very sad that the ship should go down," Martise offered.

People were taking seats around her. Peggy had moved on, and was now serving ale to the men as they took their chairs. The woman who had been sitting in the corner with the child had moved forward, too, and now sat in the arms of one of the young sailors.

"Ships do come, and ships do go down," the man with the red cap said. Peggy handed him a mug of ale and he smiled. "Why, 'tis the way of such a land, ye know!" he told her.

Katie, no longer quite so awed by her presence, pulled out the chair opposite her. Her merry blue eyes danced with the crackle of the fire from the hearth. "These be the Highlands, milady. Not just Scotland, but the Highlands. Why, Vikings came to our shores, they did, and brought their gods and goddesses, but the Romans didna dare to touch us, for our chieftains then were fierce and more bloodthirsty than their own."

Micky bounded into the conversation. "Aye, indeed, ships do wreck upon our shores!"

"Perhaps we shouldna be tellin' the lady aboot such happenings," the man with the red cap said.

"No, it's all right, it's fascinating," Martise assured him.

"Why, the laird himself has boasted that Lady St. James fears no ghost!" Peggy proclaimed proudly, as if Martise were of her own making.

"Are there many ghosts, then?" Martise asked with a smile.

"Oh, aye, milady, that there are!" the red-cap man promised. He introduced himself then as George Mahaffy, and then went on. "They say 'tis the land, they do. Sheltered, private, fierce!" His eyes twinkled. "When the Vikings came, we werena so Christian, as it were, prefer-ring the gods of the Druids and those of the harvest. Why, milady, days gone by, 'twas said that our virgins were sacrificed to the harvest, that there were dances about the

May pole, and when All Hallows' Eve came, lasses were taken, here and there, each year."

"Aye, and even now," Peggy murmured, her eyes far away, "virgins disappear."

"And ships wreck upon the shoals." Katie sighed. "But then"—she laughed—"we are all of Creeghan, eh? And the castle has its own haunts. Why, 'tis like it has stood forever, for in ancient times, they *were* our chieftains, the Creeghans. We've legends and stories galore, and all of them fascinating. We do love our Creeghan lairds, that we do."

"The good ones, and the evil!" Micky agreed happily. He smacked his lips around his ale. "Eric Creeghan did fight the later horde, and 'tis said that he impaled thousands of men upon his sword that he named for the rock and the castle. And Jarrett Creeghan, hundreds of years later, defended us from the English and from the Orangemen, and kept us independent, no matter who the monarch sitting on the throne down in London! Our throne!" he muttered, "with the Stone of Scone beneath it." He was both confused and outraged at such an idea—Micky was certainly one citizen of Britain who would not have himself associated with his English neighbors. "No matter, they have always defended us."

"Dark and fascinating, and always!" Katie told her, leaning forward.

"Aye, dark as devils, and with their devils' own eyes," Peggy said. She winked at Martise. "Always seducing the ones they would have, as if there was some power within them. Many, many a lass has borne a Creeghan bairn—"

"So we think ourselves Creeghans often enough," Micky interrupted.

"Ah, but they are handsome, are they not?" Katie said wistfully. "And the lairds are always tall and fierce, and they will have what they will!"

"Strange sometimes," the young woman murmured suddenly. She rose and walked over to stand before Martise. Her eyes fell full upon Martise's, and even as she stood there, it seemed that the wind began to rise outside. The fire flickered warm and bright, but outside, the day darkened. Night was coming.

The pretty girl smiled, and as the fire touched her face, it seemed that there was something magical about her and that she wasn't just speaking, but performing. "We are a strange people ourselves, Lady St. James. Catholic—when most of our land is Presbyterian. We've eked out a hard life, and that's a fact. And our ancestors at times made their living by the sea—by the shipwrecks that cast their salvage upon our shores. And our great Creeghan lairds have been known to go through one wife after another, and there have been rumors aplenty that the castle is filled with bones other than those of the dear departed lairds and ladies!" She smiled, laughing. "On nights with full moons young lasses do disappear! In ancient times our priests practiced strange rites, and we danced naked beneath those moons! The laird was the god of the ceremony, and he alone was dressed in a dragon mask, and wore a black cape, until he chose his virgin for the night that all might find fertility for the winter."

"I dare say that I canna imagine our laird this day in a dragon mask!" Micky hooted.

"I see our present laird as easily as any other!" the girl said. "He is a Creeghan, and such men beckon, and women come. He is no different than the others. He is perhaps more powerful, and more beguiling, as fierce as any before him . . . aye, and strange! Stranger than ever since God—or the devil—did claim his lady wife from his side . . ." Her voice trailed away. Martise could not tell if there was a twist of suspicion to it.

But they were all very still and silent, as if a ghost had come among them.

And then a deep rich voice bellowed out with amusement, and they all turned with a jump toward the door.

"Strange, Cassie? Thank you, lass, I dare say."

The laird of Creeghan was among them. Dark—as

dark as the tales had been. He was dressed in black again, a black cavalry shirt, black breeches, his black boots, and a black cloak about his shoulders that must have reminded them all of that worn by the dragon deity who ruled the ceremonies by the light of the full moon.

His hair was again windswept and wild about his forehead, his features as bold and striking and handsome as any god's might be.

And his sharp eyes, green-gold, burning their fierce and startling fire, and falling upon them all, one by one.

He was smiling. Subtly, the curve of his lip adding to the deep and dangerous fascination of the man.

"Oh, me lord!" Cassie gasped, hopping back from the hearth and keeping her distance from the man. Her husband, Martise noted, did not leap to her defense, but kept to his chair, his mouth open as he gaped at Bruce Creeghan. "I meant no harm, me lord, and surely I didna, I swear it! We were telling tales—"

"So I heard."

"And the storyteller within me came a wee bit carried away, and that's it, I do promise."

He arched a brow, still smiling. " 'Twas a good story, Cassie, I'm sure. We've many of them hereabouts." He swept off his cape. Micky was quickly at his side to take it from him and hang it from a hook by the door. Katie was instantly upon her feet.

"Laird Creeghan, will ye speak yer pleasure, will it be whisky or ale or brandy, heated and sweet?"

"Whisky, Katie, please." He took the seat across from Martise that Katie had just vacated. He seemed to sprawl slightly, and stared at her with his lashes heavy over his eyes, his gaze intrigued. "Have you enjoyed yourself, then, milady?"

"I always enjoy a good story," she told him.

He nodded. Katie brought his whisky and he sipped it, still staring at her. He smiled, and glanced to George

Mahaffy. "Did any of you tell her just how strange some of our clans can be?"

"Ach, the story from last week!" George said.

Bruce smiled at Martise, his eyes glittering. "Indeed, we'd had a fine family among cliffs and tors like this, above a road, the only road, for some, into Edinburgh. It seems they'd send out their lasses, fair and beautiful, and their lads, young and strong, and equally beautiful. And they'd find unwary travelers and see that their horses were lamed or their carriages broken. And then they'd solicitously promise aid and invite the poor weary travelers to a meal. And seduced—and beguiled—the men and women would stay, blessing the Lord that they should have had their problems among strangers who were so very kind."

He leaned ever closer to Martise. The fire seemed to rise and flash in the hearth, and his eyes might have been part and parcel of the flame.

"Then they were slain by the very beauties who seduced them, and indeed, they were there for supper, they were there to *be* supper, and it seems that this clan survived by cannibalism for years and years, selling off the goods of their victims when they did not need them, using all parts of the bodies."

Martise, caught up in this tale as well as any other, gasped. "Cannibalism! I don't believe you!"

He leaned back. "'Tis true. We are a barbaric people, don't you agree?" he asked pleasantly.

"Ah, but my dear Laird Creeghan!" she exclaimed. "I've heard that ghosts do roam the castle, but from all accounts, these ghosts are in full possession of their flesh and all their limbs!"

He laughed, and the men within the room laughed. Even poor Cassie seemed to relax, and her husband welcomed her into the crook of his arm once again.

Katie assured Martise, "We've no rumors of anything quite so horrid around here, I promise ye, milady!" she said. Then she turned to Bruce and said, "Milord, we've venison steaks this evening, fine and sweet and tender as the Virgin Mary's own sweet heart. Will you and Lady St. James stay to sup?"

"Aye, fine, if Lady St. James is willing," Bruce agreed, watching her. She nodded, wishing that she could tear her eyes from his to smile at Katie. She could not quite do so.

But then he turned from her, and he talked knowledge-ably to some of the men about their catches, and he even flashed young Cassie a smile that caused her to flush and lower her eyes. But when Cassie's eyes fell upon him again, Martise saw that they carried a certain adoration.

Cassie might love her handsome young husband, but just as Clarissa had done, it seemed that she had set her dreams upon the laird of the castle.

And if he, as a dragon god, had chosen her as the one to go with him, she'd have gladly lain naked beneath the light of the full moon.

They ate Katie's delicious venison and vegetables and warm hearth-baked bread, and Bruce seemed at ease and comfortable, and the wind picked up and the true darkness of the night came upon them.

And then he rose, reaching for her arm. "We should return to the castle, milady."

She accepted his assistance from her chair, and thanked Katie and Micky and smiled at George and Cassie and the others. In the entrance hall, as Micky set Bruce's cloak about his shoulders, she turned suddenly to Peggy, who had grown silent with the tales, and hugged her fiercely. "Clarissa will come home," she promised her in a whisper.

"Aye, and that she will," Peggy agreed. But the woman did not believe her, Martise could tell. Peggy was con-vinced that her daughter was one of the lasses—virgin or other—who had disappeared with the light of the full moon.

Bruce, too, told her a gentle good night, and then Martise and he were out on the porch. Martise shivered fiercely as the night wind swirled around her.

"You've no coat?" Bruce demanded irritably.

"No, I came out earlier. It was not cold."

"Then you'll ride with me. Desdemona will follow along."

"No . . . I . . . I'm all right, really!" she protested. The shadows of the night lay across his face. She was not afraid of him, she told herself, she was not.

But he was everything that the girl had said, handsome, seductive, beguiling . . . beckoning her, stealing her heart and her soul.

And when he held all of her within his hands . . . ?

What, then?

But he emitted a furious, impatient oath, and before she knew it, she was swept up into his arms, held fiercely and passionately in the startling warmth. And then she was set upon the bay, and he was behind her, strong, powerful.

He nudged the bay and whistled softly, and Desdemona, with her reins tied loosely upon her back, followed obediently. Bruce led the bay along slowly enough until they passed the village, then he nudged the bay, and they rode like the wind, hard and fierce. The ground was dissolved beneath the horse's great hooves, and in the mist of the night, they might have ridden the clouds or the darkness itself. She didn't feel the cold, for his arms and the cape were sheltering her. She did feel the man. Felt his heartbeat, along with that of the driving hooves. Felt the steel of his arms and the vibrance of his chest.

Then, suddenly, in the shadows of the castle, he reined in, leapt from the bay, and pulled her down into his arms.

"Bruce!" she cried out.

But his mouth descended upon hers, with fire and urgency, and her lips parted, and it seemed that the consuming heat of his tongue filled her. And she would have protested . . .

If she had not been so swiftly, so completely, seduced. The power seemed to ravage her. His hands were upon her, cupping her breast beneath the fabric, holding her tight, molding her to the length of his form.

Suddenly, the kiss was broken, and his eyes seared into hers even as he held her.

"You're trembling, milady. Do you think, then, that I am in truth a beast?"

"No!" she protested. There was darkness all around them. His hands were so very strong. And now he gently, so gently, stroked her throat.

"You are a liar!" he said heatedly.

She was shaking. Shaking because she had to continue to challenge him. "Mary is dead!" she cried out with an equal anger and fervor.

"She died of heart failure!" he lashed back. "I do not seize upon lasses by the light of the full moon, nor do I wear the mask of a dragon!"

Martise moistened her lips, staring up at his face, seeing the passion and tension within his striking features. Feeling it. Her lashes were heavy, falling. The passion remained within her, too, but her anger was fading. She wanted to feel the heat and moisture of his lips and tongue again, wanted to know his kiss . . . and more.

"Not a dragon!" she exclaimed softly.

"What are you looking for, then?" he demanded. But she didn't really hear the words. She felt his touch, and the sweet growing ache inside of her. And then she was on her toes herself, her tongue just flickering over his lips, her body pressed full and flush against his, her arms winding around his neck. The pulse of his body seemed to leap within her own, and she felt the power of his thighs, of his chest, of his arms, wrapping tightly around her. She felt the fire of his kiss, eclipsing all else, and felt his hands, slipping beneath her bodice and her blouse, a blaze upon her bare flesh.

He would have her . . .

There upon the cape, beneath the darkness of the night sky. Against the rocks and the tors and the wildflowers. She would fall, as others had fallen . . .

She tore her lips from his. He shook her and met her

eyes, and then he thrust her from him in a fury. "Don't think to seduce me from the purpose of my questions ever again, milady. Understand me, and understand me well. Next time, milady, I will have you, as I have promised."

"Me! Seduce *you*!" she protested in a gasp.

"Indeed, you, Milady Innocence!" He pulled her close. "I will know what you are about!" he promised. And then his voice softened just slightly. "And I will know you."

She wrenched free. She swirled around, feverishly adjusting her clothing. And then she shivered because he was gone and the wind was cold.

She jumped when he touched her again, but he was not a man to allow protest, and even as she gasped and tried to mouth a "no," she was in his arms again, and set upon the bay.

And in the darkness, they rode for home.

Eight

❧

The ride with Bruce had left Martise feeling desperate, and she spent long hours of the night going through Mary's things once again. She found nothing.

The emerald was eluding her. Bruce was home, and it would be difficult to search the library. But she didn't believe anymore that the gem could be there.

It had to be in the master of Creeghan's private quarters. In the other tower. In the days to come, she was going to have to discover when Bruce was occupied elsewhere, and search out his rooms.

But she was too restless to sleep, and so she drew out some of the letters Mary had sent her. She glanced over the early ones, when Mary had been so very much in love. She closed her eyes and imagined Mary writing the descriptions of her lover, and she started to tremble and set the letters down. There was no way for her to deny what she was feeling for Bruce Creeghan, no matter what suspicions and fears came along with the fascination. She hurried on to Mary's later letters, when her unease was beginning to come through.

And then she paused, her heart thudding against her

chest, when she read that a girl had disappeared from the village, and they had searched for her day and night, but she had not been found.

Martise glanced at the date and saw that the girl had disappeared almost a year and a half ago now.

Then her eyes skimmed down the page and she noted with chills that Mary had even mentioned when she had disappeared.

On the night of the full moon.

And there was more. There had been rumors in the village about the hazy past of the lords of Creeghan. Maidens had been known in centuries past to disappear behind the walls of the castle, never to be seen again. The lords of Creeghan were strong and powerful, defending their people, caring for them. They were also striking and seductive, with demanding, insatiable appetites. Sensual, dangerous . . .

To Mary, the rumors were ridiculous. Even in her fear, Mary had defended Bruce. He was a handsome man, a sensual man who was admired by other men, attractive to women. And because the people couldn't forget ancient legends, they liked to imagine that their lord was nearly a god himself—a god, or a demon, so seductive that only the devil could create such power.

And I defend him, too, Martise thought. No matter what I see or hear, I defend him. Because I am attracted to him, too. Entrapped by his eyes, by the sound of his voice, the feel of his arms.

She put the letters away, nervously tested the doors, and then curled up in the bed, holding the covers tight beneath her chin.

But for long hours she didn't sleep, and she wondered if she should confront Bruce Creeghan with his deceased wife's letters, or if she should keep her information secret.

And wait . . .

And watch . . .

Sometime in the night, she dozed. In her dreams, he was

with her again. She was cold and shivering, and she realized that she was naked on the stone. People were dancing around her, and they were naked, too, just swirling forms in a gray-misted world. And the gray mist moved away and he was coming toward her.

He was dressed in a black cloak. It draped him from neck to toe. He wore the dragon mask, but she knew that it was the lord of Creeghan; it could be no one else. He paused beside her and touched her, and where he touched her, the coldness was gone, and she should have screamed and fought because it was not the warmth that was the truth of the man.

The truth lay in the dragon mask.

The coat slipped away, and his heat covered her, enwrapping her, igniting her.

Then she saw the blade in his hand. The long sharp blade with the jagged edge, glittering despite the grayness and the mist. And his eyes were touching hers, eyes of fire . . .

She tried to struggle. She could not. She was bound to the coldness of the stone.

His lips touched hers. His fingers raked along the length of her body, over her breasts and her hips, between her thighs. And where he touched, there was fire . . .

Then he was straddling over her, the blade between his hands as he stretched and reached to heaven. Once again, his gaze touched her, and he leaned down to her slowly, achingly slowly.

She did not know if he intended to free her from the ties that bound her to the stone . . . or slide the blade across her throat and let her blood run red to feed the ravenous hungers of ancient gods.

She awoke, strangling, gasping, somehow knowing that it was a dream, that she mustn't cry out. If she did, he would be there, be there in truth, and she could not face him.

She sat up and stared at the low-burning lamp by her side, and slowly, her breathing began to ease. Then a prickling of unease touched, and shivers ravaged her spine. She could swear that he had been near. The air seemed touched by his subtle masculine scent.

She leapt up and tried her doors once again, then leaned against those to the hall, exhaling. She was alone, and she had forgotten to slide the bolts. She went back to bed and stayed awake, staring at the ceiling.

Finally, with the dawn, she closed her eyes and slept a dreamless sleep.

When she awoke at last, she knew that she had slept until at least noon. The sun was warm as it filtered in through the balcony drapes.

It was still hard for her to rise. But soon she heard a soft knocking at her door and she rose to let Holly in.

"Ah, and at last, milady," Holly teased. "I've been at the door a good ten times, milady, and ye've been sleeping like one dead!"

Martise really didn't care for any reference to death that morning, but she smiled at Holly and sat down with the tea the maid had brought her. Holly chatted as she laid out Martise's clothing and collected things to launder or press. "There's a bit of a ruckus going on, then, today, that there is! There's been a wall has caved in below. Oh, 'tis happened before. The water, ye see, and the dampness, weakens the structure here and there. Oh, 'tis a constant battle to keep this house up, I do tell ye! But today, Laird Creeghan has called in the workmen, and there's been some secret room or passage found. So exciting, I dare say!"

"And I've slept through it all!" Martise exclaimed. Jumping up, she nearly unsettled the tea, caught her cup, and placed the tray on the bureau that flanked the wall. She hurriedly scrubbed her face and doffed her gown, dressing quickly with Holly there to lace up her corset and tie her petticoats.

"Ye're going on down, then?" Holly asked, laughing.

"Oh, indeed! Secret passages. How could I miss such an event?" She grinned and swirled around and left the room.

The corridors were empty as she hurried to the stairs, past the great hall, and down the cold and curving stone steps to the cellar far beneath them. Even as she reached the landing, she could hear voices. They were coming from one of the crypts, and as she hurried past the chapel, she realized that it was the newer vault, the one where Mary lay in her coffin.

She hurried in to find that they were all there, Bruce and Ian and Conar and Peter, and even Hogarth and a number of the men from the farm and stables, the huge man with the scar, Robert McCloud, among them. He nodded to Martise, with that smile upon his lips that made her uneasy. The lad Trey McNamara was at his side, along with two older men with weathered and rather weary faces.

Elaina was in the crypt, a bit apart from them all, sitting on an empty coffin slab, her face buried in her hands.

And young Jemie MacPeters was there, silent, staring. Bruce's hand rested upon his shoulder, and they all stared at the wall where bricks had crumbled down.

They were curiously silent, just looking at the opening. Then Bruce spoke, nodding toward one of the workmen. "Go on, then, break down the rest, and we'll bring her out as gently as we may, though it seems a bit too late for the lass."

"What!" Martise gasped. She hurried forward, anxious to stare into the cavity herself.

"Martise, don't!" Bruce cried out harshly, but she had slipped past them all, and his workers weren't about to stop her. Bruce did, catching her arms and pulling her against him, but it was too late. The break in the wall had displayed a tiny nook beyond it. A lamp had been lit, so the contents of the small nook were visible.

They were bones. Bones held together with fragments of flesh and material, soft cotton, touching lace ribbons, even the remnants of a bonnet. The bones leaned against the far wall of the crevice, as if the stance had been taken in a last desperation.

As if the girl had died, walled in there, screaming . . . and when her screams went unanswered, gasping, seeking the last breaths of air to be had.

A scream rose in Martise's throat along with the taste of bile. For once she was glad of Bruce's arms about her, and she sagged hard against him and swallowed back her scream.

"For the love of God, let's get the lass out of the wall and decently beneath a blanket!" Bruce demanded roughly. "And be careful, MacTeague will need to see her."

Bruce swung her around, seating her beside Elaina, who looked up at last, ghastly white. "Elaina found the chasm!" Bruce remarked angrily. "What are you doing down here?"

Martise stared at him, gathering her wits about her as quickly as she could. His gaze was upon her, hard and firm, and her hands were rested in the warmth of his. She suddenly felt like a wayward child, and she also felt his concern, and something almost tender from him. Something different from the taunting and the passion. Something gentle and caring. Also rather stern, as if she were flagrantly defying a parental order.

He was waiting, and irritatingly, she found herself stammering out an excuse.

"I—I heard about the chamber. The idea of it was fascinating," she said defensively.

"Well, you can both go on up—"

"I'm all right!" Martise protested. "Really, I am. I was just startled. I didn't know what—what to expect!"

Elaina was looking at her woefully. She rose, staggering somewhat. "I don't know about you, Martise, but I'm going on up."

"I'd like to stay—" Martise began.

"Bruce!" Conar called, excitement and a trace of amusement lacing his voice. "Come see this!"

For the moment, Bruce left her sitting there. Elaina smiled wanly. "I don't wish to make any more discoveries today," she told Martise.

Martise squeezed her hand. "I'll be up soon," she promised. Elaina smiled wanly and walked briskly from the crypt.

The men, Martise saw, were disappearing into the hole.

The bones, the pathetic remains of the young girl, were now on the floor, covered in a blanket.

Martise leapt up and hurried past the body and the workmen and into the jagged cavity in the wall. To her left was the now empty cavity. To her right was what seemed to be solid wall.

And before her . . . was a scene out of the worst nightmare.

Gas lamps now cast a bright glow over a dirt floor and cavelike ceilings and walls strewn with misty spiderwebs, which continued over all the contents of the rooms.

Machines, creations, horrible structures in wood and brass or tin or other metals. Martise did not know what they all were. She did know that they had come upon a torture chamber.

"I'll be damned, I will!" muttered Peter, breathing in. His eyes touched upon Martise and he tried to smile. "I dare say that we know now that Castle Creeghan does have her skeletons in the closet, eh, milady?"

She tried to smile. Bruce spun around. "Martise!" he said irritably.

"It's all right," Ian said, stepping to her defense. "There's nothing here, really."

"Nothing!" Conar sounded as if he were strangling. "By God, this is horrible!"

"Ah, indeed, horrible," Bruce agreed, walking toward Martise.

Uncle Peter, his kilt swaying, spoke up. "But no bones or bodies about, Bruce. Nothing that the lass might not see in one of the Queen's new collections in London, eh?"

Bruce arched a brow, but Ian was saying, "My God, Bruce, look at this!" Bruce turned to Ian once again.

Martise flashed Peter a thank-you smile and he grinned in return and Martise and he hurried over to the contraption.

It looked like a coffin itself. It was tall, way taller than Bruce, and broad, and it appeared to be made of a time-blackened iron. She thought of the mummy tombs in Egypt, but there was nothing colorful about the structure; it was large and menacing.

"What is it?" she asked.

Ian was opening the coffinlike thing even as she spoke. The door, or lid, flew outward. Within it were long spikes.

"An iron maiden," Bruce muttered. "Here."

"Quite an implement of torture," Ian said, walking around it. "The victim was placed inside, and the door was slowly and surely closed. The spikes would impale him or her—none of them positioned where they would pierce a vital organ and make death quick! Ah, no! The poor sinner inside would perish a slow and agonizing death!"

"Ian, remember Lady St. James . . ." Conar reminded him gruffly.

"Oh! I am sorry," Ian said, meeting her eyes.

"Martise, you shouldn't be in here!" Bruce snapped.

"I'm all right!" she insisted. She flashed Conar a smile, then hurried over to another mechanism on a table. There were frayed ropes and pulleys and wooden planks. She looked over at Ian, as Bruce was still rigidly frowning at her. "And what is this?"

"Ah, the 'Earl of Exeter's daughter'!" he announced. "So called for a man determined on the virtues of its use." She stared at him blankly. He smiled. "The rack, milady. Well, well used in medieval England!"

"Ah, and Scotland, so it seems," his father said with a trace of humor. He walked around the room, indicating other pieces about them. "Whips, chains, scold's bridles, shackles . . . over there, a gibbet."

Ian laughed. "I dare say one of our esteemed ancestors *must* have been something of a beast, eh, Bruce?"

"So it appears," Bruce said dryly. Martise felt a chill,

and she shuddered fiercely. She felt Bruce's eyes. He had been watching her, and now she was sorry that she had shivered.

"We'll wall it all back up."

Peter was inspecting one of the scold's bridles, and Martise went over to him. "Now, this one, milady, was for the fairer gender, and the fairer gender alone. If a wife did talk too much, pass gossip or the like, she was locked into this hideous mask, and I wager she did learn to keep silent in the future."

"There's a chastity belt over here," Ian commented. "Our illustrious forefathers must have worried about the loyalty of their wives now and then, wouldn't you imagine?" He grinned devilishly at Martise. "Beware, Lady St. James! The master of the castle, ye laird of the Creeghan beasts, could take a fancy to keep you forever within these walls—locked with this ghastly contraption."

"Amusing, Ian, very droll. She's already convinced that I'm a beast. Thank you very much."

Ian laughed and winked at Martise. "Fear not. She doesn't seem to be quaking."

She was flushing slightly because his eyes were upon her and because . . . there was something between them. Something sexual. Tense, exciting. Always simmering beneath the surface.

"And none of us knew a thing about this place!" Conar said suddenly. "Dear God, Bruce, what else do ye think this ancient place beloved by us poor fools might hold?"

"God knows. I suppose there could be other chambers—"

"Or walled-in virgins," Ian suggested.

"I think that when she was walled in, actually, she was no longer a virgin," Peter said wryly. Even Bruce smiled, but his smile quickly faded. He was standing by the opening, surveying it all with distaste. His eyes fell upon Martise once again and he shrugged. "We called the Mongols barbarians. I wonder if any society was so adept at the doling out of torture and agony as our own."

"You can't really wall it back up, Bruce," Ian said. He extended an arm. "This is, for all its ugliness, history."

Bruce reflected on the comment for a moment and then shrugged. "Maybe you're right. I can have it donated to the Queen. They say that she is accumulating all kinds of collections. I imagine they'll have a place for such a one as this." He turned around, heading for the opening. "As long as it's out of here," he said flatly.

They all followed him back through the opening and out into the crypt beyond.

The body of the poor girl was gone, as were the workmen, Robert McCloud, Trey, and Jemie.

Martise looked at where the body remains had been on the floor and then at Bruce, and found that his eyes were already upon her. "I had Robert McCloud take the wee lass on outside. I'll take the wagon to MacTeague myself."

He stared at her, but did not seem to expect an answer. He turned around and left the cellar.

She did not hear Peter at first when he came up behind her. "Ye mustna mind Bruce, Martise. He didna want you seein' this new sorrow, not when you come for a sister departed, and have since been through so much."

"So much?" she murmured. She liked his light eyes and his gentle smile, and wondered sometimes if he wasn't the only true friend that she had found here. No, of course not. Elaina was her friend, close and sweet. And Ian and Conar were wonderful, too. It was really just Bruce, the great laird himself, who was ever rude and blatantly unwelcoming.

Not at times . . . the times when he held her. When he whispered, when he promised, when they both looked at one another and knew that it would only be a matter of time.

"Aye, lass, well," Peter was saying. "Ye come fer Mary, and soon there's a shipwreck and a man dies despite yer tender care! And then a poor girl is gone, and here today, a poor wee lass is found. It is a bit much, don't ye ken, milady? He is worried, and that is all."

She smiled. "And you are his uncle, and his blood, and would thus defend them."

Peter arched a brow. "His uncle, *aye,* his blood, *nay.* We are not Creeghans, the boys and I. I am Stuart from the far north, from a place near John o'Groat's. I married Jenny Creeghan, the sister of the last Creeghan laird, and came here, for there was much land, and the laird had need of us. I'm surprised that you did not note the plaids."

"Pardon?"

"The colors, lass, the plaids. I wear the Stuart colors. When we rode the other day, Bruce wore his Creeghan scarf. There is a difference in the patterns, with Creeghan's offering up a bit of red, and more yellow."

She smiled ruefully. "I'm sorry, I did not notice at all."

"Well, now, ye mustn't be sorry," he said.

Ian came up behind his father. "She should never be sorry, Father, for what?"

She smiled and shrugged. "Ignorance. Shall we go up? I wish to make sure that Elaina is all right."

Ian nodded, looking regretfully back toward the hole. " 'Tis just so fascinating. I wish Bruce weren't so hell-bent upon removing it all."

"I think it has more to do with the poor lass in the wall," Peter said.

Ian shrugged. "Aye, Father, but 'tis all ancient history here, don't you think? I pity the lass, but it seems that our pity for her is wasted, for surely she came here long ago, and there's naught to be done for her now. Still . . . ah, well, let's go up, indeed, let's go up. I'm fair starving, I say. We missed a meal in the excitement. I'm sure Freya will have something on."

"How could you possibly eat . . . now?" Martise asked.

"Hunger, 'twill do it every time," he said, and grinned, and she found that she was smiling, too.

Martise headed for the stairs with them behind her. Elaina was waiting for them in the great hall with a large decanter of sherry set upon the table. She served them all, and then asked fascinated questions, since Bruce had mentioned the chamber to her on his way out.

To her surprise, Martise found that she was famished herself. And the meal that Freya had indeed readied for them was another of her delicious fish concoctions, and so she ate heartily and well. Ian spoke about the collection longingly, telling her tales from the Tower of London, and more ghost stories about the castles at Stirling and Edinburgh.

"You should have seen the chamber, Elaina!" Ian told her.

She shrugged. "Perhaps I will. It was just that . . . seeing that poor dear girl's bones there . . ." She shuddered and broke off. " 'Twas well and enough for me for the moment!" she assured them.

They lingered in the great hall for some time, then Peter mentioned that he had work and Ian sighed and agreed, yes, he had to see to their foremen and managers.

The men went on to their labors, and Martise spent time with Elaina, watching her pick up a beautiful piece of needlework. She hadn't Elaina's patience, though, and after a while, she snatched a bright red apple left on the table to bring to Desdemona and wandered outside, toward the stables.

Night was coming, more quickly each day now, so it seemed. There was a mist that night, cool and smooth and rising from the ground.

It seemed that the world was gray as she entered the stables. She held still for a moment and saw that two lamps were burning just inside the heavy doors. They barely seemed to cut through the shadows. But after a moment, her eyes adjusted, and she saw Desdemona's stall. She walked down to the horse, opened the gate, and walked up to the mare's face. Desdemona shifted on her hooves, then nuzzled Martise with her soft nose. She must have smelled the apple. Martise spoke to her softly and soothingly as the mare very neatly bit the apple, snapping it in two. She ate the one half before going for the other.

Martise heard a soft rustle and, startled, she looked about. She didn't see anyone, but as unease swept along her spine, she cried out, "Who's there?"

There was another rustling sound. Suddenly, Martise could remember nothing but the sight of the corpse in the wall, and panic seized hold of her. She was a fool to be out here. It had gotten dark so quickly, and things . . . things happened at Castle Creeghan.

"Who's there!" she snapped again boldly. She could not panic, she must not!

And then, just over the wooden wall that delineated Desdemona's stall, a forehead appeared, and two very wide, very frightened eyes.

" 'Tis me," came a voice, and then, as an afterthought, "Jemie, milady. Jemie MacPeters."

"Jemie!" She almost laughed out loud with relief and pleasure. "Oh, Jemie! Why were you hiding from me?"

She came out of the stall and impulsively stroked the urchin's face, despite the dirt and grime upon it. "You frightened me by hiding!" she admitted.

He blushed furiously. "I'm sorry, ever so sorry, milady. I didna know who it was meself. I couldna—" He wanted to say more. Suddenly, he couldn't.

She smiled, thinking that the boy wasn't really retarded or daft, he was just slow, and needed help. "It's really quite all right. I understand. I frightened you, too, right?"

His eyes still wide and luminous, he nodded vigorously.

"It's because of the girl in the wall today, right?"

Again, he nodded vigorously. It didn't seem, though, that she was reassuring him. If anything, he seemed more frightened.

"Well, you really mustn't be frightened. Things happened long ago."

He looked doubtful, then he opened his mouth, trying to speak. "Na, na, lady," he managed to mutter. Then suddenly, his hand was anxiously on her arm. "Ye must take care, ye must run. 'Tis the masters. They be the sea gods and the earth gods. We must never, never go agin them, never, me ma said, for there'd be no food, no land, no shelter. But ye're not one of us. Ye mustna disappear, ye must take care, ye're—ye're kind, lady. And his eyes be upon ye. The devil's eyes, lady, he do mean to keep ye!" He was backing her against the wall, his hand still upon her. He was a youth, but he was strong, she thought. Cords were knotted in his throat. His fingers felt like steel.

She had no doubt that he was speaking about Bruce Creeghan, but he was scaring her silly himself.

She couldn't stand there any longer, feeling his touch and wondering if she might not be the fool, if he might not be dangerous himself. He was telling her things, she thought. Telling her that the master was responsible for death and disappearances . . .

And that he was watching her.

She would be next.

And still, even as Jemie warned her, his fingers were upon her. Too powerful.

She caught his hand where it lay upon her arm and tried to smile. The effort was futile. She dropped his hand and told him, "You must not say such things, Jemie, truly, you must not!"

Then she did run, as fast as she could, into the courtyard. Once there she paused, feeling the mist swirl around her feet. Night had fallen. It had not come subtly; it had rushed down upon them. In the mist and the darkness, she felt a real terror. She picked up her skirts and fled toward the doors to the hall, certain that all the demons of hell were behind her.

She reached the doors. Gasping, she turned around swiftly. There was no one behind her. The mist swirled silently in the darkness of the night. She was alone. Completely, terribly alone.

She swung open the doors to the great hall and passed through the entryway. She wanted to reach her room as soon as possible.

But the great hall was not empty. Even as she came into the entryway, she heard voices. She held still, holding her breath, and realized that Bruce had come back. He was by the mantel, and he was talking with his Uncle Peter.

Arguing with him.

"Well, ye've changed, Bruce, and I don't mind saying so. Ye're nigh on hard as nails now, stubborn, man, I say, and I canna reason with ye no longer."

"There *is* no reasoning it—" Bruce began, but he cut himself off and walked toward the entryway.

He stared at her, and she felt like a schoolgirl caught in the act of eavesdropping. Color flooded her cheeks. "I am sorry. I didn't mean to interrupt. If you'll both excuse me—"

"Ye needn't be excused, milady!" Peter said quickly, inclining his head toward her. "We were done speaking, lass, rehashing words said before. Ye two excuse me." He nodded to them both.

Bruce did not see him go up the stairs, for his eyes never left hers. "Come in, sit, enjoy the fire," he said softly.

"Really," she protested. "I was just going to my room."

"But you must not," he told her, and, smiling, he took her arm and led her to one of the chairs before the fire. He rested his booted foot upon one of the stone supports before it and set his elbow upon the mantel, smiling down at her.

"It seems that we have so little time alone," he said.

"Or perhaps too much," she murmured.

He laughed, and then left the hearth and sauntered around behind her. She felt him at her back and nearly jumped when his hand fell softly upon her shoulders. Then his thumb very gently caressed her cheek.

Fire seemed to flame throughout her. She fought hard to

remain still. There were things she wanted to say to him, things she wanted to shout . . .

Accusations that screamed within her heart.

"The games are this week," he told her lightly. "It seems that you will still be with us for the event."

"What is the occasion that brings these games on?" she whispered.

"Pardon?"

"Well, I've heard about your May pole, and the fact that the dances were once a form of worship, just as the pole itself is a—a symbol."

"Phallic?" he inquired politely. She gritted her teeth. For a man determined to shelter her from the horrors in the cellar, he had no difficulty with sexual boldness.

"Indeed. So what brings on this fest?"

"Hmm," he murmured. "Well, it is fall. It is nearly All Hallows' Eve. Surely, it must go back to the bringing in of the harvest, don't you imagine?" He was no longer behind her. He had walked around again, as lithe, as silent, as agile as a great cat. He sat in the chair opposite her, his legs outstretched, and he smiled. Complacent.

Dangerous.

"You're to win the caber throw," she said.

"Aye."

"And will you?"

"I do assume so," he said, adding a blunt "I'm good."

"Very powerful."

"Milady, why do I always feel that your words are leading somewhere?"

She didn't reply. Instead, she looked to the fire, and she felt its warmth lull her slightly. She turned back to Bruce and asked a question instead, softly, almost wistfully. "What was your life like with Mary, Bruce?"

He lowered his eyes. "Mary was sweet and bright and everything that a man might love," he replied. "As lady here, she was deeply cherished." His eyes rose again to hers. "That I swear to you," he said, a deep tremor to his voice. But then instantly, he changed again, and his smile tightened. "Ah, alas, I had forgotten. You are convinced that I did Mary in, are you not?"

"Not convinced."

"Just very suspicious."

He stood, and in seconds he had passed the distance between them. Upon his knees he caught her hand and turned it palm up. And he began to stroke it as he spoke, and she felt the hypnotism of his voice, and even as she longed to bolt, she sat still. She watched his thumb move over her palm, and she wondered how such a simple movement could seem so intimate, how it could touch her deep inside, seem to strip away her clothing and leave her bared and naked . . .

And vulnerable.

"It's been an intriguing day for you, has it not?" he said, and his voice was soft, and it seemed to blend with the flicker of the fire that warmed his face and burned within his eyes. "Alas, you must wonder about me, for the lairds who came before me do not speak well for the clan! A poor wee lass walled in, implements of torture within the walls . . . and there's more, of course. In the 1600s one of the lairds was dragged from this very hall, from his stance by this very hearth, by a neighboring earl. His people had tried to defend him, but he had stolen the earl's daughter, you see. The earl swore that the Creeghan had taken maiden after maiden. He and his men brought the laird to the town, and there accused him of crimes of lust and bloodlust, and he was beheaded by the earl's sword then and there. There are many, many skeletons within many closets, milady. It is, I think, a danger of knowing one's past so well. I do know mine. And it *is* frightening."

"Ah," Martise whispered. "But the sins of the fathers need not be visited upon the sons!"

He laughed, delighted. "No? But the warning is clear and

bold! Women beware, for women have met such sorry ends within these walls. Terror has come here."

"But . . ." She paused, moistening her lips. And then she demanded, "Is it coming here again, my lord? Is it all happening—again?"

He folded her hands within his own. "You should leave here, milady."

She shook her head. "I cannot."

"Why?"

"I—I must know."

"And what if you do risk your own life?"

"Do I do so?" she demanded.

He did not answer her, but cross-queried her instead. "What are you looking for?"

"Nothing!"

"Ye should know that the infamous lairds of Creeghan deal harshly with thieves."

"I am no thief!" she protested.

"No?" He brought her hand to his mouth, kissed the back, and twisted it slowly, then kissed her palm where he had stroked it before. Excitement seemed to sear and dance within her, and shocking sensations rushed to even more shocking and intimate places within her. And he rose, pulling her up with him, and he kissed her lips softly, and then with more passion. His fingers curled into her hair, and he loosed it about her shoulders, and his whispers touched her ear and raced hotly against her flesh. "Ye should go, milady, I warn ye again, fer if ye stay . . . I want ye as I do not remember wanting even air to breathe, or water to drink. I want you as simply as I want to wake, to move, to live. I do not know what so drives the ache and the longing and the need. I want you beneath me, naked, with this great tangle of hair spread out beneath us and between us, golden like flame, soft like silk, taunting. Aye, my dear Lady St. James, I want you hot and anxious and eager and awaiting my touch with those naked blue eyes of yours wide and seeing the beast and the man for all that he might be . . ."

"Stop!" she gasped, realizing at last that no true lady would even listen to such words, that she should have slapped him, should have escaped him.

"Aye, lass, I want you. As you want me."

"No!" she protested.

"Then run."

"I cannot."

"What are you looking for?" His voice was no longer a whisper, it was thunder.

She jerked from his touch. "Nothing!"

"If I catch you too close to the flame, lady, you will get burned, I promise you!"

"How dare you—" she began.

"Nay, lady. How dare *you*. I warn you again. Come too close, push too far, and you will feel the flame. Enter into my arms, and I will carry you where I please."

"Into a crypt where I might be walled away forever?" she challenged in a whisper.

His eyes narrowed and darkened dangerously. He swore with sudden impatience and his booted footsteps brought him striding past her. At the stairway he paused and turned back.

"Contrary to your beliefs, madam, I like my women awake, alive, and willing. Hot, even, milady, simmering hot, blazing hot, wanting—no, needing—to be loved. Do you ken, milady? If not, perhaps you will. I warned you oft enough. Yet I believe you must like some of the heat, for you are ever wandering nearer and nearer the fire." He paused, and a slight smile curved his lips. "Nay, lady, I will take you to no crypt. I will take you wherever it is that you finally taunt me too far, be it my bed, the earth, the hay. And I dare say that you will scream . . . but with pleasure. And you will certainly arise from it all very much alive and shatteringly aware of all that has been."

"You arrogant bastard!" Martise hissed.

"Aye, that. But not a murderer, milady." Then he smiled,

and bowed, and turned his back on her, and his footsteps carried him up the stairs.

Always the master he had spoken the last word.

Seething, she followed his footsteps up the stairs, and she bolted herself into her room for another night in Castle Creeghan.

Nine

❧

The next few days passed slowly, and with little incident. Martise felt curiously as if it were a time of waiting, and that there was little she could do about it.

Something would happen, something would break, soon enough. Bruce Creeghan was seldom in the castle, and Martise passed her time with Elaina, and alone. With Bruce gone, she dared to start through the library again.

And then, one evening at dinner, when she learned that Bruce had gone back to the village to see Dr. MacTeague, she thought that it might have come time to try to search through his tower quarters.

She yawned and excused herself to Elaina early, and then hurried to her own room. She waited there a while, and then slipped out, remembering what Hogarth had told her that first night in the castle. The west tower held the great hall, her room, and, she had learned, Elaina's suite. And then he had said, "The lower floors of the north tower house the servants, the east tower holds the family rooms, and the south tower is the sole domain of the lord of Creeghan."

She slipped from her room, and turned, not to the stairway, but along the corridor leading the way to the south tower.

Rich maroon runners led the way here, and the walls were well set with lamps, tapestries, and paintings. As she reached the end of the corridor, she found that the hallway narrowed, while to her right lay handsome double doors that were inlaid with gilded designs of mighty Highland warriors at battle, and at feasts.

She hesitated, turned about, and assured herself that no one had seen her. The hallway behind her was empty. A breeze came through the narrow arrow slits that still lined the corridors, despite the tapestries hung to keep out the cold. The gaslights flickered.

Martise opened the doors and entered the master's chambers. She closed the doors behind her, then leaned back against them, barely breathing. But even as she did so, she froze, certain that she heard footsteps in the corridor. She didn't dare walk out into the hallway.

She clutched the elegant gold timepiece she wore around her throat and noted with dismay that it was midnight. She had lost all track of time, and it was possible that the master would be returning.

She couldn't run out into the hallway, so she turned and hurried through a doorway into a dressing room, and for a moment she waited there. Then she heard the great carved doors open and she fled through to the bathroom.

The doors beyond closed.

She held still, barely breathing. She heard the footsteps again. Heard them enter the dressing room. With a few more steps, he could be in the bath.

She opened the back door quickly and started back along the narrow corridor, thinking that within seconds she would be able to stand there and pretend that she was about to knock if he should appear.

But then she heard someone coming, someone else, down the corridor. One of the servants, she thought. But she couldn't be caught there. Whoever it was would know that she hadn't just walked down the same corridor.

And if anything, she had discovered, these people were loyal to Creeghan. She would be handed right over . . .

That thought spurred her into motion and she turned around and stared down the dark, dank stairs that led from this tower. She wished fervently that she had a light.

The footsteps were nearly upon the lord's room.

She started down the stairway.

She couldn't see, not a thing, in front of her. There was no rail, and so she placed her hands tentatively against the cold stone wall. Gingerly, she tested each step, and then she paused, breathing deeply. How many had she come down? Even the pale light from above was disappearing.

She heard a scurrying and caught her breath. Rats, mice, what else? Then she thought that something brushed over her hand where it lay against the damp stone, and she nearly screamed aloud. She wrenched her hand from the wall and almost unbalanced herself. She went down hard to sit upon one of the steps and remained there shivering. She had to pull herself together. She could not fear spiders or rats, or she would plunge into the Stygian darkness below her.

She inhaled and exhaled slowly and thought for a moment about casting her head back and screaming. Bruce would come for her.

And then he would have every right to oust her from his house, for he would know that she had been in his chambers. And he'd already accused her of being a thief.

No, she couldn't go back. She had to go forward.

She rose slowly and started down again. Carefully, taking the steps one at a time.

Then she was startled and relieved that once she had turned along the spiral she saw a whisper of light.

She had come to a landing, and there was an arrow slit here. She paused by it, gasping in the cool night air, and staring into the night. She was above the cliffs here, cliffs that led straight out to the crashing surf.

And she could see, along the coast, the cave where they had gone to search for Clarissa, where they had found the injured sailor. The man who had whispered a name before dying.

Creeghan.

She caught her breath and blinked. She thought that she could see light out there. Lights flashing from the rock below her. Once, then twice, then disappearing. She waited, but saw nothing more. She looked to the sky, but the moon was not yet full. It would be full once again after the games, probably on All Hallows' Eve, she thought.

Panic started to settle its icy fingers over her. It was unreasonable, she told herself, but suddenly she wanted nothing more than to reach her room and bolt her doors and hug her shoulders tight before the warmth of her fire.

Her fingers tightened around the stone, and she looked down. She realized then that she knew where the darkness and the steps would lead.

To the crypts.

And still, she had no choice. She followed the stairway down.

As she came closer to ground level, the stone seemed ever colder. She could imagine her breath misting in the air before her, but it was too black to see it. Then, as she rounded another spiral, she saw a filter of light. Pale and wavering . . . candlelight.

She stood still, certain that she heard voices. Not whispers, voices so low that she could not make out the words.

She continued down, and at last, she could see in the wavering light that she had come to the last step. Before her, there was a wall, and within it, a high arch that seemed to lead to a corridor. The light came from there. She started across the floor and heard a squealing sound. She looked down and caught her breath as a rat crawled over her feet. She swallowed back a scream and looked around wildly.

That was when she saw where she was.

It was one of the truly ancient crypts, hundreds of years old. Its walls were lined with slabs—waist-high slabs that were all around her.

All of them were covered with bodies, covered with the long-dead of Castle Creeghan, creatures in ancient costume, misted by the gauze of their shrouds. Men and women and children, their decaying hands folded atop their chests, their sightless eyes aimed toward heaven. Swords were laid at warriors' feet, and infants rested upon their mothers' breasts . . .

"Oh, God!" she cried aloud, and spun around, suddenly overtaken by the thought that they could come alive, these pathetic creatures, in their medieval headdresses and ballooning breeches and elegant hose and tunics. They could come alive and whisper through the room, their bony fingers clawing upon her, their misted shrouds covering her, choking her . . .

No! she thought, and once again, she turned, this time toward the corridor where she could see the meager light.

But even as she turned, a sharp, staggering pain cut into her temple.

Then she was falling, falling to the cold, damp floor.

Moments later—or was it hours?—she awoke. She tasted blood upon her tongue and felt the ringing pain that now haunted her skull. She opened her eyes, and there was darkness. She blinked, but the darkness remained. She felt the awful cold beneath her and fought back a scream as she realized that she was still in the crypts.

And she could still hear voices. But they seemed so very far away. So furtive, and so far away. Almost as if they were part of the stone of the castle.

She reached out a hand and found stone and then staggered to her feet. She reached for support, and her fingers curled around something . . . something.

It was when she realized it was bone that she started to scream.

Suddenly, she heard her name whispered. She spun around wildly, flailing and swinging. But arms swept around her, hard and punishing and confining. She opened her mouth to scream again, but too late. A hand settled over her mouth.

"Martise!" she heard her name whispered again, and she stood still, then started to fight wildly. "Shh, shh! Stop, wait, listen!" came an urgent whisper in the darkness.

Then she knew that he was with her, that Bruce Creeghan was with her, and that it was his hands settled over her mouth, his arms that wound so tightly around her.

"Don't make any more noise!" he warned her. They were unnecessary words. She couldn't have spoken. She couldn't have moved. She thought again of the strength of the arms holding her, and never had she felt such fear. If he wanted, he could crush her. Crush her and leave her to lie with the bones and the corpses in the crypt . . .

Her eyes widened, and though she couldn't speak or move, she saw that this was not the same crypt where she had fallen. There was one of the wrought-iron gates before her, and guarding the walls, like mythical sentinels, were two full suits of ancient armor. And when she managed to twist just a shade, she saw that there was an old altar at the rear of the crypt.

And right beneath it was a new coffin. A fine oak coffin, the wood so new that she could smell the fresh scent of it.

"They're gone," he said at last. His hand eased from over her mouth. She instantly inhaled to scream, but even as she did so, his hand fell back upon her. He hugged her tightly against his body, and she could feel the heat and the unleashed energy and passion within him, and breathe in the very male scent. "Don't!" he warned her in a whisper. "Don't scream. I'm not going to hurt you. I want to know what you're doing here. I want to know what you saw. Hush!"

He was waiting, waiting for something. All that she wanted to do was get out of the crypts. She nodded her head frantically up and down.

Slowly, he eased his hand from her mouth. His arm was

still about her, locked tight beneath her breasts as he stood behind her. "Don't scream," he said.

"No," she whispered.

And then she was free. She heard the striking of a match, and the tiny room came swiftly aglow as Bruce lit one of the wall torches.

Looking around in the light, she felt sick. The pain in her head returned, and then savagely seemed to attack her stomach. The darkness had been better. The mist and the darkness. Now she could see too clearly. Bones only partially covered with flesh. Beautiful long hair that streamed from skulls with empty sockets for eyes.

"Oh, no," she murmured, and she was starting to fall again, to black out all of the horror around her.

She didn't fall. She was swept up into his arms. His eyes burned down into her while his touch and his arms warmed her. She stared into his face, into his eyes, and she tried to tell herself that the dead were not a threat . . .

And that this man, with his towering shoulders and searing gaze, might well be the greatest danger. Laird Creeghan. Laird of these crypts and passages and walls where women were entombed . . .

Her lips were dry, she could not breathe. And even then, as he touched her, she felt the fire within her. Felt the excitement snaking into her. Felt the desire . . .

"Please!" she whispered. And then she found her voice. She didn't try to struggle from his arms. "What is going on?" she demanded.

He didn't answer her, but turned toward the gate and started to take them from the place of death.

"Bruce! You have to tell me. What is going on here?"

"I can't tell you."

"You must."

"I don't know!" he flared down to her angrily. His eyes held hers as he fumbled with the gate and took them from the crypt. She wasn't about to give up so easily.

"Whose coffin was that?"

"Martise, there are hundreds of dead—"

"The new coffin."

"It isn't new. And it's there . . . because there wasn't space elsewhere, I imagine." And before she could ask him another question, he had taken them outside the gate, and began to climb the stairs that led to the great hall. "Quiet now!" he warned her.

He started up the steps, holding her. She could walk very well, she thought, but he didn't set her down. His eyes held hers, and she whispered, "You're lying."

"I'm not."

"That coffin is new!"

"Martise, trust me."

"How can I when—"

"Shush!" he said heatedly again. They had come to the landing, to the great hall. The fire still burned there, very low, but no one was about. Bruce paused momentarily, searching the hall with his eyes, and then he continued upward. His long strides brought them to her room, where he laid her out gently upon her bed. He checked her skull and found the lump upon it and exhaled in a soft whistle. He soaked a cloth in her cool clean wash water and set it upon her forehead. She watched him all the while, chewing her lower lip.

"Bruce, what—"

"What were you doing down there?"

He sat back, staring down at her, and his voice told her that he was asking his questions as the laird of the castle, and that he meant to have answers. He had distanced himself; he was cold, hard. Ruthless, she thought.

"I—I came down, that's all. I wanted to say a prayer—"

"In the middle of the night?"

"It was just past midnight."

He leaned back, crossing his arms over his chest, a brow arching doubtfully. "Do you often go down to cold, dark crypts in the middle of the night to say prayers? I wonder why I doubt it of you so very completely."

She sat up, catching the soothing cloth as it fell from her head. "What were *you* doing down there?"

"You forget, I am the master of this house. I may roam where I please."

"I did not know that I was not supposed to do so!" she cried out softly. Then she caught herself up. "Really, I do not care to discuss this at this time—or at this hour, as you have pointed out. Please, leave my room."

"Not, milady, were you to bargain your soul," he said flatly. "What were you doing down there?"

"I—I heard something," she said. "You know that I did. You must have heard the voices when you found me. You must have heard them. Bruce, what *is* going on here?"

He shrugged. "I don't know. Maybe you're imagining things."

"A bump like this on my head? Or"—she hesitated, then threw out the accusation—"did you hit me?"

"Don't be daft!"

She leapt up, swirling away from him. She moved close to the door, passion causing her breasts to rise and fall in rapid heaves. "Did you kill Mary?" she demanded.

He was instantly on his feet, staring at her. He walked toward her, and suddenly she found herself imprisoned between the searing hardness of his body and that of the wall. His one hand fell on the left side of her head, his arm a bar, while he snatched up a soft tendril of her hair and moved it very slowly, very sensually, between his fingers. And when his eyes touched her, she was mesmerized still by the thought of his touch, by his fingers, by his hands . . . by the implication in his eyes that his touch could go on and on.

"No," he said simply.

She inhaled and exhaled, feeling him there, feeling him with heart and soul, and feeling as if she lay naked before him in all things.

"Have you ever killed anyone?" she managed to whisper. And his hands ceased their movement and his eyes seemed to impale hers. "I have never murdered, that I swear to you, Martise. And now I'm telling you, you've got to trust me."

"How can I."

"You must."

"But someone was down there—"

"Aye, someone was down there."

"But—"

"You were down there, girl. And you've still not answered me about why—and where you came from." His voice was soft, subtle, insinuating. She trembled, and she knew that he felt the shivers within her body, and she wondered if he thought that she moved so with fear . . .

Or with longing.

She moistened her lips. "Who is in the coffin?"

"Forget the coffin."

"But—"

"For the love of God, trust me, Martise!"

"I'll trust you," she said swiftly. "I'll not say a thing, I swear it. But someone will know something. Someone attacked me tonight. Unless . . ."

"Unless?" he inquired.

"Unless it was you," she said.

He was silent for a moment, studying her.

"Nay, girl, I did not hit you," he said at last. And for a moment, the hardness, the arrogance, the ruthlessness, were gone. He leaned down toward her, and his lips found hers, formed over them completely, hot and open-mouthed. And his tongue invaded her mouth, raped and ravaged it, and she found herself within his arms. His hands moved rapidly, hungrily, over the length of her body, exploring swells and curves, lingering over the rise of her breasts.

Then she was up, up in his arms, and her lips were still fused with his. His fingers were within her laces, touching flesh, bare flesh, caressing and discovering the fullness of her breasts, teasing and rubbing her nipples to hardening peaks. His lips moved from hers, and ravaged down the length of her throat, and paused there, in the dishevelment of her clothing. His mouth pressed tightly, erotically, over her breast, and she felt the fullness of the pink tip taken into his mouth, and played with there, his tongue circling it again and again until the suction upon it became hard and caused a hot streak of fire to shoot straight to her loins.

She cried out with the shocking fullness of the sensation, with the longing and desire it created. She wanted him. Wanted—this. Wanted it to go on and on . . .

But then his dark head rose above her, studying the abundance of her body, and she cried out suddenly in distress, and the words were not really those that she should have uttered, but they were filled with the truth of her emotion. "No, no, not here!" Her head tossed upon the pillow, sending her hair cascading about as her blue eyes watered. "Not in Mary's bed!"

She might have splashed icy water into his face. His features hardened as his eyes grew cold and narrowed sharply and then he was on his feet.

"Not here, not anywhere!" he snapped ruggedly. "You're getting out of here. Do you ken, girl, you're going to leave!"

And with that, he slammed his way out of her room. Martise bit her lip, leapt up to bolt the doors, then pitched back into her bed.

There was no mention in the morning that she should leave, nor did anyone seem to be behaving in the least suspicious manner.

If Bruce hadn't struck her, who had? She might have tried to pretend that her panic in the crypt had swept her senses away, except that beneath a fringe of her hair, she was still wearing a big bruise.

I might have fallen, she thought. I might have fallen and struck one of the slabs . . .

Except that she had not.

Bruce was not in the castle during the day. The next day,

nearing the feast of All Hallows' Eve, would be the games.
Bruce was out practicing with the caber, Elaina told her.
Together, they planned their outfits for the event. Martise
would wear Mary's colors, she decided. Creeghan colors.
There was a beautiful ruffled blouse and a long wool skirt,
matching shawl, and bright green tam.

On the day of the games, she donned them all. She left
her hair loose, cascading around her shoulders.

There was a knock on her door. She answered it, and she
was startled to find Bruce there. She backed away, a bit in
awe, because he was, indeed, the Highland laird that day.
He was kilted, rather than wearing a kilt, she knew, because
Peter had explained the wearing of the colors to her. He was
in full regalia, from his deep green jacket and balmoral to
the dress sporan that hung low from his hips. The outfit
became him well, as it should the laird, she thought. With
his startling eyes and dark hair and muscular structure, he
seemed the fierce warrior of ages past. She shivered
slightly, remembering the feel of his arms and the brush of
his chest. His shoulders seemed even broader today, and his
legs were hard as young oaks, lean but tautly muscled and
rounded from constant use.

She realized then that his eyes were likewise studying
her.

"Our colors becomes you, milady," he told her quietly.

"Thank you."

He offered her his arm. She accepted it and tried not to
tremble beneath his touch. She lowered her eyes, unable to
forget their last meeting. It seemed that each encounter
became more intimate. Or that she still dreamed, of a man,
of a beast, of a dragon, breathing fire, fire over her naked
flesh as he came to claim her with his kiss . . .

He escorted her down to the great hall where the others
were waiting, Ian and Conar and Peter and Elaina. Ian
whistled sharply and Elaina clapped her hands with delight.
"Oh, 'tis perfect, Martise, indeed it is!"

"Shall we go?" Peter suggested. He was carrying his

bagpipes, a beautiful set, his own colors covering the skin bag. They came outside, and Bruce helped Martise to mount Desdemona. Her eyes met his as she adjusted herself to her seat.

"Does this mean, milord," she asked softly, "that I am to stay?"

His gaze narrowed. She bit her lip, realizing that she had spoken in a taunting fashion, and that he was not a man to taunt.

"The games will be over very soon," he replied. And then he added, "You stay at your own risk."

She did not know what it was he implied that she risked, but she knew that she should be afraid.

Yet she forgot her fear during the day, for she had never had so much fun. When they reached the village, the festivities were already in full swing. The sounds of pipes, strident, wistful, sad, beautiful, filled the cliffs. Every man and woman and child sported some piece of their colors. Booths were set up with all kinds of delicacies, pastries, and meat pies, and the Scottish dish, haggis, which Martise could not help but avoid once Elaina cheerfully told her that it was made from sheep bellies. Bruce and the men soon disappeared, joining in with the others who drank dark ale and bet on horse races. Elaina took Martise in tow, locking arms with her as they strolled along the paths between the booths. They watched the girls' competition for the dancing, and then the boys', listening to the flutes and bagpipes as they did so. Peter, up on a dais, winked down to them and then played a sad lament. There was thunderous applause, and the older man was awarded a medal for his playing. Elaina and Martise both kissed his cheeks in congratulations, and they wandered on, sampling cider and more pastries as they did so. Then Elaina murmured that it was time for the caber throw, and they hurried to watch the spectacle.

Martise wondered how such a game had come about as she watched the first player. He was a stocky, muscular fellow who wore the colors of a Cameron. The caber, or pole, was huge, and Martise wondered how he could balance the rod, much less toss it. But with a startling force and power, the man did so. The distance was measured, and the next contestant stepped forward.

Ian and Conar played, and Martise clapped especially hard when Conar took the farthest record. Then he was back by them, grinning. "I think I'll take a medal at the least," he said.

Martise's eyes were wide. "You should take the grand prize," she said.

He shook his head, smiling ruefully. "Nay, lassie, ye've not seen Bruce up there yet. 'Tis inbred in the Creeghan heir, I do believe. Wait. Watch."

"But you were wonderful."

"Watch," he warned her. "Bruce is coming now."

The great laird of Creeghan, his plaid now wrapped low about his hips, his jacket discarded, his shirt sleeves rolled to the elbow, stepped forward for his throw. There was, Martise thought, a certain magic about him. A magic like the cliffs and hills today, all dressed in gold and purple heather, the sky so blue, the rock so gray and shimmering, the grass so incredibly green.

Bruce handled the caber almost tenderly. Like a child. And when he tossed the massive log, it seemed to fly.

Indisputably, his went the farthest. Martise didn't need to hear the numbers called to know that it was so. There was wild cheering and applause, and while they waited for the awards to be called off, Ian told Martise with a wry smile that winning didn't matter. "The prize is so much lamb and mutton, and we turn it back over to the village every year anyway. Conar's medal is worth more."

Conar shrugged and Ian laughed. "And me, I've earned a sore shoulder. And I'm ready for supper. Ah, here comes our laird and master, without whom we dare not dine!"

His words were somewhat bitter, but his smile remained,

and he easily clapped Bruce upon the shoulder and congrat-
ulated him as he approached them. "And well done, me fine
Laird Creeghan! We shall hold sway for another year now.
Shall we move on for some tender spitted lamb?"

"Thank you, cousin, and aye," Bruce said. His eyes had
found Martise's quickly. "Come, then," he said, and he
offered her his arm.

Darkness was falling, and yet the village was alight with
burning tapers. In a clearing before the cliff, several spitted
lambs cooked slowly over open flames, and there were huge
black pots of late vegetables, simmering fragrantly. Bruce
had just taken her to make a plate when a cry went up, and
a young blond girl rushed forward with a crown of flowers
in her hand. She laughed and leapt up and placed them atop
Bruce's head, and kissed his cheek and cried out, " 'Tis our
laird of Creeghan, and King of All Hallows' Eve!" And
then she turned to Martise, placing a second crown upon her
head. "Queen, milady! Be our queen this eve, and forever
the spirits will watch over ye!"

Before Martise could protest, the girl had disappeared,
and wild cheers were going up again. Someone struck up a
fiddle, and then a lute joined in, and she found herself
turned into Bruce's arms.

"Queen, milady?" he murmured. "They've honored you.
And as my queen, I fear that you are expected to dance with
me to open the evening celebration."

She didn't say anything, and she prayed that he didn't
mean a Highland dance, but she needn't have feared. She
was swept into his arms and led along, and it was very
much as if she were back home, enjoying a Virginia reel.
Suddenly people were all around them, dancing and laughing beneath the stars. And the moon was out, not quite full,
beautiful and benign, and it looked down upon them. He
smiled at her, and she was breathless, and she found herself
smiling in return.

"You're a beautiful queen, lass."

"Thank you. And you've a handsome king. But then, you are always the king, are you not? Laird of Creeghan . . . the king in truth, as far as it matters to these people?"

He arched a brow. "Aye. Perhaps. But the queen," he said, his voice low and mischievous, "is usually a sweet and virginal young maiden."

"To appease the dragon, the beast?"

"So I am a beast?"

"We are discussing custom and legend, so I thought."

"All right," he said lightly. "Then a maiden, pure and innocent, given to appease the dragon, the beast, the laird, however you would have it. But a widow . . . this is quite different."

"A widow?"

"You, milady."

"Oh, of course!" she said quickly. "Well, times do change," she said sweetly.

"Alas, that they do," he said.

But he was smiling, and she knew that he taunted her, and it felt delicious just to be in his arms, and to enjoy the moon and stars and the coolness of the night and the delicious smell of the roasting meat. She tossed her head and lifted her chin to him. "Then thank heavens that I am a widow. Perhaps this ferocious beast needs to be slapped hard in the nose rather than appeased."

"Ah . . . and do you think you're the one to do such a deed? A dragon slayer, then, milady?"

"I've not come to slay the dragon—"

"Merely tame it?" he suggested. She flushed and he laughed, the sound deep and melodious, truly wicked. He swirled her in his arms and warned her with a soft whisper, "Creeghan dragons are not to be tamed, milady. They remain forever ferocious and terrible, and the strong of heart can merely learn at best to keep upwind of their fire."

"That seems to be because they keep acquiring sweet

innocent maidens," she replied, undaunted, her chin raised impudently, her eyes sparkling.

He laughed again, and they swirled around, and finally, he danced her from the center of the clearing to a long trestle table where two high-backed chairs had been prepared for them so that they could sit at the head like a true king and queen while their subjects arrayed themselves around them. Plates were set before them, heaped high with food, and wine-colored chalices decorated with ribbons and lace and late flowers were brought to them, filled to the brim with home-brewed ale. He toasted her, and she sipped her ale, and found it very heady and strong. As she swallowed the delicious potent brew, she felt the searing heat of his eyes upon her, and she did not care. It was fun to be here tonight, exhilarating to be at his side, to tease and laugh, and feel his arms . . .

In the safety of all of these people around her.

The night went on. There was more food and more dancing, and she was claimed by Ian and Conar, and even a few of the lads from the village. Bruce dutifully danced with all the young maidens who would not be queen this year. And she danced with Dr. MacTeague, and even Father Martin, and she chose to take young Michael Cunningham as a partner, and then his father, Henry, too. Even Peggy seemed happy that night, although her eyes remained haunted. Clarissa had never returned.

Acrobats leapt and jumped about, and a trained bear danced. Young men practiced careful swordplay and wrestling. And there was more ale and more dancing, and Bruce whispered to her that she moved exceptionally well for an outlander, and she cast her head back, feeling the ale, smiling mischievously. "The dance is very much like the dancing back ho—in America!" she corrected herself quickly.

"Ah, in Virginia?"

"Yes, in Virginia. You've copied the Americans."

"How dare you presume such a thing, milady. The Americans have copied us," he told her. And she laughed, and he started to lead her back to her chair.

Suddenly, she sobered, for an old woman stood in their path.

She was withered and very small, and looked to be ancient. Her eyes were pale blue, watery and rheumy, and she stood with a long bony arm extended, pointing at Martise.

" 'Tis ye!" she exclaimed. "Aye, All Hollows' Eve will come, and the spirits will rise, and ye will be next! Ye've come to taunt, to delve, and the devil will take ye. Run, lass, lest ye be like the others! Swept away by his fire in the night. Taken from the cliffs, dashed downward into an eternal hell! The laird of the darkness has chosen ye, and yer blood will feed the rock and the earth!"

Her hand fell. Everyone was silent, absolutely silent. Nothing could be heard except the crackling noises made by the various fires.

Bruce stepped forward. "Mattie!" he murmured. And the old woman burst into tears and allowed Bruce to take her gently into his arms. Bruce led her from the circle. She looked up into his eyes. "She should go," she said.

"Aye, she should," he agreed, and he disappeared with the woman. Martise, standing alone and shivering, felt an arm slip through hers.

"Mattie," Elaina whispered. "Poor woman, she lost a daughter a year ago or so, and she hasn't been the same since. You mustn't mind her, Martise. She means you no harm."

Martise nodded. "I didn't think that she meant me harm," she said. No . . . hadn't Elaina listened? The woman said that she had been chosen by the laird of darkness . . .

The laird of Creeghan.

She wanted to run, to hide. The night had been so beautiful, and now it was nothing but nightmare.

Then Uncle Peter was with them, smiling grimly. "Well, Mattie has managed to put a damper upon another fine eve, so she has. Bruce will sit with her till she calms herself once again. We should head now for home."

Martise was agreeable. Once again, she wanted only the solace of her room.

But they did not travel alone. MacTeague said that he would come back to the castle and await Bruce for one last drink. He rode silently beside Martise while the others rode ahead, yet when they reached the courtyard, he held her back when the others entered the castle.

"What is it?" Martise asked.

He looked at her earnestly. "Ye do need to go, milady. I'm sure that Bruce would agree with me. It's dangerous here. He has told me himself, he thinks that you should leave."

Martise watched Jemie and Trey move away with the horses, wondering if either of the boys had heard the exchange. "Why are you telling me this? You're the one who said that Mary died of heart failure, and nothing more. You assured me that she wasn't murdered—"

"Mary wasn't murdered, Martise. But someone was."

"What are you talking about?" she cried in dismay.

"The girl bricked into the wall, Martise. This is confidential. You mustn't say anything at all. You—"

"Well, of course, she was murdered!" Martise said, feeling a rise of anxiety within her. "She was murdered years and years ago! And walled in and—"

She broke off because he was shaking his head. "Nay, lassie, she was not. She's been there no more than a year and a half. I'm not a fine pathologist, but I'm a fair enough doctor to know a young corpse when I see one. The poor wee thing has been sent down to the city now so that the fancy doctors can take a good look. I can assure you of this—she was murdered within the castle walls, and that spells danger for anyone, especially an outsider." He stopped speaking because they could both hear the sound of horse's hooves clattering up behind them. He swung around, and together they watched as Bruce Creeghan came up on the massive bay. He leapt down from the horse, quickly and easily, and leaving Martise with no true answer to the question of what a Scotsman might wear beneath his kilt. He strode toward them. "Ah, MacTeague, glad you could come. Did you tell my guest that it was time she leave this place?"

"I did, indeed," MacTeague said solemnly. She didn't know if MacTeague had confronted Bruce with his accusations. She didn't even know if MacTeague suspected Bruce.

But who else . . . ?

She was shivering. Both men noticed, and MacTeague suggested that they go inside.

"Warm brandy will sit well," MacTeague agreed pleasantly.

Bruce's arm touched down around Martise, and she jumped. His smile was mocking, and she remembered that she had danced in his arms all night. She forced a smile in return. A flirtatious smile, teasing, inviting. One meant to allay his suspicions about her thoughts.

They walked into the hall and found that Peter, Ian, Conar, and Elaina were there. Hogarth had already warmed brandy, and blue-patterned crockery mugs awaited them. MacTeague and Bruce and Martise joined them by the fire, and they talked a while, reliving the evening, until Mac-Teague said his good-nights, bowing to Martise.

"Good-bye, Lady St. James. I do hope you choose to leave soon."

She smiled, feeling wooden, like a puppet jerked around by strings. Bruce was staring at her, his gaze cutting through her, golden and bright. She wanted to shout at him. To scream and shout and tear her nails into his flesh and demand to know the truth about everything that was going on. But he just watched her, and she was careful beneath that scrutiny.

"Perhaps, Dr. MacTeague," she murmured, and she felt his kiss upon her hand, and then Bruce walked him to the door.

"Well, I'm for bed!" Elaina announced.

"And I," Ian said wearily. Bruce was striding back into the room, pouring himself a straight whisky, tossing back his head to swallow it down neat. "What about you, O great laird of Hallows' Eve?" Ian asked.

Bruce shook his head. "I'm going to change. Then I'll be in the library, working on accounts. And I'm afraid, Ian, that you're going to be with me. For the first hour, at least. We need the count on the wool shipments for Flanders."

Ian swore beneath his breath. Bruce was turning toward Martise, but she was already on her feet. "Well, then, good night, all, I am going to turn in. I'm afraid that I can't help you." She smiled. Bruce was walking toward her. "We'll talk tomorrow," she said hastily, and then she turned and fled up the stairs.

She paced her room for what seemed like hours, paced it and paced it. She weighed the evidence, and was very afraid.

The girl in the wall . . .

She had been murdered, and recently, by someone within the castle. Someone here was a murderer.

She had to go. She didn't know where. Maybe to Edinburgh. Somewhere where she could perhaps find help.

She clenched her fingers into fists. She didn't want to flee. It was the coward's way out.

She had no choice. To stay, she would be a fool. Falling further and further beneath Creeghan's haunting domination.

She stopped her thinking and began to shed her clothing, convincing herself that there was no other way. She slipped into the long white gown that Holly had left out on her bed, but she could not crawl beneath the sheets.

The emerald! she thought, with a rising dismay. But was

the gem worth her life? Was even Eagle's Walk worth her flesh and blood? What good could she do, rotting beneath the earth?

Or within the cold stone walls of Creeghan Castle?

She tentatively opened her door, then listened at the next one. Bruce was in the library with Ian, and he would be there for some time, he had said. This was her last chance to find the emerald.

She held still, waiting, she knew not for what. Then, from the great hall far below, she heard the clock chiming midnight.

Midnight. The witching hour.

She didn't hesitate. She ran along the castle corridor, her gown trailing behind her, soft and ghostly, to the master's tower.

She threw open the great doors to his room, raced in, and scanned the room. She stared at the dragons, the insignias, the beautifully carved one atop the armoire, the claw feet upon the furniture.

A single candle burned upon his desk. A single flame to lead the laird to his bed.

The desk! She rummaged through it. Whisky, tumblers, inks, blotters, nothing! Nothing!

She sank to the floor, dismayed, desolate. Time! She needed time!

And she was wasting it. She leapt over to the bed.

Desperate, she wrenched aside the covers. She tugged at the pillows and searched beneath them. By God, where was it, where was it? No brilliance greeted her eyes, no stunning, lustrous green . . .

"Lady St. James!"

Soft, taunting, the wicked drawl came to her in the night, and she spun around, a cry on her lips.

He was there. Smiling with a cruel twist to his lips, a satyr's grin. And his words came huskily, wrapping around her.

"Are you so eager, then, to share my bed that you would ready it for me?"

She didn't answer, she just stared at him. But then his voice snapped out again, rich, deep, a quiet tone of thunder. "Well?"

"No!" she cried.

But his eyes burned into her, never leaving her, as he strode surely into the room.

INTERLUDE

Laird of Creeghan

Since she had come to Castle Creeghan, since that very first night, he had known that she was living a lie.

But what she wanted and why she had come, he couldn't say. Sometimes the suspicion and the accusations lay open and naked before them. And sometimes they hid them and politely danced around them . . .

And sometimes . . .

Sometimes the wanting had gotten in the way. He thought himself so hardened, so jaded. He hadn't thought that a woman could get through to him, any woman. But she had. And he wished he didn't know the things he did: that she couldn't possibly be the woman she claimed to be. That Lady St. James had died in Richmond, soon after her husband.

And so he had known. From that first blustery and tempestuous night when he had swept her up onto his bay, he had known that she had come . . . as a spy, as a thief . . . as a lie. But from the first moment that he had seen her, seen the sweep of her lashes over the liquid blue dazzle of her eyes . . . he had known, too, that he wanted her. The intrigue and her beauty and the sweet sound of her voice haunted him in his dreams.

But he was living a lie himself.

Creeghan was his, and the responsibility was his, and even the death, if it came to it, was his. He belonged to rugged tors and cliffs; he had been born to the wind. She did not belong. And yet, she had come from the war-torn Confederacy, of that he was certain. She had to have learned something of hardship.

So what was she? A gold digger, a fortune seeker? Despite her angel's face and flaming hair, her soft smile of innocence, was she a harlot or a thief?

Aye, she was after something.

Something she believed to be in the castle, something that she wanted badly enough to risk her life to obtain.

What?

He intended to find out.

She played him for a fool time and time again. He had listened to her lies. But he had let her slip through his fingers.

No more.

Tonight . . . tonight, he had her. Here. In his bedroom. Tearing apart his very bed.

And still, she somehow seemed the innocent, rather than the deceiver. She was dressed in white. In a long white gown that was edged in fine lace, beautiful. Soft, whisper-thin fabric that molded to her form, that enhanced and teased at the lush secrets of her body, secrets he had just begun to discover with his touch. She stood there elegant, as her hair waved and cascaded down her back. It touched upon the shimmering blue of her eyes and shadowed the finely chiseled loveliness of her features. And the light teased over that white gown, darkening the proud rise of her breasts and swirling around the haunting shadow at the apex of her thighs. And even as they stared at one another, her chin rose, and he felt the temper rise within him as well as the passion. She was still going to deny everything. Deny that she was searching for something, deny that she was an imposter.

Not tonight. By God, tonight she would deny nothing.

He slipped off his frock coat, hanging it over the back of the desk chair. He stood before her and faced her in the white ruffled shirt and the ebony riding breeches and boots he had donned upon their return from the games.

Tonight, she would answer him. He smiled and placed his hands on his hips, watching her. "Then, pray tell, dear lady, just what are you doing between my covers?"

Her lashes fell over her eyes.

"I . . . I . . . uh . . ." she began. Her voice faded and he smiled, his lip curling mockingly. He arched a brow politely, waiting for her to go on. She had barely moved. He could see her agitation in the rapid rise and fall of her breasts. In the pulse throbbing swiftly against her throat.

She was beautiful. Her flawless cream-colored skin, her sky-colored eyes, her elegant throat . . . her breasts, rounded, firm, peaked with the exquisite rose tips that had taunted him beyond the devil's own imagining. And staring at him, so defiantly, she was ever more appealing.

He gritted his teeth. "Yes?"

"My . . . earring!" she said.

"You lost it in my bed?" he said incredulously. His smile deepened with the heat of his anger, with the swirl of passion deep inside him. He fought for control, fought to ease the tension. But he felt on fire. Felt the fire in him, remembered it in her laughter, in her taunting eyes. She had known. When she had left him tonight, she had meant to flirt and tease, and cast him off guard. He spoke softly, tauntingly, in return. "Nay, my lady! I promise you, I would have remembered the occasion."

She inhaled and cast him a withering glare. "Lord Creeghan, I meant no such thing. I thought perhaps it had caught upon some piece of your clothing—"

"You are not wearing any earrings," he interrupted her. He casually sat at his desk, crossed one booted leg over the other, and waited, his hands together, his fingers tapping against each other.

"How very rude of you to notice," she commented, and in the soft slur of her defense, he heard the strength of her Virginia accent. Oh, he knew that accent. Knew it well. He'd spent so much time there, with so many Virginians. And like a Southern belle she was playing him for some gentleman fool.

But these were the Highlands. She would not play him so.

"But alas, Lord Creeghan," she continued sweetly, "when I lost the one, I removed the other."

"So . . . you think you might have lost the one upon my person earlier?" he asked politely.

She flushed angrily. "Perhaps—"

"But why would you assume that I had been in my bed already?"

"Sir, I say that you are no gentleman."

"And madam, I say that you are no lady."

He rose swiftly, with purposeful, lazy menace. She stiffened warily, watching him.

He must have come too close. She cried out softly and sought to run by him. He reached for her and missed her arm, but his fingers curled around fabric, the silk of her gown. The gown was wrenched from her shoulder as she tried to flee, but then she caught herself up, swirling back to face him.

Too late, perhaps, for the gown was already off her shoulder, and her breast was bared to him in all its naked and candlelit splendor. His gaze moved from the seduction of that naked beauty to her eyes.

Bright and blue, they returned his stare, widening. He didn't know what she saw within his face, but it must have been a warning. Perhaps it was the soaring flame that kindled within him. Perhaps it was a memory of the constant friction and tension that had risen between them . . .

Perhaps it was simply the fire, the desperate, searing fire, that was ignited and created there. Perhaps spawned of anger and spun to passion, he did not know.

"No!" she murmured.

But there was no denial. Not this night! He had vowed it.

His hand fell upon the bared flesh of her arm, and he swept her hard against him. He caught her chin and tilted back her head and kissed her lips, and then availed himself of the long white column of her throat. She was warm, and the taste of her flesh was sweet, and the flowery scent of her soap that lingered upon her was an essence that seemed to sweep him to madness. It was his anger, no . . .

It was his desire, stark and hot, and simmering too long within him. Potent, tearing into his soul, it ripped into his muscles and his loins, and he could not let her go.

She moaned slightly. She pressed against him, and he felt the soft pressure of her breasts, the rising pulse of her heartbeat. She was mercury against him, soft and fluid and exciting, and she trembled within his arms. Her fingers touched upon his shoulders, then threaded into his hair, and the touch ignited his senses.

His lips moved further upon her, stroking her collarbone. His tongue created a trickle of fire upon her naked shoulder, and at the sound of her gasp, he shuddered, and felt the need sweep through him with an urgency both dark and desperate. He wanted her there, now. Spread out upon his bed in all her golden glory and beauty. She was his, and the lie was still there between them, and so, tonight, he would brook no denial.

"No!" She pulled away from him, her hair tumbling wild and free around. He felt his features constrict. She shook her head, backing away.

"Martise!"

"No! Leave me be!"

He shook his head, fury and tempest building. "Lady, you have lied and cajoled and taunted me for the last time! If nothing else, by God, I will have the truth!"

She cried out, but there was no mercy within him then.

He seized upon her ruthlessly. She beat against him, but he ignored her touch, he could scarcely feel it. By God, he would have answers!

His hands gripped about her waist and he carried her across the room, throwing her upon his bed. She tried to sit up, but he fell atop her, his anger now unleashed and free.

"What are you doing in here?" he demanded.

She seethed as his captive. She gritted her teeth and snapped out, "I told you."

"Liar!" he charged.

She tried to strike out against him, but he saw it coming and caught her hand, pinning it to her side. He straddled her and stared down at her, teeth gritting against the growing extent of his rage. "Tell me the truth!"

"I have told you—"

"Lies!" he finished.

Lies, indeed. She did not bother to answer him. She twisted beneath him frantically.

Yet as she did so, she played more havoc upon his senses. Her gown was wrenched up high along her thighs, and her limbs were long and sinewy and soft beneath the hardness of his own. The gown had fallen again from her breast, that sweet morsel he had tasted before.

She suddenly went still. And her eyes were on his, huge, furious, yet not afraid. Nay, she was never afraid, this one.

He smiled grimly and secured both her wrists with one hand, high above her head. He waited, watching her eyes, then he allowed his own to travel over the body bared to him. Inwardly he groaned, and wondered at the magic, at the silvery beauty within her that captured and held him, when he never should have fallen at all. It was in her voice, in the grace of her walk . . .

It was in her eyes. Eyes he met boldly now.

She did not fight. She stared at him. And so he touched her, using his free hand upon her. He wrapped his fingers around her breast and explored the nipple with the pad of his thumb. Fascinated, he watched as the color deepened, as the sweet pebble hardened to his touch.

Then he lowered his head against her, and took it into his mouth, and felt the satiny texture with his lips and tongue, breathing in the erotically feminine scent of her.

A cry escaped her and he felt her trembling, and he knew himself that they had gone too far this time.

They would not turn back. His loins were burning, his hands ached to know more and more of her, nay, he needed just to be one with her, to fill her with his seed.

He moved against her body, freeing her wrists. And he caressed her with his lips and tongue, stroking with his fingers, exploring the length of her. Her fingers curled hard into his hair.

Then he rose, pulling her with him, annoyed now by the silken garment that had so enraged his senses. She stood before him, those eyes on him, and he swept the garment from her shoulders so that it fell to the floor in a soft swirling cloud of white.

Then he stepped away from her. He had to see all of her. To drink in the beauty of the woman. And then he thought, Fool! She will run again, she will deny . . .

But she did not.

She remained there, naked and proud. The moonlight swept in to spill over her shoulders and touch them with ivory, while her hair took on the glorious colors of a sunset, spilling over her high firm breasts.

He emitted a guttural cry, and felt indeed as if Castle Creeghan might house a beast, for all thought had left him except the stark necessity to possess her. The sound of his cry was harsh and hoarse, and brought her to life.

She was going to flee . . .

Nay, lass! he thought with determination, and he pulled her back into his arms, and his lips descended upon hers with force and hunger . . . and seduction. And when he released her from the liquid magic of his mouth and tongue, it was only to bear them upon her again with the swiftness of Mercury.

He encircled her breasts with his hands and sank before her on his knees.

He would have her, all of her. With no inhibitions, and no denials, and he would taste all the sweetness that she had to give.

His lips moved over the bareness of her belly, and with a savage tenderness, he demanded more. He felt her quivering tension, felt her fingers fall upon his head. He caught her hands with his own, and holding her, sought the very heart of her womanhood, the soft dark petals and the tiny bud of her desire.

She cast back her head, gasping. He boldly demanded still more, taking her with ever greater intimacy, and knowing sweet haunting triumph in the tremors that began to shake her body, in the whimpers and denials that escaped her lips . . .

She fell against him, spent and confused, and he quickly swept her up into his arms.

"Aye, lass," he whispered gently, laying her upon the bed. "No denials this night, the truth between us. All of it."

She did not move as he shed his clothing and came down beside her.

"What I have done . . ." she murmured.

What she meant, he wasn't sure. He caught her chin and held her eyes to his. "'What I have done,' my lady? You are a liar, and perhaps a thief, but a beautiful one."

"No!" Color flooded to her cheeks. She tried to rise, and he knew that he would never let her. He caught her firmly against him, letting her know the fullness of his arousal, then finding that his temper was fading, and the fascination was taking flight. He studied her eyes, the beautiful blue orbs that so enchanted, that raged like the sea, and softened to a sky on a cloudless day. "Martise, what are you, witch or angel? I am enchanted against all wisdom, desperate to have you against all sanity." His lips found hers again and he kissed her heatedly, burning now, and fevered and savagely demanding in his touch. And her fingers knotted into his hair again as he bore down upon her, his body pressed, nay, formed, to hers.

He buried his body between her thighs, and as his lips held hers, he probed her with his maleness.

He felt her tension again, and he stroked her and spoke softly to her. And then he could bear no more. The wind had swept into him, and was part of him, and he had to have her, or be damned. He moved swiftly, entering into the warmth of her body, startled, and pausing only slightly when he felt the resistance, when he discovered her maidenhead. He groaned, for it could not matter, not now, not this night.

She cried out, and buried her head against his shoulder, and he whispered anew to her, holding still, and letting her accept him. And then he caressed her again, knowing that if he had awakened the passion within her before, he could do so again now.

He swept her again with his touch and caress and stroke. The searing dampness of his lips aroused new fires. With liquid warmth he licked and caressed the beautiful length of her body, demanding intimacy again, bringing her body alive.

He joined with it once again, and at long last gave free rein to the hungers that ripped and tore inside of him.

He moved within her like the wind. He stroked her with his sex, made love to her with it, and then allowed the tempest to sweep through them both. Her limbs were wrapped around him, and incoherent words tore from her throat. The molten seed built up in him, and still he held, drawing out the explosive desire for release.

He waited. Waited until he felt her shudder in spasms beneath him, and then he let the fantastic climax tear and sweep from him. It shook him as no other had, as he had never imagined.

She was staring up at the ceiling. Tears still shivered within her eyes. He was angry with her, angry with himself.

He had not believed that she could be a virgin. But saw how wretched she was after all that they had shared. He wanted to touch her, to bring her against him, to hold her tenderly.

But remembering that she had lied and betrayed them all, he spoke out instead. He rose above her, staring at her.

"What are you after? And who are you? Damn it, who are you?"

A sob burst forth from her, and she leapt from the bed.

He reached for her, and she jumped away from him, the fall of her blazing hair the only cover against her naked beauty.

"Damn you—" she began to swear to him.

"No! Damn you, Martise. We'll start at the beginning. Who are you really?"

"Lady St. James—"

He swore savagely, cutting her off. He leapt up to come after her. By then she had found her gown and slipped it over her shoulders. She gasped out a furious sound as she discovered it torn beyond repair.

He ripped the top sheet from the bed and threw it to her.

"Martise—"

"No! *You!* Don't you dare question me! Who are *you?* Lord of Creeghan? Man or beast? You tell me, milord, what in God's name is going on here!"

She was wild. Furious, tempestuous. "Martise—"

"No!" she shrieked. "I will find out for myself!"

"Martise, no!"

She did not listen. She fled into his dressing room. He heard the lock click.

He tried it, and knew that she had bolted him out. Then he heard her moving onward, into the bath, then back into the hall.

The steps, he thought with an inward groan. She knew the way down to the crypts from this tower.

He broke the door, then swore as he tripped over a chair. She was already gone, through the next door. She had probably made the stairs already.

He tore into the bath and grabbed his smoking jacket and then burst into the hall and started after her.

"Martise!" He took a lantern from the hallway and hurried on down, thundering out her name.

The coffin!

She was heading for the new coffin in the fourteenth-century crypt. And if he didn't hurry . . .

"Martise!"

He heard her scream. Heard the terror of it. Heard it rise and echo against the cold stone walls of the crypt.

She had opened the coffin; he knew it instantly. Oh, Martise, I told you to trust me! he thought with agony.

She screamed again, and the sound rose higher and higher . . .

He reached her at last. She turned and saw his face before her, identical to that in the coffin.

Her blue eyes were wide and dilated and panic-filled. But seconds later her rich lashes swept over them, and she began to swoon.

A deep, agonized sigh of regret left his lips. Then he lifted her up into his arms.

The night was far from over.

They'd met the naked truth of their desire this night.

And now they must face the naked truth of the secrets they had both been keeping.

He carried her surely up the winding steps and back into his room.

The master's chamber.

Oh, aye. The master's. For he was laird now.

To his eternal sorrow, he was laird of Creeghan, *now*.

PART II

My Lady Creeghan

Ten

୫ଽ

She'd been in a nightmare, Martise thought, awaking slowly. A horrible nightmare in which white-shrouded ghosts misted through the halls, touching her hair with decaying, ethereal fingers, following behind her as she ran and ran and ran . . .

Until she came to the long dark corridor, and the hall lengthened and darkened even as she stood there. She moved forward slowly, and then quickly, and then she was staring down into the face she had come to know so well. The face of Creeghan. A lock of dark hair over the forehead. The sharp angles and rugged planes of the face . . . except that this face was cloaked in death.

Her eyes opened, and she saw the hand-painted dragon sitting on the armoire. Her fingers moved over the black velvet spread with the red dragon emblazoned upon it.

She saw his eyes. Creeghan's eyes. Eyes of fire, gleaming brightly in the candlelight as he studied her pensively, and she wondered if she had lost her mind or if, when the corpse in the crypt below opened its eyes, the same fire did not blaze.

A scream welled in her throat. She braced herself up in

the bed in a panic. She was here, she was back with him, in his own room. Enwrapped in the sheet that slipped from her shoulders. Laid upon his bed.

"Nay, don't scream!" he commanded, and the burr in his voice was very strong. He was by her side, his hand clamping over her mouth. And he was close against her, clad in his smoking jacket. She could feel the rich texture of it against her flesh, could feel the heat emanating from him, and she knew that this man, at least, was very much alive.

Even now, the passion was in his eyes and in his touch. She began to tremble, and she heard his long soft sigh. "If I meant you harm, milady, I'd had done so by now."

His hand eased from her lips. She spun to face him, clasping the sheet tightly around her. "Who was that? What in God's name is going on here? Who are you?"

She wasn't going to scream, he determined. He stood, leaving her on the bed, a disturbing and desirable distraction with the sheet leaving her shoulders bare and the wild tangle of her hair curling over it. He knew now all that lay beneath that sheet, and the desire had not been sated; indeed, it had grown and flourished.

He clenched his teeth down hard and paced toward the door, then turned around and stared at her, a crooked, wry, and humorless smile curving his lips. "Milady, I am, indeed, the Laird of Creeghan."

Her lips trembled. She was fighting for courage, well he knew. Her delicate face remained pale, her eyes wide and luminous. "You cannot be. Lord Creeghan must lie in the coffin. But how—"

"I am laird of Creeghan," he repeated. Then he added softly, " 'Tis my brother, Bruce, who lies in the coffin."

"Bruce!" she murmured. "But—"

"We were twins, Martise. Quite identical in looks, though different in personality, so my mother often said. Bruce was the elder by three minutes, I believe. And so he was the laird of Creeghan. But with his death, I am laird."

Martise sat silent for a moment, staring at him. That he

and his brother were twins, she did not doubt. Even when one lay in death, the resemblance was uncanny.

That he had cared for his brother, she could not doubt either. Emotion tore his voice ragged when he spoke. But as to what was going on, she still couldn't begin to fathom.

Her throat went dry. She was in love with him, she had known that, and that love had now been consummated, but the circumstances in which they were entangled made her ever more afraid. She wanted the truth, she feared the truth.

Perhaps he had not murdered Mary. But perhaps he had murdered his own brother. No, surely not. Please, God, surely not.

His smile, caustic and bitter, deepened. "Believe me, milady, were I a beast, I'd have taken the opportunity to brick you into a wall below, when you were, for once, silent."

Color flooded to her cheeks. "You've not explained anything at all!" she snapped.

"I am Bryan Creeghan, laird in truth. I am not so much the imposter. But madam, I am fully aware, as I have been since you arrived, that you are not Lady St. James."

Her color deepened and she bit her lip.

"Who are you!" he thundered with a sudden, ruthless vehemence. He strode toward her and she cried out as he sat before her, his fingers tangling into her hair and lifting her eyes to his.

"I am Martise St. James!" she said.

"Margaret is dead, I know that," he told her bluntly. "So who is Martise?"

"Her cousin-in-law!" Martise said. His fingers were still so taut, his eyes ablaze. "I swear it!" she gasped out, and she reached for his hands, that she might free herself from his touch. The sheet slipped and suddenly his gaze was upon her breasts again, and all the fires that they had so recently sated seemed to come alive in his eyes once again and he stared upon the creamy mound with its quickly hardening coral peak. She swept the sheet back up against her, and he rose, turning away, filled with a simmering, explosive tension.

"So it is your name," he said dryly. "Who is the real Lady St. James, then?"

"I—I believe that my father's brother's wife, somewhere in England, now holds the title," she murmured. "But my name *is* Martise St. James. And—" She broke off.

"And what?" he demanded.

"I loved Mary very much. She was my very good friend. As was Margaret."

Something seemed to have eased a little about him. He leaned against the double doors and watched her, his arms crossed idly over his chest. "Well, then, we are both just half imposters. Your name is real, your title is not. I am indeed Laird Creeghan, but I am not Bruce. Well, well, what else shall we learn?"

"You seem to know everything!" she cried passionately, kneeling up on the bed to face him. "By God, I don't understand—"

"I saw Margaret in the States," he told her. His eyes fell over her. Up on her knees, in the swirl of bedclothing, that hair radiating all around her, impassioned and demanding, she was so tempting that he wanted to forget all that lay between them and sweep her hard into his arms, ignoring any protest, knowing that she was made for him to love. Even had he known that she was innocent, he could not have changed anything that had passed between them. He closed his eyes and inhaled deeply. He hadn't wanted her here. There was a murderer about, and he had to discover who. Creeghan was his now, but it was in Bruce's memory that he had vowed to find the killer.

But she was here, and she was involved. She had cast herself into the fire. It seemed that he had no choice now but to try to explain it all.

"I knew your cousin well, though I knew others better," he told her. "I went to school in the States, and I spent a great deal of time in Virginia. I was there, thinking about a purchase of land, when Virginia voted to secede from the Union. I wasn't alone. Elaina's fiancé, Niall MacNeill, was with me. And in the wild scramble of everything that was going on, I promised certain friends that I would stay and fight. I was able to recruit a cavalry unit, and we joined up beneath Jeb Stuart. I didn't expect to be gone so long," he said.

"No one expected the war to go on so long," Martise murmured. She had sat back upon her haunches. Her lashes were swept low over her cheeks. And for that one moment, it seemed that they each rested their hostilities and found a plateau of peace. For a moment he held silent.

"It was a long, long war," he said at last. "Much longer than any of us had intended. And being in the midst of it, following Stuart, from Manassas to Antietam to Gettysburg, I didn't receive letters very often, but I did receive them. I knew my sister-in-law well, and she tried to write often. Cheerful letters usually, sometimes letters telling me that I should come home, and sometimes letters that were just genuinely happy." He hesitated. "She and Bruce were very much in love. She thought that he was the sun, and she was everything in life to him. But then the letters started to change."

Martise inhaled sharply. So it had been with her.

"She was worried," Bryan continued. "She was vague at first, but there was something in the letters, something between the lines. And when I'd hear from Elaina, she'd tell me that nothing was the same, and that she wanted Niall and me to come home. I didn't know how to tell her that, even as a foreigner, I couldn't just walk away from the war. Even when we knew that it was lost, we couldn't walk away. We'd seen too many men die."

He paused, and then Martise realized that he wasn't looking at her anymore. It was as if she wasn't even in the room, as if he spoke to himself. "Then I heard from Bruce. You should have known my brother. His honor, his people, his responsibilities toward bettering their lives . . . they were all the things that governed his life. He was diligent, and fine, as fine a man as I could have ever hoped to claim as a brother. And he was afraid of nothing.

"But in his last letters to me, he, too, had changed. He was frantic, telling me that he thought that he was losing his mind. That there were ghosts at Creeghan. Lights in the middle of the night. Movements in the corridors, sounds from the crypts. And he searched, but it seemed that he could never find anything. I wrote back that he should hold on, and never doubt his own sanity. Petersburg was falling, Stuart was dead, Jackson was dead, and more than half of my own men were dead. Then Lee surrendered, and I came home as quickly as I could.

"I'll never forget the night. It was raining and cold. And when I came in, I thought that I would find warmth. Mary and Bruce by the fireside, maybe the sounds of Uncle Peter with his bagpipes somewhere, Ian and Conar about. But only Hogarth appeared when I came into the hall, and he was drooped and pathetic and his hair was whiter than ever and he seemed exhausted. His eyes were damp, and he told me that Mary had died soon after her last letter to me. And Bruce was ill then, desperately ill. I told Hogarth that I was going to my brother, and then I warned him not to tell anyone else that I was back. I hurried here, to this tower. Hogarth had told me that Bruce had been melancholy since he lost Mary, but it was only the night before that he had taken so gravely ill. You see, Hogarth had found him down in one of the crypts—the fourteenth-century crypt."

Martise felt the blood drain from her face. The crypt. The crypt where she had been struck down herself.

She said nothing, and Bryan continued. "Dr. MacTeague had already been in; he had done everything for Bruce that could be done. Elaina had been with him, but she had stayed up through the previous night and all day, and Hogarth had sent her to bed and stayed with Bruce himself. And so, when I reached him, Bruce was alone. But my brother didn't awaken while I was with him. I brought the chair up to the bed, and I sat there. I talked to him. I thought that I'd keep him alive by talking."

He paused, then started off softly again. "I was back behind the pillar—Bruce had draperies on the bed then. And I had dozed off. Then I awoke, knowing that someone was in the room. I couldn't tell who, because the candle had burned out. I didn't realize at first what was happening because I was barely awake . . . and then I saw that the figure was trying to smother Bruce. A pillow was pressed over his face.

"I leapt up and threw myself on the form and dragged it away from Bruce. But I was barely awake, and the person was strong and got away. I would have pursued the attacker, but . . . there was Bruce. I could not leave him. Not that it mattered in the end. Death was not to be robbed. By dawn, Bruce was ravaged by fever. I held him while he breathed his last and stayed at his side. I was bereaved, and then mystified, and then horrified and furious. Something was going on in the castle. Something serious, something so serious that someone had been willing to kill Bruce because of it."

"Who?" Martise whispered.

"I still don't know."

"But why did you claim your brother's identity?" she asked.

"Because I needed everyone to believe that I was Bruce, in case Bruce had known something, or seen something. In case someone inadvertently gave himself—or herself—away, thinking that I was Bruce."

She was silent, still staring at him.

He cocked his head to the side, his arrogance showing in his smoldering eyes. "Well, milady?"

"I—I don't know whether to believe you or not. How can this be? Surely, someone must suspect."

"There was nothing to suspect."

"But, surely—"

"Hogarth knows who I am. And, I suspect," he added, "Elaina does, too. But she will not say anything, and perhaps she does not even admit it to herself. It is easier for her to believe that Bruce is alive, and that there is still a prayer that Bryan will return. But she knows. I believe that she knows."

She was trembling, wanting to believe him, not knowing if she dared do so.

"Well?" he demanded again.

"I don't know—" she began.

"And neither do I, milady," he retorted. "I've given you all that I can. Now it is your turn. Some things are easy. 'Tis a strong Virginian accent with which you speak. And you are a St. James—so you claim—and other than the fact that you came here lying a blue streak, I've no real reason to doubt that you are a St. James."

"How very kind of you to give me such faith!" she retorted, deepening her accent and allowing it to drip with scorn. He ignored the tone of her voice. His eyes narrowed as he watched her, shimmering golden in the candlelight.

"Let's have it, shall we?" he said softly. His tone rippled danger, and it infuriated her.

"I was in Richmond when Lady St. James died of the typhus," he reminded her sharply.

"I've told you—"

"You've not told me why you are here!" he snapped.

"And I've nothing else to say to you!" she flung back. She needed desperately to be away from him. She needed to try to understand all that he had told her . . . she needed time to sort it all out, and to try to decide if she believed him or not. His story rang true . . .

And yet there was still so much going on in the castle. She didn't want him talking to her any longer.

Making demands upon her.

She swept a tail of the sheet over her shoulder with all the dignity she could muster and stared at him as she rose from the bed. "I've nothing else to say to you tonight. You're still an imposter, and—"

"I'm an imposter! I, at least, madam, belong in the castle!"

She shook her head, staring at him, but his back was still against the wall and his eyes held a definite warning gleam. "I am not an imposter. I am Martise St. James. Let me by."

"Nay, lass. You've yet to answer a single thing."

She swore softly, slamming a foot upon the floor. Then she remembered that she could go through the dressing room and bath and reach the stairway. She glanced toward the doorway, but he saw the direction of her eyes and her thoughts. She dashed for the dressing room door, but he was upon her.

Kicking, flailing, she was swept up in a tangle of the sheet, and in seconds flat she was flung back upon the bed, and he was straddled over her. She struggled against him and then went still, realizing that she wore nothing but the sheet, and that he, too, was dangerously bare beneath the smoking jacket. And God forgive her, but she could not think logically when he touched her so. It was far too easy to remember vividly everything that had passed between them. She did not want to love him, not now, not when he seemed so ruthlessly cold and determined. Not when his eyes held that very dangerous spark.

No, she had fallen once . . .

But his thighs were powerful and hot as he straddled her. There was an electifying vibrance about him, and despite herself, she felt color flood her cheeks. She was not horrified by anything that happened between them. She was still in wonder, still in awe, and she wanted to taste and feel every sensation again.

And she dared not . . .

"What are you doing here?" he demanded.

She could never tell him about the emerald. Never. He would probably not believe her. Or he would think that the emerald had been Mary's, and that Martise was a thief, come to steal it away in the night.

"You know why I'm here!" she cried out.

"Why?"

"Because of Mary."

"Because of Mary?"

"Yes! Because of her letters. Because she wrote to me so often. And because at first she was so much in love. Because she adored Bruce Creeghan. And then because she was so very much afraid! And then she died!"

He shook his head, and then he seemed furious again. "Bruce would never have hurt Mary. Never. He loved her."

"But someone—"

"Nay, Martise, I would have known. I trust Mac-Teague—"

"No, Laird of Creeghan, you do not!" she accused, twisting her wrists against his hold once again. "If you did, you would tell him who you are!"

"I have told no one who I am."

"Then—"

"Nay, I have not told him, for I would not have him give me away inadvertently. And you must not do so either."

She inhaled, furious, wishing desperately that she had the strength to cast him from her. She had not. The deep V of the smoking jacket displayed the rippling power of his chest muscles and she could feel the force of his thighs as they locked around, as relentless as the twist of his jaw.

And so she lay perfectly still, challenging him with her eyes. "How do I know that you are not Bruce? That you have not lost some of your senses, that you are not as debauched as some of your ancestors, that you didn't murder your brother upon his return, and take on this charade?"

She should never have spoken, she thought swiftly, not if she valued life. For his eyes were like golden blades, and they sliced into her with an intensity that she could feel. He did not move, not visibly, but she felt the fury and the tension that stole over him, tightening his muscles, knotting his body. He leaned close to her, and she fought desperately not to lose her courage. She would not quiver before him, she vowed, even if he did close his fingers around her throat and squeeze . . .

But he did not touch her throat. He smiled slowly, with a hard and bitter twist to his lips. "Perhaps you cannot know," he told her. "Perhaps you will have to trust in me."

She moistened her lips, returning his stare, praying then that he would let her up, and let her run.

But he did not move. And at last she murmured, "Let me up. The night is nearly over. I need to return to my own room and—"

"You are a fool," he interrupted her quietly.

"How dare—"

"You're not going anywhere," he informed her flatly, steel in his tone.

"Oh, but I am!" She felt a heated flush rising to her cheeks. "If you think that I am going to remain here with you—"

He leaned against her. "If you're not afraid, milady, then you should be. I've told you that oft enough. Despite what you do or do not believe, I am not going to be the one to brick you into a wall. But, Mistress Martise St. James, someone here must be very aware that you do know something. You were struck down in the crypts. What were you doing in my room that night?" he demanded.

Her eyes widened at the sudden attack. She had been moved, she knew, from one crypt to the other. So how had he known that she had come down the spiral stairway from this tower?

"I wasn't in this room—"

"You're a liar."

"But how—"

"I was in the great hall, Martise," he said coldly. "After I saw the lights, I was in the hall, and I came quickly below.

You did not pass me by, and so you came by the spiral stairs. So why were you in this room?"

She lifted her eyes to his rebelliously, the blue dazzling in her defiance. "*You* tell *me*, my Laird Creeghan. You say that I am so anxious for your company—"

"I am anxious that you quit lying!" he hissed.

She fell silent, then told him sharply, "Let me up."

"Nay."

Her cheeks reddened. "I'll not sleep with you again! I'll not be so ravished—"

"You call that ravished, mistress?" he inquired with such a trace of mockery in his voice that she wanted to hit him. "The kiss was forced!" she insisted.

He looked as if he was about to laugh and she slammed her fists hard against his chest. "I will not sleep with you again, great laird of Creeghan!" she insisted desperately. "If you touch me again, I swear that it will be by force, against my will—"

"Milady," he murmured, catching her hands and holding them hard against his chest as he met her eyes, "I've no desire to force you to anything. But you're not returning to your room tonight. Things are moving too swiftly . . . and frighteningly. You are going to stay in this room."

She paled. "I'll not—"

"Cease, milady. I do not intend to sleep with you. I intend to keep you alive, until I can see you safely out of here."

She forgot that she herself had been intending to flee. But she couldn't believe now that Mary had died of natural causes when so much was happening here. When she knew that she was not imagining the lights at night. When she knew that a young girl had been murdered recently.

"I'm not going anywhere!" she informed him tensely.

He still held her hands. He pulled her even closer. "I am not leaving!" she repeated, but her voice held less conviction, and she was trembling.

"If you do not leave, you play it all my way."

She clenched her teeth and felt the chill of the room touch her back and sweep along it.

"And know if you stay that I shall haunt you. Far worse than any spirit, my dear lady. You will do as I say, and you will stay where I tell you."

"You are an arrogant autocrat, Laird Creeghan," she returned.

"I intend to keep you alive," he said bluntly. She was beginning to shiver. He suddenly dropped her hands and strode back to his door, checked it, then came over to the bed to stare down at her again. "You did not search well enough," he informed her.

She cried out softly as he nearly unseated her, lifting up the mattress and pulling a weapon from beneath the bed. "It's a Colt revolver, heavy, but accurate, and a six-shooter. Have you ever fired a weapon?"

She stared at the pistol, and emotion welled in her throat. It was an American weapon, and yes, she knew it well. Many Rebel soldiers had carried breechloaders, rifles that needed to be loaded for each shot with balls and powder or a cartridge, slow weapons, even when fired by experts. But many cavalry men, many of the guerrillas, had managed to obtain the revolvers. War had given the world many new weapons. There was the Winchester and the Gatling gun, and the Colt weapons had been improved to such speed that they could truly rain down their death upon men.

"Yes," she said. "I've fired a gun before." Her father had seen to that. She had fired many different kinds of guns during the war. There were renegades and deserters from both sides who had preyed upon women alone.

He grunted and shoved the Colt back beneath the mattress. "If anyone comes after you, do not hesitate to shoot."

"Does that include you, Laird Creeghan?" she asked.

He paused, staring at her. And then he smiled. "That must be at your discretion—milady."

Then he turned and walked toward the dressing room

door, and suddenly, she felt fear constrict her throat, and she called out to him quickly. "Where are you going?"

He paused and turned back to her. "The dressing room. I've a cot I can pull out. Good night—milady."

And he disappeared. But he left the door open between the rooms, and though she was anxious, she was glad.

The candle was burning low, the fire in the hearth was all but out. She pulled the covers close about her and stared up at the ceiling, wishing that she could call out to him.

She closed her eyes tightly against the night, and she was forced to realize that she was still in love with him.

No, she was more in love with him than ever.

And the memories of the night were a fresh torment, filled with both sweetness and anguish. She trembled suddenly, and realized that she was different, she would never be the same. He had changed her tonight, forever.

She should have been ashamed, she should have had regrets, but she did not. Indeed, he was dark, he was dangerous, but she knew in her heart that she could not have found a more passionate, seductive, and tender lover than the man who had claimed her. The laird of Creeghan. He had touched and awakened her. And in her heart, she could not believe him a ghost.

Yet even then, knowing her heart, she could not sleep. She lay awake and remembered the sight of his face, a true reflection, in the coffin. Nor could she forget the lights at night.

Or the rumors of things that happened on the nights when the full moon reigned. Rumors . . . and things she had seen with her own eyes. Downed ships and a girl buried beneath the brick of the walls of the castle.

But Bruce was innocent. He had to be. No, not Bruce. Bryan. Bryan Creeghan . . .

She should not think it, because she must not say it. She must keep his secret.

She believed him, she thought. Or she believed *in* him. She must not do so too easily! she chastised herself. She had to take care with him. Grave care. In all that happened, she still did not know what he felt for her. His whispers had been gentle, tender, even, in the act of love . . .

But his words later had been taunting, and he was still as suspicious as she.

She could not tell him about the emerald.

And she knew, as she settled into sleep, that even more than her life, she truly had to guard her heart. She was going to stay, and so he would haunt her, day and night.

And she could not let him know how much of her he held already within his hands. She dared not.

Not if she meant to keep her very soul . . .

Sometime in the night, she slept. And yet she was exhausted when he rather rudely awoke her, shaking her shoulders.

He was up and dressed, handsomely attired in navy trousers and cotton shirt. He was freshly shaven and looked none the worse for wear despite the night. She was certain that she had not survived it so well.

She groaned as he shook her. "Have a heart," she pleaded into the pillow. "Let me be."

"I cannot," he argued. "It's time I return you to your own room."

He pulled her over and she belatedly remembered that she was sleeping naked in his bed. She swept the sheet around her and realized that she was not so emotional by daylight. The fire in his eyes betrayed nothing as he watched her, and she suddenly wanted nothing more than a bath. The sensual male scent of him still seemed to cling to her flesh. Or was it simply that he was standing before her, smelling of soap and shave lotion?

She rolled, bringing the sheet around her body, and rose with an air of grandeur. "Seriously, sir, I do believe that I should have returned last night!"

To her annoyance, he laughed. "Ah, is it better to walk

the halls in naught but a sheet by the light of the moon rather than risk the betrayal of daylight?"

She didn't reply, but tossed her hair over her shoulders and headed for the door. He was right behind her, and his stride quickly matched hers. She grated her teeth.

"This is truly marvelous, milord. It will definitely allay suspicions if you walk along with me while I am cloaked in a sheet!"

"I'm not waylaying suspicions, milady," he told her, his eyes still sizzling with amusement. "I am seeing you safely to your door."

They had walked the corridor and stood before it even then. There was no one about in the early dawn.

He bowed to her with exaggerated courtesy. "We need to talk, but we'll do so later. As always, bolt yourself in," he told her.

She closed the door tightly behind her and bolted it securely, then cast herself down upon her bed. She began to tremble as it struck her anew that she could never be the same again.

She had met the dragon in truth, and she had been filled with the sweet flame of his breath . . .

She hadn't thought she would sleep again. She had meant to just lie there until she found the energy to rise, but when she closed her eyes, it seemed she fell instantly asleep, unplagued by any dreams.

Much later, she heard a tapping at her door. She called out, and Holly answered her. She arose to pull the bolt and then remembered that she was still wearing a sheet. She tore quickly through a drawer and found another gown, slipped it over her shoulders, and allowed Holly to enter. Holly had tea, hot delicious tea, and crumb cakes.

Martise thanked her and devoured the tea and crumb cakes, amazed at the extent of her hunger. As Holly chatted, Martise interrupted to ask that the bath be brought and Holly promised that she would attend to it immediately.

While she waited for the bath, Martise stood on the

balcony and looked out upon the cliffs, listening to the
sounds of the sea crashing against the shore. She heard
voices, yet she remained on the balcony, aware that Jemie
and Trey and the giant McCloud had brought up the tub
and the water. She closed her eyes and felt the breeze, and
waited for them to leave. When they were gone, she closed
and bolted the balcony doors.

Holly awaited her, but Martise assured her that she meant
to soak until the water cooled, and that she would be fine by
herself. When the maid was gone, Martise bolted the door,
then stripped and stepped into the bath. She felt the water
sweep around her, bathing her thighs, steaming away the
touch of soreness but not the memory.

She leaned her head back, and then, despite the heat, she
shivered as she wondered just who in the castle could be a
murderer. She swallowed against the memories of the poor
sailor who had died by the caves, and of the pathetic bones
that had been walled within the crypt.

There was a slight noise, and she sat up suddenly, tension
tingling down her spine. She swirled around, and a scream
of amazement caught in her throat as she saw that Bryan
Creeghan was in her room. Cocky, arrogant, his hands on
his hips, his dark hair askew upon his forehead, his eyes
bold and challenging her.

She pulled the sponge to her breasts and glanced to the
balcony and the entrance, but all the doors were bolted. Her
eye shot back to his with amazement. "By God, how on
earth . . . ?" she asked incredulously.

He bowed slightly to her, raising an arm. "The armoire,
milady. There is a spring on the side, which slides it and a
secret doorway open."

She stared at him, feeling an intense fury growing inside
of her. She sat up, her eyes snapping. "You laird of all
bastards!" she hissed. "You've been in here before!"

"Aye, that I have."

She flung the sponge at him fiercely, calling him every
evil thing she could think to mutter. He caught the sponge

easily enough, and seemed amused rather than daunted by
her words. He walked to the tub and stood over her and she
ended her tirade on a furious note. "How dare you. How
dare you! You've no right in here now or ever, you
barbarian Highlander, you—"

"Ah, but I'm standing here now to return something that
you too carelessly cast aside," he told her, his eyes flashing
his amusement as he plopped the sponge back down upon
her. And then, to her great distress, he knelt by the tub, his
fingers idly curled around its rim, his eyes a wicked flame
as they caught hers. "And I never came to do you harm,
milady—"

"Stop that!" she hissed to him. "You know that I am not
'milady,' and you mock me with it again and again!"

"Ah, but in truth, I do not mock you. I find you to be a lady
indeed, fascinating, beautiful, beguiling. I am bewitched."

Her eyes widened. She never knew when he
taunted . . .

When he was serious.

When he merely intended to seduce.

"You came into my room at night!" she accused him.

"From the very first night," he admitted frankly. "I came
to see that you were safe and well each night."

Her eyes narrowed. A shimmering sensation swept
throughout her, just from the heated caress of his gaze. She
wondered how he could affect her so without the slightest
touch, and yet, inside, she knew . . .

She knew where such a bold glance could lead, what
delight sensual laughter could foretell. She knew the feel of
his eyes raking down her nakedness, and that it was a soft
reminder of the sensual sweep of his hands, the caress of his
searing kiss.

Her breath was coming too quickly. To her dismay she
felt her breasts swell within the water, her nipples tighten to
hard peaks, and her pulse begin to beat wildly against her
throat. She forced her voice to hardness. "I am fine. You
need not be here now."

But he had seen that pulse against her throat, and he leaned toward her, sweeping back her dampened hair and placing his lips against the frantic blue vein where that pulse so beat. She caught her breath, leaning back, feeling his lips slide over the steam-dampened length of her throat. She fought the swirling desire that seemed to burst forth like the bloom of a rose within her. "I told you!" she whispered desperately. "I will not sleep with you—"

His lips covered hers. His mouth was open, his tongue swept her mouth with an unceasing demand, finding every sweet crevice, invading, demanding, seducing . . .

No! She would not be so easily led astray, even if she had already traveled the forbidden path before. She twisted from his touch, and still she could not breathe, but she fought hard to do so. "Out, Laird Creeghan!" she demanded imperiously. "You've no right here. And if you think to come furtively through a secret door ever again—"

She broke off threateningly. But the threat did not disturb him. He arched one of his autocrat's brows. "Do tell, milady."

"Take care, milord," she warned, her eyes narrowing, her voice a warning purr, "I shall slap that arrogant face in two seconds."

"You may try."

"And I may succeed." She modestly crossed her arms more tightly about her breasts, drawing in her knees.

"And what do you hide from me, lass?"

"Out, Laird Creeghan! You are a dragon, I do believe."

He shook his head, and the amusement faded away, and he seemed very tense when he said softly, "I warned you, milady, that if you stayed, then I would have you." She flushed, startled by the new passion within his voice that held no taunt, and no hint of laughter. "Well, milady, it has come to pass, and I'll not forget that it has, nor shall I allow you to forget."

"I told you—"

"You've nothing left to hide from me, lass. And I warned you, too, that I would haunt you, day and night."

He stood suddenly and sauntered to the armoire. "I'll never force you," he promised softly, and his gaze burned her flesh far more thoroughly than the steam that rose from the water. "But I will have you again, and willing, I vow it. Nor shall I cease to haunt you, as I have promised."

"But—"

"Are you still determined to stay?" he demanded.

"Yes, yes!" she cried out, and her fingers wound tightly around the rim of the tub.

Bryan Creeghan clenched down hard upon his jaw. His fists knotted at his back as he watched her. Did the lass not know that she drove him to distraction? Her hair curled and waved about her forehead in a damp splendor, as if she were some sea goddess. And now that she had moved her hands, the water just crested the fullness of her breasts, framing the coral aureolas, teasing the taut peaks. A tightness constricted his groin and his limbs, and he wanted nothing more than to deny his words, and wrench her damp and dripping from the tub and into his arms. He could bring her willing, into his arms, giving and eager and pouring the sweetness of herself upon him, by God he could!

He clamped down with a greater vengeance upon his jaw, and locked it in a twist. Nay, he could not! Not now . . .

For if she was determined to stay, then it must be at his side, in accord with his every whim. And she had to understand that.

"Then I've come to talk!" he told her harshly.

She sank back into the water, wariness creeping into her eyes.

"Yes?"

"Someone in this castle is guilty," he reminded her. "And if you're going to be here, you must help me discover who. Trust no one. Be ever wary. And remember, above all else, whatever I say, and whatever I do, you must agree with me."

"All right," she said after a moment.

"Whatever I say, whatever I do," he repeated in a stern command. "Swear it."

"All right!" she repeated. Then added through her teeth, "I swear it!"

He bowed to her, and she watched as he walked to the armoire and slipped his hand in back to slide a panel at its rear.

Martise choked as she saw how swiftly and silently the wall, with the armoire, slid open two feet. Then Bryan disappeared, and the panel closed, and she was left to glower at it in a newly rising fury.

"Whatever you say, indeed!" she muttered. "Beast!" But he was gone, and so it was easy to defy him.

She finished scrubbing herself with a fury, and still the memories remained. Impatient with herself, she rose from the tub and toweled herself dry with a vengeance.

Despite her simmering anger, when she dressed and came downstairs for the midday meal, she meant to keep her vow.

They were all assembled at the table. Elaina, Ian, Conar, Uncle Peter, and Bruce—no, Bryan!—Creeghan. And even as she looked at them, she could not believe that any of them could be guilty. Not Ian with his laughing ways, nor Peter with his kindness, nor Conar with his sense of responsibility. And certainly not gentle Elaina . . .

The talk was of the games, and she found that she could still laugh when Ian remarked that he really needed to invent a new game so that he needn't feel obliged to toss a caber. Bryan was silent, sipping his wine, watching the others.

And then suddenly, he spoke, his voice a soft and casual burr, his gold-green gaze moving slowly around the table.

"By the by, there's something I feel I must share with you all immediately," he said.

He rose, and Martise watched him as he came around to stand behind her chair. His hands rested on her shoulders while his thumbs moved with a startling intimacy and affection along her throat. And then, to her amazement, he bent low to place a gentle and tender kiss upon her cheek.

"Lady St. James has consented to become Lady Creeghan."

Eleven

❧

There was silence, absolute, dead silence at the table. It seemed to stretch forever and ever and ever, and Martise thought vaguely that they were all in shock.

Except that no one could be in a greater state of shock over the announcement than she was herself.

It was Uncle Peter who spoke first. He rose to the occasion gallantly, lifting his mug of ale high and smiling down upon them both benignly.

"Congratulations, nephew. You've captured another great beauty to grace these halls. Martise, milady, I warmly wish you well, and welcome you to our family."

The words seemed to break the frost that had fallen over all of them. Elaina leapt up and kissed her brother and hugged Martise. There were tears in her eyes. "I am so delighted! Oh, Martise, we shall be sisters now. It is wonderful!"

Martise rose, hugging her back. Bryan stood just behind them and she tried to glare at him with all the fury that she could muster. What right had he to say such a thing? She should deny it this very second. What he had done was cruel, horribly, horribly cruel.

But when her eyes met his, she knew that she could not deny him. She had sworn that she would go along with him, no matter what he said or did. No matter how it hurt Elaina . . . or herself. And the glitter in his eyes, the searing warning within them, told her that she must keep her vow. Or else . . .

Or else he would see that she left the house, and it seemed more important to her now than ever that she discover the truth buried within the walls of the castle.

"I, too, am delighted!" Ian told her, sweeping her from Elaina's enthusiastic hug. He kissed her soundly on the cheek and grinned at his cousin. "I do say, Bruce, you have managed again to do the castle proud." He shook his head mournfully. "And I thought that I had a chance this time! Ah, well, as long as the great Creeghan beast brings the beauty into our lives . . . welcome!" Then he hugged her, too. And then Conar was hugging her and congratulating her, and Elaina wanted to know when they were going to celebrate the nuptials. Her brother gave her a rather vague answer, but promised that it would be soon, very soon. "The period of mourning for Mary is over," he said softly, looking at his family from one to another. "I see no reason that Martise and I should wait very long. However, I've business to attend to at the moment, so if you'll all excuse me . . ." He smiled, the rogue's smile that was not without its lulling charm. He paused behind Martise once again, and his lips brushed the back of her neck. She felt a soft whisper of flame there, against her flesh. "I'll see you soon, my love," he murmured. Casting his gaze over the others once again, he was gone, heading hurriedly toward the stairs.

Once again, the silence fell.

"Damn!" Ian exploded after a moment. Then he smiled at Martise and laughed. "Well, the laird has been known to possess his devil's ways, but I hadn't realized at all how close—I mean, I just hadn't seen—I didn't—"

"Ian, you're babbling, lad," his father told him, and

asked that Martise pass him the bread basket. He grinned at her and added, "Ye've na said a word yerself, lass. Be happy. Don't let the tales of evil Creeghans and dark and mysterious deeds within these old stone walls steal a single whit of your happiness."

Ian laughed. "That's right! Don't let a one of those stories disturb you—even if they are true!"

She smiled. It was a tremendous effort. She stood up, anxious to escape them all, especially Elaina, who was so very happy with the news. She was dying to get her hands on Bryan Creeghan.

"Surely, there were evil Creeghans in plenty!" she exclaimed, her eyes wide, as she winked at Peter. "But then, at least, they're interesting men. If nothing else, I shall not be bored."

"Ah, here, here!" Ian toasted her, his eyes dancing. "Perhaps the castle itself has met its match at last!"

"Perhaps," she agreed, and she pushed her chair in, trying to maintain her forced smile for them all. "Thank you, thank you all for being so very kind and warm," she said. "Now, if you'll excuse me, too . . ."

She didn't have an excuse, and so she simply fled up the stairs. She wanted to see Bryan immediately, while the blood was boiling within her.

She tore past her own room and down along the corridor to the master's tower. When she reached his door, she flung it open, ready, anxious, to wage war.

Even as she stood in the doorway, he appeared, walking in from the dressing room, slipping his scarf over his shoulders. He stared at her and must have seen the blue fire sizzling in her eyes. "What now?" he cried, and made a *tsk* with his tongue. "Martise, you are ever welcome in this room and in this bed and your very eagerness just flatters me to the teeth, but really, I do have an appointment. Oh, never mind, the hell with the appointment. If you're willing to fall within my arms once again . . ."

She felt as if she were strangling. She wanted to shout,

but was dismayed to discover that all she could manage was a choking sound. And that sound escaped her as she tore across the room in a sizzling dark fury and threw herself against him, trying to pummel and claw him, and not managing to do either. The force of her weight and her flight across the room did catch him off balance. He caught her, though, and they swirled around, and crashed down hard together upon his dragon bed.

He called her name, but the wildness of her rage was still with her and she twisted and fought beneath him until he was forced to catch her hands. He tossed a hard-muscled thigh over her hips and shook her, and she finally went still, staring at him furiously. For the rogue who had started all the trouble, he seemed to be annoyingly amused. His eyes were flecked with golden flames that danced while the fullness of his mouth was curved into a well-humored and sensual smile.

"How could you!" she managed to say at last.

"How could I?" he repeated blankly. "Easily. You're a wildcat, I'll admit, but I am by far the stronger. And actually, *I* didn't—you did."

"I what!"

"Well, you came catapulting at me. I did my best to defend myself. Even though I was stricken to realize that you came to beat me to an early demise rather than bed with me."

She twisted, determined to catch the flesh of his hand, so tight upon her own, between her teeth and bite until he wiped the smile from his face and screamed for mercy. But he was too quick, laughing as he spread their hands far from the neighborhood of her teeth. "My dear lady, what behavior for such a fair, innocent damsel."

"You've already commented, my lord, that I am no lady!" she snapped. "Now leave me be!"

"Leave you be! Martise, you are dangerous!"

"Me! I repeat, how could you! How could you sit there

with your family, with people you love, and make such a horrid announcement!"

Shadows flickered across his eyes. A startling tension filled him and she felt it in his hold upon her, from the tightening of his fingers to the heat of his thigh. "I've yet to hear that the announcement of a marriage was a 'horrid' thing."

"You know what I mean! You were ungodly cruel to your sister, making her think that we will be wed!"

Suddenly, he released her and stood. He combed his fingers through his ebony-dark hair and walked toward the door. Martise hadn't realized that it was still open. He closed it softly and then turned around to face her.

"We probably shall be wed."

"What!" she exclaimed, sitting up and trying to smooth back the dishevelment of her hair. "We cannot be! You cannot be serious!"

"I am deadly serious," he told her, and catching sight of his eyes, she knew that he was.

"But I cannot marry you!"

"It may be the only way."

"The only way to what?"

"To let you stay here. Safely."

"Safely!" she cried, hearing a hysteria rising in her voice. She clenched her fingers into fists at her sides and hardened her tone. "Mary—the laird's last wife—is dead, I remind you. Is that safety?"

His gaze narrowed coolly as he watched her. "I need you near me," he said flatly.

"You wish to use me as bait!" she accused. Then she leapt up and stared at him across the room. "That I do not mind, but to go so far as marriage—"

"Temporary marriage," he interrupted coldly.

"Temporary!"

"Martise," he said impatiently, "I am not without influence. I can arrange a divorce when this is over. But in the meantime, I am deadly serious, and I want the legalities handled as quickly as possible. I am interested in your safety, milady. I want you under my eye at night—and especially beneath the full moon."

"Well, you've gone too far! You're an insolent bastard but you've gone too far this time! I am not one of your simple village girls, and I'll not follow your orders or play your games or be seduced—" She broke off. She had already been seduced.

Into bed, and into love.

And *there* was the truth of the matter. She was in love, and he was talking about expediency. Her heart was aflame, and his words were as cold as ice. And even now, while she thought that she would explode within, his eyes danced once again with amusement. Aye, indeed, she had been seduced.

"Pray, do go on," he encouraged her softly.

"Get out of the way," she told him.

He arched a brow. "It's an ultimatum, Martise. You do know that. I warned you before. It's my way here, or no way at all."

"I could go out and denounce you for an imposter!" she cried.

He smiled. "But I am an imposter who belongs here, Mistress St. James. You are not."

"And perhaps I do not care any longer!" she challenged him. "Mary is dead. I cannot bring her back."

"That's true. And it's been true since the beginning. And still, you have not left." He paused, then inquired politely, too politely, "I wonder why?"

She started to stride for the door, heedless of the fact that he blocked it. "Let me by," she commanded.

To her surprise, he stepped aside and opened the door, his gaze burning into her as he did so.

"Don't forget that I have given you an ultimatum," he reminded her.

"Umm, so you say. I believe I should much rather leave than marry you, milord."

"So you say, lass. Yet how curious, I don't believe that you will do so."

"Leave—or marry you?" she asked sweetly, pausing in the doorway.

"Always the little Rebel," he murmured. "Well, love, the war is on. And I do not suggest that you rebel against me."

His eyes touched hers. They saw far more than she was willing for him to see. Something about his gaze was more disturbing than usual, and she wondered why.

Wondered what he knew . . .

"Good day, Laird Creeghan," she said, and swept on by him. But as she walked along the corridor, she knew that he was still watching her. She felt his eyes. Felt their fire and their power. Felt them seep beneath her skin. Aye, he watched her! She knew it.

And she knew that he saw . . . something.

What?

She shivered, because she did not know.

When she was gone, he sat down at the desk. His desk now.

His brother's desk before.

He took out Bruce's notebook, the private journal that Hogarth had just discovered in the library and brought to Bryan minutes before Martise had come to the room.

He flipped through the pages, and his mouth tightened into a tense line. He clenched down hard on his teeth, and he realized that his fingers were trembling even as he held the book.

What a fool he had been.

Oh, aye, he had known from the beginning that she was not who she said she was. And he had determined to discover her identity.

But he had not realized that she would slip beneath his skin. That she would capture his passions and his heart, and softly, surely, wind him about the evocative beauty of her whispers and her form. Yet there was no innocence about her. Nothing real, nothing tangible. Oh, aye, he had taken something from her. Innocence. Yet it seemed that she had bargained it freely enough, he thought, his anger growing. She had come here purely and simply for personal gain.

He leaned back, throwing his booted feet up on the desk, and closed his eyes.

It might have been the war! God knew, the war had warped and hardened enough people. It might have been the bloodshed, and the waste and the devastation. He should understand her, if anyone should understand . . .

He did. In his way. Or he would have . . .

If she didn't lie so easily. With her eyes straight upon his, the murky lashes framing them so sweetly. If her voice didn't tremble, if she didn't quiver in his eyes, if she didn't look at him with such a tangle of emotion seeming to mirror the tumult of her soul.

If he wasn't in love with her.

A fool in love, he thought bitterly.

All these years, all these women. And now, when life itself was at its most deadly, he was falling. Hard. And there was nothing left to do but fight the fascination.

And to use her—as she used him.

He swore out loud bitterly. And then he rose and strode angrily from the room.

He hurried for the stables, barely acknowledged Jemie, nodded to Robert McCloud, and leapt onto Lucian's broad back. He raced the stallion from the castle, the hoofbeats from his reckless gallop seeming to echo the furious thunder that ruled within his heart.

She paced her room until she couldn't stand it any longer.

Holly had already been to see her, tears in her eyes, too. She was so happy. Martise was going to stay. No one could take dear Mary's place, but that Martise had come, Mary's sister, must surely allow Mary to rest far more gently within her grave. Freya had been up to knock hesitantly upon her door, and then welcome her with enthusiasm. Hogarth had been the worst. He had actually beamed. Hogarth! Hogarth, who knew so much of the truth—

About Bryan, at least.

When he was gone, Martise sat down upon her bed, shivering. She thought that thank God he was Bryan and not Bruce, and that he had never been Mary's husband.

How could she be certain about anything? She got to her feet and began pacing again. Mary had died of heart failure. The sailor had died after he had been wrecked upon the shore. Clarissa had disappeared, just as a girl had disappeared before . . .

And a young girl's body had been discovered in the castle walls. A girl killed not two years ago.

She was shivering violently. The girl had been walled in the crypt. Where she had ventured and been struck down. And Bryan had found her.

Had he really stumbled upon her?

Or had he knocked her out himself, and then appeared at her side, pretending to rescue her? Was he really Bryan? Or was it Bryan Creeghan who lay in the coffin in the crypt?

She covered her face with her hands and sank onto the bed, certain that she was losing her mind. Perhaps she had been seduced by the devil.

No . . . she had made love to a flesh-and-blood man, one who was passionate and hard, with gleaming fire eyes. With fingers that could stroke tenderness and bold demand, with whispers that could ignite the very soul. Dangerous, devastating . . .

But a murderer . . . ?

She didn't know. She just didn't know anymore.

Suddenly, she was desperate just to leave the castle. She changed swiftly to riding clothes—her own. She would never don Mary's clothing again, she swore. And when she was dressed she barely glanced at her reflection in the mirror and hurried out. She was white, she thought as she raced down the stairs. White and pale, much paler than a blushing bride-to-be should appear.

The great hall was empty as she hurried through it. She walked across to the stables and was pleased to see that Jemie was there. Except that he wasn't smiling. He looked at her gravely and nodded a greeting, and then he said, as if it was something that he had been coached to do, "We're pleased to have ye as mistress of the castle, milady. Aye, indeed, we're pleased."

She stopped and stared at him. "Well, Jemie, if you don't mind my saying so, you don't seem to be terribly pleased."

He shook his head wildly. "I'm pleased, milady!" He had flushed a very dark color. He looked around, almost as if he expected the stable walls to have ears. "Ye're kind, milady, so very kind. Like t'other one, aye, that ye are. But she died. Died because the Devil's Teeth must have their fill, because the cliffs must take their blood, do ye ken, milady?"

A faint, eerie feeling rippled along her spine. The breeze was picking up, and with it, she could hear the moaning. It was a sound that came with the castle and the cliffs and the wind, and she knew it, and still it sounded like a woman's cry, low and chilling and despairing.

She stiffened her spine. "No, Jemie, I know no such thing. Cliffs do not need blood." She stared into his stricken eyes and lowered her voice. "Jemie, it's all right, you are afraid for me, aren't you? Because you know that Mary was afraid. But land can't be evil, Jemie. And the castle can't be evil, either. Only men can be evil. Do you understand me, Jemie?"

He shook his head. He looked around quickly, and she thought that he was going to speak again.

"Jemie," she said urgently. "Do you know why Mary was afraid? Was she afraid of someone in particular? Or something? Jemie, please, can you tell me?"

Suddenly, he stared past her shoulder and clamped his mouth shut.

Martise spun around. The huge groom, the towering Robert McCloud, was coming their way, long legs bringing him fast upon them. "Taking a ride, milady St. James? Jemie, where be yer manners, lad? Get the lady her horse, and quickly."

Jemie turned around to do as he was bidden. Martise stared at McCloud, and the unease she had felt with the rising of the wind swept along her spine once again. His scar stood out lividly against his flesh. He might have been a good-looking man without it, and Martise wondered briefly how he had obtained it. Probably a barroom brawl.

Perhaps she had no right to judge.

"Lady St. James, the master has been to see us, he has, and we wish to extend ye our best wishes and our loyalty. Long may we serve ye, lady!"

He bowed to her, as if greeting royalty. But to these people, the laird of Creeghan was their royalty, and if he sat as their king, then she, indeed, would sit as their queen.

She felt the chill of the breeze, but she smiled and thanked him.

"So ye're riding this day," he commented when Jemie came forth with a groomed and saddled Desdemona. "The master wouldna like it," he said, and there was disapproval in his voice.

"Oh, and why not, Mr. McCloud?" she asked.

He shrugged. "Seems there might be a storm brewing."

She led Desdemona to the mounting block and leapt atop the mare before McCloud could determine to help her. She smiled down at him. "Why, Mr. McCloud, it seems that there is always a storm brewing hereabouts."

"Aye, such is Creeghan, milady."

Martise noticed the insolent crook of his smile, and she wondered if he was referring to the place or to the man.

"I am a very good horsewoman, Mr. McCloud. The laird himself recognizes that fact."

"Still, the laird might well protest."

"Might he?"

"Maybe," he acknowledged with a smile that she wasn't sure she liked. "But keep to the main roads, milady. Take care. 'Tis easy to lose oneself here."

"Thank you for the warning," she told him. She cast Jemie a quick smile. The lad was standing there, silent and pale. He didn't respond to her smile.

"Keep to the main roads!" Robert McCloud repeated.

She didn't acknowledge him this time, but nudged Desdemona. The mare leapt into a trot, and Martise urged her into a canter. She glanced up to the sky. It didn't appear that there would be a storm.

When she first left the stables, she kept upon the road to the village. It felt good, very good, to leave the castle behind her. She maintained her smooth canter, glad then of the wind that whipped through her hair and cooled her face, glad of the feel of the spirited mare beneath her. Desdemona was real, and solid, a fey creature perhaps, but one with which Martise felt she had much in common this day.

When she at last pulled the mare in, she saw that the sky had darkened somewhat, but she didn't think there would be a serious storm. And she was feeling defiant. She'd be damned if she'd listen to the likes of Robert McCloud.

There was a forest path leading off to her right. She was certain that it was still Creeghan land, a wilder, overgrown section that surrounded the plateaus of grass where they brought their livestock to graze.

She turned in along the path, and when she did so, she was pleased. The trees formed a natural arbor over her head, with flecks of sunlight filtering through the leaves. The world around her seemed suddenly filled with a beautiful green darkness. And best of all, she could no longer hear the womanish wail of the wind.

She traveled deep in thought for some time, secure in the surroundings about her. She felt as if she were at along last sheltered from the eyes of the castle. Desdemona moved along with no thought of direction from Martise. The earth beneath her was blanketed in brush and fallen leaves, and there was quiet and peacefulness about the forest that was very comfortable.

And quiet enough that she should be able to think . . .

What was she to do?

Forget the emerald, forget about Mary! a voice cried from within her mind. Forget . . . and run! Run for your life, as fast as you can!

But from deep within her heart, another voice arose.

I cannot run, I cannot forget Mary, I need the emerald and . . .

There was nowhere that she could run, nowhere far enough away, that she could ever forget Bryan Creeghan. Forget the sound of his voice with its rich husky burr. Forget the bold feel of his lips against her, the raw demand of his touch, the fire of his eyes and his body when it joined with her own . . .

The fire touched her cheeks, and she knew that, all alone in the forest, she was blushing. And then she realized that she had been deceiving herself for a long time. She had not stayed for Mary. And she hadn't even stayed for the emerald. She had stayed because of Bryan Creeghan.

And now he was demanding marriage.

Marriage. He was not sweeping her off her feet, nor was he kneeling down before her. He was not whispering words of love, or declaring that his heart and his life would be empty without her. He wanted her as a bride. As a Creeghan bride.

Bait . . .

For a Creeghan murderer.

And as he spoke so flatly and coldly about marriage, he could not know that he was sliding a knife deep into her heart, and ripping the cold blade cruelly out once again.

"No!" she suddenly whispered aloud. "He is a hard, cruel bastard, and I will not love him, I will not!" she declared to the forest. Desdemona's ear flickered back. "What is it about him?" Martise exclaimed to the mare.

And then, more desperately, "What in God's name is it . . . ?"

And then, even as the sound of her own voice faded away in the denseness of the green forest, she knew that she was not alone. There were voices, coming from a shadowed cove that broadened out from the trail before her.

She reined in on the mare and held very still for a moment. Then the breeze shifted, and she heard it again, the murmur of voices. And in the very quiet of the voices, and that of the forest, she felt the edge of something sinister.

She knew that she should turn her horse and race away.

The breeze rustled through the trees and touched upon her cheeks. She dismounted from Desdemona, her booted feet falling softly and carefully upon the leaf-strewn trail. Slowly, slowly, she edged toward the clearing. The trees, the bracken, the rustle of the autumn leaves, were her cover.

She moved closer and closer. The sound of the voices rose, and yet she still could not understand what was being said. She came closer.

Through the brush that surrounded the copse, she saw that some meeting took place. There were at least ten figures there, surrounding a fire. Each figure was decked in a dark and hooded cloak. She could see no faces.

She needed to get just a little closer. But if she moved much farther, she would lose the cover that she needed, and she somehow knew that the meeting was extremely secretive. Some sixth sense warned her that it would be dangerous indeed to be discovered listening in upon it.

She held her breath, straining to hear. She could just begin to catch snatches of conversation.

". . . All Hallows' Eve . . ."

". . . if the moon be full . . ."

". . . Creeghan . . ."

She couldn't quite make out enough words to understand what was going on, but already her heart was pounding out a furious beat. She had to know! The very secret of the castle might lie before her.

She took another step.

And that was when a twig snapped beneath her feet.

The hooded heads lifted sharply. She still could not see faces in the shadows of the forest, but she knew that eyes were upon her. Each and every figure had jerked up its head like a rocket, and now stared directly at her . . .

Or at least to the place where she stood, spying.

She had to run. She turned on a heel and started to tear back toward Desdemona.

There were footsteps behind her. Footsteps pounding after her. She ran harder. She dared not look back, for she could feel them, sense them all, the dark-cloaked creatures coming with deadly intent behind her. Her lungs burned, and she was gasping, trying to call for the horse, too terrified to find voice.

The mare looked up from her grazing. Martise cried out, and the mare backed away. "No, no, please! Stand still, oh God help me, God help me . . ."

She had leapt up on a horse unassisted often enough in her life, but not upon a sidesaddle and not when she was filled with panic. She grasped the pommel, and the mare, now snorting and prancing with fear, stepped backward and forward nervously. "Please!" Martise murmured. "Please!"

She could hear the grass and bracken flattening. She turned around and saw that two of the figures were close upon her. She knew deep in her heart that if one of them touched her, her body would be discovered—perhaps hundreds of years from now—bricked into a wall. In the crypts of Castle Creeghan.

"Please, God!" she shouted again, and she leapt up with all of her strength and managed to throw herself upon the horse.

Desdemona instantly bolted.

Martise tried to right herself as the mare tore into the brush, straight for the figures. Hands, clawing fingers, reached for Martise. They knotted into her clothing. They twisted into her hair. She grasped tightly and blindly to the mare. Desdemona, now in panic, raced wildly. Martise could see nothing but the earth, flying up from the horse's hooves. The world spun. And still, things grasped at her, tore at her, tried to wrench her from the saddle . . .

It was no longer hands, she realized. The mare's flight was bringing her beneath a multitude of oaks, and it was the branches that seemed to reach and claw for her. She laughed, and the laugh caught in a sob. She tried to right herself and became aware that the darkness was richer here, an even deeper green. She had entered the true heart of the forest.

She righted herself at last and leaned forward to try to catch the reins. "You had to run this way!" she said to the horse. "You just had to run this way! We needed to reach the road, and you've brought us deep into the forest instead. Now we're going to have to circle around them to get out of here."

If they weren't still pursuing her. After all, they knew the forest. She did not.

And they meant to kill her. Of that, she was certain.

"All right, Desdemona," she said aloud. She needed to speak aloud. To calm the horse.

To calm herself!

"All right, all right, it wasn't your fault. It was my fault. I should have been calmer. I shouldn't have been so damned stupid. If you'll just stand still long enough for me to catch your reins . . ."

But even as she leaned ever further forward to try to catch the straggling reins, Desdemona suddenly stumbled. She pitched downward as her front left leg buckled beneath her. Martise, totally unprepared and stretched out in her awkward position, went flying over the horse's lowered head.

She landed on the soft leaf-covered earth and was dazed. Then the world ceased spinning about in a green web, and she righted herself upon the ground. She was not hurt, she realized, moving her arms and legs. But she could be if she stayed too long within the forest.

She leapt to her feet. Desdemona was just feet away. "Come here, you—" Martise began. She reached out to grab the reins. The mare bolted, jerking away. She wandered a few feet.

"Desdemona!" Martise cried out more desperately. "Don't! Please, please, don't do this to me!"

The mare turned to her, her eyes wide and soulful, almost as if she had understood every word. "Good girl, sweet girl, that's right, you just can't leave me here!"

She had to keep the fear from her voice. She had to speak softly, soothingly. She managed to do so, taking tiny step by tiny step toward the mare.

"You traitor, you!" she accused the horse, but she still kept her voice low and soft and lulling. "Yes, you little sweetie, you prancing around when I was trying so hard to leap upon you. Now please, don't you understand? Those awful people are not after you, they're after me . . ."

The mare was just standing there. Martise stretched her hand out. Desdemona tossed her head in the air as if she were nodding. She even took a step toward Martise. And then, just when Martise was about to snatch up a trailing rein, a blackbird rose up from the bracken, screeching away.

"No!" Martise cried desperately.

It was the last straw for the frightened mare. Desdemona reared high into the air, almost toppling down on herself. But she landed on all four feet, and for a moment, she hesitated—before bolting out of the clearing.

"No, no, no, no!" Martise cried out, and she sank down to the ground in despair. "How could you! I'll see that there is horseflesh on that table for dinner if you don't come back! Do you hear me! There will be horse steaks and horse stew and—oh, hell!"

She stared broodingly after the mare. Then she murmured, "Please come back!"

The horse didn't return. And even as Martise sat upon the ground, it seemed that the forest darkened around her. She thought that the trees were conspiring against her, growing together, interweaving their leaves, to surround her with their green darkness.

But it was not the trees. The afternoon was waning, and the sun was fading away. It was going to be completely dark soon, and she didn't know where she was.

Yes, she was in the forest. Alone.

Not alone. The figures in the dark cloaks were in the forest, too.

Creatures who wanted her . . . dead.

With that thought, she leapt to her feet. She had to walk, out of the forest, away from the green darkness. She had to escape before they could find her.

She gazed up again. The sun was setting to her left. The castle would lie to the west, too, right upon the coast. She started to walk. With each step, it seemed that the day grew darker. She heard her own footfalls and something else. It was, she realized, the sound of her own heart.

And then she thought she heard more than her heartbeat. No . . . it was the night. The forest playing tricks. There were things to hear, of course. The scurry of mice. That soft whistle of the wind through the leaves. Squirrels, birds, owls, perhaps, night birds, those that could see in the dark. Fly in the dark. Beat their wings in the dark.

But it was not the beating of wings that she heard, she realized. The ground was trembling. It had come alive with the sound and tremor of hoofbeats.

She was being pursued.

She spun around and cried out. In the darkness she could see a figure clad in a dark cloak, riding hard, bearing down upon her. The cloak flew in the breeze, and in the darkness it seemed that the horse and the figure were one. A giant dragon, bearing down upon her, seeking her.

The cliffs needed blood. Creeghan needed blood. And she was being pursued, the sacrifice to obtain it.

"No!" she cried out with terror. The dragon rider had

seen her. He had known where she was, and he had ridden straight to her, and now he saw her.

She turned again, stumbling in the darkness, and started to run. The hoofbeats came closer and closer. Her breath rose raggedly against her breast, and came from her in gasping little sobs.

The figure was shouting to her, but she couldn't hear, the thunder of her heart was so great.

She swore. She would fight, fight, until the very end, but they were right upon her, almost trampling her. She screamed, trying to zigzag.

Then the rider leapt from the horse, and flung itself upon her back, and she was screaming again, and falling. Falling forever, it seemed, into a rich carpet of the green, green grass.

Hands were upon her. Strong, powerful hands. Trying to grasp her. She screamed and thrashed, flailing and kicking. A weight bore down heavily upon her and she was imprisoned by a searing heat, enwrapped and entangled within the huge and engulfing folds of a dark cloak.

"No!" she shrieked. "Please!"

"Martise! Martise!"

She went still at the sound of her name and stared into the face of her captor. Dark hair, ebony with the night, fell down upon a broad forehead, and gleaming, shimmering eyes of fire stared into hers.

Bryan's eyes . . .

"Dear God!" she cried out, and she tried again to struggle free, to leap away.

But his thighs locked around her, his hands caught upon her wrists hard, and he held her beneath him. "Nay, lady, nay. This night you are mine. 'Tis time to return you to Creeghan, milady. The castle awaits you."

Twelve

❦

"No!"

In utter panic, she shrieked the word again. Her eyes were wild and she trembled desperately.

Shaken by the deep-seated terror in her voice, Bryan sat back on his haunches. "Martise! We're going to leave the forest—it's all right. You're not lost anymore. I've come to take you home."

"No, no, no! I'll not feed the cliffs with my blood! I'll not be the one within the walls. I'll not let you—"

"Shh, shh!" he whispered gently. He shifted his weight from her and wrapped her warmly into his arms. She tried briefly to struggle, but she was already exhausted and he held her tight, smoothing back her hair. "It's all right. I am here."

"You're one of them!" she cried. Pulling back, she studied his eyes. Her voice trembled. "One of the figures within the copse. In the cloaks. Coming after me, to kill me."

He shook his head, alarmed that she seemed so terrified of him. In all of the time that they had held their separate suspicions, in all of the time that they had danced around one another with their knowledge and their wonderings, she had never been afraid like this. Of him.

"I have not been in the woods, lass. I came when Jemie told me that you had ridden out and that the mare had come back without you. One can be lost on these cliffs and rocks and moors quite easily, as you have discovered, Martise."

She pushed away from the strength of his chest. "I was not lost! I came upon a meeting. A devil's den . . . something! In the copse. And you were there—oh, no! Please, God, tell me that you were not there! Make me believe you." She had risen, and stared down at him now, and whatever else about her was a lie, her distress was very real.

He stood, facing her. "I was with no meeting in the glen, Martise. I came here after you. Now, if there was some meeting out here, I've a need to know of it."

Her eyes were liquid, her lips were starting to tremble again. She shook her head, then she waved a hand behind her. "I took a side trail and then I came to a copse. And . . . and they were all there. Maybe ten of them, maybe twelve. I don't know. They were all wearing that same cloak. I tried to listen to what they were saying and I couldn't really hear them but it was something about Creeghan and the full moon and, I think, All Hallows' Eve."

"Twelve," he murmured. "The number for a coven."

"Witchcraft!" she cried.

He shook his head ruefully. "I don't know. I don't think so, even here, in the Highlands. Unless the coven hides something even more sinister." He took a step toward her, and she gasped, leaping away. He felt his own fingers tremble. He had wanted to tell her about what he now knew. But not tonight. Not now. She was like a badly scalded cat, afraid of being burned again. Smudges of dirt marred her face, and her hair was wild and free in a magical tangle that was incredibly sensual in the verdant forest. Her eyes were huge and startlingly blue against the dirt and the darkness.

Tension seemed to have sprung taut and heavy on the air. He had to ease the fear. Had to touch her.

"Martise," he said very softly, "come here." She did not make a move, but stood poised like a young doe, beautiful, wired, ready to run. He reached out a hand to her, and the softness of his burr rang gently with his words. "I swear to you, I was not within these woods tonight until I came for you. I will not hurt you. Come to me, lass, and take my hand. I will bring you safe home."

Her eyes were upon his, so blue, so liquid, so tormented. She raised her hand slowly, very slowly, until just their fingers touched. And they stood there so, while the wind picked up the tendrils of her hair and whipped his cloak about him. Then some choked-out sound escaped her and she was in his arms, held there close against his chest, feeling the sure beat of his heart with her damp cheeks. He stroked her hair for long moments, then touched her cheeks and smiled down at her as her head fell back and her eyes met his once again. "It's all right. I swear, it shall be all right." His fingers moved over the smudges. "I'll bring you to the brook," he murmured. He did not expect her to walk. He swept her up into his arms, and she was silent as he walked with her.

The laird of Creeghan knew its forests, knew the trails of green darkness, even in the night. It seemed that they moved not at all, or moved just briefly, their gazes still locked, his arms strong about her, her fingers entwined about his neck.

She heard then the soft and melodic rush of the brook, and the sound mingled with that of the night breeze rustling through the leaves and the trees. It no longer seemed a frightening place, but rather an Eden of green and sweetly secretive magic.

Some inner voice warned her that he might have been among the figures in the cove, he might be lying, he might be the very essence of evil.

But she could not believe that, not in her heart. Not when

he held her, not when his eyes touched hers. Not when the moon, very nearly full, rose high above them and the world was blanketed in a kelly-green splendor. Not when the softness of the breeze caressed her face, and his hands were so tender upon her.

He laid her down in the thick carpet of grasses by the narrow tumbling brook. He swept off his cloak and set it out beside her, then drew his scarf from about his throat and soaked it in the cool waters. He hunched down upon the balls of his feet to smooth the scarf over the smudges on her face, and smiled when they were gone. He took her hands into his own and, turning them over, bathed the palms. When he was done, he kissed each finger gently. The searing moist heat of his kiss swept through her, and into her being, into her blood, eliciting, demanding a response. Their eyes met. He sat upon the cloak and pulled her into his arms. And then it was her mouth that he sought with his lips. His kiss was tender and coercive. His mouth moved subtly against hers and he broke away and kissed the corners of her lips and her eyelids and her cheek and her throat. His tongue gently teased the lobe of her ear, and the hot breath that accompanied the sensual play awoke and aroused her anew. His teeth grazed softly across her lower lip before his tongue plunged deeply into her mouth, stripping away the last of her defenses, passion taking away the soft stroke of tenderness.

He bore her down to the verdant earth upon his cloak, and there he kissed her again, his fingers splaying out the lush bronze beauty of her hair against the darkness of the garment. She trembled slightly, and he rose above her, promising, "It is all right. I am here."

"Even into the darkness of the night," she murmured. Her mouth curled into a soft and wistful smile, her lips damp from his kiss, the curve of them so inviting that he shuddered violently with the sudden, gripping force of longing.

"Forever into the darkness of the night," he vowed. His

eyes remained upon hers while he slowly unclasped the frog
hooks of her bodice and loosed the ribbons of the chemise
she wore beneath. The fullness of her breasts spilled out
over the bone of her corset, the globes of perfection of
alabaster and ivory in the soft glow, the nipples and aureolas
blush-dark and hardened and as enticing as any sweetly
forbidden fruit. And again his hand trembled as he moved it
over her flesh, the palm connecting with the nipple first, his
fingers closing over the rise of flesh, his thumb coursing its
naked beauty. Her breath rose quickly, soft, sighing gasps.
Her eyes remained upon his. He cupped her breast within
his hand and lowered his head and slowly, slowly suckled
the hard rose crest into his mouth, bathing it with his
tongue, drawing upon it with a greater and greater strength
that brought a soft moaning sound from deep within her to
mingle with the melodies of the wind and the brook.

Her fingers moved into his hair, entangling within it,
smoothing out the ebony locks. He wondered how he could
touch her there, there, upon her breast, and yet she could
feel it, the heat of it, shimmering down the length of her
body, warming it, setting it alive, and igniting that secret
place between her thighs. A place where fire now burned,
where the night and the green magic had entered, where she
knew she must be touched and fulfilled.

And she would be . . .

Even as his lips caressed her, his hands moved upon her.
Her skirt slid against her thighs. His fingers found the tie to
her pantalettes and his hand delved beneath her clothing.
His touch played over her belly, and below. She gasped as
he found the dampness at her center, teasing, caressing, so
softly it might have been the breeze, so knowingly that she
burned anew, and shifted against him, wanting more of
him.

His eyes rose above hers and he watched her face in the
moonlight, the color of her eyes, the hurried, desperate
catch of her breath. He moaned raggedly and took her lips
with his own again, and even as he did so, the stroke of his

touch moved suddenly hard and deep, deep within her. He caressed her with a rhythm, building upon the sweetness of the rhythm, then brushed and stroked the tiny bud nestled between her loins.

Her moans were no longer soft, but something sweet and wild that rose against the green magic of the night. Her head tossed, sending the copper beauty of her hair in a sunlit rain to pour down upon them and between them.

He rose above her, fumbling with his breeches. Her eyes closed then, but he hesitated, hesitated with the burning in his loins so strong he could scarce maintain it, and yet, when he lowered himself over her, he forced the pulsing tip of the rod to hold still at the soft and wet and welcoming portals. And her eyes opened at last, and a soft blush filled her features and he smiled. "Tell me, lady, do you welcome me as a lover?"

She groaned, and her arms wound around him and she murmured, "Must we speak . . . oh, please . . ."

"Aye, and we must," he whispered tenderly, and nuzzled her throat, yet moved just a sweet and fiery thrust against her. "I'd not be some beast of Creeghan, or of the night, or of the forest. I'd be welcomed love, aye, even here, and I'd have your eyes upon me as I make us as one."

Indeed her eyes were upon him, very wide, as blue as heaven and the surefire promise of eternal delight. And she managed something of a smile and murmured, "Beast, dragon, lover, demon of the darkness, aye, laird of Creeghan, I welcome you!"

His lip curled slowly, and then he thrust, full and strong against her, moving the full erotic length and hardness of himself deep within her, so deep with that single stroke that she cried out, stunned and sweetly shattered, reaching a little crest with the simple movement. And his eyes burned down on her, glowing golden with pleasure and a certain wickedness, and he began to move again and again, and she did not think that she could take it all, that she would tear and shatter and die, and still the sensation was delight in the extreme, anguish and beauty, and she felt that he reached within her to touch her to the heart. She locked her limbs about him, and her nails raked down his shirt, and he swept her so high that she beat against his chest, nearly sobbing. But he pressed her back to the ground and promised that they had just begun. The thunder of his body seemed to fill the earth beneath her, and the rhythm of his love collided and cascaded with the night and all its magic. And she soared again, this time reaching for a peak that spiraled and curled deliciously within her, and she cried with both the agony and the splendor as the sweet, sating climax burst upon her, raining down in a shower of nectar, so volatile that the darkness closed around her for endless moments as she shuddered with the startling aftermath. Consciousness was gone; perhaps she had died with the pleasure. But then she could feel. Feel the earth, and inhale the verdance of the green ground, and the rich masculine scent that was the man. Her lover.

Dimly she heard his cry and felt the great rocking chasms as he reached his own climax. Hoarse and breathless, he murmured against her ear, his great body thrusting against hers again and once again, and the sweetness of his seed warming her body as it spilled heavy and hot within her. His fingers curled within her hair, and as she opened her eyes against the darkness that had claimed her, she met the golden probing force of his own, and she cried out once again, looping her arms around him and pressing her cheek tightly against the fabric of his shirt.

He shifted his weight from her, but brought her curled against his form. He stroked her hair as their heartbeats slowed, as the frantic pace of their breathing ebbed.

And the sounds of the night came alive once again. From somewhere nearby, an owl hooted out his ancient wisdom. The ever-bubbling brook seemed closer and louder. And the wind, the ever-present wind of Creeghan, rose whistling against the trees.

"You are," he murmured, his fingertips stroking back the

hair at her crown, "the most beautiful creature I have ever seen."

Her eyes opened, crystal and blue, upon him. "But I am not a creature, Laird Creeghan. I am nothing more than a woman while you, sir, are the dragon, the beast, the creature of night and day, of the sun, and more, the moon."

He smiled. "Alas, none of the above. A man very simply myself, and it is something that you must know."

She shivered suddenly and he wrapped his arm more tightly about her.

"I should take you home," he said, and there was a tone of regret to his words. He didn't want to face the light himself. There was wonder here, kelly-green, forest-green, night-green wonder and magic, and they were bound to lose it by the garish light of lamps or candles, or that blinding, truthful light of day.

"I'm all right," she whispered, and she rolled up to sit upon her haunches, plucking at the strands of grass and leaves that were tangled within her hair and clothing.

He rose himself and came down on his knee beside her. "Let me help," he said.

She met his eyes, smiling. "I'm afraid there are leaves in my shoe." He untied her boot and pulled it from her foot. He meant to empty it and return it to her foot, but he did not. He reached for her other leg and caught hold of her ankle and freed her from the second boot. She watched him, but did not protest.

She had thought that she could feel no more—not that night. He had touched her inside and out, and surely she could feel no more. But her breath caught as he slid his hands along her thighs, finding her garters, stripping down her stockings. "Leaves," he told her solemnly. His fingers feathered over her naked flesh. She could feel. Beyond a doubt, she could feel. Silvery tremors snaked along her spine, and warmth was reborn within her.

The breeze stirred as she met his eyes. They were silent and still, and then she rose, and found the hook to her skirt and undid it, and the velvet riding garment fell to the earth. She tossed aside her bodice and chemise and stays and then stepped demurely from her disarrayed pantalettes.

The wind struck against her naked body. She leaned her head back and she felt it. Felt the moon kiss down upon her and the whispers of the air as they plucked at her hair and played it around her.

He watched her, naked and straight, and proud against the night and the wind. And he thought that she was a match, indeed.

For himself.

For Creeghan.

She stepped aside him and came to her knees at the brook, scooping up the cool water and delighting in the feel as she let it fall upon her, creating succulent, shimmering pearl drops upon her breasts in the moonlight. She turned around and smiled at him. "There's little I can still claim to be," she said softly, "and yet it amazes me that we have . . . done what we have done, and done so almost fully clad. Milord . . ."

She looked back to the water, and yet . . .

The invitation was there. Not to be denied. He rose and cast off his shirt and his boots in a flurry, and stripped down his breeches and discarded his hose in seconds.

When she looked back, he was naked and magnificent in the moonlight. And as her eyes fell from his to his dark furred chest and below, she felt her heart begin to thump again. Aye, it was possible to arouse anew. Even after what they had just shared.

He strode to her, confident, a great forest beast with his glittering fire eyes and hard-muscled form. He pulled her up, naked, in his arms, and where their flesh met, it burned. "What we have done," he murmured, "is make love. And what we're going to do," he added softly, "is make love again."

He started to wrap his arms around her, and yet she eluded him, slipping beneath his hold and coming around to his back. There was so much she longed to do. And only now, tonight, in this green darkness, did she dare. She slipped her arms around his waist and moved her lips over his shoulders, and as she did so, the peaks of her breasts moved over his bare flesh. He was still, allowing her to explore. She slipped lower against him, stroking her fingertips upward against the harness of his buttocks while the seduction of her kiss traveled down the length of his spine. She heard his jagged breath, and then he cried out, catching her arms, pulling her around before him again and into the heady demand of his kiss. Yet even then, when their lips broke, she would have her way. Her eyes met his.

Dear God, she knew exactly what she was doing, what she wanted to do. She could be so wanton . . .

She met his eyes, and she moved slowly downward against him again, brushing his flesh with her hair, with her breasts, with the softest caress of her lips and teeth. Downward, downward, until she was on her knees. She longed to take that pulsing shaft of life into her mouth . . .

And she did. Savoring it, savoring the wicked shudder and spasms and hoarse cries that claimed him. And she relished the sweet victory of her own power, and loved him, uninhibitedly, stroking, touching, tasting.

He wrenched her up and into his arms, and his eyes were wildly ablaze. She cried out as he nearly dragged her to the ground and thrust into her, hard, careless, magnificent, and wild. And he moved with the wind again, bringing her to a startling precipice that brought tears to her eyes.

Then he withdrew, and she was lost and confused and aching. She opened her eyes seeking him, but gasped when she felt his hands upon her knees, drawing her to him, lifting her, and making love again with the searing wet heat of his tongue. He teased and licked her until the stars shattered above her head, and she passed out once again.

She awoke in his arms, awoke to the thunder of his fierce lovemaking. Awoke to his kiss, awoke to climb and soar and reach across the heavens again. And when he exploded within her, it brought about her second shattering peak, and even as she drifted down from the ecstasy of it, she felt the racking waves of his body, tight against her own.

This time, she could not look at him, dared not acknowledge all the intimacy that lay between them. She turned to her side, facing the brook. But he was not a man to let her be, not a man to allow denial.

He drew her back around to face him, and in those curious moments, there might have been no Castle Creeghan, no mystery, no death—no world, in fact, other than that which lay between them this night.

"Martise!"

He lifted her chin to his. At last she opened her eyes. And he smiled.

"You must not be ashamed," he told her.

"I'm not!" she lied.

"Most men wait an entire lifetime, and never know a beauty such as you have shown."

"I—let me go, please. I cannot talk about it!" she cried in dismay.

His eyes were intense, golden. "Nay, if you choose it so, I'll not talk. But I beg this of you, Martise, don't let the night slip away. Don't hide from the magic. We've discovered it here. In shadow, in darkness. I'll not let you take it from me."

She shivered violently and moistened her lips to speak. "My dear Laird Creeghan, I am lying naked on your cloak in the woods, so there is little I can deny."

"But, alas, I cannot *keep* you naked in the woods," he said, and grinned. "It's quite cold, and when the fires of our bodies have diminished, you are going to want your clothing."

She flushed. "I am cold now."

"I will warm you—"

"You have warmed me well and enough!" she vowed, and he laughed when she rolled to escape him. She hurried to the water, shivering with greater violence as she tried to rinse herself with it. She didn't hear his footsteps, but he was quickly at her side, comfortable with his nakedness. He hunched down beside her and touched her chin. "Martise, I cannot be washed away," he told her gently.

"I know. I did not mean to. I mean—" She broke off, and he laughed, and splashed his face with the water, seemingly oblivious to the cold. It grew with the night. With the shriek of the wind.

He stood and left her, and she splashed her breasts and her arms. When she turned, he was already clad in his hose and breeches and boots again, and awaited with her chemise, ready to slip it over her damp breasts. He did so without saying a word, then turned aside for his shirt as she found her stays and stockings, her pantalettes, skirt, and bodice. When she had gotten that far, she realized that he stood waiting with her riding boots, and he knelt down to slip them upon her feet, tying the laces for her. He stood and swept his cloak from the ground and shook it free of leaves, and then wrapped it around her shoulders.

"You have nothing now," she told him.

"Ah, but I am still afire, Martise St. James," he told her. "And I fear that I will burn for all eternity. Come, let's find Lucian. He'd best not have headed back without us!"

The animal waited behind the trees where Bryan had left him. He munched grass and stared soulfully at Bryan, then ambled toward him.

"There's a lad for you now," he said, proud of the horse. "Come, I'll boost you up, Martise."

He mounted up behind her, and she realized that she was warm again, and very glad to rest against him. Bryan led the horse into no brisk pace, but allowed him to walk along sedately, by the light of the moon and the stars.

"Bryan, I swear that I saw what I saw," she told him then. The memory of the night was still with her. It would always be with her.

But so would the memory of the day.

"I believe you, Martise," he said after a moment. Then he reined in and asked her, "You believe that I was not among them?"

She nodded. He nudged the horse and they moved forward again. "Bryan, once before you told me that you had never murdered."

"Aye," he said.

She twisted around, meeting his eyes. "But you have killed," she said softly.

"In the war, Martise. That is what happens in war—men kill one another."

The sound of his voice was bitter. "Why did you fight?" she asked him. "It was not your battle."

She felt his shrug. "I fought because I was there, and because I was among friends, because a man cannot run when the battle comes to the door of a friend and you are staying within that door. And I stayed when it was lost because . . . because it was necessary to see it through to the end."

She hesitated. "Bryan, if you have come home, where is Elaina's fiancé?"

"I don't know," he told her. "I just don't know. Niall was taken prisoner at Gettysburg. I have friends searching for him, but no one has heard from him since."

"Oh, my God," Martise said. "Then he is dead. Surely, he is dead. The prison camps—"

"I survived a summer in a Georgia camp," he told her roughly. "Niall might well be alive. Don't bury him on Elaina until it must be done."

"But she must know—"

"Nay, you must know. She loved him. Elaina loves fiercely, and completely, with all of her heart. She will wait forever, if need be."

"But she should not!" Martise said. "By God, can no one in your house be happy?" she demanded, twisting around to see his face.

"We all have moments," he told her. "Moments. Such as

tonight." His eyes were glittering, and not upon her, but staring straight at the trail ahead. She felt a blinding of tears dampen her lashes and she swung back around.

Moments . . .

They were leaving the green magic behind them, the shadows of the night. And the moment was over.

She blinked back the tears. "I shall have more than moments!" she announced coldly. "I pity Elaina, for she has lost one brother, a fiancé, and must live beneath your thumb!"

"You will live beneath my thumb, too, my love. Are you forgetting our forthcoming nuptials?"

"Indeed, I am, for they shall be entirely forgettable. They will not be real, milord—"

"But they will. By law. For the moment."

"Then I'll not—" she began, but he had suddenly reined in Lucian and gone tense. Fear—gone so long from her now!—invaded her system once again. "What is it?" she asked tensely.

"The cove—this must be the cove. Stay here," he told her. He leapt down from the horse.

"Bryan! Bryan, no!" she cried. But he was gone. In the moonlight she could see him hurrying through the trees. She saw only the darkness of his form as he paused and kicked aside the remnants of a fire. He stood very still for several moments.

She started to breathe again, realizing she had held it from the second he had left her.

He strode back for the horse and leapt up behind her. "Aye, there was something there. A group of some kind." He nudged the stallion into a smooth, slow canter. The gait brought them quickly to the main road, and once they were upon it, he slowed again. They were nearly to the castle.

"Why do you deny witchcraft?" she asked softly. "Your people are superstitious. I think that they do still believe in ancient gods and prophesies and—"

"Martise, would you turn the whole of a good and

God-fearing people into a clan of murderous lunatics? Aye, they have their quirks, and we have our games, and we tell tales by the full moon. But none is practicing witchcraft. Not sacrificing maidens and the like, and all. And besides, if they needed a maiden, you'd not fit the bill a single bit."

She wanted to hit him. " 'Tis only been recent," she murmured, and added indignantly, "I came as a widow—"

"Aye, 'twas your mistake. Had I believed in your purity, you might still maintain it."

"Really?" she demanded, tossing back her head. "Would anything have stopped the laird of the castle from his desires?"

"We'll never know, will we?" he cross-queried, and she felt the warmth of his gaze, and the laughter within his words.

"You should be slapped."

"You've tried oft enough," he reminded her.

"Take care. One day I shall succeed."

"Indeed, perhaps you will. And yet, I wonder, here I am offering a perfect solution. I wish to wed you for reasons of my own, perhaps you should wish to wed me as well. After all, mistress, you have been seduced, debauched, some might say. And marriage is the customary remedy for such a thing."

She stiffened. The walls of the castle tower rose before her. Lucian walked them ever closer.

She lifted up on the pommel, turning to him. "Your reasons, and my own, milord, are not the right ones!"

"They're not?" he demanded.

"You wish a wife for bait to catch a killer—"

"I wish your safety, I swear that!" he said heatedly, his eyes narrowing.

"Aye, you intend to keep your bait safe!" she snapped back.

"I would think you'd want to catch the killer," he said.

"I do! But it is not a reason for marriage."

"But what of the destruction of your innocence?" he queried politely. There was a hard edge to his voice.

"Oh, I should learn to live with it, milord. It is not the right reason for marriage!"

"And what is?" he demanded.

"Love," she returned, her eyes on his. Then she leapt down from the horse.

He could have stopped her then. It seemed that he chose not to.

"Good night, Laird Creeghan," she told him.

"Good night? Is that all?"

"Indeed."

"Ah, well, perhaps I can be more eloquent. Good night—and thank you. Mistress, I have never known such a lover," he said gallantly . . . and mockingly.

She turned quickly on her heel, her hair and his cloak flying out around her. She entered the great hall and found that Elaina had been there, all this time, waiting for her.

"Martise! Oh, we were all so distressed. My brother was beside himself, thinking that you were missing. But he found you!"

She accepted Elaina's hug. "Oh, yes, he found me," she said.

"You're shivering. I'll tell Holly that you're home. There'll be a warm bath in minutes. Brandy, I must get you some brandy. Hogarth! Martise has come home. Bring something quickly, please!"

And Hogarth did bring something quickly, his warmed wine with cinnamon, and a huge lamb chop with mint jelly and potatoes and greens. To her surprise, she was famished. She thanked Hogarth and told Elaina only that she had wandered in the woods, and yes, the laird of Creeghan was home, too, but she did not know why he had not come in.

"Probably seeing to that stallion of his himself," Elaina told her, and poured her more wine. "Oh, I was so very worried! You mustn't frighten us like that again, Martise. Please!"

"I didn't mean to frighten anyone, truly," she said. "I just needed to go riding."

"Well, Robert said he warned you to stay to the main roads, but he knew you intended to take the trails."

"He did, did he?"

"Aye, he told Bruce that he could see it in your eyes, and Bruce rather angrily agreed that you liked to defy people."

Martise flushed. "That's not true." She stared down at her plate. Robert! Robert McCloud with his evil, knowing grin! Had he known that she was in the woods . . . because he had been in them himself?

She shivered and Elaina leapt up. "Come on, I'm sure your bath is ready by now. I'll walk you up."

Holly was within the room, adding the last of the water. She welcomed Martise back warmly, with tears in her eyes. Martise hugged her maid and promised that she would be very careful in the future.

Both women would have stayed; Martise shooed them out, wanting, needing, to be alone.

She stripped away her clothing and sank into the bath. The steam whirled around her, and she luxuriated in the sweet-smelling rose soap that Holly always remembered to bring her.

You cannot wash me away . . .

He had told her that. And she knew that she could not.

Nor did she want to. No matter what came in the future, she did not want to forget. She knew herself that what they had shared was extraordinary.

Was it because she was in love with him? Or was there something else that ruled such things? Was passion her own mistress?

It did not matter. Just as she had been famished, she was exhausted. She leaned against the bath and closed her eyes. When she opened them, she nearly screamed. He was back in the room, leaning against the mantel, watching her. His eyes were fire, his hair was still tousled, and he was very nonchalant and entirely too comfortable and casual in his stance. "Shh!" he warned.

"I should scream!" she hissed to him angrily. "How dare you dance in and out of a guest's room—"

"I didn't 'dance.' I came by the secret passage."

"Damn your secret passages!"

"I merely wish that I knew them all!" he returned.

She groped for her towel and drew it to her breast as she stood.

There was no reason to hold a towel against him. None at all. They both knew it; his mocking gaze conveyed it. But he made no comment about it, merely stepping toward her. And when she would have cried in protest, thinking that he meant to snatch it away, he merely pulled it up higher upon her shoulders.

She jerked away and almost toppled over the tub. "What are you doing in here?" she demanded breathlessly as he righted her.

An ebony brow shot up. "I warned you that I would be your shadow."

She trembled. She needed to be away from him so badly, and he was back here with her. And when she stood naked and wet, the memories were almost more than she could bear.

She shook her head strenuously. "I don't want you in here. Not tonight. Maybe not any night. I'm not denying anything that has happened, I'm just not ready for it to happen again. You have to go. Please. I—I will not make love with you again!"

His lips curled in a very slow, taunting smile. "I did not come to make love, Martise." He walked away from her and tossed her the nightgown that Holly had set out for her. It fell to her feet, and she stared down at it stupidly. "Put it on!" he ordered hoarsely.

She hated to obey him, hated to obey anything that he said. But she reached down and secured the gown. The towel fell as she slipped the gown over her head.

Her eyes met his again.

He had not looked away. He walked over to the door and tried the bolt, then went to the balcony doors and assured himself that they, too, were secure.

Then he strode back into the room. She still stared at him. He smiled and swept an arm toward her bed. "You bade me good night before. I imagine that you are tired. Please, don't let me keep you awake."

She didn't move. He was in the process of stripping off his shirt.

"What are you doing?" she demanded anxiously.

"I'm going to take a bath."

"Here?"

"Well, the tub is here. And the water is still steaming. And it was quite cold out there." His shirt fell to the floor.

"You've got your own very elegant bath!" she reminded him. "You're the master of Creeghan, remember?"

"I remember. You seem to forget," he taunted. Then his patience seemed to leave him. "Go to bed, Martise. I'm going to take a bath and sleep in the chair. I'll not disturb you or awake you. But I will be here."

"Your cloak is downstairs, if that is what you're looking for," she grated.

"Thank you—and I do not need my cloak at the moment. Now, if you will, Martise, please go to bed. Tomorrow promises to be a very long day. And for this evening, I am going to be here."

She didn't move. She stared at him. He couldn't just come in here like this and stay!

But it seemed he had determined that he could.

He pulled off his boots and started with his breeches. He smiled. "Martise, one more time. I will be here—whether you like it or not."

She fled across the room, leapt into the bed, and pulled the covers to her chin. She heard a whisper of air as his breeches fell, and then she heard him sigh with pleasure as he stepped into the warmth of the tub.

She closed her eyes, but she heard him still. Bathing, resting, luxuriating in the water.

Her water. It wasn't fair.

He couldn't stay forever!

"You know," she said primly from beneath her covers, "you can't wash me away."

She didn't dare look at him, but she could sense his slow smile.

"But I'm not trying to wash you away," he said softly. And then there was silence.

Minutes later, she heard him rise. Heard him drying himself before the fire.

Then she felt the coverlet being drawn from her bed and she tensed.

He had lied! He was going to come sweeping down beside her!

But he did not.

Even as she clenched her eyes tightly closed, she heard him move across to the chair and settle within it.

Hours later, she dared to open her eyes to see him there. Her body trembled. If he had touched her, she thought with amazement, she would have easily fallen into his arms.

Yet . . .

Even this was good. Just having him there was good.

She closed her eyes and pulled the covers back up, and in time, she slept, a smile curving her lips, her sleep as peaceful as that of a child.

Because he watched over her, by night. Until the morning's light . . .

And yet, if she had only known what the morning would bring—the tempest and the anger—her dreams might have never been so sweet.

Thirteen

◈

In the morning, he was gone.

Martise had very much expected to find him in her room when she awoke, but she was alone. She dressed quickly and hurried down to the great hall.

It was early, and though the rest of the family was in the hall, Bryan was nowhere in sight. Elaina was at the table, stirring sugar into her tea. Ian was across from her, and Conar and Peter were at the buffet, preparing plates.

Peter looked up as she came in. "Ah, lass, and good mornin' to ye! We heard ye had a bit of trouble last night, so it's good ta see that you seem well enough from the episode. 'Twas the forest ye were lost in, eh?"

"Yes, it was the forest," she said, coming toward the table.

"A dangerous place at night," Peter said.

Ian chuckled and rose, pulling out a chair for Martise. She smiled and allowed him to seat her as he said, "Dangerous! For our Lady St. James? I think not! The beasties and goblins had best beware when she walks about! Shall I get you tea?" he inquired.

"Please."

"I should have been quite terrified," Elaina said. "I might well have died of fright. Like Mary."

"Elaina!" A voice came sharply from the stairway. Martise twisted around to see that Bryan was joining them. His dark hair was smoothly combed back, and he was immaculate in black breeches and frock. His eyes were upon his sister, and they barely skimmed over Martise as he strode across the floor to her.

He set his hands upon Elaina's shoulders. "Elaina, you must not think that."

His sister's lips trembled as she stared down at the table. "She died in the crypts. She fell in the crypts. She saw something down there."

Ian reached across the table, his fingers curling around hers. "Elaina, come! You know that the dead don't rise! The tales about the castle are for the village children. There are no ghosts that roam the halls."

Elaina looked suddenly to Martise. She seemed stricken. "Martise! I'm so sorry. I didn't mean to open the wounds. I don't know anything, truly I don't. I just miss her, you see, and I was so very worried about you last night."

She smiled at Elaina. "You did not hurt me, Elaina, truly." She cast a defiant glance to Bryan. "Usually, I am not frightened by forests."

"Usually?" Ian said, his eyes dancing. "Usually. What happened? Did you come upon an altar in the woods? A ghost, a creature, a fanged beast?"

Bryan's eyes were narrowed sharply upon her. Martise tossed her head back and smiled brilliantly at Ian. "More than that, Ian. I came upon a cult."

"A cult!" Conar exclaimed. Martise thought that he looked down the table, at his brother, his cousin, and his father—with fear. But she couldn't be sure.

"Come, tell us!" Ian urged her mischievously.

"She saw things in the darkness, nothing more," Bryan stated, irritated.

"Aye, 'tis green out there, is it not? Why, the man with

the very stoutest of hearts might well imagine things," he said, and winked at Martise. "But do tell us, what did you see?"

"Martise—" Bryan began.

She pretended that she did not hear him. He was not her keeper, no matter what he seemed to think.

And something was going on here. He wanted her to be the bait for the killer at Castle Creeghan. She might as well begin to play the game this way.

"I came upon a very strange grouping in the forest," she told Ian earnestly. "They had formed a circle around a fire, and they were all dressed in dark capes."

"Witchcraft!" Elaina whispered in horror.

"So one might think," Martise agreed.

"Ah, but if it was a coven of witches and warlocks," Ian said, "then there is devil worship hereabouts. We must thank God that they did not see you, for devil worshipers are known for extremely ghastly deeds."

"Oh, but they did see me," Martise announced simply, sitting back and sipping her tea. From the end of the table, she could almost feel the heat and strength of Bryan's anger.

"They saw you?" Conar said, startled. "And then what?"

"They chased me, of course," Martise said. "But I did manage to reach Desdemona, and gallop deep enough into the forest so that they could not find me."

"And then . . . ?" Ian said.

"And then that rogue mare tripped and deposited me upon the ground and returned home without me," she said with a smile, and Ian laughed.

"And the laird of Creeghan rode into the darkness and rescued you, his fair damsel in distress. 'Tis wonderful, the very stuff of legends."

" 'Tis not wonderful!" Conar exploded, rising. "Cults are dangerous. Witchcraft has risen its head in Scotland oft enough, and 'tis never anything but frightful."

"Come, Conar!" Peter said. "We've not burned ourselves a witch here since the early 1700's."

"Aye, Father, and that's true." He rose and looked around the table. "But the practice is dangerous, nonetheless. Down Glasgow way just a few years ago there were a group decided they were the devil's own. You know of this, Bruce. Several lasses were slain on white stone altars— given up to the demon god."

"But in Creeghan, the laird is akin to the god—be he heavenly or sent straight from hell," Peter commented. He shrugged. "I think ye should look into it, Bruce."

"Indeed, I intend to," Bryan replied, and Martise felt his eyes upon her, hot with the fury he leashed in his voice.

Peter swung around to Martise, wagging a finger at her. "And ye, lassie, ye must take greater care. There are them what believe in the supernatural, and so forth. Why, Jemie, that poor daft stable boy of ours, believes that the dead of Creeghan rise every night! He slips in to assure himself at times that the gates in the crypts are locked, lest the dead rise and escape their ghostly boundaries. There's just no telling what goes on in the minds of men. No more excursions into the forest, lass!"

"She won't be riding out, I can guarantee it," Bryan said softly. Then he rose. "I'm into the village. I shouldna be late for supper." He stepped by Martise, then his hands touched her shoulders and he bent down behind her. His kiss brushed her neck. "Take care, my love. Elaina will be with you through the day."

And then he was gone. Conar announced that they had to get to work, and Ian grudgingly agreed, smiling at Martise. "'Tis interesting ye've made things, since ye've come, Martise St. James. The ghosts had best beware." He winked to her and followed his brother from the hall. Martise felt Peter watching her, and she looked up to see that his eyes were, indeed, intently upon her. She smiled and rose, and Elaina, too, got to her feet.

"I thought we might spend the morning in the library," she told Martise.

"Pardon?" Martise said.

"Well, I'm not to leave you, my brother's orders." A look of dismay and anger must have crossed Martise's features for Elaina quickly continued, "I am sorry, but I do promise to be entertaining. Oh, please, Martise, spending the day with me cannot be that bad a fate!"

"Elaina, I did not say that it was a bad fate at all!" Martise assured her. It is Bryan who seems to be my sorry fate! she thought.

She had no plans. Not today. She had cast out her story about the coven in the woods, and there was nothing to do but wait.

Wait . . .

For what?

Someone within the castle was in on the secrets. And she would not allow herself to believe that it was Bryan. And if it was not, then it had to be Peter or Ian or Conar . . .

Or Elaina.

No. She refused to believe it of Elaina, too. "I'd like to fetch a shawl, then I'll meet you there. You do mean Bry—the laird's library by my room?"

"Aye," Elaina told her.

She smiled at Peter and turned toward the stairs. She started up them, still feeling his eyes upon her. When she reached her room, she was shivering. She opened the armoire to search for a shawl, and as she did so, there was a rapping upon her door.

Without thinking she called, "Come in!"

She expected Holly or Elaina, but was surprised to turn around and see that Peter stood in her doorway. He stepped into the room and closed the door behind him. And then he strode toward her and gripped her by the shoulders.

"Lass, ye must take very grave care!" he said intently.

"Peter, what—"

"I don't know what, lass, only that the wind blows very cold, and that ships wreck in from the sea, and that strange lights and haunts do roam this castle. Ye canna be safe, not with the laird, not with anyone. When the wind blows, and the moon rides high, ye must bolt yer doors, and close yer eyes, and bring the covers close to yer throat. Ye must do this, and forget all else."

"Peter, what are you telling me?" she demanded, frustrated.

"Stay far from the crypt, Martise St. James. Perhaps Jemie has the truth of it. Perhaps the dead of Castle Creeghan do walk the halls at the night. Perhaps they seek souls to bear down to hell along with them, I know not. I only know what I'm telling ye—when the moon rises, stay safe within yer room. Do you ken, girl?"

"I understand that you're worried, but you have to tell me more, Peter, please! I—"

He lifted a finger to his lips, and she fell silent. They could both hear footsteps beyond the door.

He bowed to her suddenly. "I've work meself. Have a pleasant day, milady."

"Peter, wait!" she cried, but he was gone. Her door closed as he left, and when she followed after him and opened it, he was halfway down the hall, almost to the stairs.

She moved back into her room, found her shawl, and curled her fingers around it. Peter knew something. He had come to warn her. And he would not say all that he knew. Because, she thought, to do so would be to condemn someone that he loved. Ian or Conar, his sons.

Or the laird of the castle himself.

The shawl did not help. She was still shivering when she hurried from her room to the one beside it. Elaina was already there, sitting before a new and crackling fire, her fingers busy with embroidery.

She looked at Martise anxiously. "I was just beginning to worry about you."

Martise walked over to Elaina and knelt down before her. "Elaina, why would you worry about me in broad daylight, right here, in the castle?"

Elaina's beautiful eyes seemed to cloud. "There is no

reason, Martise. None at all. I must still be thinking of last night." She smiled. "Isn't it beautiful here today? Feel the sun coming through the windows?"

Martise nodded and rose. She would get nothing from Elaina. Elaina only saw what she wanted to see.

And, aye, the day was beautiful. The sun was very strong, coming through the glass panes of the doors to the balcony.

But even then, even with the warmth of the sun upon her face, she could hear the wind. The wind that always ripped and tore through the castle.

Moaning, crying out. Whimpering . . . screaming.

She chose an American novel and sat down with it, near Elaina. As the hours ticked away, she wondered who in the castle Peter was trying to protect.

Or was it any of them? She closed her eyes and leaned back against the upholstery of her chair.

Perhaps she needn't fear any of the family. Not when there was Robert McCloud. The huge groom with his scarred cheeks and his insolent eyes. He had seen her ride away yesterday, and he had warned her to keep from the forests. He had to have been one of them. He was dangerous. She could feel it every time she was near him.

And then there was the greatest danger of all.

Bryan . . .

Whether guilty or innocent, he was still the greatest danger she faced. He held more than her life in his hands. He held both her heart and her soul.

Later in the afternoon, Hogarth brought them tea and light sandwiches. With delight he handed Elaina a bundle of beautiful wildflowers and told her that he had picked them on the moor. When Hogarth had removed the trays, Elaina glanced at Martise and flushed. "I haven't been able to gather many flowers lately. Winter comes quickly here. There's little of a true autumn. I'd like these for Mary's grave. Will you come with me?"

"Of course!" Martise agreed.

They went to the crypts by way of the great hall, passing the chapel and coming to the most modern vault. As soon as they stepped into it, Martise saw where the wall had been opened and then resealed with fresh bricks and plaster. No hint remained of the young girl who had been buried within the wall, nor was the remotest trace left of the passage that led to the torture chamber.

Elaina noticed the direction of her gaze. "That was so upsetting," she said.

"But ancient history, Elaina," Martise told her gently.

Elaina shrugged, kneeling before Mary's coffin to arrange the fresh flowers upon it. "I suppose. But Bruce is so easily annoyed by the legends that surround the castle. And he is the laird. The rumors fall back upon him, you see? The laird is born to be the 'beast' of legend. I suppose our harsh and cruel ancestor brought that about. Or perhaps the dragon beast came into our history with the Welsh princess. I don't know." She actually grinned. "Women don't carry the stigma, though, only the Creeghan males. But I am glad that he sent those instruments away, and that he has sent the poor girl's body down to Edinburgh for proper care and disposal."

"Yes," Martise murmured. The poor girl . . . alas, she was not ancient history.

She leaned against the wall, waiting with Elaina, and she wondered if Dr. MacTeague had told anyone but her that the girl had been murdered recently.

Had he told Bryan . . . ?

Her eyes wandered beyond the gate as she waited for Elaina to finish with the flowers. There had been a walled-up passage here. And the night that she ran from Bryan's bedroom to discover that his twin lay in a coffin, she had surely seen another such passage. Perhaps the crypts were riddled with them. If so, they must lead somewhere.

Suddenly, she wanted only to escape the crypts. She

stepped forward and gently set her hand upon Elaina's shoulders. "Shall we go up?" she asked softly.

Elaina glanced at her, then nodded.

As they left the crypt behind, Martise thought that even Elaina seemed nervous. She paused on the stairway to the great hall and shuddered, then offered Martise a tremulous smile. "I'm so glad that Bruce has had the wall closed."

"Yes," Martise agreed.

But again she wondered how many passages lay within the shivery cold walls of the crypts.

Elaina planned to lie down before dinner. Martise told her that she would probably lie down, too, but the moment that Elaina left her, she changed into riding attire and headed for the stables. She had determined to go see Dr. MacTeague.

As she approached the stables, she called for Jemie. A shadow stepped out into the silence, and she stood still. It was not the lad who appeared, but Robert McCloud. He blocked the entrance.

Martise paused before him, noting that his arms were folded over his chest, and his smile seemed smug. "Mr. McCloud, I'd like to ride, please," she said politely, but with an edge of superiority to her voice. "Would you saddle Desdemona for me?"

She gritted her teeth as the massive man shook his head.

"Mr. McCloud, perhaps you did not hear me. I wish—"

"I heard ye fine, me lady. But orders 'tis orders, and them what come from the master do come first."

"What orders came from the master?" she asked sharply.

McCloud's grin deepened, stretching out his scar. "He said as how he didna want ye taking off away from the castle this day, Lady St. James."

"But that is ridiculous! I am not a prisoner here!"

"Nay, lady, that ye're not. But ye must understand me position here. I'm not to give ye a horse. I couldna stop ye from walking, lady, but I warn ye, night is coming quickly, and 'tis a sorry long walk to the village, so it is."

She held still, wanting to run past him and steal a horse. Of course, he would stop her. Laird Creeghan's word was law, it was sacred. And any struggle on her part would merely serve to entertain this man.

"Thank you, Robert," she said politely, and swung about, seething. She could not wait to see Bryan, yet she dreaded seeing him, too. She would not be able to sit with him before the others and maintain any pretense of a smooth relationship between them.

But Bryan did not return for dinner. Martise sat with the others and tried to enjoy the meal. Ian told her that he had ridden into the forest and that he had found her cove. "At least, I did find the remnants of a fire. 'Tis interesting. I've been here me entire life, and I'd not have suspected. But Bruce will get to the bottom of it all, fear not."

"I'm sure he shall," Martise agreed politely.

Conar was quiet, Elaina was withdrawn. As soon as it was politely possible, Martise excused herself and headed for her room. She tried to think, and she could not. She came out to the balcony and stared up at what would soon be a brand-new and very full moon.

And when it came . . .

She must stay in her room. Ignore the sounds and the lights, pretend that they did not exist. That was what he had told her.

When the full moon came, other lights haunted the castle. And men who spoke in whispers moved below in the crypts.

She stared down upon the castle walls and the cliffs, and she listened to the sound of the surf crashing against the rock far below. The Dragon's Teeth were out there, waiting.

She shivered and returned to her room. As she locked the balcony doors, she heard footsteps in the hall. Soft, furtive footsteps. They came nearly to her door, and they stopped. She paused, waiting, listening.

Again she heard the footsteps, receding this time.

She raced to the door and flung it open. There was no one in sight.

She wondered if it had been Bryan, and her fury got the best of her. There were so many things that she had to say to him. She started down the corridor that led to his tower and his room. His door stood slightly ajar and she slammed it open.

He was there. Newly arrived from outside, so it seemed, for his black greatcoat still covered his shoulders and his ebony hair was slicked back and damp. He was at his desk and looked up, startled by the sound, as one of the massive double doors to his suite cracked hard against the wall.

He stared at her for a moment, slowly arching a brow. Then he swept off his coat, tossed it over the desk chair, and bowed to her politely. "My Lady St. James. How nice of you to come and visit."

"Is it? If you wished to speak with me, why did you pause outside my door? Why didn't you come in?"

He frowned. "I was not by your door."

"Someone was. Just minutes ago."

"I should have seen him. Or her."

"Someone was there, I tell you."

He shrugged, circling around the desk. "Well, you are here now. Come in. We need to talk."

She strode into the room, keeping the desk between them as she faced him. He was all in black, from his silk shirt to his breeches and boots.

"*You* wish to talk!" she spat out incredulously.

"Indeed. But it seems you believe that what you have to say must be more important. So, pray, milady, do go on."

"All right!" She slammed a fist upon his desk. "You've no right to keep me here!"

He lifted his hands. "I see no chains upon your person."

"I went for a horse today and your insolent groom informed me that you had left strict orders that I was not to ride."

His eyes narrowed. "May I remind you that you rode out yesterday—and disappeared."

"Oh! It is my safety only that concerns you!"

"What else?"

"Perhaps there are places—or people—you would prefer that I do not reach!"

"Such as?"

His arms were crossed over his chest, his feet were firmly planted upon the ground, and he seemed dangerous indeed as he stared down at her, his eyes very much aflame. She inhaled sharply, wishing that she did not feel the shivering inside of her, the trembling. Wishing that she did not know him so well—and yet, not nearly well enough.

Wishing that she did not love him.

She moistened her lips. "Dr. MacTeague," she said softly.

"MacTeague?" he said, frowning anew.

"He, he told me——" she began, but her voice failed her.

"He told you what?" Bryan demanded sharply.

"He told me that he was a country doctor, but that he knew an old corpse from a new one. He—he said that the girl discovered in the wall had only been there about a year or so."

Bryan lowered his head. For a moment, all she could see was the stygian darkness of his hair, and then he raised his face to hers once again. "Martise, I know that. Believe me, girl, MacTeague came to me first."

"Then why are you afraid that I should see him?"

"Why haven't you shared this information with me—or with others—before now?"

She shook her head. "Whom would I tell?"

"Indeed," he said softly, "whom would you tell?" He took a step toward her, and his smile seemed bitter. "No matter. You shall have your chance with MacTeague tomorrow." He paused right before her. The pulse of her blood took flight. He did not touch her, but stood before her.

She didn't want to run or shrink from him. "Will I?" she said, tossing back her head and lifting her chin. There was something about him tonight. Something careless, something reckless.

He nodded to her. "He's coming to our wedding tomorrow."

She gasped, so startled that she stepped away, her fingers winding tightly into fists at her sides. "Tomorrow!" she echoed with dismay. "But that's not possible! You can't—"

"Mistress, I am the laird here—I can do almost anything."

"But this whole thing is absurd! I will not marry you!"

To her surprise, he turned away, taking the seat at his desk. He tossed his legs up upon it, stretching them out and crossing them comfortably. He steepled his fingers and touched them across his lip.

"You will marry me tomorrow, at twelve noon precisely. The good father will be here, along with much of the village. We will be married before them in the chapel below."

She shook her head. "It is insanity!"

"Ah. You're still afraid of me."

"I am not afraid of you!"

"Not afraid of the laird of the castle, the beast, the demon, the keeper of bones within walls and searing instruments of torture? Laird of cliffs and rocks—and death?"

"Stop it!" she hissed.

He shrugged. "You've no reason to fear me, Martise. As you should well know," he added on a bitter note, "I have not been the deceiver."

"I don't know what you're talking about!" she declared. Suddenly, the urge to run was strongly with her. Something in his speech, in his words, in his actions . . .

Was she afraid of him?

Aye, tonight, she was.

But she sensed that there was no way past him. If she made a move for the door, he would be up. It was in his eyes, in the tension that gripped his body even as he gave the pretense of sitting so casually to study her.

"Ah, you do not know!" he murmured.

She was going to get past him, she thought furiously. She was not going to run, she was going to stride by.

"Indeed, I do not know," she said coolly. "And I am weary, and ready to retire—alone, milord." And with that she started to stride from the room with a swift arrogance.

But she had not misjudged his mood, or his reaction. He was swiftly on his feet, and his fingers wound around her arm before she could pass him. She cried out as he swung her hard against his chest and into the tight constriction of his arms. She gripped his arms tightly, trying to free himself. "I said that I wanted to retire, milord, if you will please let me go."

"Nay, girl, I'll not!"

"This is nonsense. I've not promised you anything, and I will not participate in a grand charade."

"You will not participate in a charade! You, milady?" He shook with his fury. "Why, mistress, the wedding should absolutely delight you. It will give you access to all of my private concerns, and that is what you desire, is it not?"

She struggled more fiercely. "I don't know what you're talking about!" she shouted, quivering.

"You don't?" He shook her hard to still her, and his eyes blazed down into hers with a piercing wrath. "Ah, but think! Could it have something to do with a very large emerald?"

She gasped, going still as death, and he seemed to take it as a sure admission of her deceit. Swearing out an oath, he tossed her back with such a violence that she was sent sprawling up the dais and back upon the bed. She rolled to defend herself lest he come for her, but he remained standing, aloof and remote. Yet the passion still burned from his gaze. "So you are a thief, mistress. Nothing more. You came for Mary, bah! You came to steal her jewel!"

She rose to a sitting position and returned his gaze, nearly choking on her fury. "I came for Mary!"

"You came for the jewel!" He strode for the bed and it

was all she could manage to do to sit still, and not cower to the other side. If he touched her, she swore, she would scream. But he did not touch her. He remained before her.

"Ah, for poor Mary's sake you ransacked the library. And 'twas for Mary's sake that you came to this bedroom and invaded my papers and my desk!"

"Your brother's paper!" she cried in defense.

"Nay, lady, for all here belongs to the laird of Creeghan, and I am he now. You are nothing but a grasping, fortune-hunting, little bitch!"

She swung at him and her hand connected with his flesh. Startled, he lashed a hand out at her, stopping only when she cried out, ducking away. He did not strike her. His hands landed upon her shoulders and he jerked her to her feet.

"Let me go!" she cried.

"Now that I have discovered you!"

"You have discovered nothing. The jewel is mine!"

"'Twas Mary's. It belonged to my brother, and to Creeghan."

"No! It is mine, and Mary held it for me. If you have it, give it to me!"

"And you can flee back to America with it."

"Yes! Yes!" she vowed passionately, lifting her chin, blinking back the tears that stung her eyes. "If that's what you wish—"

"'Tis not what I wish! You came here with your games and your deceits, and now you have managed to become a part of the castle and the mystery here. You will wed me tomorrow."

"How can you make me do this when you think me a thief and—"

"A whore?" he queried.

Stunned, she gasped out loud and struggled anew. He pulled her closer against him with a startlingly furious strength and his words where whispered just above her lips.

"Aye, a whore, for you came to me to find the gem. Goods delivered for goods you hoped to receive."

"I'll never marry you, never!" she swore. "I want the gem—"

"I have not got the gem!"

"Then how can you know of it?"

"Bruce wrote that he must take care of it for Mary, Lady St. James," he spat out caustically. "But I do not have it. And so, if you would take riches away, you must pay an even greater price. Who knows, as mistress here, you might even find the precious bauble that you considered worth your innocence and your life!"

She pulled away from him with a force she did not know she possessed. She backed against the wall and leaned there, her eyes warily upon him.

"Why?" she whispered.

"Because there is a murderer in the castle," he said softly.

"You say you want my safety, but you seek to use me!" she cried.

"Have it as you will," he said coldly. "You must marry me. The full moon is coming." He stared at her a long moment, then turned away. Opening his desk drawer, he pulled out the bottle of whisky and two glasses. He poured them both a portion and walked toward her, offering her a glass. She did not take it at first. He pressed it toward her and she lifted her hand and curled her fingers around it, meeting the blaze of his eyes. "To our wedded bliss," he said.

"I cannot marry you tomorrow," she said. "I cannot, even if you wish it. No matter how the moon will rise at night. I am not prepared. I have no dress—"

"You will be prepared," he assured her, and tossed down his drink with a single swallow. He turned away and headed toward his door, closing and bolting it.

He turned back to her, a sardonic smile giving a dark and Satanish twist to his handsome features. "And believe me,

I will care little what dress you wear, or if you bother to dress at all. Weddings are, after all, my love, to give blessing to what is shared with the spirit—and the flesh. And, mistress, I have grown quite fond of your flesh already, as it were."

She hurtled her glass at him. He ducked in plenty of time, and the glass crashed hard against the door. He straightened, and laughed softly.

"Indeed, milady, until tomorrow. Imagine, the emerald might be found, and there might be great rewards in all this, after all. The bed is yours—for tonight. If you desire me, I'll be on the cot in the dressing room." He bowed and strode that way.

"I shall not desire you!" she hissed. "Ever." And then she added as an afterthought, "Again."

He paused by the dressing room door and turned back to her, and she could not tell if he was angry or amused.

"But you will marry me tomorrow."

She stood silent, and he cocked his head. "Mistress, you should be vastly relieved by this opportunity."

"Opportunity!" she exclaimed with horror.

"Aye, well, you say that you will not desire me. But I have not forgotten certain sweet and forbidden things that we have shared. Such things do, mistress, upon occasion, bear fruit. You might want to take that into consideration— along with Mary's emerald. Damn, mistress, but you did deceive me so well! But if our relationship has brought about the planting of a seed . . . well, then. I would imagine you would prefer your child's future to be that of heir to a castle, rather than a bastard born and bred."

She stared at him, for once at a lack of words. He bowed to her once again, then disappeared through the dressing room door.

She found her voice and fury at last and stormed across the room, slamming hard upon the door. "I think I'd rather have a bastard than the heir to this particular castle!" she cried. "Do you hear me, Laird Creeghan?"

His soft laughter was her only response. She slammed upon the door again.

To her surprise and then dismay, the door opened. He was shirtless and bootless and she stepped back and he smiled. "'Tis your last night of freedom, lass. May I suggest that you retire and enjoy the bliss of an empty bed?"

"I'll not marry you."

"I think that you will."

She swore savagely. "It is *my* emerald."

She could read nothing from his burning eyes or rock-hard features.

"I hope it is important enough to die for," he said.

"You would die for this pile of rock!" she cried. And then her lashes fell as tears burned behind her eyelids. "Well, there is dirt and rock that I would die for, too," she whispered.

"What are you talking about?" he demanded.

"Nothing! Nothing. It's none of your business."

"Martise—"

"Don't! You think that you always have your way. That you can order and manipulate others at will. Well, things in my heart are my own, Bryan Creeghan. And that you cannot command."

"There seems to be nothing that I can really command from you," he said, and his burr was suddenly soft, and even tender.

She didn't want to look at him. She twirled around and headed back for the bed, and stretched out upon it, not even removing her shoes.

He did not close the door.

"You are going to go through with it, aren't you?" he asked her.

She was silent for several seconds. Then she whispered, "Aye."

"Why?" he demanded.

She did not look back to him. "Because the laird of

Castle Creeghan has commanded it, why else?" she retorted.

And she fell silent. His eyes remained upon her back, she
knew, for a long time.

And then the door closed softly between them.

She rolled over and stared at the dragon motif upon the
bedcovering and ran her fingers over it. She was going to
marry the man she loved.

And that would be the greatest charade of all.

Fourteen

❧

Martise dozed on and off through the night. Her sleep was restless, filled with dreams. He was there with her, her lover, the laird of Creeghan. And he came to her, walking through the mist and the wind, walking over the rock. She knew that she awaited him, awaited him naked and vulnerable around a sheet of ancient rock. And she should be running, but she could not run, because he was coming.

Clad in a dark cloak and the mask of the dragon. And all that appeared of the man beneath the mask was the fire of his eyes.

But still she waited . . . waited because she knew the sweet succulence of his touch. Waited because she could not run. Whether he brought pure ecstasy or the silver flash of death, she would wait, because she could not run.

He came nearer and nearer, and still she held. Whispers surrounded them, gentle on the breeze, growing louder. She heard the sound of the surf, crashing far below. The salt taste of the sea sprayed against her face, and there were no more whispers as the wind rose to a high crescendo. He spoke to her, in the burr of the Highlands, and he told her that Castle Creeghan awaited her, that the castle needed a bride. That it was her last night alone . . .

And then he was before her, and she saw the deep-bronzed strength of his long-fingered hands fall gently against her breast and travel to her throat. He cast aside the dragon mask, and his features were bare and handsome as he moved low against her. His fingers caressed her throat, and she didn't know if he meant to kiss her . . . or to kill her.

There was no kiss. She awoke with a start, and suddenly she was angry, very angry. A candle burned from the desk, and outside, the darkness of the night was just beginning to fade as the rising sun struggled to cast a pink glow into the room.

She leapt up, not taking the time to think, and burst into the dressing room upon him.

The second the door opened, he shot up. He stared at her, dark hair tousled and disheveled, his gaze sharp. The blanket fell from his chest, displaying its hard-muscled nakedness. "What is it?" he demanded harshly.

"You!" she told him, her hands on her hips. "You! How dare you threaten me."

Both dark brows shot up, a small smile curved into his lip, and he leaned comfortably upon an elbow. "Would you care to elaborate on that?"

"Indeed, I would. Yes, I need the emerald. It was never Mary's, it was always mine. Margaret kept it for me for a while, but then she thought that she, being in Richmond, was in an even more vulnerable state. She arranged to get it to Mary. Mary must have asked your brother to keep it safe. Maybe he didn't know where it had come from, although I cannot believe Mary didn't tell him. That, my Lord Creeghan, is the truth, and you better believe it!"

"Will I?" he asked politely.

"Yes, if you expect me to exchange vows with you in order to catch a murderer. I did come here for Mary, too. And that you will also have to believe. She sent me letters about how very frightened she was, and she was my friend, my very good friend. If someone here did kill her, then that someone must be punished."

"Someone . . ." he murmured. "So does that mean that you no longer believe that it was me? Or Bruce?"

"Bruce is dead. He could not have rendered me unconscious in the crypts."

"Ah, but I could have. I was there with you, soon after the deed."

She didn't reply immediately. If she had any sense, she would consider him the prime suspect.

But love had stripped away her common sense. She shivered, remembering her dream. If he did mean to harm her, would she be able to regain her soul and run?

"I am in this room," she offered.

He cast aside the covers and stood. He had slept naked, but he seemed not to notice his state as he gripped her wrists and forced her eyes to his by the power of his will. "I do not suspect you!" she said, wishing now that she had not come. It was too disturbing to be held by him so.

"Only upon occasion," he said.

"I don't know what you mean."

"All right, Martise. It's nearly dawn. We are about to wed. So I will believe in you, believe your words, if you will put your trust in me."

"But I—"

"Your total trust. Not sometimes, but always. Not 'I do not wish it to be him, but perhaps it is.' Nay, lady, believe in me, and I will help you."

"Help me what?"

"To find the emerald. You must want it very badly. To have risked my room, believing that I might be the murderer . . ."

She wrenched her hands free and moved away, leaning against the door. Perhaps it hadn't been such a wise move. The laird of Creeghan lacked not one bit of his power and arrogance in his naked state.

She tried to keep her eyes steady with his, and not to

allow them to fall. "Yes, I need it very badly. I have a home in Virginia that means very much to me. I'll lose it if I can't pay the new county and state taxes on it." She paused just briefly, her lashes falling, then rising swiftly again. "I need something other than, er, Confederate currency."

"A house? A plantation, I imagine."

"Yes."

"Good tobacco crops, cotton?"

"Yes." She had forgotten just how well he must know Virginia. "Some of the richest soil in the state," she told him.

He was silent for a moment, watching her. "Perhaps, if I survive, and Creeghan survives, we can save this place of yours, too."

She lifted her chin very high. How could he carry on a conversation so nonchalantly?

"I don't want your charity," she told him. "I just want my own emerald."

"Perhaps it can be found. But," he added on a note of wry humor, "I imagine that you've searched very thoroughly for it already. I don't know where to begin to look myself."

"It must be here!" she said desperately. Then she couldn't bear standing across from him so, and she spun around to leave.

"One moment!" he said sharply. She paused with her hand upon the doorknob.

"What?"

"I never threatened you over the emerald."

"I don't know what you mean," she said.

"You came in here telling me that I had threatened you. And that you weren't going to let me do it. What were you talking about?"

"Oh," she murmured. Her knees felt weak. She needed to escape.

She had come in upon him in a sweeping fury.

She swung back around, bracing herself by the door.

"Last night," she began softly. There was no substance in her voice. Her eyes fell again despite her best efforts and she felt a riddling of sweet excitement rip throughout her. Like an Apollo or a Zeus, or any classical god crafted of marble or granite, he was truly beautiful in his naked form. But he was not made of marble, and muscle and sinew rippled within him, and the pulse of his heart was evident in his veins, and all that was rugged and masculine and rawly seductive about him was very much in evidence.

"You threatened that last night should be my last night alone," she snapped out, drawing up her eyes.

He smiled, and crossed his arms over his chest. "I wasn't threatening," he assured her, and added softly, "I was promising."

"You are really an insolent rake," she retorted heatedly.

He shrugged and walked toward her. "All right, then, it was a warning."

He stood right before her. She felt the radiating heat of his body, so very close.

"You are forcing this marriage, Laird Creeghan, and beyond that, you would threaten—"

"Warn," he interrupted.

"And bully."

"I do protest," he said, and by then, he was very close to her. Flames leapt in his eyes, and he leaned forward. He did not touch her lips, but his tongue flicked over her lower ear, and then his mouth formed in a soft kiss at her throat.

She felt the pulse leap and stagger within her, and she knew that he felt it too. She wanted to move her hands upon his shoulders, to taste the bronze flesh there. But she held very still, and when his eyes met hers again, she reminded him, "We're not married yet."

"Nay, we're not," he agreed.

But a hand was now on either side of her head, palms against the door. She could feel the heat and hardness of his loins, pressed close, through the various fabrics of her clothing. He touched her lips lightly. "I can wait," he told her. "For I know that the prize I await is greater, and perhaps all the sweeter for the torment."

"I must get back to my room," she whispered.

"Why?"

"Because we shall be discovered."

He shrugged. "And if we were? What then? I am the laird of the castle. No one questions my will."

"But they whisper and they talk."

"It is not yet six. No one will be looking for you."

How could anyone infuriate and seduce so damn easily? she wondered. And yet it had become a point of her will, and her pride, and she would not give in to him. Well, whatever came from this alliance, she would not be among those who instantly obliged the laird of the castle.

She lifted her chin and managed a sweet seductive smile of her own. "We're not yet married," she repeated.

"There's still no reason for you to run, lass," he said softly. Then he pressed his finger to his lips. "Shh!"

She went still, feeling him against her, hearing the hallway door to the bath being twisted open. Her eyes opened wide with alarm, but his gaze upon her was lazy, decadent, and amused. She heard the splash of water and frowned.

"'Tis Hogarth and the lads with water," he said. "This morning, we can share my bath."

"I'll not—"

"Shh!" he repeated. And a second later, there was a tap upon his door. "Bryan, Bryan Creeghan?" Hogarth called softly. "'Tis six, and yer bath is ready."

"Thank you, Hogarth," Bryan called loudly, his eyes never leaving Martise's. "I am awake."

"Is there anythin' else, then, me laird?"

"Nay, I'll be fine on my own, Hogarth. Thank you."

The door closed. He still stared at her, smiling. "Come, join me."

"I don't care for a bath."

"What? My bride does not intend to bathe for the nuptials?" he said in mock horror.

"Well, you see," she retorted, "I was not given time to respond with a proper gown, or shoes, or hose, or chemise—so it would seem futile to pretend this shall be a customary wedding."

"Alas! And I'd dreams that my Southern beauty would smell as sweet as a rose against a winter's day."

She arched a brow in disbelief. "Am I to believe that Hogarth would give you, the laird of Creeghan, rose-scented soap? I had imagined a bridegroom with some alluring, spicy scent, something a bit more to his gender than roses."

"One never knows what Hogarth might have supplied, Mistress St. James. He is a very keen and astute fellow."

"Too keen," she commented dryly.

"He is our only other conspirator in this charade, Martise. But never mind, we've only to talk. So come," he said, "indulge me while I bathe."

He turned around and left her against the door, striding with the confidence of a sleek and muscled cat across the room to the bath. He opened that door, and within seconds she heard him sinking into the large tub.

She could have turned away. No ropes bound her, no arms held her, not even the power of his eyes kept her there. But she walked on through the dressing room and perched upon a hamper. From her spot she could see his shoulders and head and neck, but little more. It seemed a comfortable enough position.

He knew that she was there.

"The full moon comes tomorrow night," he told her.

"And it coincides with All Hallows' Eve!"

He shook his head with irritation. "You are still convinced there is witchcraft, and there is none, I tell you."

She was standing, angry. "You don't want to believe that there is witchcraft, and you have blinded yourself! I tell you what I saw—"

"And I tell you that it is a ruse to cover some other crime."

"What other crime?"

"Wreckers," he said softly.

"Wreckers?" She came to his side.

"The *Lady Mae* will be sailing near our shore tomorrow night. I'm sure her captain has not thought of All Hallows' Eve."

She was shivering suddenly. "The last ship—it was on the night of the full moon. But I don't understand! Wouldn't they need darkness for the ship to cast upon the rocks. Oh, you must be wrong! I saw those men in their cloaks making their circle about the fire. And the girl, the poor girl buried within the castle wall! What has she to do with such a thing?"

He shook his head. "I don't know," he said. "But it's by the light of the full moon that one usually sees the other lights appear upon the cliffs. Perhaps the men need some light to carry out their devilish deeds, to set the traps, to lure the ships. There have never been any survivors."

Suddenly she remembered the sailor who had washed ashore near the caves. With his last, dying breath, the man had whispered, "Creeghan." And then Bryan had come . . . and the man had died.

She almost leapt up. He caught her wrist. Her eyes betrayed her as she stared into his.

"What is it?" he demanded harshly.

"Let me go."

"Nay, not when you're afraid of me again like this. What, what is it, tell me!"

She tugged upon her wrist, trying to rise, trying to escape him. He rose with her, and as he pulled her back, his foot slipped and they both came floundering into the tub, Martise soaked to the teeth and locked within his arms.

"Now look what you have done!" she charged him.

"No matter." His arms tightened around her. "What is it that you're not telling me?"

"My God, my clothes are soaked. How shall I explain—"

"I'll bring you clothing," he said. "Talk to me, Martise."
His words were warm against the dampness of her ear. His
hand wedged beneath her breast, holding her tight.

"But how shall you explain—"

"I am the laird of Creeghan. I never need explain," he
said with exasperation.

She spun in his arms, heedless of his wet, slippery body,
or the pain of his hold upon her. "Aye, you are the laird of
Creeghan! But there are certain things that *you must
explain*. Like dead men, Laird Creeghan. Dead men who lie
upon your shore!"

"What are you talking about, lass?"

Tears stung her eyes. "The sailor! The sailor they found
upon the shore. He whispered your name. And he was
alive. And then you touched him. And then . . ."

"And then he was dead," Bryan finished, his mouth in a
tight line. And he added bitterly beneath his breath, "So
now I am a murderer again—and you are a thief!"

"I'm not a thief—"

"And I'm not a murderer! I've told you that oft enough!"

She exhaled slowly. They were so close, her gown
covering them both in a sodden cocoon. "He spoke your
name!" she whispered.

He arched a brow in disbelief. "He said, 'Bryan'?"

"No, no! He said, 'Creeghan'!"

"But that could mean anything!" Bryan told her with
exasperation. "Creeghan is the castle, and Creeghan is the
village, and the fishing dock, and the land. Girl, he did not
accuse me—" He broke off, and ended softly, speaking
almost beneath his breath. "He accused someone, something, within Creeghan."

"He was alive—"

"I took the body to Edinburgh, Martise, and had him
examined by an expert. No one could tell me the true cause
of death, though exposure was a part of it. There was a
wound, a horrible wound to his temple. Perhaps he was

struck with some weapon—and perhaps he crashed upon the rock. Not even the doctor in Edinburgh could tell me that." He stared at her sharply. "So you thought that I had killed him while you lay in the cave."

"I thought nothing—"

"You're lying."

"I am soaked, and I would like very much to get out."

He shifted, coming to his feet, bringing her along with him. So much water was caught within the folds of her clothing that the tub seemed barely filled. Waves of water cascaded from her body. He smiled, but she thought that the humor was gone from his gaze. She tore her eyes from his and tried to draw up her skirt, wringing water from it.

He spoke her name, and she looked back to his eyes. His hand moved over hers, his fingers curling within her own so that she dropped the skirt. Then his touch moved to the tiny buttons at her throat and he began to undo them. When the gown lay open to her waist, he slipped his fingers beneath her shoulders and peeled the wet material down. She shivered, standing in chemise and petticoats and corset and pantalettes and hose, but she did not move. He reached for the limp laces of her corset and untied them, and tossed the garment heedlessly from the tub. And she watched him still as the delicate ribbons of her chemise came undone, and that garment, too, was cast to the floor. The cold air moved over the dampness of her bare breasts, and his eyes still met hers while his hands cupped and curled beneath the fullness of the mounds.

He bent his head, and his lips pressed against the deep and shadowed valley he had created, then wandered lightly over the full globes, licking away the remnants of water that clung there. She lifted her hands, bracing herself upon his shoulders, sighing softly. His mouth moved, hot and wet. It covered the cold and achingly sensitive peak, and a soft sound escaped her. Her fingers tore into the sleek ebony dampness of his hair and she pleaded softly, "Bryan, no!"

His whisper moved against her flesh. "Because we are not married—yet?"

"No, because I shall fall and perhaps drown," she told him honestly.

He looked up into her eyes, laughing. "Mistress, how could I not force this?" he murmured, and he swirled her around, untying her petticoats, shoving them down to the froth in the water, and then releasing her pantalettes.

"Bryan—" she protested anew, but he was busy picking up the volumes of material, wringing it, and tossing the whole sodden bundle from the tub. Then he stepped from it himself and pressed upon her shoulders so that she went down to take the position that had once been his. He went to the cabinet for a huge towel to wrap about his hips and when he turned back to her, he had a lump of rose-colored soap in his hands.

"Well, ye canna deny, lass, that you're already halfway there. And I did have dreams of a rose-scented bride."

She didn't have a chance to protest. He was kneeling at her back and his hands were upon her, stroking the soap over her shoulders.

"Someone in this house is guilty," he said softly.

He spoke again of the mystery within the castle. Of life and death. And now, it seemed, they were conspirators in truth. The lies were over between them, and the suspicions, and the things once best left unsaid. It was like her dream, for even as he spoke of the danger, she felt the stroke of his touch. If she had turned to see that he had grown horns, she could not have moved. Soap, sleek and silky, scented like roses, moved over her flesh with the sensual brush of his fingers behind it. Slowly, evocatively. She wanted to lie back as he eased the tension from her neck and shoulders.

She closed her eyes.

"Robert McCloud," she said aloud.

"Robert!" he said sharply.

She nodded. "I've noticed him since I came to the castle. He—he stares at me peculiarly."

"He is a man, and you are a very beautiful woman."

"No . . . he stares insolently. As if he knows something. Secrets. And there is his scar, and the manner in which he behaves. And—"

"Martise, I brought Robert here from Glasgow. He grew up an orphan on the streets with nothing; and trust me, Glasgow can be a cruel and vicious place. He had a way with horses, and he was loyal to me. I brought him here."

"But he knew that I was riding out. And he warned me to stay away from the forest. He is guilty, I know it!"

"I thought that a man was innocent until proven guilty, even in the aftermath of war, in the States," he said.

"But you don't know the way that he looks at me! And if he is not guilty, then who?"

"I don't know," he said. "But if the cloaked figures you stumbled upon in the forest are involved, then it is more than just one person."

She shivered violently. He pressed his lips against her shoulder. His kiss moved up the length of her neck as he wound her hair high, and held it from her flesh to bare it.

"There are your cousins!" she whispered.

"Aye, if *I* am *not* guilty . . ." he agreed against her flesh. The soap moved over her within his grasp. Over her breasts, sweeping below, to her waist, to her thighs, between them. She gasped softly, and she tried to keep speaking, seeking his hands to cease the flow of sensations that were only heightened by the fading heat of the water and the mist of steam that surrounded them.

"What are you going to do?"

"Do?" he said, and joined her in the tub, pulling her to her feet. He stood before her, taking her hands into his. "I am going to discover the truth," and he pulled her into his arms, and his lips formed hotly over hers. He kissed her with a searing passion, drawing away to bathe her face with the touch of that kiss, joining his lips to hers once again and drinking so deeply from her that his tongue reached every sweet crevice of her mouth. He drew away, her chin cupped in his hands, and bathed her lower ear with the searing damp moisture of his tongue. Against her naked flesh, she could feel the hard pulse of his desire as it brushed against her. She caught hold of his arms and felt the tension and ripple of muscle within them, and she cried out again. "I shall fall!"

But he caught her up in his arms, and as her fingers entwined about his neck, he looked down into her eyes and promised her, "I shall not let you fall."

He stepped from the tub, and his long sure strides brought them from the bath and through the dressing room and into the bedroom, and there, soaked and gleaming, he laid her down upon the bed. He stared at her for a moment, his eyes sweeping the length of her, the damp but glorious tangle of her hair, the deep rough peaks of her breasts, the slimness of her waist, the flair of her hips, and the golden shadowed valley of her sex. The long, long limbs that stretched out beneath. Her flesh was touched here and there with tiny droplets of water from the bath.

"A rose-scented bride," he said, crawling atop her, his great throbbing rod now a pulse that could not, would not, be denied.

He curled his fingers within hers. Blue eyes like a cloudless day, lazy, just dazzling with a subtle humor, met his. "We are not married yet!" she reminded him huskily.

"So?" he murmured.

He parted her thighs, resting his body between them, then lowered himself. He pressed his lips against the inside of her knee and slowly moved that caress along her inner thigh.

She gasped out loud as he moved along and found the flower-scented center of her very being. With his touch he stroked and parted the hot damp petals, and seared them anew with the hunger and pleasure of his mouth.

She cried out loud, gasping words that had no meaning, protests that had no substance . . .

And deep, deep searing ecstasy that could not be hidden or denied.

With a longing, a yearning, a thunderous need deeper than he had ever known before, he brought himself high against her, and there looked into her eyes while his sex teased the burning warmth.

"You said—" she whispered.

And he smiled, his lips a curl of fascination, for he knew it was more than her beauty that drove him on so deeply, that it was her whispers, her sweet burning passion, the honesty of this, at least, between them.

"Be damned with what I said," he told her. And he plunged within her. Deep. So deep that he felt he went into her forever, more than his body, more than his heart . . .

All of his life.

Then the blinding desire swept hold of him, and he thought no more. A wind ripped through him, the wind that was part of Creeghan, part of himself. Wild, raging, passionate, untamed . . . and soft and sweet and low and whispering. She met him in ardor and urgency. Damp and musky, their flesh rubbed together, ground hard together, and their breath mingled with the kisses they gave and received until their lips could touch no more, until his hands were still upon her shoulders, until there was no more play at all . . . just the last, shattering thrusts. He rose above her, watching their bodies where they met, and then the climactic waves washed over them. The flow of their passion, spent, mingled as their breath had done, and he groaned out the depths of his ecstasy and desire, and fell hard against her. His arms about her, he rolled, and carried her with him so that his weight would no longer bear down upon her.

And they were silent as the last pink streaks that had heralded the dawn faded away.

Daylight had come. Full daylight.

Their wedding day.

"Does it matter so much?" he asked her.

"What?" she said softly.

"That we were not wed now?"

"No," she replied. But her eyes did not meet his. She looked across the room to the dragon that sat atop the armoire. "We shall not truly be wed at all later, not truly."

His arms tightened and his voice hardened. "What do you mean? Father Martin would surely disagree."

She rolled around to face him, her eyes suddenly very old, and very wise. "I shall be marrying *Bruce* Creeghan."

He fell silent, then told her lightly, "Nay, lady, don't think that it shall be so easy, quickly promised, quickly over. You came here pretending to be a lady. Well, I shall make you one today in truth."

He rose and returned to the bath, thinking that she would follow. She did not.

Bathed anew, he came back to his room, but she was not there. Puzzled, he looked about, and realized that she had taken one of his coats from a hook by the door.

He walked out to the balcony, but she had not left that way.

He stared out upon the cliffs of Creeghan and shuddered suddenly. Where was his conviction now? Once, it had seemed the only way, and it had certainly seemed like no less than she should deserve. Marriage had meant nothing to him, nor had any woman.

He had fought a foreign war and lost. And in the losing, he had betrayed the brother who had been his best friend all of his life. He had betrayed Creeghan itself.

He owed Creeghan everything. Most of all, he owed Creeghan honor, for that was what had been stripped away. No matter what his ancestors had been, his father and his grandfather had brought prosperity to the people.

He knew in his heart that Mary *had* been frightened to death. That, if her heart had not failed her, she would have died nonetheless. A fall to the cliffs below . . .

Fingers tightening around her throat.

And so it had seemed that to protect Martise, he had to be

with her. To sleep with her. And she had come as a schemer, hard, boldly voicing her own lies. But the lies now seemed to crumble beneath him. He had taken her and used her, and now . . .

The marriage would be legal, he vowed. It was too late to send her away—she would not go. They were in it together, entangled, entwined.

And he loved her. Loved her with a greater passion than he could give to this house, or even, for that matter, than he could give to honor. Loved her with a rage like that of the wind, with a tenderness like the salt-breeze caress upon a gold and glorious dawn.

And tomorrow night was the full moon . . .

It would be over! he swore. It would be over. He would fine the right passage this time, the right passage within the honeycomb mazes of the crypt that led to the sea.

He turned back into his room to dress for his wedding.

She might not have had time to plan, but he was convinced later that no bride had ever been more beautiful. Elaina had helped her improvise. She wore a cream-colored gown, one with delicate lace and satin ribbons. It swept long behind her, and the bodice was low, trimmed with the lace. The slimness of her body and the fullness of her breasts were emphasized, and still, no bride had ever appeared more innocent, more pure. Her eyes were blue and wide beneath the soft sheer veil that she wore.

Her hair was a cascade. Gold and fire, swirling down her back, free and simple, and incredibly glorious.

Elaina attended her, and Peter walked her down the aisle, to hand her over to him. Her eyes met Bryan's with such honesty that he was stunned. He knew that she would not falter, nor did she. Words were spoken, songs were sung.

It seemed that all of Creeghan was there, crowded into the tiny chapel. Spilling out into the hallway. All these people, come to celebrate a ceremony of life.

The servants were there, Holly softly weeping, Hogarth

grinning from ear to ear, Robert with his wry smile. And Jemie and Trey, and the young maids who came by day and left by night. And Freya, beaming proudly, as if her cooking had brought it all about.

And the villagers. The fishermen, the sheepherders, and the merchants. The Cunninghams were there, smiling, but Peggy was still wearing that pinched look of pain that had been with her daily since Clarissa's disappearance. And MacTeague was there, somber as he watched the ceremony.

And the family . . .

Peter, so proud, having given away such a stunning bride. Ian with his ever-ready smile, Conar so grave. Elaina, tears in her eyes, tears of joy and tears of sorrow. Bryan could see in her face that she was remembering both Mary and her own Niall, and wondering if she would ever be a bride herself.

He had given Father Martin careful instructions. Perhaps some might have thought it curious that Martise gave her vows to "Laird Creeghan" rather than to a man with a given name. And yet, he was the laird of Creeghan, and it was true, few would ever question his desires.

Martise spoke the words softly but well, and faltered only once: when she swore to love him forever.

His own vows were steady and strong. He could not falter. Not, he thought wryly, as the laird of Creeghan.

When they signed the license, he was careful to write "B. MacKenzie Creeghan, Laird of Creeghan."

None could ever deny that it was he.

Her fingers shook as she wrote down her name.

There was cheering anew, and Peter called out that Laird Creeghan must kiss his new lady once again.

Her eyes met his and he swept her into his arms. And he murmured, "Lady?" before kissing her with all of the audience before them.

They cheered and applauded as his kiss went on. Friends, loved ones, a close community, they applauded, with smiles and with tears. They welcomed a new bride to

Creeghan. And yet among their number, there was at least one who might very well try to slay her . . .

Their kiss parted at last, and again her eyes met his. Grave and blue, naked and beautiful. It was done, this thing between them. Born of fear and lies and deceit . . .

And taken this day in dangerous passion.

She turned away from him, managing to smile. He had lost her, he thought. In taking her as his wife, he had lost her completely. There was a coldness about her again, a distance, and his kiss could not erase it.

And yet, as she moved away, he smiled.

There came from her a soft and beautiful scent. Subtle, sweet, alluring.

The scent of fresh roses.

Aye, the scent of roses.

Fifteen

❧

The feasting went on throughout the day.

Elaina kissed her cheek and hugged her warmly as they stood in the great hall above. It had been cleared for dancing, with the large oak dinner table pulled close to the fire, and delicacies of all kinds heaped heavily upon it. There was smoked and pickled eel, pheasant, potent-smelling fish stew, and the ever-present mutton. Ices had been formed in elegant shapes, a bride and a groom, rearing horses, the Creeghan dragon, and hounds and kittens. As the day wore on, the ices slowly melted and the children broke off pieces to suck upon.

Martise stood with Bryan near the fire. She felt as though she had married into royalty, as all the people came before them, bearing best wishes and gifts. Then they moved onto the dance floor where the men had set up with fiddles and flutes and the inevitable bagpipes, and even a stray harmonica or two. The music was loud, the guests were gay, the mood was festive.

Elaina paused beside them, smiling, watching the dancers on the floor. She turned to Martise and hugged her impulsively again. "I'm so glad you're my sister in truth now, Martise. Like Mary."

"But I am not Mary," Martise reminded her softly, suddenly feeling uneasy.

"Look at them," Ian murmured from behind her. "All in their best plaids and laces, welcoming a new bride to Castle Creeghan." His eyes were shimmering; perhaps, Martise thought, from the aged Scotch whisky brought out for the occasion. "Think of it—tomorrow they'll be lain out on their fields or in the bows of their little fishing vessels, scarce able to open their eyes."

" 'Tis the laird's wedding day," Bryan reminded him. " 'Tis not something they do often."

Ian laughed. "Well, 'tis becoming something that they do oft enough!"

Bryan's jaw twisted and held. He reached out a hand to Martise. "Lady Creeghan, come dance with your laird," he invited, and they stepped past his family.

The guests moved aside as he swept her into his arms and began to swirl her around the room. Martise cast back her head, smiling up at him. "What are we trying to prove?" she inquired sweetly.

"Prove?"

"Why this grand affair?"

He arched a brow. "How else does one watch people?" he asked her quietly.

How else, indeed. He, the laird, had eschewed his Highland dress for his nuptials, and was striking in the black she had come to associate with him. Aye, black, the color of the night, the color of his hair. The color of a lord of darkness.

She had married him and had to trust him now. She had cast herself into his keeping and agreed to play this game. Nor could she regret it now, sweeping about within his arms as if she danced on air, meeting the wildfire of his gaze. His black frock coat and slim silk tie were elegant over the fine ribbed lace of his shirt, but beneath the texture of the fabric, the heat and pulse of the man were filled with an electric tension. If she were to cast all, including life, into this charade, then so be it, she thought, for she could never turn back now.

"Whom are we watching?" she inquired.

"All of them, my love," he answered, expertly turning her into a twirl. "All of them. Ian who is drinking, Conar who is surly. Peter who is playing his pipes . . . Robert McCloud, the man you find so suspicious. And there—we have the Cunninghams and their proud sons. And Katie and Micky Douglas. And young Cassie and her sailor husband, Richard. They're all here. The boys, Trey and Jemie. The villagers, all of them, watching you, Lady Creeghan."

She swirled beneath his arm again. "How can you be so cynical and cruel! Clarissa Cunningham is still missing, and you would cast such a slur upon her family!"

He smiled and pulled her close and his whispered words brushed over her temple. "But I am the one who has supposedly buried Clarissa within a wall. That is what you suspected, is it not?"

She pulled back. "I never thought—"

"You most certainly did," he said, and his eyes sparkled their dangerous fire. "But now, my dear and charming bride, we have sworn our trust in one another, have we not? And now, you are a lady in truth, Martise. My wife."

His soft taunt sent chills sweeping along her spine, and she did not know if they were shimmers of fear or desire.

"We've spoken words," she said uneasily. "We've agreed upon a dangerous game. We play at charades. We have joined together for that game, and for no other reason."

He stared down at her, his gaze seeming to blaze. Then he said softly, "Ah, but the playing of the game, milady! 'Tis most enjoyable. I do say—let the play continue."

She met his gaze. But she said nothing more, for a hand fell upon her shoulder, and Peter spoke at her ear.

"Nephew, will ye let an old man take on a beautiful young lady?"

"Aye, Uncle Peter, my lady is yours," he agreed politely, and stepped aside.

Peter was an able dancer with a willing energy. They were soon halfway across the floor. His eyes were bright, and his smile was wolfish as he teased.

"Ye're one of us now, lass."

"Aye, Peter."

"And welcome ye are."

"Thank you."

"Remember to take care."

"Will the ghosts of Creeghan harm me?" she asked him.

"Nay, lass. They will protect their own, when they may. I'm an old man, lady, but trust in me."

She laughed. "Old! Why, Peter, you put the lot of us to shame with your wit and style and grace."

"Charming and bright as well as beautiful." Peter laughed. "Och, and here comes that son of mine, set to steal you away. Well, and then, 'tis your wedding. I must give in." He paused and kissed her hand. "Conar, the lady is yours!" Peter said gallantly, and she was suddenly within his son's arms, and Conar was smiling, and seeming as pleased with the events of the day as any man there.

"So, Lady Creeghan," he said. "Now ye're the bride of Creeghan. No regrets, I hope?"

"None, Conar. No regrets."

He was very serious when he spoke next. "Martise, we are all glad to have you. You are beautiful, intelligent, kind, and determined. Aye, we're glad to have ye. But take care within this house. Let us solve the problems within it."

"I don't know what you mean," she told him innocently. But her heart was beating hard, and her fingers closed more tightly upon his arms as they danced. "What problems?"

He shook his head and laughed, his seriousness vanishing. "Things that go bump in the night, milady. Truly, I shouldn't have spoken. There's nothing to worry about. Bruce will care for you."

Bruce will not, she thought, for Bruce is dead. And

Bryan now is laird, and everywhere I turn, it seems that I must be afraid. "I must let you go, so it seems," Conar murmured. "Henry Cunningham comes this way, and 'twill make his entire lifetime, I believe, if you will dance with him."

He turned her over to Peggy's aging husband, bowed, and left her. She smiled radiantly at Henry, and swept forth into the music once again.

Over her shoulder she saw Bryan. The beautiful young Cassie was in his arms. Her head was thrown back and her laughter was long and low and husky. Where was her sailor husband? Martise wondered, and she was surprised at the depth of the jealousy that tugged upon her heart.

He had married *her*, not Cassie. He had made her his bride.

No, he had given Creeghan a bride . . .

Was it one and the same, or was there a difference?

She didn't know. She spun, a bit clumsily, in Henry's arms, and as she did, she saw Ian disappearing down the stairs. Back to the wine cellar perhaps? Or back to the chapel?

Or to the crypts?

She didn't know, and she was suddenly eager to discover his purpose.

"Oh!" she gasped, smiling at Henry Cunningham. "I do declare, this dancing has gotten the best of me at last. I must sit out a spell."

"Aye, lady! Come, I'll bring ye ootside fer some air, and I'll fetch ye some punch—"

"No, no, Henry, I shall be all right."

He wasn't going to leave her, she realized. She smiled. "All right. Fetch some punch, please. I'll find some air myself, and be right back with you."

He left her upon the dance floor and headed for the buffet table. Martise watched him go, then turned and fled through the crowd, smiling here and there, taking a hand, greeting the guests anew even as she did so.

She at last made the stairs. Seeing that no one seemed aware she was fleeing her own reception, she looked down the stairway. There was still light down there. The lamps that had led the guests to the wedding in the chapel burned in their sockets along the wall. She swept up the fullness of her skirt and started down the stairs.

She reached the landing and moved tentatively to the arched stone doorways leading to the wine cellar. "Ian!" she called softly. She shivered, for the cellar was very cold. She stepped away and hurried across to the chapel.

The candles had burned out, just as the daylight beyond the beautiful windows had died away. Now shadows entered the chapel. And the figures within the windows seemed to stare down at her with a dark and haunting visage. She was not afraid of the chapel, she assured herself.

But she was.

She backed away. "Ian!" she called again.

She turned and ran back out into the hallway. She started running along the stone floor and came to the modern crypt. The gate hung open.

"Ian!"

She heard a burred and slurry reply. "Come in, come in! said the spider to the fly!"

She stepped through the gate. Ian was perched upon the slab where Mary's coffin lay. He held a bottle in his hand. He had worn his family's colors that day. His tam sat askew upon his head, yet there still seemed to be a dignity about him.

"Ian, what's wrong?" she asked him.

He waved the bottle toward her. She shook her head, refusing it. She came in and sat beside him. Her eyes fell upon the repaired wall and she shivered, remembering the body of the poor young girl as she had appeared the day they discovered her.

Where else were there passages? Where else were there rooms, or crevices within the wall, where skeletons might well be hidden? Family skeletons—a literal term in Castle Creeghan.

"Ian, what are you doing down here?" she asked.

His eyes, a paler version of his cousin's, more green than fire, touched hers. "I told you. I loved Mary. I came to be with her today."

"I loved her, too, Ian. I'm—I'm sorry if I offended you. I am not trying to take her place."

He cocked his head as he looked at her. "Well, ye canna really, really take her place, can ye, now?"

"I don't know what you mean."

He studied her intently, and she wondered just how drunk he might be. Was it all an act? He seemed to be reading into her soul. And at that moment, he seemed very wise. "Ye do know what I mean, Lady—Creeghan," he said softly.

"Ian—" she began uneasily, but he was standing, setting his bottle down upon the slab. "A toast to us, eh, Mary?" he said, speaking to the coffin. He turned toward the coffins beyond Mary. "And to ye, Ma—there's me mum, Martise, have I shown ye that grave? She was a Creeghan born and bred, and so she rests here. But then, Da shall rest here, too, along with her." His eyes shot back to hers and he smiled. "And now, Martise, you will rest here, too. Rest with the Creeghans. For eternity."

She leapt up, suddenly very frightened by him. She wondered briefly why she had come here alone. She had been warned often enough.

He was stepping back to her now, and suddenly his hands were tight upon her shoulders and his urgent whisper was hot against her cheek and smelled of whisky. "There's more passages here, Martise. Did ye know? There must be, catacombed within the walls. Passages made by the lairds of Creeghan. To hide royalty, sometimes; to hide Catholics and priests and others. But ye mustna doubt that the lairds know of their passages. For sometimes, lady, 'tis not been for honor that men have trod these steps! Indeed, this is a place of death! Come with me, Martise. Come with me, help me discover them. Come with me, deep, deeper into the very bowels of the castle. Ah, lady, the truth must be known!"

"Ian, let me go!" she insisted.

He shook his head, holding her tight, and his voice lowered to an even more urgent whisper. "Ye don't understand. The full moon is coming. It must be now!"

"No, Ian, no! You must let me go."

"But Martise—"

"Martise!" A voice thundered out, rich and deep, filling the caverns of the crypts with its life.

Bryan was coming for her. She heard his footsteps upon the cellar floor, heard the long hard length of his stride.

Ian's hands fell wearily from her shoulders. The light left his eyes and he turned around, taking his seat upon the slab by the coffin once again, picking up his whisky bottle.

Then Bryan appeared. Tall, dark, and towering in the archway of the crypt, only his eyes ablaze in the shadows at first. Martise meant to walk, but she rushed to him, shivering violently as his arm came around her and he swept her against the warmth and strength of his chest.

"Ian, what are ye doing down here, lad?" Bryan asked.

Ian laughed. "Getting drunk. Come, Bruce, allow me the same folly as the fishermen and sheepherders! Ah, Bruce, come on! Ye're ever the one with the bride, ever the laird of the castle." There was the slightest trace of bitterness to his voice. "First there was Mary, and now there is Martise. To the laird of the castle. You are the laird."

"This has always been your home as much as mine."

"And I thank ye for it, I do." He smiled and the bitterness was gone. "Aye, for everything."

"Ian, I dunna want ye sleeping here among them, man. 'Tis not healthy."

Ian stared at Bryan and smiled, and his smile was warm and charming. "I'll not, Bruce. I'll be up soon enough." Then his eyes fell upon Martise and he said softly, "I did not mean to hurt ye, Martise. I loved Mary, but we all love ye, too. Ye ken that, do ye not? We're glad to have ye. We pray for ye, aye, lady, that we do!"

"Aye, Ian. Thank you."

She could stay in the crypt no longer. She turned, heedless of Bryan's touch, and started across the floor. She nearly screamed aloud when his hand landed upon her shoulder and he spun her around to face him.

"What the hell happened?" he demanded in a harsh whisper.

"Nothing! I—"

"What in God's name were ye doing down here?"

"I saw Ian come. I just wanted to speak with him—"

"You fool, girl! I've married ye for safety, and you defy me at every turn. Never, never follow anyone into the crypts! Never, Martise, do you understand?"

She tossed back her head. "Does that refer to you, too, Laird Creeghan?"

A darkness crossed over his features. "Aye, lady, that refers to me, too."

He stared at her hard. She felt her trembling begin again and he pulled her hard and taut against him. And still he offered no comfort. "Why did you come?"

"I told you. To speak with Ian—"

"He didn't hurt you?"

"No, no—"

"What did he say? Why were you so terrified?"

She shook her head. "He really didn't say anything. He—he babbled. About Mary. And the crypts. He said that there are more passages."

He leaned back. "Aye, there are more passages. And so help me, these nights I will know them!"

He stepped past her and started for the stairs. She stood still and he paused, swinging back at her. He reached out a hand and seemed to bark, "Come!"

She stiffened. "Don't yell at me!"

"Yell?" he said incredulously. "I'm ready to *throttle* ye, lass. Come now!"

She ground out an expletive and, ignoring his hand, rushed up the stairs. He was behind her as she hurried back to the great hall.

At the top of the stairs, Henry Cunningham was waiting, still holding her punch. Peggy was standing beside her husband, and they both appeared anxious.

"Ah, there ye are, lass!" Henry said, relieved.

"Henry, yes, thank you!" she said, taking the punch from him. "I'm sorry, I didn't mean to disappear."

"As long as you're all right, lass," Peggy said.

Martise gave her a hug. "I'm fine, and you're a dear to care. Especially when—" She broke off, and her thought remained heavy on the air.

Bryan had come behind her; she could feel him there long before his hands fell upon her shoulders.

"Martise, my love, what are you saying to these poor people?"

"Nothing, Laird Creeghan, not a thing at all," Peggy said quickly. "Drink your punch, love. 'Tis nearly midnight, and the bedding will take place."

"The bedding?" she said. Midnight was the witching hour, she thought. At least, so it had proved at Castle Creeghan. She spun around to stare at Bryan. His eyes fell upon her with no apology. "An old custom, my love. They do die hard in the Highlands."

Even as he spoke, the clock began to chime. A wild cheer went up, and there was suddenly an array of people around them. Uncle Peter and Conar, Dr. MacTeague, and even Father Martin and old cadaverous Hogarth at the head of the men; Peggy, Katie, Elaina, Holly, and a very mischievous Cassie gathering around Martise. She had one chance to cry out a protest, and then she discovered that she was soundly lifted into the air by the efforts of the women.

The crowd surged up the stairs and along the ancient hallways, laughter spilling out, raucous, wanton, wild. Bryan was ahead of her, rushed along by the men.

At the master's chamber, the door was burst open. With

a growing sense of horror Martise felt herself carried ever forward, and she thought that if they stripped them both together, she would surely die of the humiliation.

But it was not to be so bad as all that. Bryan was rushed through to the dressing room and the door was closed in the wake of the men. But there was nothing to be spared her among the women. Though tender care was taken with her gown, there seemed to be a hundred hands upon her. Her gown was gone, her shoes were tossed aside, then her corset, her petticoats, her chemise, and she was down upon the bed as her pantalettes were stripped away. She shivered at her nakedness, distressed that so many eyes, even feminine eyes, should be upon her.

But she wasn't to be left so for long. Holly was quickly at her side with her bridal nightgown.

It was not white, but a shimmering, see-through blue in a silk as soft as butterfly wings. Elaina slipped it over her head and drew her back to her feet, smiling warmly. "What a beautiful bride!" she exclaimed, and swept back, holding her new sister-in-law's hands. "Oh, Martise, truly, you are beautiful!"

Cassie was walking along behind Elaina, her eyes not nearly so warm. "Aye, Castle Creeghan has another stunning bride. May this one last!"

"Cassie!" Katie Douglas chastised her.

"Her hair, and quickly!" Peggy said, taking over as the silence became charged. A brush was brought forward and Peggy made quick work brushing the length of Martise's hair. There was a knock upon the dressing room door and Peggy cried out, "Ready!" as she swirled Martise around to face the door. The women fell away as the door opened and Bryan appeared, surrounded by his people.

Her heart hammered, her breath caught. She was still nearly naked, for the gown was so diaphanous that she was defined in the lamp- and candlelight.

And she knew that beneath the dark black velvet cape that covered her husband's shoulders, Bryan was naked, too.

He stepped forward. He stared at her a long moment, his fire eyes burning into hers. And then his fingers threaded hard into her hair and he tilted her head back to his leisure and kissed her with a dark and staggering passion.

She heard the cries go up around them, the laughter, the taunts, the ribald comments. She wondered desperately where else this display would lead, and she brought her palms hard against his chest, her fingers curling against the velvet of his robe in a silent pleading.

They were married now.

And he had threatened, warned, and promised what would come when they were man and wife . . .

He raised his head from hers and met her eyes. And though she said nothing, perhaps he read something within her heart, or perhaps he had never intended to allow a true show here this night.

"My friends, I give you my bride, the new Lady Creeghan. A true beauty, in any age!"

There was a roar of approval.

"And now—out!" he demanded. He released Martise's hand and waved the onlookers toward the door. There was an outpouring of groans; but with good humor, the guests began to disperse. Holly turned to Martise and winked, then disappeared with the other women.

Hogarth gave her a knowing smile and disappeared with a promise that they would not be disturbed in the morning.

Then the door was closed, and Bryan bolted it. Leaning against it, his eyes caught hers and swept slowly over the length of her. She felt the warmth of his touch, felt it seep into her being.

He stepped toward her, his strides taking him ever closer. He stopped an arm's length from her, his voice a hot whisper in the night.

"Have I ever told you, my lady, that you are beautiful, indeed? Beyond the imagination, beyond the depths of desire." He reached out and his fingers just brushed her cheek. He lifted a tendril of her hair and brought it over her shoulder. "The gown is exquisite, Elaina's choice, I imagine. And beneath it you are silk and alabaster. I could not bear for others to stay a second longer." Still away from her, he cupped his hands beneath her breasts, molding his palms and the silk around them. His touch sent her senses reeling. He was slow, so slow. Gentle, tender. And distant. And so his slightest touch seemed an ecstasy and an agony, and she longed to throw herself against him, and yet she could not move. For the game had begun. She was his wife.

He came closer, his whisper hotter still, their breath mingling on the air. "Aye, lady, what this froth of silk doth do! There was indeed murder in my heart when I saw the looks of the men upon you. Custom be damned. This must be for my eyes alone."

He caught her hands and pulled her forward at last. And his eyes met hers again and he whispered, "Now, lady, now you are my wife."

"Aye, so you say," she murmured.

"'Tis still a charade?" he said harshly. She felt the searing heat of his body beneath the velvet of his robe. A robe that very much resembled the cloaks worn by the men in the forest.

Or a cape . . . like that worn by the laird in her dream. The laird who came to claim her in the dragon mask.

To claim her, to love her, or to slay her . . . ?

She tried to pull away from him but his arms held her tight. "What is this?" he cried. "You would deny me now?" A husky, boldly sexual tone gripped his voice. "After all that has been between us? When now I have raised you up and made a lady of the temptress!"

"I was ever satisfied as Mistress St. James!" she retorted.

He smiled. "Nay, lady, never! For you came as Lady St. James, if you will recall. And still, no matter. You are the bride of Creeghan now, my lady. Mine now, my love."

He swept her up into his arms. She was torn between vast excitement and the edges of fear. "You would force me to do your will, then, Laird Creeghan?" she demanded.

"The Bride of Creeghan always does the will of the master," he reminded her.

And he laid her out upon the bed, upon the black velvet spread with the emblazoned red dragon.

"Not *this* bride," she vowed stubbornly.

"I would never force anything from you, milady," he murmured, smoothing back her hair. "But always, my love, the laird of Creeghan will have what is his."

He leaned toward her, and she closed her eyes, her breath moving quickly and softly through her parted lips. He would kiss her, she knew, kiss her and sweep her to the forbidden world of enchantment that he had so thoroughly introduced her to before. A world where she could not tell the difference between love and danger. When the line drove her endlessly higher to peaks unknown . . .

His lips did not touch hers. She opened her eyes and discovered that he was studying her with both amusement and desire.

"Alas," he said. "Even the laird of Creeghan cannot always have what he wants exactly when he wants it."

He stood and shed his velvet robe, but not to return to her side. Despite the obvious arousal of his body, he went to his armoire and pulled out a pair of breeches, climbing quickly into them.

Martise stared at him in disbelief.

He slipped on a shirt and walked over to the bed. He bent down and kissed her lightly. Feeling like a fool, Martise twisted from his touch and edged up on the bed. "Where— where are you going?"

"Down below."

"Below?"

"Into the crypts," he said, sitting to pull on a pair of socks and his boots. "No one would expect me now. This might be my best chance."

"Suspect you of what?" she demanded, shivering.

"Of searching out the crypts," he responded on a note of aggravation. He rose, but then he paused. In his dark shirt and breeches and boots, he resembled a pirate more than a dragon laird, and he smiled with a rogue's curl to his lips. "My lady, I am ever so glad to see you distressed at my departure."

"I am not distressed!" she protested.

"I shall hurry back."

"Please, don't bother. Contrary to the laird's opinion," she said coolly, "he cannot always have what he wants. At any time."

"My love, you wound me."

"I am not your love. This is a game we play."

He waved a hand in the air, and he no longer taunted her, but spoke seriously. "The Colt remains beneath the bed. If anyone comes near you, do not hesitate. Shoot."

"What if you are the first to come near me?" she asked sweetly.

"If you choose to shoot, then do so with deadly accurate aim, or rue the action until your dying day," he warned her. "Martise, do you hear me? Stay here. Do not leave, not for anything. Not if there are lights, or cries, not if the wind screams, and the very castle threatens to catapult into the sea. Do you understand me?"

"Aye!" she cried out.

"Good. And the Colt—"

"The Colt is beneath the mattress. And I am a very fair shot," she assured him.

He smiled and stepped toward her again. He leaned down and she tried to roll from his touch but his arms pinned her down and his lips seared fire against hers despite her effort to elude him. He kissed her until the breath was swept from her, until she could fight no more.

"I will be back," he promised.

She gritted her teeth. "Do not return on my account, Laird Creeghan."

"Aye, but lady, I shall," he promised again.

He straightened, then slipped through the dressing room,

and the door closed, and his voice hoarse and low warned her that it must be bolted.

She rose and slid the bolt, and she leaned against the door and then sank slowly against it.

The laird of Creeghan was gone.

After all of his threats and promises, he had left her. She was his at last, legally a bride of Creeghan. His wife, no matter what the game.

And he was gone.

Gone into the caverns of the darkness . . .

She was very much afraid, and no amount of denial could change that fact.

She wanted him back that night. She wanted him back, alive and vital and lustfully demanding . . .

Making her his bride in truth.

Sixteen

❧

The dream began with the mist.

It swept and crawled around her, brushing against her flesh. Dove gray, hazy, cool, like a vine, it grew up from the shadows that lay beneath her, and caressed her.

Then she began to hear the wind.

Soft and low it began, a whisper, words she could not really hear, thoughts she could not comprehend. Then the sound rose to a moan, to a cry.

And as the wind grew louder, the mist began to creep away.

And he was coming.

Walking across the rock, wrapped in a black velvet cloak. His stride was slow and easy, lazy . . . sensual. She could not see his face, for he wore the dragon mask. All that she could see was his eyes . . .

Eyes of fire.

Blazing and burning, and promising heaven and hell.

The mist had cleared, and she was on the rock, naked and alone. And the wind was the cry of the villagers, below on the cliff, watching, chanting, waiting . . .

Waiting for the blood to feed the earth.

She did not move, she could not move. She was imprisoned by the very stone of the cliff. He was coming closer and closer, and then he stood beside her at last, staring down at her with the flames of his gaze scorching her flesh. She wanted to scream, but she could not. She wanted to deny him, but she could not. He swept aside the folds of the cloak and she closed her eyes, awaiting the sharp feel of a knife to pierce her throat before her body could be tossed to the waves below . . .

Softness . . .

Softness caressed her. Searing heat stroked against her nape and over her shoulders. Sweet, arousing, a touch now upon her thighs, curving around her buttocks, stroking. Her eyes opened, and there was no rock beneath her, only the softness of the feather mattress of the laird of Creeghan. She was awake, and yet still so weary, so hazy, as if she had awakened in the mist.

The laird himself was at her back, naked, no black cloak upon his shoulders, no dragon mask upon his face. His kiss, hot and sultry, warmed her neck and shoulders, and coursed over the sheer silk along her spine. His hands swept up the soft blue folds to bare her limbs and hip, and stroked her naked flesh. He rolled her to him, the bareness of his lower body meeting hers. And he smiled, seeing that he had awakened her. With mischief, with a rogue's pleasure.

With eyes of fire . . .

Of passion, of promise.

"I was dreaming," she murmured.

"Of me?"

"Aye," she whispered. And her eyes closed again. "You were a witch, a warlock, a dragon lord. And you meant to take your blade against me."

His lips touched hers and whispered against them. "Indeed, lady, I mean to bring a blade against you, but one of flesh and blood and desire rather than steel."

She smiled, and her lashes just barely lifted over her eyes. He had never ceased to touch her. To stroke her with the silk between them. Slowly, so slowly that every stroke was luxurious and sweet. And ever more intimate.

" 'Tis a charade, a game, and nothing more," she whispered.

"If it be a game, lady, then let's begin to play." And with those words he sank between her, and within her. Slowly again, so slowly that she ached with each small movement, so slowly that she closed her eyes and drifted again, and felt the wind surround her, and bring with it the lazy caress of the breeze . . .

Then his hands molded about her buttocks, and his body entered fully into hers, and she cried out softly, for at first it seemed that she would be torn asunder . . . and then it seemed that fire had exploded within her, and that she would die if he should leave her.

The magic swept her, urgent, gentle, urgent once again. Bursting within her and all around, fire to dispel the mist, heat to ward away the cold. The feeling so high and so sweet that she had never known life more acutely . . . the world fading and spinning so that it was blackness again, and mist. And still . . .

He was within her, part of her. His arms were around her and they slept together until she dimly awoke, aware of movement again, of magic, and the wildness, the cry, that was the wind, the passion that was the very Highlands.

And then again, she slept. Soundly, deeply. The wind had grown quiet, and even the waves washed gently upon the Dragon's Teeth far below.

She was alone when she awoke suddenly, with a start.

Sitting up, she looked around. Daylight was filling the room. It was late, she imagined.

The soft blue silk gown was still upon her shoulders and she closed her eyes again, trying to remember the night. She had dreamed. Dreamed of witchcraft and dragons and the cliffs and the rocks and the waves that touched the shores. And in her dream, he had come to her.

No, that had not been the dream! she assured herself.

She swept her hand over the spot where he had lain. The bedding was cold. But his scent remained, husky, elusive, and still warming to her, and she knew that she had not imagined him. She hugged her arms about her chest and she knew, from the telltale feel of her body, that she had not dreamed the dragon laird in truth.

She jumped out of bed and came to the balcony. The cold wind instantly tossed and buffeted against her face. The temperature had dropped overnight.

All Hallows' Eve had brought its own chill.

She slipped back into the room and crossed through the dressing room to the bath. Steaming water awaited her, as if the very minute of her awakening had been anticipated. She slipped off the gown and climbed into the delicious steam. She sank into it, and allowed it to warm and soothe her. All Hallows' Eve. It was upon them, and she could feel it. In the air, and deep within.

Her teeth chattered and she told herself that she was allowing the castle to seep inside of her. She could afford no flights of fancy, not here. Not today.

She decided not to tarry in the bath long and rose quickly to take a huge towel from the cabinet. Wrapped in it, she came back into the bedroom and then sat at the foot of the bed, perplexed, wondering what she was to do for clothing. She rose and looked tentatively in the armoire and discovered that a few of her dresses had been brought over. She searched through drawers and found her underclothing as well and dressed quickly. Finding the laird's engraved silver brush upon his dresser, she swept it through her hair, then left the room.

In the hallway she paused, certain that she heard whispers.

It was the wind, she told herself.

But it was not. Low, genderless whispers were coming from the stairway that led down to the ancient crypts.

She moved against the wall, trying to hear. The burrs

seemed very thick. The ghosts were talking, she thought. And then, irritated with herself, she moved closer to the winding stairway.

"It canna be, 'tis come too clear—"

"It must be! 'Tis when she comes to the rocks—"

"He knows!"

"The Dragon's Teeth will have their due, and that be it. Only we are privy to the trail. The walls will close around all others!".

She moved still closer. Her feet must have scraped against the floor, for the whispers were suddenly silent. She swore to herself and hurried for the stairwell and looked down.

Darkness greeted her. She could see no one, no one at all. Had it been the ghosts of Creeghan? How could anyone have disappeared so quickly?

The whispers had been swallowed up into the darkness. She hesitated at the brink of the stairway, and then she sighed. Only a fool would travel down into that darkness alone.

She bit into her lip, thinking that someone had been in the master's bath to fill it with the steaming water. That someone had surely been Hogarth. Could he be among those who donned dark cloaks and whispered in dark passages? Bryan believed in him. He was the only one in the castle besides herself who knew Bryan's true identity. Or was he?

It was an incredibly complex tangle, and one she dared not try to solve alone. If only Bryan were here! But he was not, she thought crossly. It seemed that he only crawled the tombs and chambers of the crypts in the dead of night.

Unless . . .

Unless he had been among the whisperers on the stairs . . .

She started through the tower across the long corridor to her old room and then to the main stairs. She hurried down those to the great hall. Only Elaina was present, sewing before the fire. She looked up at Martise with a warm smile. "Good afternoon."

"Afternoon, is it?"

"Aye, you've slept the morning away. But then brides are supposed to do that, I hear," she said, and grinned impishly.

Martise smiled. There was tea on the buffet and she moved forward to pour herself some. "Elaina, you'll discover yourself someday, I'm sure of it," she promised her new sister-in-law.

Elaina flushed. "Maybe," she said. She set down her sewing. "Bruce said this morning that you would be going to America."

Martise almost dropped her cup. "What?"

Elaina smiled. "He said that he thought the two of you needed to take a honeymoon. He said that you have property in the States and that the two of you should go look at it. And then, of course, he could look for my Niall MacNeill, and for our brother, too." Her voice went very soft. "He warned me that I mustn't hope too greatly that they live, but he will search . . ." She broke off again, shaking her head. "My brother is dead, I am certain."

Cold shivers ripped through Martise. She did not know how to answer. She couldn't lie. Elaina's brother did lie in a coffin below. Her brother Bruce.

"It was a long, hard war," Martise said.

"You didn't know that you were going back to America?"

"No, I, er, didn't," Martise said, sitting across from Elaina. The fire snapped and crackled.

"Ah, well, Bruce must want it to be a surprise. He probably warned me in case you two decide to disappear mysteriously in the middle of the night. Riding away by the light of the full moon, disappearing into thin air . . ."

Chills shook her. Was Bryan planning that she should disappear into thin air this very night?

Cast upon the shoals below . . .

Buried within the castle walls.

She felt ill. How could she suspect a man who loved her so passionately and tenderly?

How could she not suspect him?

Because she loved him.

"Where is Bry—Bruce?" she asked Elaina.

"Gone, out. There's much to be done today. Tomorrow is a high holy day for us, which means that tonight, the villagers will play."

"Oh?"

"Aye, 'tis great fun. They come to the castle in masks and disguises, and we provide marzipan candies and pasties and treats."

"It sounds wonderful," Martise said uneasily.

"We can dress, too, if you like."

"Perhaps."

"Let's!"

"But—"

"Come on!" Elaina said. She reached out a hand to Martise. "We'll find costumes."

"Where?"

"In the wine cellar. We've a lot of old clothing stored there, very old clothing. Some from the twelfth century."

"In the crypts?"

"In the wine cellar!" Elaina repeated.

Martise rose with her. She had wanted to go to the crypts. The wine cellar was in a different direction down the broad hallway, but perhaps she could see something.

"This shall be fun!" Elaina promised her.

They ran down the steps, past the chapel, still fragrant with the flowers from the wedding service. While Elaina opened the gate to the wine cellar, Martise stared down the hallway. But she could see nothing. The hallway was too long, and too dark, and the crypt, which the circular stairs from the master suite descended to, was shadowed in absolute blackness.

"Come on, back here!" Elaina encouraged her. Martise

turned around and followed Elaina into the wine cellar, past the bottles and racks, some of them covered in dust.

"Back here!"

Behind all the rows, there was a cavern in the wall. It was lined with trunks. Elaina blew the dust off the top of one and plunged into it. "Oh, look! These are beautiful, aren't they?"

Martise took the gowns from Elaina. They were both from the Napoleonic era, elegant silks trimmed with fur, with high bodices and low necklines and slim skirts.

"And there are hair crowns in here!" Elaina said. "Oh, they were so pretty! However did we come to wear these monstrous skirts after these beautiful sleek things were worn!"

Martise shook her head. "I'm sure I don't know," she murmured. Then she fell silent, leaping to her feet. She was certain that she had heard someone else down here with them. Footsteps . . . that led toward the crypts.

"Elaina!"

"What?"

"Did you hear that?"

"Hear what?"

"Footsteps?"

Elaina held still, listening for a moment. Then she shrugged. "Nay, I heard nothing. Give me a hand, Martise, let's bring this trunk off of this one. I believe that the really old gowns are down here."

Martise dutifully helped her. They both laughed, looking at one another, realizing that their faces were smudged with dust.

"Oh, well, 'tis worth it—" Elaina began, then she paused, frowning, listening.

"What is it?" Martise asked tensely.

"Someone *is* down here," Elaina murmured.

Martise left her, hurrying through the wooden racks of wine to the entryway. She burst out into the hall and stared down the long corridor.

Nothing greeted her but silence. Silence and darkness.

Still, she felt as if her skin were crawling. She hurried back to Elaina. "No one is here."

"Maybe Hogarth was down here, cleaning up the chapel, setting flowers, I don't know." She smiled. "It could have been anyone. Look at what I've found. It's perfect for you."

She lifted up a gown that resembled a tunic. It was white and soft and exquisitely crafted, with shimmers of material falling upon one another. There was a golden braid belt beneath the breasts, and then the gown fell in a soft sparkling splendor to the floor. "And there is a circlet, a crown of jewels, with a train of the silk, to go with it," Elaina said.

"It's stunning."

"Wonderful! I shall be the Empress Josephine and you—well, you shall be Queen of the Castle, of course!" Then she broke off again, frowning. She looped the gowns over her arm and smiled. "I do hear something . . . Excuse me, Martise."

Martise sat down upon a trunk and heard Elaina's footfalls grow softer and softer. She waited several minutes, wondering where Bryan was, and when he would return.

Then she heard something else. A whisper of sound. A grating. A sliding, and then a grating.

It seemed to be coming from behind her.

She leapt off the trunk. She gasped, certain that the wall was starting to move, that stone was scraping against stone. She backed away and closed her eyes. She heard it again, the grating.

But even as she stared, the wall became one again. As if it had never moved.

She stepped forward, touching it, leaning against it.

Then she heard a clanging.

The gate to the wine cellar had slammed shut. "Elaina!" she screamed. She swung around and raced through the racks of wine once again. She reached the iron gate and threw herself against it. It had been locked, padlocked, from the outside.

"Elaina!" she screamed. "Elaina!"

There was no answer. Her voice echoed through the empty halls.

She swore, she kicked the gate. Cold crept along her spine. Elaina . . . she had never suspected Elaina. Beautiful, melancholy Elaina. Perhaps she was just barely on the edge of sanity. Perhaps . . .

She clenched her teeth and sank down to the floor. She was panicking, and it was foolish. She was locked in with bottles of wine this time, no corpses. And surely there was some mistake. Elaina would come back for her.

But already, the dim light that filtered in through the chapel windows was fading from the hall. And if she wasn't locked in with the corpses, they still were not very far away.

"No . . ." she mumbled aloud.

Someone would come for her. Hogarth would need wine for dinner. There was no reason, absolutely no reason, for her to panic.

Then she heard it again. The grating. As if the wall, far back in the little storage chamber, were moving. And she knew. There was a passage here. Like the passage from the laird's library into her room. Like the sealed passage to the torture chamber, where the poor girl's body had been discovered. There was a passage. And whoever had locked her in was coming for her now. Coming from out of the stone of the castle.

She threw herself against the grating, and she screamed. There was a figure there, a figure in the darkness, coming toward her. She screamed again. She was trapped, from within, and from without . . .

"My lady!" a voice cried out. The gate rattled.

The grating was silenced.

"Lady Creeghan!" the voice repeated. She blinked, because a match was lit against the wall, and a lantern came ablaze. It was Hogarth, the lamp in his one hand, the key to the gate in the other.

"Martise!" Elaina's soft voice called out. And then, behind Elaina, she heard Bryan's voice, breathless, angry.

"What in God's name is going on down here?"

The gate swung open. She stepped out, and the mad pulse of her heart slowly subsided. She wanted to throw herself into Bryan's arms.

He had been the last one to appear—after the grating sound had ceased. She didn't know where he had been. She could only see in the shadows and the glittering lantern light that his ebony hair was tousled over his forehead, his eyes were aflame, and a furious pulse beat against his throat. And he was winded, as if he had come running.

"Bruce! I didn't know that you were back!" Elaina cried.

"What's going on?" he asked again.

"We were looking for costumes," Elaina explained. "How did the door get locked?"

"You didn't lock it?" Martise said.

"Of course not!" Elaina protested indignantly. "Martise, how could you think that I would play such a prank upon you?"

Hogarth cleared his throat. "Please, ladies, my Laird Creeghan. Forgive me—I locked the cellar. I'd no idea that the ladies were into the costumes. Forgive me, please. I should have called out first."

Martise stared at Hogarth and felt relief flood through her. He smiled apologetically, uneasily, and she wondered if he was telling the truth.

Or if he was shielding someone.

Elaina shivered. "Let's go up."

"Aye, supper is ready to be served," Hogarth said. "Early this eve so that the villagers might play."

Martise turned and hurried for the stairs. Bryan set his hand upon her back to lead her up. She quickened her pace, avoiding his touch.

Ian and Conar and Peter were in the hall when she

reached the top of the steps. "Aha, there's the wayward bride!" Ian called cheerfully. "Holding up the meal," he said, stepping toward her and taking her hands. "That's not the way to our hearts, cousin-in-law," he teased.

"Martise was locked in the wine cellar," Elaina told them.

"First the crypt—then the wine cellar?" Peter inquired.

"'Twas my fault, sir," Hogarth quickly explained. "I brought out the wine and padlocked the gate."

Bryan was behind Martise again. He pulled out her chair, and she felt the warmth of his touch. "They were acquiring costumes, Martise and Elaina," he said. He took his own seat at the head of the table. "And did you find something?" he asked her.

"Aye, wonderful things!" Elaina said. "Bruce, shall you dress?"

"I think not, Elaina."

"I shall wear my colors!" Peter said.

"That's no disguise!" Elaina protested. "All right, then, be boring, my beloveds. But we shall be magnificent. I found Martise the twelfth-century bridal gown. She'll be exquisite."

"The bridal gown?" Bryan said, stiffening.

"Aye, Bruce, wait till you see her! A bride yesterday, a bride today. But you canna see her till we're ready. We'll dress in my room."

"Indeed?" Bryan said.

Elaina nodded happily. "And you really must wear something out of the ordinary. All of you."

Peter snorted, and Ian laughed. And the conversation moved onward to the festivities and the treats. "Tomorrow should be endless," Ian commented. "All those men today worthless from the wine and ale and whisky of yesterday. And now, after tonight! Why, it shall take those drunkards a week to recover."

"Ian," Conar protested sternly, "the villagers are hard workers and not drunkards."

"No more so than yerself," his father taunted.

There was an awkward silence, then Ian laughed. "Aye, well, that's a fact. I did overindulge yesterday. But then, I gained a new cousin. And a delightful one." He winked at Martise.

Elaina pushed back her chair and tossed her napkin on the table. "Martise, are you done? Shall we?"

"Yes, I'm quite finished," Martise said. She rose. Bryan's eyes were bright and probing upon hers. He smiled, and his gaze remained upon her even as he spoke to his sister. "I do not mind my bride being stolen for a few hours," he warned her, "but remember, all, that midnight is the witching hour this night above all nights, and I will have her back at that time!"

Elaina laughed.

Martise felt chills race down her spine.

"Of course, laird of Creeghan!" Elaina assured him, then hooked her arm in her sister-in-law's and drew her toward the stairs.

As they entered Elaina's room, Martise wondered if she shouldn't find time to talk to Bryan alone. There was so much that she should tell him. About the whispers on the stairs. About her certainty that there was a passage behind the wine cellar.

And still . . .

She didn't know! Damn, but she didn't know. What if he had caused the grating? What if he had become her lover, and even her husband, just to give her as a bride to the castle, her blood to feed the stone?

She almost groaned aloud. She was going to have to see him later. What was she to do at midnight? Grow frantic and say that she would not sleep with her husband? Disappear in truth into the night?

She needed to see him.

"There we are," Elaina said, pointing to the gowns upon her bed. "I gave these to Holly when I left you so that she could freshen them. Oh, Martise, when I ran up the steps,

I'd no idea Hogarth might lock you in by accident. I am so
sorry."

Martise shook her head. "It's all right, Elaina. Really."

But was it? Had Elaina lured her there?

She was losing her mind, suspecting everyone. She
forced herself to smile and began to disrobe. "We can't
wear these petticoats," she muttered.

"Nay, we canna!" Elaina agreed with laughter. "Martise,
ye must not wear anything beneath that gown. The silk is to
hold and to cling."

Martise arched a brow to Elaina, but her new sister-in-
law laughed and indicated the dressing screen in the corner.
Martise strode behind it and hesitated as the gown came
flying over the screen to her. Then she slipped the silk over
her shoulders and marveled at the feel of it.

Surely, the Creeghans had always been wealthy. But this
gown was truly exquisite for its day. The material did seem
to fall around her, to caress, to fit as if molded and formed
for her alone.

"There's the crown, remember!" Elaina called to her.

Martise stepped around the screen. Elaina was gorgeous
with her dark hair and light eyes in the elegant gown.
Martise smiled and applauded.

"Aye, thank you, but you must see yourself!" Elaina told
her. And she excitedly caught her arm and led her before a
gold-rimmed floor mirror. "Now wait, mind you, for the
crown!"

It was perfect, Martise thought. She didn't seem quite
real, or real to this world. Her hair flowed out like soft
wings of fire over the sweeping white folds of the gown.

"A Greek goddess, that's it!" Elaina whispered. And
with a flourish, she set the jeweled crown atop Martise's
head. " 'Tis glorious!" she pronounced.

She had never looked better, Martise knew. More enticing, and more innocent, perhaps. The jewels danced with
her eyes, and the silk train from the crown enhanced the
luster of her hair beneath. The material molded beautifully

to her form, and yet moved with her when she moved. There seemed to have been some magic spun into the thread, for the gown itself shimmered when she moved.

"I cannot wait for the laird to see you!" Elaina declared, delighted.

Martise made a quick decision. "And I must not wait," she told Elaina suddenly. "I've got to speak with him for just a minute—"

"But you must make a grand entrance down the stairway!" Elaina protested.

Martise smiled. "Elaina, I will. For Conar and Ian and Peter—and Hogarth!" she promised. "But right now, I must see my husband."

She hurried out of Elaina's room. Her teeth chattered, but she wanted desperately to see Bryan. She had to meet the fear within her.

Or else she would have to run from him at midnight . . .

She hurried along the corridor, passed her old room and the library, and started across to the master's tower. She was nearly running.

And then she stopped, a scream forming against her throat.

Someone was there. A figure was there, at the door to Bryan's room, clutching something against its chest.

Clutching something . . .

What? She couldn't see, she couldn't tell. The figure was in shadows. It was clad in black. In a black cloak with a hood.

It turned and saw Martise. And for a moment, it held. She could not see its face, or its eyes, but she knew that it was staring at her.

And then it turned and fled.

"Wait!" she cried, and she started to run after it. "Wait, please, wait!"

But the figure had reached the stairway, and in the absolute and total darkness, it disappeared.

Martise paused at the head of the steps, staring down.

She could not follow. She would be a fool to do so. She bit her lip and ran back to the bedroom doors, throwing them open. "Bryan! Bryan, where are you! Oh, please, damn it, where are you?"

There was no answer—except that he wasn't in the room, that was for certain. She sighed with frustration and sat down at the foot of the bed. "Laird Creeghan, where in God's name are you? Never about when I need you, only appearing in erotic dreams!" she muttered.

Then an eeriness seemed to steal around her. She was sure that the room was empty, and yet . . . she suddenly didn't want to be alone within it. She leapt back up and left the room and started walking along the corridor.

And then she was running.

She came back to Elaina's room and knocked upon the door. Elaina was there, smiling expectantly.

"Was he duly impressed?" she asked Martise.

"He—he wasn't there."

"Then I imagine he's gone down already. He is the laird, and must greet the revelers," she said. "Come, we'll get to make a grand entrance, after all."

They walked to the stairway together, then Elaina prodded her. "Go down with you, now. Alone. And slowly!"

Martise started down the stairs. She could hear many voices, and she surmised that there were many people in the hall. Then suddenly the voices faded away and stopped altogether, and Martise realized that everyone within the room was staring at her. Then she heard a hoarse male cry. "Martise!"

Bryan came to the bottom of the steps, his features tense. He reached a hand to her and led her into the room, his eyes condemning as he stared at her. Then he turned around. "The bride of Creeghan anew, my friends!" he announced, and an uneasy laughter arose, and then a puppet show which had apparently already begun was resumed. Martise tugged upon his hand, demanding of Bryan in a heated whisper, "What is it? It is as if you had seen a ghost!"

" 'Tis nothing," he said. "You simply surprised us all.",
"Why?"

"Because one of our ancestresses—the bride married in
that gown—threw herself from a balcony to the rocks
below. There's a painting of her in the smaller hall beneath
my room."

"Oh!" she cried, startled. And then she looked back at
Elaina, who had also made her entrance, and now stood
laughing beside her cousin Ian while she watched the
puppet show.

"But it is stunning upon you, Martise. Truly stunning."

She pulled away from him. He was in black. Black
breeches, black silk shirt, black frock coat. And then,
looking around the room, she gasped.

Many of the men were dressed in cloaks. Cloaks like
those worn by the figures that day in the forest.

"What is it?" Bryan demanded sharply.

"The—the cloaks," she murmured.

He did not reply, for there was thunderous applause as the
puppet show ended. The front doors were cast open and the
people went spilling out to the courtyard. Bryan caught
Martise's hand and dragged her along.

Outside, there was a giant pole set up with gaudy
streamers about it. Twelve of them. Each was held by a girl
who danced with it. No holy dance, and no Highland fling,
but something far more subtle and sensual. Decadent.
Erotic. Each girl was clad in white, with sleeves and shirt
cut and slashed as if the gowns were elegant rags. The
bodices were low, the skirts were slashed, and young flesh
was very much in evidence.

Twelve . . . the number of a coven, Martise thought.

The girls let go of their streamers, and they ran within the
crowd. One of them sidled against a masked Roundhead,
and another paused to press a kiss against the cheek of a fat
Punch. One of them—Cassie, the fisherman's wife—came
before Bryan, and cast her arms around him, and came
shimmering down the length of his torso and limbs.

The girls raced back to their streamers, and the dance began again, reaching a frenzied crescendo. The music died, each girl fell to her knees, and again, the applause was thunderous.

"I thought May Day was for fertility," Martise murmured sweetly to Bryan.

His eyes caught hers and he smiled. "This is the harvest, you must recall, my love," he said. And then suddenly, pipes were playing and a fiddle was strummed, and beneath the full moon, dancing had begun. Bryan was swept away by an unknown girl, and Martise found herself in the arms of a young sheepherder with a handsome face—but the scent of sheep still about him.

Then Hogarth appeared, dressed in one of the dark cloaks. He made a wonderful figure of death, Martise decided, watching as he threw out the marzipan candies to the crowd. There was laughter and chaos as the candies were caught, and then one by one and in pairs, the people began to drift away toward the carts and wagons and horses that awaited them along the road.

The clock began to strike. Twelve tones.

"Midnight, the witching hour," came a husky voice behind her. And Bryan's warm hands slipped around her. She swirled around to face him. He now wore a dark cloak about his shoulders, though the hood was pressed back from his head. He smiled, the devil's smile, and he swept her up into his arms.

"No!" she said.

"Ah, but I demanded you back for this time!" he reminded her. "Good night, all!" he called to his family, and strode back through the double doors and to the stairway.

Panic seized her as he mounted the stairs. Her eyes met his, and she desperately sought the truth in them.

They reached the second floor and the corridor. He swept her forward still, into the darkness. She began to tremble and shake within his arms, and still she could not speak.

And still his eyes burned into hers.

He kicked open the double doors and carried her to their bed. He left her there to stride back and close and bolt the doors.

Her lashes fell over her eyes and clamped tightly. In the dream she lay upon a cold slab and he came to her. And then he brought the chill of his knife against her throat . . .

She opened her eyes. He was striding toward her, the cloak flying from his shoulders. "No!" she screamed.

He sat at the edge of the bed and pulled her against his shoulder. She kept trembling. His kiss fell upon her forehead and upon her cheeks and upon her lips. She wanted the kiss, she despised the fear. Hungrily, desperately, she kissed him in return. Her tears bathed his hands where they stroked her cheeks. "My God, what is it?" he asked huskily.

"Bryan, dear God, tell me again that you're innocent, I beg of you!" she gasped.

He pressed her back against the bed. "I am innocent," he told her intently. He touched her shoulders and pressed his kiss against them. "Tell me, what has happened?" he whispered against her flesh.

She moaned softly. He stroked her to soothe her, to ease the chills and the trembling from her.

"I am afraid," she whispered.

"I am with you," he told her.

And she forgot the fear, and was warmed. He touched her everywhere with his kiss. He discovered her nakedness beneath the shimmering silk, and he swept his hand beneath the fabric. "I have never seen anyone more beautiful or erotic or enchanting than you in this gown," he said. Then he stripped the crown from her head and the silk from her body.

She could not deny him.

He seduced her with his touch. With the whisper of his breath against her cheeks, against her breasts. His tongue traced a molten stream over her limbs, between her breasts.

He lifted her against him, and brought that same searing heat intimately against her. Probing with his touch, with his kiss. Having her so, demanding all from her so, stroking, licking, ravishing, invading . . .

Never, never ceasing to touch. And he became one with her. Invading anew, kissing, caressing. And the desire mounted and rose and crashed and danced within her. She trembled and shook with the force of it. And when his rhythm quickened to a wild and reckless, near brutal demand, the wind and the stars swirled within her being, and with the ecstasy that enwrapped her, she was ready to die.

He allowed her to fall, and then he filled her and made love again. Completely, thoroughly, until she lay naked beside him, shivering again as the searing heat of his warmth, of his tempest, of his desire, faded from her body. And then her eyes opened to his, and she felt the brooding power of their fire upon her.

"Now, tell me," he prodded her softly. His arm swept around her and he held her close. "Tell me. Talk to me."

"There were whispers," she said, "this morning, on the stairway to the crypt."

"About what?"

"About tonight. About the danger. About a ship coming close to the shore. I don't know, I couldn't hear, I was afraid. And then today—"

"Today what?"

"Elaina had me wear this gown. As if I should be cast to the sea—"

"Elaina would not hurt you."

"I don't know anymore, I don't, Bryan. Perhaps Hogarth locked that door, perhaps he did not!"

"I cannot believe—"

"And someone was in this room."

"Who?"

"A figure in a cloak."

"Doing what?"

"I don't know, I couldn't tell." And she couldn't really tell if he believed her or not. "Bryan, I swear it."

"Go on, Martise, I am listening."

"And then . . ."

"What?"

"When I was locked in the cellar, it—it—"

"It what, Martise? Please, help me!"

"It—it moved."

"What moved, Martise?"

"The wall. The wall within the wine cellar. That's why I was so afraid. There's a passage beyond the trunks, I know it. Then you appeared. And I was so afraid that—"

"That I had come from the passage, having discovered I was no longer alone to slay you?"

She was silent for a moment. "Yes," she whispered painfully.

"But you let me make love to you now."

"Yes," she repeated, still meeting his eyes.

His mouth closed over hers. Gently, tenderly. "I have to go," he whispered.

"I'll come—"

"Nay, by God, I'll not risk it!" he swore. He held her close. "When I'm gone, get the gun. Hold on to it. Wait for my return. If anyone comes through the door—"

"I told you, I know how to shoot," she said. "I just—"

"What?"

"I don't want to be alone. With—without you."

He caught her hand and kissed her fingers. "I have to go," he repeated. He rose, donned his clothes, and picked up the black cloak, sweeping it around his shoulders. He stood above her. "You know that I have to go, tonight of all nights. Thank you. Thank you for telling me about the passage in the wine cellar."

He turned, and the cloak swept behind him as he headed for the dressing room door. He told her to come bolt it behind him, and she did so. Then he was gone. There were no whispers, no sounds, just the call of the sea below and the low moaning of the wind about the rock.

Shivering, Martise hurried back to the bed. She picked up the old silk bridal gown and slipped it over her shoulders, but the material brought her only more chills. She was frightened, truly frightened, as she had not been before.

She had to relax. Had to. She had to wait. She understood. She could not help Bryan by making him have to worry about her.

She reached under the mattress for the Colt. And even as she did so, her eyes widened.

The knobs upon the double hallway doors to the room were twisting. Someone was out there.

She dug more furiously beneath the mattress. She couldn't grasp the gun.

Then she heard a slow, persistent scraping, and she realized that someone outside was digging the lock from the doors.

"God help me!" she whispered frantically. She wrenched the mattress from the bed, but there was no gun beneath it.

Then she knew what the hooded figure had been doing in Bryan's room earlier, what it had stolen, and what it had been cradling to its chest.

The gun.

The weapon she so desperately needed now.

The grating sound was louder. In a matter of moments, someone would break through the door.

She raced across the room and unbolted the door to the dressing room. She slipped inside just as the doors shattered open behind her. She hurried on into the bath and then into the hall.

She didn't dare try to race along the corridor. There was only one route left open to her. She stared down into the ebony darkness of the stone circular stairway. She heard the footsteps behind her. Someone in pursuit . . .

And she tore down the steps, plunging into the absolute darkness to reach the crypts of death below.

Seventeen

❦

The darkness was terrible, eerie, and all-encompassing. Martise set her hands upon the walls to guide her along the continuous curve, moving as fast as she dared. It seemed then that all she could hear was the beating of her own heart and the desperate surge of her breath.

Then she paused as she heard a noise coming from behind her.

Her pursuer had come through the rooms, discovering her gone from the bedroom, the dressing room, and the bath.

And now, whoever it was had come to the head of the stairs.

And was descending.

She gasped in a new breath and hurried along again. In seconds she came to the arrow slit in the tower wall, and moonlight spilled in upon her. The steps just below were illuminated for her, and while she had light, she raced along them heedlessly.

And still . . . the footsteps kept coming. Soon, the moon would illuminate the steps for the pursuer, too.

She plunged on downward and discovered in the moonlight a very small landing and a door. She realized that the door must lead to the smaller hall in this tower, the one that

Bryan had mentioned, where the portrait of his ancestress Creeghan bride, in the very dress she now wore, was hung.

She threw herself against the door, but it held tight. She tried again, praying beneath her breath. But the door would not budge, and she was wasting valuable time.

She could still hear the footsteps, closer now, upon the steps.

She swore softly and raced downward again. Once more, the darkness came against her intently, heavy, wrapping around her. Still she curved around on the steps, hugging the wall, moving as fast as she could.

Then there was light. Not bright light, but pale light filtering through to the stairway. She was nearly to the ground floor, nearly to the crypt.

She hurried on. The crypt with its slabs of stone and shrouded dead lay almost before her, and beyond it, a passage. And it was from that passage that the light seemed to be coming.

She stumbled from the last step, looking desperately about for an escape route. The gate to the crypt appeared to be locked. There was nowhere to go but forward. Yet even as she took a step, a dark form loomed up before her. For an instant, it seemed that her heart ceased to beat, and she thought that one of the shrouded creatures had arisen from death to fly before her. But then she realized that it must be a living creature, one clad in a dark cloak with a low hood. She screamed and turned about, facing the stairway again.

By then, her pursuer had also come to the bottom. And this figure, too, was clad in a dark cloak with a low brimming hood . . . and more.

The figure wore a mask. All-concealing, bloodred and black, like a horned dragon. Tight-fitting, the mask rode just beneath the overhang of the hood. Small . . . terrifying. Shielding even the eyes in shadow.

"No!" she screamed, and spun again, darting to elude the creature before her and streak toward the hallway.

"Stop her!" called a husky, burring voice. " 'Tis the bride

returned, trying to escape her tomb, trying to escape death! She will bring down destruction upon us all."

She screamed again as a hand knotted into her gown, wrenching her backward. She turned, and to her amazement, she stared into young Jemie's face.

"Jemie! 'Tis me, Lady St. James—Lady Creeghan—"

"Aye, Lady Creeghan," he agreed. "Ye canna escape the tomb, lady. Ye were buried hundreds of years ago, and ye must be buried again."

"No, Jemie!" she cried, trying to wrench free from him. She knocked against a slab, and a spider-boned hand, covered in gauze, fell upon her. She shrieked again and tried to spin.

And she met the creature in the dragon mask. She barely stared upon it before she saw the hand rising and saw that there was a stone within it. She tried to scream, tried to duck, but it was too late. The stone struck her temple, hard. She felt the pain, and then it seemed that she felt nothing at all. The light faded, and she fell, grasping onto the only hand offered out to her . . .

The hand of bone.

It fell with her, tiny fragments littering the floor.

And then darkness descended around her again.

Dimly, from the darkness, she heard a scraping sound. It was slow, easy, pausing now and then, but rather constant. At first she just lay there, not really conscious, but aware of the sound.

Scrape . . . scrape . . . scrape . . .

Then she felt the pain against her temple again, and slowly, she became aware of other things around her. She was cold, very cold. And she lay upon something very hard. Stone. A cold stone slab . . .

She opened her eyes. Pain struck her mercilessly, and she closed them again. Slowly, she opened them once more.

There was light. A dim light, cast from a lamp not far away. She stared up at a ceiling of stone.

At her feet was a wall of brick.

Scrape . . . scrape . . . scrape . . .

She heard the sound again and allowed her lashes to fall, and then she slightly turned her head toward the sound. She kept her lashes low, but opened her eyes, and nearly allowed a scream of terror to escape from her.

She had been taken from the old crypt to the new. Mary's coffin sat no more than twenty feet away. But the wall that had been repaired had been broken down again, and one of the heavy funereal slabs had been drawn back into the crevice of the wall. The crevice where the body of the young girl had been found. The girl who had died just a year ago. The poor creature they had found in a state of partial decay . . .

The scraping sound was that of mortar being applied to brick by the cloaked figure of young Jemie. Slowly, methodically, carefully, neatly . . . he was now walling her into the crevice, burying her alive.

The bricks already rose at least three feet from the ground.

She tried to move, and discovered that she was tied to the slab by ropes that held her hands high above her head. Desperately, she began to tug at them. They tightened about her flesh.

Jemie placed another brick upon the wall and smiled at her. "Ye mustna leave the tombs agin, ye know. Ye mustna. 'Tis the living ye harm when ye do."

She bit her lip, trying to stay calm. Even if he managed to wall her up, there would be some air. And Bryan would discover that she was gone, and he would come for her.

Unless Bryan was the figure in the dragon mask.

She fought down the rising hysteria within her and began to move her wrists, scraping the rope against the rough stone and praying that Jemie would not notice. Then she spoke to him, firmly, quietly.

"Jemie, I am not any ancient bride. I am wearing this gown as a costume."

Jemie smiled. "The dragon laird said that ye'd be wily as a fox, tryin' to trick me poor mind."

"Jemie, there is no dragon laird. I swear it."

"Aye, there is! He brings us the harvest from the sea, and if we disobey him, the crops themselves will rot, and the sheep will die."

"Jemie, Jemie! Someone is using you, can't you see it! Those poor ships are no man's harvest! Your dragon laird is a wrecker, just using you. Ah, Jemie, you're not an evil lad!"

"Nay, lady, I am not evil!"

"But what you're doing is evil, can't you see that? I am Martise. Mary's friend. Mary Creeghan. Jemie, remember Mary? She was kind to you, so kind."

He stopped in his work and looked at her with a troubled frown. She kept moving her wrists. She could feel the rope fraying.

"Aye, I remember Mary," he said, and he seemed troubled.

"What happened to Mary, Jemie?"

He waved the hand with the trowel in it in the air. "Mary, poor Mary. She came running down the stairs on the night of the full moon. And she ran into the dragon laird, and she screamed and she fell. She was dead, he did say, and so no sacrifice would be necessary for a long time. She was a Creeghan bride, given to Castle Creeghan. She would look after us for some time."

Martise closed her eyes. So Mary had died of fright. Heart failure, yes, but brought on by terror. She had been murdered as simply as the girl who had been bricked into the wall.

Just as she was being buried within it now . . .

"Jemie, stop this nonsense. Laird Creeghan will be furious with you. He's a Christian laird, Jemie, and he'd be furious with this paganism!"

He gazed at her sadly and her heart seemed to freeze. Whether he was or wasn't, it seemed that Jemie at least believed that Laird Creeghan was the dragon laird.

"None is greater than the dragon laird," he told her.

She swore, suddenly furious, tears stinging her eyes.

Poor Jemie! Someone had worked piteously upon the weaknesses of his mind, and used him cruelly. More desperately, she worked upon her ropes. She jerked hard then as another brick fell into place. The rope burned her wrists, but she ignored the pain. She wrenched hard again, and her one wrist was free.

Jemie had not yet noticed. He set another brick upon the last. She spoke again while she worked frantically to sever the second tie. "Jemie, you were in the woods, weren't you? You were meeting there."

"Aye." He paused, looking troubled again. Then he stared into her eyes. "You came. And he said that you must be found."

"He? He . . . who?"

Jemie smiled. "The dragon laird."

"The head of your group of twelve?" she asked.

"Oh, nay, lady! 'Tis not twelve. Well, there be twelve of us followers, and then the dragon laird. He is the thirteenth. The laird, you see, and we are the twelve disciples."

The rope broke free. She leapt up from the slab and threw herself against the brick. The wet mortar gave, and the bricks fell back down upon a very startled Jemie.

"Nay, lady! Ye canna escape yer tomb!" he cried with true distress.

He was lunging at her, trying to stop her. Martise eluded him, leaning against the fallen brick. Her fingers closed over one, and as he pounced toward her again, she brought it down hard upon his head. To her amazement, he sank down before her. She stared at him and dropped the brick. "Oh, Jemie, I am sorry!" she murmured.

She stepped away from him and hurried to the gate. To her relief, it was open. Within seconds she could run up the stairs to the great hall above and find help.

If there was any help to be had! Twelve of them . . . and the dragon laird. Twelve apostles and the laird himself. Aye, witchcraft, but witchcraft in truth? Or a pretense of devil worship to trick the poor unwary like Jemie?

Who were the twelve? Dear God, was the entire household involved? Or the village? Whom did she dare trust?

She had to leave the crypts behind.

She swung open the gate and started into the darkened hallway. She heard footsteps, and she stared down the corridor toward the tower that faced the ancient crypts.

They were coming . . . Two of the figures, silent, secretive, furtive, were coming down the hallway. She could not make the stairs.

She sprinted across the hallway, the white medieval gown flowing behind her, and she reached the wine cellar. She tore frantically at the gate, and it gave to her touch. She slipped inside, closed it, and hurriedly slipped behind a rack of wine. She heard nothing more.

Someone swore.

They had discovered Jemie, she thought. And the fact that the Bride of Creeghan had risen again.

She flattened herself against the wine rack, praying that they would not come for her. She heard running footsteps, then their sound faded as they ran in the opposite direction. But it was only one set of footsteps, she thought.

One of the cloaked figures remained in the crypt. She still could not make the stairs.

She turned and saw that there was light coming from the rear of the cellar. Silently, she walked toward it.

The costume trunks had been dragged away from the wall, and the wall itself had turned, baring a foot-wide opening and a passage beyond it.

"Martise!" she heard her name called in an urgent whisper. Then it was shouted. "Martise! If you can hear me, come out. It is Ian. Martise, dear God!"

Ian! He was down here, one among them, seeking her out. Calling her by name . . .

She slipped through the opening in the wall and into the passage.

Shadows lay here, shadows along a long and curving corridor. Tapers burned along the way, but at great distances, creating an eerie world of darkness and light. Spiderwebs combed the low arched ceilings, and there was an unearthly chill that swept around her.

And still, she started down the corridor. It seemed that she had little choice.

As she walked, she began to hear a gurgling sound. A rush and fall, and then a humming. She kept moving, hemmed in by the shadows, and tried to understand the sounds.

And then she did.

The corridor was leading her toward the sea. Deep, deep beneath the very bowels of the castle, it was a tunnel. The humming was the wind, coming through the entry. And the rush was the sound of the surf, high now upon the Dragon's Teeth.

The walls became damp. She could smell the salt of the water.

She moved close to the wall and kept coming, knowing now that she would arrive at the opening of the cave where she had rested on the day that she had found the poor battered sailor. The sailor who had whispered the word "Creeghan" before he died.

She began to hear voices then, and she saw that there were lights, a multitude of lights, set out upon the rocks before the cave. Out to sea, she knew there was a ship. The ship that Bryan had mentioned.

And the lights would lead it to the Dragon's Teeth, where it would sink, and its men perish, buffeted by the sea.

Or murdered if they would not die.

She stepped closer still, wondering what she could do to stop what was coming. And then, even as she stood there, something was thrown over her head. She screamed as she was dragged forward, blinded and helpless, her hands and arms caught within the folds of some dark material.

"I 'ave her, I do!" cried a voice at her ear. A feminine voice.

But she didn't have time to ponder her attacker's gender, for she was thrown down upon the rough ground, the material pulled away from her. She fell upon her hands and knees.

There was a pair of boots before her. She stared at them and looked up slowly. She was staring again at the figure in the dragon mask. He stared down at her. "Tie her to the rock," he ordered.

She screamed, but it seemed then that there were at least a half dozen of the figures upon her. She fought wildly, knocking hoods from heads and managing to stare into several faces. There were two of the fishermen she had seen at Katie's inn. A man and a woman she thought to be sheepherders she had met briefly at the fest, a young lad, perhaps their son . . . and the woman who had captured her.

She gasped in amazement, ceasing to fight, as she stared into Clarissa's eyes.

"Aye, me!" Clarissa laughed. "Ye should ha' stayed in the crypt the first time I locked ye there, eh?" She chuckled with wicked pleasure. "Creeghan is mine, ye'll see."

She clawed at the girl and was delighted to catch Clarissa across the cheek, creating long, wicked scratches. Clarissa shrieked with fury, and would have pounced upon Martise, but one of the fishermen pulled her back.

"Tie 'er like he says—we've work to do!"

Martise kicked, she scratched, she fought anew. But soon she was upon cold rock again, tied hand and foot, her gown so disarrayed and torn that she might have been naked. Screams ripped from her throat, but all who could hear her were those who tied and bound her . . .

She closed her eyes, and she felt the fury of the wind and heard the endless crash of the sea.

It was so very much like her dream. Except she was not dreaming. The cold salt spray that landed upon her. The lights, the chants, or whispers all around her . . . all so real.

"What will he do?"

"Cast another Creeghan bride into the sea, eh?"

"Spill her blood upon the rock . . ."

"Let the tide take her upon the rock, she'll not interfere again!"

Numbness was covering her. She was cold. Terrified and cold. And helpless. Nearly bent upon the rock and tightly tied. With no hope of loosening the bonds.

She opened her eyes.

And then she saw him.

The dragon laird, in his dark cloak, in his dragon mask, walking slowly toward her.

Stalking her where she lay, helpless, vulnerable.

It could not be Bryan, it could not!

But aye, who not, the laird of the castle.

He had come to her to love her . . . and now he came to kill her. The cloaked figures gathered around him as he approached her. Closer, closer . . . pausing before her. Standing there, staring down at her. Pulling a knife from the folds of his cloak.

She screamed, loudly, endlessly, hysterically. The sound rose with the wind and ricocheted around the rock. And he laughed. The dragon laird laughed, and cast back his hood, and ripped away the mask. And even as she knew that her death loomed imminently, she prayed, and screamed again, hoping that the man she had married might find some mercy for her . . .

"No, please—" she cried.

Then she gasped out loud, and even in her danger, she felt a sweeping relief.

"Peter!" she shrieked.

"Aye, lass, 'tis me. I warned ye to keep ta yer room, to stay away."

"You came after me!"

"I came after the laird, fer he was onta us, lass. Ye needn't have run. But now . . . I haven't much time. The ship comes in. And we must be quick."

"No!" she pleaded.

"Aye, lass," he said softly. " 'Twill be good, ye see.

Another Creeghan bride given to the cliffs. 'Tis sorry, I am. I liked ye, Martise."

"Then don't!"

"Kill her!" came a cry. Clarissa's cry, Martise realized. And then the chant went up. "Kill her! Kill her! Kill her! Kill her . . . !"

"Why?" Martise demanded over the growing chant. "For the love of God, why, Peter?"

"Why?" His brows arched high. "I have danced around the lairds for long enough. Soon, my wealth will be tremendous." He leaned close to her, his blue eyes shimmering, then he rose, touched her cheek, and drew his fingers caressingly along her flesh, to her throat, over the curve of her breast. Then he lifted the knife.

She screamed and closed her eyes, not able to face the blade as it plunged within her.

But the knife did not fall. Instead she heard a cry, and a crack, and a sharp impact, like flesh meeting flesh. She opened her eyes. Peter no longer looked at her. He had turned, for all around him, his followers were falling to a vicious whirlwind of motion. Someone had come. Someone seizing upon the cloaked figures, striking them to the ground, avoiding all blows, and pressing through six of the figures at once.

Peter swore in a ragged fury, and his blue gaze burned down on her anew. He lifted the knife again.

She screamed.

But there was another whirl of violent motion, a slam, and she opened her eyes to see that Peter had been wrenched away from her, that he was engaged in a brutal struggle, climbing the rock with a figure in black. The figure who had torn away the others and rendered them unconscious to the ground. A figure who had fought for her . . .

Willing to die for her.

Black frock coat, black boots, black silk shirt . . .

Dark ebony hair.

Bryan. Bryan had come for her at last.

A shot sounded. Then another and another. Into the air. The cloaked figures began to scream in wild panic. Tied to the rock, there was little that Martise could see.

One of the figures came before her, a knife also in his hand. Her eyes widened with terror and her scream rent the air. It was Ian, Ian come to finish what his father had begun . . .

"Nay, Martise!" he cried, and the knife fell, severing the ropes that bound her wrists. He reached down to help her from the rock. "Martise, I tried to call to ye before. I didna know ye were taking the passage . . . Thank God we reached ye!"

He was not going to hurt her, she realized dimly. He was not in it with his father. He had come with Bryan . . .

"Oh, Ian!" she cried, and she threw her arms around him, and he helped her from the rock.

As she stumbled, quivering in the aftermath of fear, trying to regain her balance, she saw that Peter and Bryan were climbing ever higher on the rock above them. Peter was still trying to use his knife upon Bryan, but Bryan caught his wrist with his left hand and slammed Peter's jaw with his right. And upon the rock, Peter fell down to his knees, looked up at Bryan, and smiled.

"So ye've caught me, Laird Creeghan! But Bruce Creeghan, ye're not, eh, nephew? Ye've caught me, but I bested yer brother. Did ye hear me, I bested yer brother. And I've known, aye, I've known that I bested him, do ye hear me, Bryan Creeghan!"

But Bryan had turned away in disgust. With grace and ease he had begun to descend the cliff to which they had risen.

"Do ye hear me, Bryan Creeghan!" Peter shrieked out again. And still, Bryan did not turn. And then Martise screamed in horror herself, for Peter had inched forward to pluck up the fallen knife, and he meant to send it flying against Bryan's shoulder blades.

A shot rang out. So close to Martise's ear that she could feel the hot spit of the powder.

Peter seemed to poise there upon the rock, a sculpture in stillness and time, a red stain sweeping across his dark cloak. Then he pitched slowly, surely, down to the rocks and the sea below, a sacrifice himself, to the jagged edges of the Dragon's Teeth.

Martise and Bryan both swirled around to face Ian. Ian, who had shot Peter to save Bryan. He shrugged to Martise and to his cousin, as Bryan leapt down beside him, reaching out his arms to enfold Martise within them.

"He wanted to die," Ian said simply. "He wanted you to kill him, that was why he was goading you."

Bryan nodded. "Aye, I know. And still, thank you, cousin," he said very softly.

"Ye are Bryan, eh?"

He nodded again. "Bruce is dead."

"In the coffin in the old crypt?"

"Aye."

"Conar told me so. But we thought ye must have a reason for keeping yer counsel, and so we played along."

"I knew that you were with me. I should have trusted you," Bryan said. "But I couldna, you understand, for he was your father."

Ian nodded. It seemed to be all that they needed between them. And then Bryan's arms tightened around Martise, and his eyes touched down upon her.

Eyes of fire . . .

Brilliant, fathomless, and still, so very warm. "By God," he said fiercely, and still his voice trembled, "I came so close to losing you . . ."

Ian cleared his throat. "The fires, Bryan. We must put them out."

"Aye, before the ship comes too close!" Bryan agreed fervently.

"And we've these—" Ian said furiously, nudging one of the cloaked figures on the ground near his feet.

"Where's Conar?" Bryan asked.

Ian indicated the area below them, and there stood Conar. He was the one who had fired the first shots, the warning shots, she realized. He had gathered the remaining men before him and had already begun to order them to douse the fires.

Conar was not alone. Robert McCloud was with him, using his great weight and strength to break up the deadly bonfires.

"Are ye all right? Can ye stand with Ian?" Bryan asked her.

"I'm—I'm fine," she assured him.

"Ye're not fine, ye're half naked and shaking like a leaf," he said, something like a smile coming to his features. "Ian—?"

"Aye, me cloak!" Ian said, and stripped it from his own shoulders to sweep about Martise. Bryan nodded, then leapt along the rock, hurrying from fire to fire.

Martise smiled briefly at Ian and then hurried after him. She kicked up the wet sand over the fires on the rock and doused the tapers within it.

"Martise!" Ian called to her.

She turned and waved to him that she was well and fine. And so Ian began to rouse those whom Bryan had rendered to the ground, and group them together.

Slowly, the lights began to disappear, and there was no light upon the coast at all except for that of the moon. Conar came to her and hugged her closely, and told her gruffly that he was glad that she was well. Robert McCloud tipped his cap to her and smiled, and she smiled in return and thought that she should apologize, but that, she knew, could come later.

"There be four dead," Robert told Bryan softly. "Yer uncle, and three here who tried to run and were shot."

"Who were they?" Bryan demanded.

"Fishermen." He was quiet for a moment. "Peter was careful. He wooed his villagers, and he took in Clarissa because he promised her that she could have you when it was done. She was delighted to 'disappear,' and Peter thought that her disappearance might frighten Lady Creeghan. Ye were becoming far too involved," he told Martise with an awkward smile.

"And Jemie!" she told Bryan suddenly. "He's in the crypt. He tried to wall me in—"

"He what?" Bryan seemed to roar.

She clasped his hand. "He did not mean to, I know that he did not. Peter had him so confused, he thought that he was returning a ghost to her grave. Bryan, you must not—"

"I'll not hurt Jemie," he assured her. "And," he added softly, "it will break my heart for Peggy and Henry Cunningham to have to watch Clarissa go to trial. But she must. Robert—"

"Aye, Laird Creeghan. I'll bring in our 'coven' here."

"We'll give him a hand," Conar said, "eh, Ian?"

"Aye."

They turned away, going for the seven men who now sat cowed on the darkened rocks. Bryan called to Conar. "I'm sorry, Conar. Ye know that I didna mean that he should die."

Conar shrugged. Then he grinned ruefully. "Nay, Bryan. I am sorry. I suspected, and I could not bear to discover the truth until I knew that you meant to do so tonight. And I—" He hesitated. "To my everlasting sorrow, Martise, I stole the gun from beneath the bed. I was afraid that Bryan would shoot me da. And yet, there really wasna a thing to be done. I am the one who might have cost ye yer life, and I am dearly sorry. I didna want to face the truth."

Martise escaped Bryan's hold and came on tiptoe to kiss Conar's cheek. "I am sorry about your father, Conar. And truly, I forgive you with all my heart."

He nodded, glanced back to Bryan, and started down the rock. He, Ian, and McCloud would lead the men and Clarissa to the village through the same path they had taken on that day they searched the rocks for Clarissa and discovered the poor broken sailor instead.

They stood upon the rocks alone then, Bryan and Martise. He set his arm around her and pulled her very close, his chin resting upon her head. She felt a trembling rake through him. "I canna tell ye how I felt, girl, when I came from seeking out Ian to discover that ye were no longer in the room."

"It's all right," she said softly.

"Nay, 'tis not! I left you. And Peter nearly killed you, and then I hear that Jemie nearly bricked you into the wall!"

She pulled his arm more tightly around her. "You would have found me. I know that you would have."

He turned her around in his arms. "Ye mean, lass, that I should imprison you within the castle wall meself to be sure that I know where ye're at?"

She started to smile, but then she was taken with trembling and shuddered instead. He swept her up into his arms and started back for the path. "I need to get you back into bed, with a cold cloth upon that bump and warm covers to yer chin," he told her. His eyes were still warm, very, very warm, a greater blaze than she had ever known before.

Then he paused, and he turned back to the sea. And exhaled softly. "There she goes, Martise," he said. "There she goes. The ship. Do you see her out there, far from the shore?"

And she did see the ship, far out to sea.

Safe from the Dragon's Teeth.

"Aye!"

"Ye've saved her, my love, as much as any of us."

"No, I—"

"Aye, I could not find the right passage. I could not trap the wreckers without knowing where they came. Robert and I searched night after night forever, it seemed. And I became ever more certain that my uncle was the head of the ring. I could not go to Conar and Ian until I was nearly certain that I could trust them—and until I had some proof.

And you gave me that. So those poor souls upon that ship survive tonight because of you."

"And I survived," she whispered, "because of you."

He smiled. He kissed her lips very gently and walked with her through the long tunnel that no longer seemed so evil. In the warmth of his arms, she closed her eyes, and by the time he had brought her from the cellar to the stairs and along the corridor to the master's chamber, she was lost in a world of darkness, sunk deeply into a deep and dreamless sleep.

When she awoke, someone was with her, bathing her forehead, making her warm, making her comfortable.

She opened her eyes.

Elaina was there. "I didna mean to waken you!" she said softly. "Just to make you sleep more easily."

"Elaina," she murmured. And then she knew that Bryan had told his sister everything. And Elaina must know now that Bruce was dead and that Bryan had taken his place.

And her uncle, too, was dead.

Martise sat up. "Elaina, I am so sorry—"

"Don't be," she said. "Lie back. They were both my brothers, ye know. I've thought for a long time that our laird was Bryan, and if that was so, then Bruce was dead. The truth now is better, Martise. Aye, there is pain. But I think we are closer for it, Bryan, Ian, Conar, and me. And you, Martise. I lost Mary, but I have you."

"I'm not really her sister—" Martise began.

"I know. Bryan told me everything. And dear God, but I am sorry I had you wear that dress! It might have caused Jemie to—"

"It caused nothing, Elaina," Martise assured her. And she shivered, thinking that there had been a time when she even suspected Elaina. She hugged her impulsively. "Oh, Elaina, I hope that there will be some happiness for you soon. Truly, I do!"

"I am happy," Elaina assured her.

"But I hope that you fall in love—"

"As you are in love?" Elaina asked her shrewdly.

Martise smiled. "Aye, as I am in love, Elaina."

"But I am still in love," Elaina said, and she smiled. "I will wait forever." She blew out the candle at Martise's side, and rose. At the door she added softly, "One must always have faith," she said, and left her.

She awoke warm and secure, the cloak and the remnants of the old bridal gown stripped away, a soft flannel nightdress in their place. Her sister-in-law had seen to her comfort. She touched her temple, and there was still a lump there, but even it was small.

As she struggled to fully open her eyes and sit up, she discovered that Bryan was with her. Bathed and dressed in a fawn frock coat, white shirt, and fawn breeches, he seemed younger than she had known him, handsome with his dark hair smoothed back, his fresh-shaven features set in a tender smile.

"Good morning," he told her.

She smiled.

He took her hand into his own. He was silent, uncharacteristically silent, for the longest time. Then he said softly, "You know that I love you, Martise, do you not?" He rose, walking to the window, his hands in his pockets. "I know that ye canna love this castle, Martise. Aye, or this place, for it has brought you nothing but pain and heartache. And I doubt, too, that ye could really love the laird of this castle, for it seems that I, too, have brought you little but trouble and heartache." He turned back to her, leaning against the wall. "But ye are my wife in truth, ye know. And I do love you. I do not know when you so seduced my heart, for I was certain you were a thieving tart when you first arrived. And even then . . ."

His voice trailed away. Her heart pounding, she stood, facing him. "Even then, my lord?" she murmured.

"Even then, I wanted you," he said bluntly. "I wanted

you with a burning that threatened to destroy my very soul. And when I touched you . . ."

She took slow, sure steps that brought her standing directly before him. She slipped her arms around him and came up on her toes, pressing the softness of her breasts and the length of her body against him. She brushed his lips with her own.

"When you touched me . . . ?"

He groaned, sweeping her tightly into his arms, returning her kiss with a wild and vivid passion that rocked her and rendered her trembling, and wanting in return. But he lifted his lips from hers and whispered above them, "Once I touched you, I was yours forever. I could not bear not to touch you again and again. Not to have you. Not to force you, to keep you, to demand you . . . Not to love you," he said at the last, and his breath mingled with hers.

Her lips curled in a subtle smile, and she could not move away. "My laird?"

"I love you, Martise."

"Oh . . ." she whispered.

"Damn!" he swore suddenly, vociferously. "Will ye not say it, lass!"

Her smile deepened and he swept her off the ground and back to the bed, and he lay over her, and his lips seared hers again, and his thumb stroked her cheek and parted her lips, and he broke away and kissed her forehead and her chin and her earlobe and her throat and the hot wet fire of his demand came over her, creating desperate trails of desire throughout her blood, throughout her limbs. And she tried to grasp hold of him, running her fingers through his hair, but he could not cease to touch her. In a frenzy he swept the gown from her, tearing fabric and tiny delicate buttons, and not caring in the least. And straddled over her, he cast aside his own shirt with the same careless abandon, and came down upon her again, his chest muscles rippling against her bared breasts, the dark hair upon him teasing her flesh and eliciting an ever-surging spiral of desire to beat more strongly within her. His lips coerced, demanded, ravaged, and came tender again, and then he paused, just above her lips. "I have to tell you . . ."

"Tell me!" she demanded heatedly.

"Nay, not now!" he cried, "for I will have it from you, little Rebel, I shall!"

She smiled and stole his kiss again. And she begged him to breathe his fire within her, but he ignored her, sweeping her body with his desire, with raw, ragged demand. With a kiss and a stroke, with an intimacy that brought her trembling and undulating beneath him, and no longer taunting, but begging anew.

And he rose above her, strong, so strong, and pulsing at the very apex of her need, and he smiled. "Nay, love, I'll not be had so easily," he teased. And so she cried out in frustration and caught his lips, nipping, licking, kissing . . .

And whispering at last, "Aye, Laird Creeghan, I love you! Love you so much that I followed you no matter where you led. I dreamed that you were the dragon laird, sworn to take my life, and still, I could not leave you. Aye, Bryan Creeghan, I love you. With all of my heart, all of my soul, all of my life!"

He let out a cry, something like a Rebel yell, yet something wilder still, more ancient, like the Highlands themselves.

And then he was within her, part of her.

And the wind took them. The wind that was the beauty of Creeghan, wild and exciting, dangerous, sometimes violent, sometimes tender, and always, always, filled with the passion of the sea and the sky and the thunder . . .

He loved her deeply and well, and when she thought that she was sated beyond belief, he loved her once again. And she was filled, and trembling, and so swept by the ecstasy that she clung to him, unwilling to be parted. Unwilling to ever leave his side.

His hand cupped her head and pulled her close, and he

placed a gentle kiss upon her hair. "I had thought that we should go to the States," he said.

She bolted up. "You meant that?"

Dark lashes shielded his fire eyes as he stretched back lazily. "Aye, of course. We both need to be away. Ian and Conar know more about the castle estates than I do." He frowned suddenly. "Why? Elaina mentioned it to you—she told me."

Martise flushed furiously. "I thought that—"

"Ah. Saying that I was taking you to the States would make it possible for me to have you disappear—into a castle wall, I imagine."

"Well, I—"

He swept her back into his arms. "I do have quite a bit of mistrust to forgive you for, you know, girl."

"I didn't really say—"

He rolled over her and said intently, "I think it is something we both need to do."

"Aye," she whispered, her eyes shining. "And I'll bring you to Eagle's Walk."

He pushed away, rising, and for a moment she wondered what she had said or done to cause him to leave her. He padded naked to his frock coat and reached within a pocket. He cupped something within his palm and then smiled ruefully as he laid it between her breasts. He lifted his hand away and she gasped, stunned, as she stared down at the green fire lights of her emerald, dazzling in the morning light.

"My God! You found it! Why didn't you tell me?"

He shrugged. "I tried to. Well, all right, I didn't try very hard. I had to hear you say that you loved me. The emerald was what you wanted. And I didn't actually find it. Jemie knew where it was all along. Bruce had set it in the folds of Mary's skirts when he entombed her. He thought it would be the safest place. Bruce knew that something was going on. He couldn't quite catch Peter. I believe he knew that you might come, and I think that he meant to keep the emerald safe in the only way he saw possible. When I talked with Jemie, he told me."

"Jemie! What of Jemie?"

"I've sent him to Edinburgh, to a friend, a doctor. He's going to work with him. Peter played horrible tricks on his mind. But with time and care . . . perhaps, in a few years, he will be back with us. I don't know."

He paused, staring at the gem. "I wasn't sure that I wanted you to have it. It was your escape. And yet, if you would just say that you loved me, I knew that I would never let you leave me. Not even for Eagle's Walk."

Her fingers closed around the gem and she threw her arms around him. "I'll never leave you!" she whispered. "Not even for Eagle's Walk."

"But we will go back to Virginia. And without your emerald. It's to be saved. For our children. My love, I am a very rich man. A dark, dangerous laird, mayhap, but a rich one at that. And you forget, I fought your war. And I still love your land."

She smiled, her eyes a dazzling blue upon his. "Laird Creeghan, I love your castle, too. Oh, Bryan! I am delighted that we will keep Eagle's Walk! But I will live with you wherever you desire. I do love you. With all of my heart!"

She kissed him. And he kissed her in return. And fires might have risen between them all over again.

But there was a fierce tapping on the door, and Ian called out excitedly. "Bryan! Bryan Creeghan. I donna mean to interrupt you, man, but get yer pants on!"

Bryan's brows shot up as he looked down at Martise. "Impertinent bloke, I dare say."

"See what he wants," she urged, pulling the covers to her chest as he rose to slide into his breeches. He strode to the door and threw it open.

"What the bloody hell is it, Ian?"

Ian grinned, undaunted by his tone. "Ye'll not believe this. Ye must come down, and now." He looked past Bryan to Martise and winked. "Niall MacNeill has come home at last. He and Elaina are down in the hall together. And if you don't come, and quickly, and make some arrangements, well, I'll not answer for my ability to keep your sister chaste!"

"Niall is home!" Bryan exclaimed.

"Aye, and that he is."

"Jesu!" Bryan exclaimed. "We'll be right there!" He closed the door and came back to the bed and lifted Martise up and swung her around the room. Then he buried his face against her throat, and he murmured, "Thank God! There's always a give-and-take, is there not, my love? God took my brother and Mary and . . . Peter, but now he has given us back Niall, and most importantly, he has given me you."

She smiled and tousled his hair, and she thought of Elaina's words. "One must always have faith!" she had said, and she hugged him fiercely to her. "And my love, I swear, from this moment onward, all my faith shall be in you."

He kissed her gently, and then she struggled within his arms. "My dear laird husband! We must see to your sister's nuptials!"

He laughed and set her down, and they helped one another dress, and then they left the room behind them. Arm in arm, they walked along the hallway, and then suddenly, at the top of the stairs, he turned to her.

And he pulled her close and kissed her lightly. "My love, you are ever my lady!"

She flushed, and she raised on tiptoe and kissed him in return. "And you, sir, are ever my wondrous dragon laird. And I should not survive without your fire."

He smiled, took her arm again, and led her down the great sweeping stairs to the hall of Castle Creeghan, where the shadows had all been dispersed, and the light of day came pouring in.

Epilogue

Lightning flashed with a sizzling fury across the darkened sky. Thunder clapped, and when its drum had ended, the cry, the rising shriek and moan of the wind, sounded again, more fiercely, more plaintively.

The dark rider did not care. Hurrying along the trail that led to Castle Creeghan—the great stone structure seeming truly this night like part of the cliff, part of the very rock—Bryan Creeghan was absolutely heedless of the weather.

But then the wild weather had never bothered him. Neither had the roar of the surf, the call of the wind, or the hard cliffs and tors that had bred him. And tonight . . .

Tonight, he was very anxious to get home.

He'd been down to Edinburgh, receiving the last of the papers that cleared Eagle's Walk and made the property legally theirs, with no liens and no holds against it. They had traveled there last summer, soon after Peter's burial—in the castle crypt, beside his wife—and after Elaina and Niall's wedding. They had spent months there, and they had been good months, and he knew that they would come back often, probably every year. And in the future, one of their children might long to move there, as he had himself, long ago, before the castle had become his responsibility.

But Creeghan was his, his heritage, and he had wanted his son born here.

The ghosts of Creeghan were all at rest. The wreckers had all been tried. Three men had been hanged, and the others, including Clarissa, had been deported. Peggy had cried for months, but she had been grateful for her daughter's life, and her sons were here, and Michael had given her a beautiful grandchild, and so life was going on. There was warmth again, and trust, and a great deal of love.

And tonight . . .

Bryan had wanted a babe himself, and dearly. Martise had quickly fulfilled the beginnings of that wish.

He just hadn't expected that son so quickly. The babe wasn't really due for another month, but word had reached him along the way that he had best hurry, and so he was doing.

Lucian reared as lightning flashed and thunder crashed, and the great bay lunged forward. Bryan rode hard into the castle courtyard, where Robert awaited him in the pouring rain, ready to take his things.

He leapt down. "How is she?"

"Hogarth reported just minutes ago that your lady does well and fine," Robert assured him.

Bryan smiled and hurried into the great hall, shedding his sodden greatcoat. Ian and Conar and his good friend Niall walked before the fire like expectant fathers themselves.

"Bryan! Ye've made it!" Ian welcomed him, and took the offending coat.

"Aye. And—"

"Upstairs, man. Elaina and MacTeague and Holly are with her, and Hogarth is standing guard at the door like some great bulldog!" Niall told him with a grin.

He nodded, then headed for the stairs, running up them. In the hallway he met Holly, rushing for the stairway, beaming from ear to ear.

"Laird Creeghan!"

He caught her arm. "Holly, is the babe—"

"Aye, Laird Creeghan! Hurry, MacTeague's sent me with word and Lady Creeghan is resting and well and—"

He hurried past her. "Laird Creeghan!" she called after him. "Wait, let me tell ye—"

But he didn't wait. He barely nodded to Hogarth, who was indeed guarding the hallway, and he burst through into his room.

MacTeague was just washing his hands, Martise was sitting up, her features weary, but her eyes alight, her gown fresh. She saw him, and she smiled, and he came to her side, kneeling down beside her. He saw the wee bairn in her arms and met her eyes again. "A lass? A lad? Tell me, my love."

"A boy, Bryan, but—"

"A son!" He laughed, delighted.

But then he noticed that his sister, Elaina, had come to stand behind him, and she nudged him, and he murmured a bit impatiently, "Elaina, I'm just meeting my son—"

"Well and good, Laird Creeghan!" she remonstrated him. "But ye might as well meet them both at once!"

And she plopped a second swaddled bundle into his arms. He looked from one tiny crinkled face to another, at one black-thatched head to the other, and then he began to laugh.

"Twins!" he said to Martise.

"Aye, Laird Creeghan, twins."

Her eyes were blue and dazzling. His love for her welled deep within him, and he kissed her tenderly and whispered his thanks to her for giving him two such beautiful sons.

He rose from his knees, for he was the laird of Creeghan. Then he was smiling and laughing again as he sat down and met the gazes of the doctor and his sister, and then his wife once again.

"Twins! Just what Castle Creeghan needs!" he said.

She laughed, too, and the others departed to give them some peace.

Martise reached up to touch his cheeks, and she was dazzled by the love and the passion in his eyes. Haunting eyes, fabulous eyes. The eyes of her husband, her lover, and now the father of her children.

She smiled and reached for his kiss.

For her, they would always be beautiful eyes. Exciting eyes.

Beguiling . . .

Eyes of fire.

If you enjoyed this book, take advantage of this special offer. Subscribe now and . . .

GET A *FREE*

NO OBLIGATION (a $3.95 value)

If you enjoy reading the very best historical romances, you'll want to subscribe to the True Value Historical Romance Home Subscription Service. Now that you have read one of the best historical romances around today, we're sure you'll want more of the same fiery passion, intimate romance and historical settings that set these books apart from all others.

Each month the editors of True Value will select the four very best historical romance novels from America's leading publishers of romantic fiction. Arrangements have been made for you to preview them in your home Free for 10 days. And with the first four books you receive, we'll send you a FREE book as our introductory gift. No obligation.

——— free home delivery ———

We will send you the four best and newest historical romances as soon as they are published to preview Free for 10 days. If for any reason you decide not to keep them, just return them and owe nothing. But if you like them as much as we think you will, you'll pay *just* $3.50 each and save at least $.45 each off the cover price. (Your savings are a minimum of $1.80 a month. There is *no* postage and handling – or other hidden charges. There are no minimum number of books to buy and you may cancel at any time.

HISTORICAL ROMANCE –

—send in the coupon below—

To get your FREE historical romance and start saving, fill out the coupon below and mail it today. As soon as we receive it we'll send you your FREE book along with your first month's selections.

Mail to: 10530-B
True Value Home Subscription Services, Inc.
P.O. Box 5235
120 Brighton Road
Clifton, New Jersey 07015-5235

YES! I want to start previewing the very best historical romances being published today. Send me my FREE book along with the first month's selections. I understand that I may look them over FREE for 10 days. If I'm not absolutely delighted I may return them and owe nothing. Otherwise I will pay the low price of just $3.50 each; a total of $14.00 (at least a $15.80 value) and save at least $1.80. Then each month I will receive four brand new novels to preview as soon as they are published for the same low price. I can always return a shipment and I may cancel this subscription at any time with no obligation to buy even a single book. In any event the FREE book is mine to keep regardless.

Name _____

Address _____ Apt. _____

City _____ State _____ Zip _____

Signature _____
          (if under 18 parent or guardian must sign)

Terms and prices subject to change.
